W9-ABS-163

A STEAMY ENCOUNTER

Dorie heard a noise outside of her cabin, and immediately knew she wasn't alone. Reaching one hand out of the shower, she turned off the light but left the water running.

Seconds later she saw a figure emerge in front of the bathroom door. At once, she jumped out of the shower, tearing the curtain with her as she went. Grabbing the intruder around the neck, she shoved her gun to his head.

"Dorie," the man managed to choke out. "It's Richard."

She lowered her gun and released him from the chokehold. Reaching into the bathroom, she flipped on the light.

"What the hell were you thinking?" she exploded. "I could have killed you."

"I'm beginning to see that," Richard said, and reached behind her for a towel hanging on the wall. "You're crazy."

"*I'm* crazy? I'm not the one who almost got his head blown off for breaking and entering someone else's private residence. Is this the kind of thing they teach you at the DEA?"

Richard finished drying his face and took a good look at her. "No, but if they'd told us that the view was always this good, I would have tried it before now."

Rumble on the Bayou

Jana DeLeon

To my husband, René,
who believed in me before
I wrote the first word.

MAKING IT®

October 2006

Published by

Dorchester Publishing Co., Inc.
200 Madison Avenue
New York, NY 10016

If you purchased this book without a cover you should be aware that this book is stolen property. It was reported as "unsold and destroyed" to the publisher and neither the author nor the publisher has received any payment for this "stripped book."

Copyright © 2006 by Jana DeLeon

All rights reserved. No part of this book may be reproduced or transmitted in any form or by any electronic or mechanical means, including photocopying, recording or by any information storage and retrieval system, without the written permission of the publisher, except where permitted by law.

ISBN 0-8439-5737-9

The name "Making It" and its logo are trademarks of Dorchester Publishing Co., Inc.

Printed in the United States of America.

Visit us on the web at www.dorchesterpub.com.

ACKNOWLEDGMENTS

To Caren Bevill, a great friend and talented author, who taught me the first things I ever learned about the industry and told me I was good enough to sell. To my critique partners. Cari Manderschied and Cindy Taylor, your contribution to my writing is only bested by what your friendship adds to my life. To the Non-Bombs—Colleen Gleason, Diana Peterfreund, Wendy Roberts and Elly Snyder, for supporting my success and my failures and for never, ever letting me think about quitting. To Jane Graves, tremendous thanks and enormous gratitude for being so willing to help newbies learn the craft and helping me make *Rumble* worthy of a sale. To Malcolm Hebert, Louisiana Department of Wildlife and Fisheries, for answering all my game warden questions and not arresting me when I asked the best way to smuggle drugs through the Gulf of Mexico. To my test readers, Pat Henry, Adrienne Linch and Linda Stanish, for making me believe I could entertain the world if they'd just pick up the book. To RWA and DARA, the best education and motivation sources any writer could have. To my parents, Jimmie and Bobbie, and my brother and sister-in-law, Dwain and Donna, for all their support and pre-release marketing efforts—also my beautiful niece KatiAnne for just being a blessing and a joy. To my extended family, both those still in Louisiana and those who have moved on, for always reminding me where I came from and why Louisiana is different from any other place on earth—God bless those of you displaced by Hurricane Rita. To my wonderful editor, Leah Hultenschmidt, and the incredible team at Dorchester for making *Rumble* perfect, from the editing to the cover art. And finally, to my fabulous agent, Kristin Nelson, for believing in my voice and style and not letting anyone else convince her otherwise. For not being afraid to tell me the tough things that made *Rumble* so much better and for always having my long-term career in mind with every move you make—you are the best!

Chapter One

"This day just keeps getting better." Deputy Dorie Berenger stared at the alligator in front of her. It had to be the swimming pool.

Why anyone below sea level and not even a mile from the Gulf of Mexico would install an in-ground pool was beyond her. Even the houses in Gator Bait, Louisiana, sat on fifteen-foot stilts. An in-ground pool was just asking for trouble.

And trouble was just what they had.

Maylene Thibodeaux bulged out of a lawn chair next to her pool's cloudy water, jug in hand. She wore a pink bikini and was sitting in stoned silence. Which was rare when you considered her usual mouthiness, but understandable since it was almost evening and she had probably been at happy hour since before noon.

Dorie stepped right up to the pool's edge and studied the alligator more closely. He was a good-sized one, probably ten or twelve feet and currently floating like the dead in the center of the pool, with what looked like a backpack hanging out of his mouth. His eyes were half-closed, as if he would drop off into sleep at any moment.

"What do you think?" asked Deputy Joe Miller. Joe had been the first to arrive at Maylene's, but had immediately called for backup. This one was definitely out of his league.

Dorie blew out a breath. "I think this is not my usual fare. What about Curtis? This is his specialty."

"I tried. He's still on a call at the shrimp house. Turned out to be three gators instead of just one."

"Damn it, Joe, that's four times this month. Did Buster get those traps repaired?"

"Not that I'm aware of."

"Then I'm charging him this time. The taxpayers aren't paying us to keep his shrimp house running, and trappers like Curtis don't come cheap."

"I agree," Joe said, "but what about the problem we have here?"

Dorie sighed and tossed a sideways glance at Maylene, who was working her jug like a prizefighter with a water bottle. "How much homemade wine has Maylene had?"

"She was drinking when I got here."

It figured. Maylene Thibodeaux was hard enough to please sober. Drunk was a whole different story. "You didn't let her give you any, did you? That stuff's worse than drugs." And it seemed to produce the same kind of hallucinations. In the past, they'd been called out for everything from aliens in her garden to unicorns in the bedroom. Dorie had been slightly surprised to learn the gator was real.

Joe looked shocked. "No way, boss. I'm still thinking that's how she bagged Mr. Thibodeaux."

Dorie smiled. Joe was probably right. Maylene Thibodeaux had been making her own stash since she was a little girl. Rumor had it Mr. Thibodeaux had behaved oddly and had a strange tone to his skin on the day of their wedding thirty-five years ago. Folks around town said his skin was the same exact color when they buried him six months ago, making Maylene the most patient hunter in the parish.

It had taken her only minutes to trap her prey, but thirty-five years to kill it.

Maylene's ears must have been burning because suddenly she came alive and rose from her chair. Actually, the chair rose a bit with her, and there were a couple of seconds of detachment necessary. Then she glared at Dorie.

"Damn it," she said. "I did not have this expensive piece of concrete put in to swim with the gators. I could go down to the bayou to do that. And I'm at least a mile from any water whatsoever." She hiccupped and staggered a little toward the edge of the water. "What the hell is this one doing in my pool?"

"I don't know," Dorie replied. "Did you ask him?"

Maylene shook a finger at her. "Don't you get smart with me, young lady, or I'll have a talk with your daddy." She pointed back at the gator. "Now, just what are you going to do about that?"

Dorie squatted for a moment and assessed the situation. At five-foot-ten, she towered over most of the women in Gator Bait and a whole heck of a lot of the men. Sometimes getting an eye-level look at things was the first order of business. She noticed, however, that all six-foot-four of Joe didn't feel compelled to hunch down on the cement with her, but then, standing at the edge of the pool was probably much closer than he ever wanted to be.

"You poked him with the cleaning brush, huh?" she asked Joe as she rose.

He nodded. "Not a peep. If I didn't know any better, I'd swear he was drunk." They both looked at Maylene.

"Maylene, you didn't put any of your special brand in the pool, did you?" Dorie asked.

She looked offended. "Why, I'd no more waste the good stuff on a dumb animal than I would a woman."

Dorie glanced over at Joe, who tried not to smile, then grabbed the pool-cleaning brush and pushed on the gator's side. His body moved a couple of inches across the water, but only because she was pushing, not because he was helping. She shoved again. Still nothing. He seemed perfectly content to be propelled through the pool.

Dorie looked at Joe, who shrugged. "Got me," he said. "I ain't ever seen anything like it."

She continued to push the gator until he was next to the far wall, then crept around the pool, first tapping his tail with the brush and slowly working her way up to his head. When she got to the front, she poked him square in the nose. He didn't even flinch.

Dorie leaned the brush against a patio table and grabbed the long blond ponytail hanging halfway down her back. Twisting it in a knot, she secured it at the nape of her neck with a pen and rolled her sleeves up over her shoulders. Her usual "uniform" of jeans and a T-shirt would be able to withstand a splash of Maylene's pool water, but she didn't even want to consider what it would take to wash the slimy substance out of her hair.

Hair and clothes securely in place, she reached down and pulled on the backpack, but it didn't budge. "Damn. He's got it locked in his teeth."

"I hope he ain't got whoever was wearing it locked in his belly," Joe said.

Dorie shot him a derisive look. "Joe, you know we would have heard by now if someone's angel hadn't made it home from school. Besides, I haven't seen a kid around here actually carry one book, much less a whole sack of them."

Joe rubbed his forehead and nodded. "So what are we going to do?"

She studied the gator again. "Well, first I'm going to try and pry his mouth open with one end of the cleaning brush. Given his altered state, it might work. Then, I'm going to get the backpack out."

Maylene jumped up again, chair still attached. "Wait a minute," she yelled as she lumbered back toward her house, the piece of lawn furniture trailing with her, swinging from left to right. "I gotta get my camera for this one."

The chair popped off Maylene's rear as she hurried between the stair railings and up to the house. She was back a minute later, camera in hand. "Okay. Do your stuff," she said, looking excited for the first time since Dorie had arrived.

"Be careful, Dorie," Joe said from the other side of the pool. She noticed he didn't offer to come any closer.

Knowing it was now or never, she made the sign of the cross and picked up the cleaning brush again. She gently inserted the pole into the gator's mouth right beside the backpack, then pushed down on the pole, prying his mouth open. To her utter amazement, it worked, and the lethargic animal still hadn't twitched.

Reaching down slowly, she carefully lifted the backpack from between the razor-sharp teeth, Maylene clicking furiously on her camera the entire time. Dorie rose swiftly with her prize and received cheers from Joe and Maylene.

Backing a few steps away from the pool, she opened the pack. "I think I found our problem," she said and pulled out a handful of wet plastic bags containing a white substance. She opened one baggie, dipped a long nail into the powder and tasted it, then made a face and spit into the grass next to the pool. "Heroin. He's higher than an eighties rock band."

Joe stared at her in obvious surprise. "Heroin! We ain't ever had no problem with drugs in this town. Well, I mean, except weed."

Dorie nodded and began to dig in the pack again. "I know. That's what makes it so interesting." She piled more bags of heroin on the patio table, then brought out a wad of wet money. "Hundreds. It's all hundred-dollar bills, and there's more in the bottom of the bag."

She looked back at the gator. He still rested peacefully, his mouth propped open with the cleaning brush. She bent down and studied him again just to make sure she hadn't missed anything.

"Shame everything got wet," Joe said. "We probably can't get prints off anything."

Dorie nodded in agreement, then caught sight of something at the tip of the gator's mouth. It was small and cylindrical. About three inches long. "You got any salad tongs?" she asked Maylene.

Maylene put her hands on her hips and pursed her lips. "You're not putting my salad tongs in that thing's mouth."

Dorie looked at the woman's round figure. "Maylene Thibodeaux, when was the last time you actually ate a salad?"

Maylene glared for a moment, then started toward the house again, stomping as she went.

"What is it?" Joe asked.

Dorie shook her head. "I'm not completely sure. That's why I want to check."

Maylene returned shortly with the salad tongs. She handed them to Dorie who squatted back down next to the gator and gently put the tongs into his mouth, clamping down on the object and pulling it out. Taking a brief look, she smiled. Joe had finally gotten up a little nerve and crossed to her side of the pool, although he still stood several feet away.

"Well?" he asked.

Dorie tossed the object at him. Reflex made him catch it, but when he looked down and saw what he held, he immediately dropped it.

"Damn it, Dorie! A finger?"

She smiled. "Guess we can run that print now."

It took Dorie and Joe another two hours and a little help from Billy's Heavy Equipment Service to get the alligator out of Maylene's pool and back into the bayou. As they lowered him next to the water, the gator finally started to come down off the high. He began to thrash and immediately broke the duct tape around his mouth. Billy hit the release button, and the gator fell the remaining foot or so to the ground and hightailed it into the murky water.

Their job complete, the law of Gator Bait climbed into their respective vehicles and headed back to the office. Dorie begged a Styrofoam cooler off Maylene and carried the finger inside. Reattachment wasn't a concern. The guy who lost it wasn't likely to post Want ads. But she didn't want it stinking up the station and wasn't really sure how long you kept this sort of evidence or in what manner. For the first time in her eleven years as deputy of Gator Bait, Dorie Berenger had seen something new.

And she wasn't exactly happy about it.

Joe had been right when he said drugs weren't a problem in Gator Bait. The small town had its share of professional drinkers and a whole lot of amateurs, but no drug addicts. Occasionally, Dorie or Joe caught teenagers trying grass they bought off other high school students at out-of-town football games, but no one seemed to be a recurring problem.

As Dorie pulled into town, she studied the sturdy, redbrick building on Main Street. The hand-painted, wooden sign on the front of the structure read GATOR BAIT SHERIFF'S DEPARTMENT in big black letters. The building itself was representative of everything in Gator Bait; strong foundation and none of the new flash and glamour of things today.

Heroin here? It just didn't make sense.

She looked down Main Street and sighed. Jesus Christ on a stick, the whole place fit in a stretch smaller than a city block. Only eight buildings made up the entire town. How in the world had a place so small come up with a problem so big?

Pushing the questions out of her mind and focusing instead on the finger and what she hoped the print would yield, she grabbed the cooler out of her jeep and headed into the sheriff's office. It was best to take things one step at a time. Getting ahead of yourself generally only made you trip on your own feet, and Dorie was in no mood to stumble—especially over something this important.

Joe already had the computer up and running and the equipment for fingerprinting out on the table. It was getting on toward evening, and his favorite show was on television tonight. Dorie knew he hoped whatever they found from the print could wait until tomorrow, but considering the amount of drugs and money in the backpack, she didn't see Joe lounging in his easy chair anytime soon.

"You ready?" she asked, plopping the cooler on the table next to the equipment.

He looked a little uneasy, but nodded. "May as well get it over with."

She removed the finger from the cooler and passed it to Joe. He made a funny face but took the digit, dried it off and began the printing process. "You know I've seen people lose body parts," he said. "Hell, I've helped clamp off the bleeding, and that didn't bother me. But finding this finger in a gator's mouth without its owner anywhere around is creepy."

Dorie nodded. She understood what he was saying, even though she didn't feel the same. Everyone had fears to deal with. Or not deal with and just live with. It didn't really matter, she always told herself. The outcome was still the same. After all, she lived every day with her biggest fear, and no one in Gator Bait was the wiser.

"That should do it," Joe said. He handed her the card with the print, and she took it over to the scanner. She carefully scanned the print into the computer and typed in a request for a trace. Whirling sounds came from the yellowed computer tower on the table, and the screen began to flicker.

"This will probably take a while," she said.

Joe pulled a deck of cards from his desk drawer. "Loser takes Saturday night patrol?"

Dorie smiled. "You love Saturday night patrol, and you suck at cards. Make it worth my while."

Joe considered for a second. "Okay. I win, you clean my house. You win, I help paint your boat."

She opened her mouth to agree when he raised one finger in the air. "But," he said emphatically. "I will *not* play poker against you. I've seen you make professionals cry."

Busted. "Fine. So what do you think gives you a fair shot?" Besides my being drunk or dead.

He gave her a mischievous grin. "Go Fish."

Dorie laughed. "What the hell," she said as she took a seat across the desk from him. "Deal me in. It's not like you have any silver to polish."

It was almost an hour later, and Joe was already indebted for a half day of painting when the computer beeped and paper started to roll out of the printer. Dorie rose quickly from her chair and grabbed the printouts as soon as they emerged.

"Anything?" Joe asked, jiggling the change in his pocket.

She scanned down the papers, slowly shaking her head. "Not a thing. And these messages make no sense at all."

The jiggling stopped. "What do you mean?"

Placing the printouts on her desk, she motioned him over. "You see the message here from the national database out of D.C.? It says, 'No Match Found.' But the usual message for no match with D.C. is 'No Matching Records.' "

Joe shrugged, clearly not understanding. "So maybe they changed their message. It's not like they'd notify us if they did. Hell, D.C. wouldn't notify us if they shut down."

Frowning, she stared at the papers again. "I know it seems minor, but something about it really bothers me. I don't have a good feeling about this whole thing." She sat down at the desk and drummed her fingers on the old, scarred wood.

"What do you think is going on?" he asked, now looking a little concerned.

Dorie had a history of "getting bad feelings," and her success rate was one hundred percent. Her bad feelings were no longer something Joe ignored.

She slowly shook her head and looked out the front window across Main Street. "I don't know. But something's coming. I can feel it." She looked up and gave him a grim smile. "Better prepare yourself, Joe. I think life is about to get complicated."

He nodded and blew out a breath. "What are we going to do?"

She rose from the chair and gathered up the printouts. "First, we're going next door for supper at Jenny's Café. You know I can't think on an empty stomach."

Joe perked up considerably, but then everyone knew he had been in love with Jenny Johnson since the crib. "That sounds great," he said and headed out the door, his television show completely forgotten.

Dorie smiled at his retreating figure. Men were so easy. Which was exactly why she didn't have one. No challenge, so what would be the point?

Jenny's Café was busy, but it almost always was, being the only place to eat in town except for frozen pizza at Pete's Bar. Taking a seat at the counter, they studied the menu on the board and waited for Jenny to make her way over. Dorie glanced at Joe and noticed his eyes fixed on the café owner with an adoring gaze. She couldn't help smiling.

He was a goner.

A minute later, Jenny approached the counter, her long black hair pulled back into a ponytail, her big green eyes sparkling, and Dorie decided Joe could do a lot worse than hook up with her friend. Jenny was young, pretty, smart and nice as hell.

When her mother had gotten ill a couple of years ago but refused to leave Gator Bait for a nursing home, Jenny did the only thing she could to make enough money to support them both, including full-time care for her mother: She opened the café. And it had been an instant success. The population of Gator Bait was made up of a few more bachelors than married men. Added to that, the feminist movement had finally reared its ugly head, so home cooking was at an all-time low.

"What can I get for the fearless law enforcement of Gator Bait?" Jenny asked, giving them a broad smile.

Joe looked as if he'd been blinded by high beams. He sat there grinning like an idiot, not blinking at all. Jenny took one look at his face and fixed her eyes on Dorie. "Dorie?"

"I'll have a soda and a BLT on white," Dorie said. "Add a bag of chips, too."

Jenny nodded and made a note on her order pad. "What about you, Joe?"

Dorie watched Joe try to shake himself out of his stupor, but he only made it halfway. "The same," he finally managed.

She stared at him but waited until Jenny walked away before saying, "Joe, you don't eat bacon *or* tomatoes."

He sighed, clearly disgusted. "Shit. Is that what I ordered?"

Dorie nodded.

"Guess I'll be eating a lettuce sandwich then."

"I don't get it." She assessed the man next to her. With his wavy brown hair and amber eyes, Joe was considered a bit of a catch in Gator Bait and wouldn't have had any trouble holding his own in a big city. His lanky frame and soft heart only completed the picture.

"You're a smart guy," she continued. "Good at your job, dedicated to this town and its people. Why does this one girl make you an idiot?"

Joe shot a look back toward the kitchen. "I don't know. There's just something about her that gets me all tied up. It's like everything I say or do around her is so damned important."

She laughed. "And then you wonder why I don't have a relationship with anyone. Who needs the angst?"

He narrowed his eyes. "I didn't notice you having a communication problem at our annual conference with that sheriff from Texas."

She waved a hand in protest. "Sex is not a relationship. Sex is easy and satisfying, and when it's over, you're done and can move on. There's absolutely no reason to complicate great sex with a relationship."

"Oh, c'mon, Dorie," Joe said and blushed. "I hate it when you talk that way. Girls aren't supposed to think like men."

"Seems only fair since you're thinking like a girl."

He stared at Jenny, his expression softening at the sight of her. "Everyone thinks this way at some point in time. You just don't know when it's going to hit you and then—wham, you're knocked down by it."

Dorie—who had never even been gently shoved by the feeling Joe described, much less knocked down—gave him a smile. "If you want her so bad, then tell her. If you wait around forever, you might lose her to someone else. Don't take me as an example when it comes to love and such. I'm an old cynic."

"You might be a cynic, Dorie, and a hard-ass, but I'd hardly call thirty-three old. You've still got plenty of time to be hit by the love bug. You just haven't met the right one yet." He gave her a huge smile. "Boy, I can't wait till you do. It's gonna be a doozy."

She shook her head and turned her attention to her drink. He couldn't be more wrong. Her life was perfect the way it was—quiet, simple, easy. Why screw up all that pleasure over a man? It couldn't possibly be worth it.

They took their time over dinner. Wasn't much reason to hurry since both of them were unhappy over the situation and not looking forward to the work it was going to require. Finally, reality couldn't be put off any longer, and Dorie shoved her empty plate to the back of the counter with a sigh.

"So?" Joe asked.

"First off, I'm going to put a notification bulletin out to all the hospitals and see if we can locate the man with the missing finger—not that I expect to turn up anything. Then we have to make sure that finger didn't belong to anyone in Gator Bait."

"Oh, c'mon, Dorie. You know that backpack didn't belong to anyone here."

"I know. But we wouldn't be doing our job if we didn't check. It shouldn't be that hard. I figure two places will cover all the residents. We'll hit Pete's Bar tonight. It's Friday and payday. We can cover at least half of the town's people in there."

"And the other half?" Joe asked, sweat beginning to form on his brow.

"You still got your navy suit?"

He groaned, his worst fears obviously confirmed.

"Good," she said and smiled at the look of dismay on Joe's face. "Then we'll hit church on Sunday. That should cover the rest."

Joe's father had been Gator Bait's pastor for thirty-six years before he passed twenty years ago. After the funeral, Joe had made a solemn vow to avoid church from that point forward. He said he was done for a lifetime. Dorie had never asked him his reasons, but she was sure they were good. Consequently, she knew how hard it would be for him to set foot in the house of God, work or no.

"Go on home," she said, relenting a little. "Take a shower, and I promise you'll feel better. That's what I plan on doing. I'll meet you back here in an hour or so."

"Are you going to tell the sheriff?"

Dorie considered this for a minute and shook her head. "Not yet. Officially speaking, he's still on leave. I think I'll wait until we have something more concrete."

"Like a body?"

Dorie laughed. "We should be so lucky."

Joe gave her a solemn look, threw some bills on the counter, and headed out of the café. She was certain he hoped the fingerless man was in a hell of a lot of pain for what he was about to make Joe do. With a shake of her head, Dorie put her money on the counter and followed him out the door, unable to help feeling the same way.

Chapter Two

Sunday morning was bright and beautiful, and Dorie was two minutes late for service. As the choir began to enter the church, she slid in the very back pew next to Joe. He looked miserable, and she was pretty sure he wasn't faking. She gave a small sniff of amusement. Joe couldn't possibly be as miserable as she was, unless he had on pantyhose.

She crossed, then uncrossed her legs, trying to find a comfortable position in the offensive garments, but finally gave up as Joe leaned over and whispered, "I checked at least twenty people before service and crossed them off the list."

"Who do we have left?"

Joe passed her the sheet of paper. She scanned it and decided they weren't in a bad position at all. Only twelve names remained, and she'd bet a year's pay that all of them were in church this morning. They'd had a huge success at Pete's on Friday night—well, in crossing off names anyway. But so far, neither Joe nor Dorie or the hospitals had turned up any news on Missing Digit Man.

"I think they're all here," Joe said, "but a few came in late and a couple others are in the choir. I guess we'll have to wait until service is over." He sighed and sat back in the pew, tugging at his shirt collar.

Dorie shook her head. "No waiting required," she whispered. "I asked the song leader to change the opening hymn to 'How Great Thou Art.' "

He looked at her, a new respect in his eyes. "That's pretty good."

She gestured toward the pulpit and gave Joe a quick nod and a wink as the song leader took the stage and said, "Turn in your hymnals to page one hundred eighty-three. And let's all stand and lift our hands to the heavens. Direct our attention to the one on high."

The piano player began the intro and every hand in the church went up in the air. Dorie moved quietly to one side of the pew and scanned hands all the way to the front of the church. She looked over at Joe, standing at the other end of the pew, and nodded. He nodded back, and they hurried out of the building.

"Whew," he said as they stepped outside. "That was worse than the bar. At least I can drink at Pete's."

"Stop whining," she said and smiled. "You only had to listen to opening announcements. You didn't even have to sing a song. How did it look on your side?"

"All fingers accounted for. The ones that were there before yesterday, anyway."

"Yeah, my side was clean, too. I figured as much. No one from Gator Bait is stupid enough to let an alligator get the best of him. Especially not with a healthy sum of product and money tied up in the gator's mouth."

Joe nodded, and placing one hand over his forehead, looked out at the bayou. "So what's the plan for today?"

"It's Sunday. It's eighty-five degrees outside, and the sun is shining." Dorie grinned and waved one hand at the clear blue sky. "I'm going to head back home, clear off the lounge chair on my deck, pull a six-pack of beer out of the fridge and pretend to fish. Probably be some of the best sleep I've seen in weeks. Why? You interested in coming along?" she teased, knowing full well that Joe would be headed into the diner as soon as she pulled out of the parking lot.

"Nah," he said, fidgeting a little. "I thought I might stay in town a while. Grab a bite to eat or something."

She gave him a knowing look. "It's just as well, since my 'fishing' tends to make you uncomfortable." She walked down the church steps to her jeep.

"You talk to the sheriff yet?" he asked.

"No. Not yet. I guess I'm waiting for things to get worse. He's just too difficult to deal with. I'd like to avoid it as long as possible."

He considered this for a moment and nodded his agreement. "You think we should call in the feds?"

Dorie stopped and glared at him, certain he'd lost his mind. "No way. I'm not dealing with any big-city prick telling me how to run things in my town. You know better than that."

Joe shrugged. "I know, but we did run the print. The likelihood of a big-city prick showing up here anyway is pretty high. I still don't buy that anyone hauling around that much product and money is a first-timer."

"The people in this town are simple, not stupid. They're not going to give away anything to an outsider without telling me first. You can take that to the bank."

"Maybe so, but you know if the feds come here, they're gonna want to take over the investigation. Start giving orders and throwing around insults."

Dorie grinned and jumped into her jeep. "I'd like to see them try." She pulled on her sunglasses and backed out of the parking lot. "Say hi to Jenny for me," she yelled as she started down the road, leaving Joe standing in a cloud of dust, a chagrined look on his face.

DEA agent Richard Starke took his first look at the town of Gator Bait and immediately knew he was going to hate it. Bunch of rednecks and idiots, he thought as he scanned the street in front of him. The average blood alcohol content was probably higher than the median IQ. Every building was rundown, the paint peeling from constant exposure to saltwater, and from his position at the end of the street he could make out a couple of the faded wooden signs.

On the right was the sheriff's office, with a big CLOSED sign in the window. A grocery store shared one wall of the decrepit building, and a café shared the other. On the other side of the street stood a run-down motel next to a boat shop with a bar on one side and, ironically enough, a church on the other.

Parallel to the dusty road and behind the side with the church was a bayou that ran down past a large metal building set apart from the others. Unfortunately, he was downwind from that building, and the general odor permeating the air told him it wasn't a place he wanted to see any closer.

He considered his options again. What the hell kind of place closed their entire law-enforcement facility on Sunday? He'd driven into Hicksville thinking he'd march straight into the sheriff's office and quickly deal with his problem. Obviously, he was wrong.

Disgusted by his lack of choices, he sighed. The café was probably his best bet. If he turned up anything useful, he could always get a room later at the Fleabag Inn. His skin already itched in anticipation. Studying the café, he mentally assessed the few people he saw through the plate-glass window. With a final disgusted look at the sheriff's office, he started across the street.

No way was this town of morons getting in the way of his finishing his job. It had already gone on too long, and he was ready for it to end.

No matter who he had to roll over to get it done.

Joe took a seat at the counter in the café and pretended to read the menu board, while casting sideways glances at Jenny, who poured coffee for a group of fishermen at a table in the corner. This was it. Today was the day he'd ask Jenny out and put a stop to Dorie's nagging. He would not fail this time.

A minute later, Jenny headed over his way and he felt his throat go numb.

"Hi, Joe," she said, flashing him a bright smile. "Would you like a cup of coffee this morning?"

He opened his mouth to speak, but nothing came out. Damn it, this was not going to happen to him today. He tried again, but even the words, "yes, thank you" were unattainable. Finally, he just nodded, too embarrassed and frustrated to try anything else.

Jenny stared curiously at him for a moment and turned to retrieve a cup of coffee. He slumped back in his seat and tried to get a grip on himself. It must be his allergies. He could never talk right first thing in the morning because of his allergies. Only problem with that theory was that it was already after eleven o'clock, and he'd been up and talking for hours.

Jenny set the cup in front of him and pulled out a pad. "You want the breakfast special or are you interested in lunch?"

He took a big gulp of the coffee and burned his tongue. "Special's fine," he managed to blurt out. Jenny jotted a note on her pad, gave him a smile and walked over to the grill. Glancing up at the chalkboard on the wall, he gave a mental groan. Grits were on the breakfast special. He absolutely, positively hated grits.

If he didn't learn to speak around Jenny, he would starve to death. *What the hell*, he thought, giving the board another disgusted look. *After that first drink of coffee, I don't have any taste buds left anyway.*

Jenny scrambled eggs in a bowl and dumped them onto the grill. "You been working this morning?" she asked.

"Yeah," Joe managed. "Just a bit." Then curiosity got the better of him, and he found his voice. "Why do you ask?" Jenny had never asked about his job before, and it struck him as a bit odd.

Jenny blushed a little, or maybe it was just the heat from the grill, and said, "It's just that you're wearing dress clothes. There's not a wedding or a funeral, and everyone knows you don't go to church anymore, so I figured if you were there this morning, it was because of work."

Joe glanced down a moment and shook his head. He'd completely forgotten he was dressed up. The tie had immediately come off after exiting the church and was stuffed in his pants pocket, but that still left him with tan Dockers and a white button-up shirt. Not his normal dress, for sure.

"Is Dorie coming in, too?" she asked.

"No," he replied, trying to sound natural. "She went fishing as soon as we were done with business. It being Sunday and all."

Jenny nodded and stirred the eggs around on the grill. Everyone in Gator Bait knew Dorie fished on Sunday. Everyone also knew she absolutely never caught a fish. But the townspeople respected her request for solitude and played along with the fishing game. No one called Dorie in for work on Sunday unless there was no other choice.

Jenny slid the plate of food in front of Joe. "Anything else?"

He looked down at the plate of steamy food, complete with the icky grits. "No," he said and tried a smile. "I think I'm good."

"Okay," Jenny said, and moved to the far end of the counter where she started restocking catsup bottles, obviously readying herself for the after-church lunch rush.

Fifteen minutes later, Joe was halfway through all he wanted to eat, when the bells above the café door jangled.

The sound of low talking at the front of the café just reached him, but the words weren't clear. He was busy stirring the grits in a small circle, trying to make it look like he'd eaten some of them, when he heard a man right behind him say, "I'm looking for the sheriff."

It wasn't a voice Joe knew, and he turned around in his seat to see the man it had come from.

He didn't like what he saw.

The man pulled a badge from his suit coat pocket and flipped it open. "My name is Richard Starke. I'm with the DEA out of Washington, D.C. Do you know where I can find the sheriff?"

Disgusted, Joe blew out a breath. This had been quicker than expected. "I'm Joe Miller. Deputy Miller. I guess you're here about the print."

Richard gave Joe a look up and down. "Yes." He cocked his head to one side and studied Joe's face. "You don't seem surprised."

Joe returned the look. High-dollar suit, alligator shoes, two hundred-dollar pen, perfect hair. *Damn*, he thought, remembering Dorie's comment about big-city pricks, *that woman is always right. This guy looks like a walking hard-on*.

"Actually," Joe said when he finished his assessment of the other man. "My boss was expecting you. Just maybe not this soon."

Richard raised his eyebrows. "Your boss was expecting me, specifically?"

He gave Richard another quick look. "Yeah, pretty much."

"I'm intrigued," Richard said and gave him a polite smile. "So can I meet this boss of yours, the sheriff, I presume?"

Joe shook his head. "Nope. Sheriff's on medical leave. Deputy Berenger is in charge during his absence. That's who was expecting you."

Richard began to tap his foot, clearly impatient. "Great. So where exactly is this Deputy Berenger, or does he have a medical malady also?"

Joe slouched back in his stool, unimpressed with the man in front of him and already irritated by his attitude. Working with him may be inevitable, but there was no need to make it easy. "Well, you see the problem is that Sunday is Deputy Berenger's day off, and no one disturbs the deputy on Sunday. It's a general rule."

"And what does the deputy do on Sunday that can't be disturbed?" Richard's voice began to take on an aggravated tone.

"Fish."

"Fish?" Richard's voice raised a notch or two. "You're telling me you want a federal law enforcement officer to wait until Monday to conduct business because the person in charge is fishing?" He stared at Joe as if he'd lost his mind.

Joe shook his head in dismay, the conversation he had ready for Jenny long forgotten. He threw some bills on the counter and nodded to the café owner, who stood next to the grill, an anxious look on her face. "Okay. I'll take you, but don't say I didn't warn you."

Dorie stepped out onto the deck of the large cruiser she called home and cast her fishing line into the bayou. She was going to relax this afternoon even if it harelipped the Pope. The weekend's events had been far more than the norm for Gator Bait and she was ready to wash it all from her mind—if only for a couple of hours. Tomorrow morning she'd make a phone call or two, but she didn't really expect to find out much of anything. Basically, that left her with the ole sit-and-wait, something that tended to grate on her nerves.

She draped her beach towel over the lawn chair

beside her and reached for the tanning lotion on the small table next to it. Carefully setting her bra straps to the right location, she began applying the lotion to her arms and shoulders. Her tan looked very nice for so early in the year, she observed as she worked the lotion into her skin and noticed how it complemented the pink nail polish.

Moving down to her legs, she rolled up the denim shorts as high as they would go and doused the exposed skin with lotion. Dorie didn't believe in bathing suits. What was the point of spending all that money? She wasn't going swimming and undergarments worked just the same. Besides, since she went without a bra most days anyway, tanning was almost the only time the thin lacy fabric got a workout.

And everyone in Gator Bait knew not to bother her on a Sunday. It only took one interruption from Joe for him to decide that talking to Dorie while she tanned was far too uncomfortable to merit the conversation. Nothing in Gator Bait could be that big of an emergency. So that left the creatures of the bayou as her only audience, and she was fairly sure the fish didn't care. In fact, the company of alligators and fish was more preferable to her because they never offered any advice on how to live her life.

Finished with the lotion, she stretched out on the lounge chair and put on her sunglasses. The weather was perfect. Nice warm sun and a gentle breeze blowing off the gulf. Definitely sleeping weather. Aligning her limbs so that none shaded the other, she closed her eyes.

She must have been dreaming, because it took a while to realize the noise she imagined in her head was very real. She rose slightly from her chair and saw Joe about to dock at her boat. And he didn't look happy.

Now what?

As Joe guided the boat down the bayou, Richard studied the terrain. This was going to be a pain in the ass. There were probably a zillion bayous and cuts and inlets in which to hide and move down here. And from the odor wafting up off the water, he was fairly sure he wanted to finish up this assignment as quickly as possible. Of course, he'd felt that way for eight years, and he still wasn't much closer to catching Shawn Roland than he had been when he first started with the agency.

Roland excelled at his job.

He looked across the bow and realized they were approaching an old dilapidated cabin cruiser. There was hardly any paint at all left on the hull and PVC pipes ran from the boat onto land, letting him know this baby hadn't left the dock in a long time. Joe cut his speed as they approached the floating disaster, and Richard put one hand over his eyes to shade from the sun. He could barely make out a fishing pole extended off the side of the relic, and a figure in a lawn chair next to it. As they drew nearer, the figure was all too clear.

Joe pulled right up next to the cruiser and grabbed the side, bringing his boat to a complete stop, then peered over the edge of the cruiser at the woman in the lounge chair. Richard stared at her in amazement. Surely she'd heard them approaching. Why in the world hadn't she put on her clothes? And why were they stopping? Sunbathing in your underwear was hardly as serious a crime as drug smuggling.

The woman lowered her sunglasses and looked over at them. "Hi, Joe," she said. "Problem?"

"Someone here to see you," Joe said.

"Anyone I know?" she asked, her voice teasing.

Joe gave Richard a wry look. "No, but he's exactly what you were expecting."

The woman smiled and sat up in her chair.

"This is Richard Starke," Joe said. "He's with the DEA in Washington, D.C. Mr. Starke, this is Deputy Dorie Berenger. She's in charge here."

Richard stared at Joe in amazement. This had to be some kind of joke. The woman on the boat next to him couldn't possibly be in charge of this town. She was barely dressed, for starters.

Dorie Berenger was all woman—from her mass of blond hair all the way down to her bright pink toenail polish—and Richard was not in the least bit happy about how that made him feel. Where was his self-control? He was here to catch a drug smuggler, not get laid.

Dorie stood and gave him a quick assessment. "DEA, huh? You got here awfully fast for a fingerprint with no prior record. Go figure." She gave Joe a smile and he grinned.

Richard glared at the woman, willing his gaze away from her well-endowed chest. This was business—serious business and nothing in the world would interfere with him getting his man, especially not the floozy in front of him. "I need information on the print you ran," he said, "but I can't imagine you'd be the person to give it to me."

She cocked her head to one side and studied him. "No? And just what kind of person do you imagine I am, Dick?"

"It's Richard," he said, bristling, "and I imagine you're the kind of person who should be arrested for public indecency. I can't believe you're the type to effectively run a law enforcement agency."

She laughed, seemingly unaffected by his comment. "Geez, Dick. I didn't realize you city boys were so sensitive. I'd think you'd never seen a bra before. Is that it? You've never seen a bra before?"

Richard felt a flush of anger begin to creep up his neck. "It's Richard, and the bras I've seen are not the point. The point is, I've never seen them on another law enforcement officer. Particularly not in public." He looked at Joe. "You should arrest this woman."

Joe pursued his lips. "Yeah, you see, the only problem with that is that we're not on public property. Dorie lives on this boat, and it's docked in the game preserve. So technically, I'm out of my jurisdiction. This is an issue for the game warden."

"You *live* on this floating piece of garbage?" Richard stared at Dorie, trying to control his mounting anger but barely succeeding. "And I don't suppose you have a game warden available?" He looked back at Joe.

Joe gave him an amused look. "Sure," he said and nodded his head toward Dorie.

"You've got to be kidding me!" Richard finally exploded, all patience gone. He looked at Dorie, who had put on a semblance of a T-shirt, but the thin white material wasn't much better than nothing at all. "For Christ's sake, she's fishing! In the game preserve! Isn't that against the law?"

"I'm not fishing," Dorie said. She picked up the rod and began to reel in the line. When the cork popped out of the water, Richard could see there was no line or hook beneath it.

"I'm tanning," she continued. "I always tan on Sunday."

Exasperated beyond belief, Richard threw his hands up in the air. "This is how it is. I want to see what you lifted the print from and make sure you did your job properly, which is highly in question at the moment. If, after my test, the print is still a match, I'm taking over this investigation."

Dorie smiled at him and shrugged. "Well, Dick, you can certainly try."

Dorie watched Joe as he headed back up the bayou, Mr. Personality in tow, and blew out a breath as they disappeared around a corner. This wasn't going to be pretty. And since Dick was really living up to his name, it would be far more work than she was interested in—if she could even get enough information out of him to help. The idiot seemed to think he could waltz into a small town, ask questions and actually get an honest answer.

He had a lot to learn.

And that was a shame, really, because Dick wasn't exactly a bad-looking man. In fact, he ranked somewhere around downright hot in her estimation. If the situation had been anything other than what it was, Dorie would have considered passing a little time with him, but instead she just wanted him to pass through her town and take his attitude and his criminal with him.

His loss.

She stored the fishing pole and walked into the cabin. Besides, who did he think he was, making those derogatory comments about her living arrangements? Sure, it could use a bit of paint, but it wasn't that bad. She gave the inside a critical look, scanning the entire interior standing in one place.

The kitchenette was small but serviceable and had a tiny table opposite it. The bath was no more than a shower, toilet and sink, but what else did you need? And there may only be one bedroom with a single bed, but Dorie didn't have visitors—the kind who needed a guest room or the kind who wanted to sleep with her.

Okay, maybe it was a little sparse and dull, but if she put up decorations, then she'd have to dust them. What was the point? This way everything fell to the ground and she could vacuum it all up easily. Of course, with his straightlaced personality, Richard probably had a house with one of those fancy toilets that squirted water. It may be the only way to loosen up his tight ass.

Realizing she had stalled long enough, she grabbed a pair of jeans from a basket in the bedroom and threw them on along with a pair of tennis shoes. She started to change into a thicker T-shirt, but decided against it. She only had one clean one left, and laundry was not her favorite activity. Besides, Richard claimed he had seen a bra before. He could just get over the T-shirt.

She locked the cabin behind her and jumped down into her bass boat. As she hurried back to town, she thought about the situation again.

If she made Mr. Personality uncomfortable, that was just an added bonus. She owed him one for disturbing her day off. No one disturbed her on her day off. And a girl should be allowed to have a little fun.

Especially with a Dick.

Chapter Three

As they made their way up the bayou to town, Richard's jaw was set and his teeth ached from clenching them together. This was not going as planned. He had expected to find a fat, balding man in charge of this hick town. Someone who was more than eager to turn the investigation over to qualified law enforcement so he could get on with his beer drinking, or fishing, or whatever the hell they did around here for entertainment. After the tanning fiasco, he was almost afraid to know.

He tried to tell himself he was only shocked by the woman's behavior, but he knew that wasn't all of it. He was shocked by the woman herself. Dorie Berenger was the last thing he expected to find in a place like Gator Bait. She'd look more at home gracing the front page of a magazine—at least until she opened her mouth. Still, the sheriff had left her in charge, so he must have thought she was qualified to do the job. Of course, the sheriff could be on leave for mental problems, which would explain everything nicely.

He needed to focus. Check the print, find his criminal and get the hell out of this place. *If* that print even turned out to be a match, and at this point, the entire situation seemed rather grim.

Which meant he was back to square one. And no closer to catching Roland than he had been his first day on the job. If this turned out to be nothing, where did he go from here? The anxiety of starting over again left a bitter taste in his mouth, and he hoped desperately that despite the less-than-stellar actions of the local law enforcement, there was actually something to the print they had run. Something that would end this once and for all.

Richard looked over at Joe, who still wore a sour expression. "You get much in the way of crime around here?" he asked.

Joe stared at him, apparently a little surprised at the question. "No, not really," he finally replied. "Mostly fishing and gaming violations, drunk and disorderlies, domestic disputes. Your normal course of business for a small town."

"But never any problems with drugs?"

Joe rapidly shook his head. "No way. We bust a couple of teenagers for grass now and then, but nothing big has ever been through this town. I guarantee that."

Richard studied Joe's face and decided he was telling the truth. Which made the situation even more interesting. Unfortunately, he wasn't looking to be entertained. He wanted to make an arrest, and he wanted to make it yesterday. This entire case had taken too much out of his life and career. It was time to move on to something else. And despite any opposition from Dorie Berenger, he intended to do just that.

Several minutes later, they docked at the marina and headed across the street to the sheriff's department. Richard was surprised to see Dorie through the plate-glass window of the office.

"How the hell did she beat us here?" Richard asked. "She never passed us, and she wasn't even making a move to leave when we did."

Joe shrugged. "Dorie knows these bayous better than the gators." He pushed open the office door and they walked inside.

Dorie looked up as they entered the office and smiled. "Glad you could join me, boys," she said, knowing full well it would irritate the hell out of Richard and wouldn't bother Joe in the least. Joe smiled. Richard scowled and looked at the items she removed from a U-Haul box and placed on the desk. The scowl vanished and was replaced with a look of incredulity.

"Jesus Christ," he cried. "You've been storing evidence in a cardboard box? Especially this kind of evidence?" He grabbed one of the bags of heroin and held it up to eye level.

"No one's stupid enough to break into the sheriff's office, Dick," Dorie said. "Besides, we don't have any heroin addicts in Gator Bait. That product may have been moving through here, but it wasn't making any stops. Of that, I'm sure."

Richard's mouth set in a hard line and Dorie could tell he was trying to control his temper. "I wasn't concerned about someone stealing the drugs. I'm concerned that any fingerprints that were on here are now useless because of the way you've handled the evidence. What the hell kind of training do you have for this job?"

Dorie bristled, but managed to maintain her cool. "My training isn't really the issue. And since all this evidence was drenched when we recovered it, there were no fingerprints on it anyway. Not anything useful."

"Then where did you get the print you ran?" Richard asked, his neck beginning to redden around the tight collar of his starched shirt.

Dorie pulled the cooler out of a small refrigerator to her left, placed it on the desk and motioned for Richard to open it. He glared at her for a moment, then pulled the lid off the cooler and stared at the contents in obvious amazement.

"How the hell did you get a finger off this man?" he asked, his voice wavering a bit.

"We didn't," she replied. "The finger was already off the man when we found the evidence. The man was long gone."

Richard gave her a hard look. "I need to see the exact place you found this finger, and I need to see it now. If I'm really lucky, there may be other evidence you missed that hasn't been destroyed."

Dorie shot a look at Joe, who shook his head in obvious amusement. "I can't show you where we found the finger," she said.

"What do you mean, you can't show me?" Richard exploded. "Is it some kind of local secret or did the location disappear?"

"It didn't exactly disappear, but it would be damn hard to find again, and it wouldn't do you any good at all."

Richard's face hardened. "Where did you find this finger?"

Dorie gave the man in front of her a quick assessment. The flush on his neck had crept up and now covered his entire face. Frustration and anger oozed from every inch of him. She smiled. Time to drop the bomb.

"Maylene bring those pictures by yet?" she asked Joe.

He nodded and reached for an envelope on top of the filing cabinet. "Yeah, Sammy down at the grocery store did a rush. He didn't believe her, so they bet a case of beer."

She shook her head in dismay. Good God. Maylene Thibodeaux and a case of beer. It was going to be a busy week.

Dorie took the photos from Joe and scanned through them. "This is probably the best shot," she said and handed a photo to Richard.

He took one glance at the photo and the color drained from his face. "You pulled all this out of an alligator's mouth?"

She nodded. "It wasn't that hard, really. You see, he'd broken one of the bags and was high as a kite. I'm guessing that's how he made it into Maylene's swimming pool in the first place."

"You put a call into the hospitals, right?"

"Of course," she replied, annoyed at the question. "We're not idiots. But no match."

"Can I have this?" Richard asked, holding up the photo.

Dorie nodded, surprised by the change in tone and the politeness of the question.

He put the photo in his shirt pocket and walked toward the front door.

"Wait a damn minute!" Dorie yelled at his retreating figure. "Are you going to tell me what the hell is going on here?"

Richard turned to look at her and gave her a forced smile. "That information is on a need-to-know basis. And right now, I don't think you need to know." He marched out of the building, slamming the door behind him.

"Don't think we're going to sit around waiting on you!" she yelled, not believing the nerve of this guy. Who the hell did he think he was?

"That went well," Joe said.

Dorie smirked. "It's probably only going to get better."

"You think Four-fingers is still around?"

She considered the question for a moment, certain she knew the answer Joe wanted, but equally as sure she wouldn't be able to give it. "Maybe," she said finally, staring out the window and across the bayou. "We have a lot of product and a lot of money. People would kill him for losing a lot less than we have. He might just be stupid enough to risk returning for his goods."

Joe sighed. "Then I guess we'd better hide all that shit."

"For tonight, maybe, even though the alarm system on this building would raise the dead." She began placing the items back in the box while Joe put the finger back in the refrigerator. "First thing tomorrow, I'm giving the whole shooting match to Dick. Protecting it can be his problem."

"That ought to make him happy."

She shoved the box of evidence on the top shelf of the bookcase with the kitchen supplies. "I'm not trying to make him happy. I'm trying to get him to do his job so he can get this crap out of my town."

Joe fidgeted a moment and she knew what was coming. The very thing she'd been dreading from the moment they had found the finger. "Are you going to tell the sheriff?"

She looked across the street and saw Richard pulling a suitcase out of the back of his tan Honda Accord. As he walked into the motel, she sighed. "I don't have a choice. He's probably heard the gossip by now, so my ass is already in a sling for not telling him at the beginning."

Joe nodded. "You want me to go with you?"

"Nah. It was my call. No use you suffering for it, too. Besides, I want a way out of having to work with Dick. I'm hoping I can appeal to the sheriff's better side and get him to give me one."

Joe looked doubtful but a little hopeful. "You think he can do that?"

"We can only pray."

Standing next to his car, Richard made a call on his cell phone and stared at the photo again. Either Dorie Berenger was damn good at her job or crazy. He was voting on the latter for now. He walked across the parking lot and was staring at the bayou when his boss came on the line.

"What do we have?" his boss asked.

Richard filled him in on the source of the fingerprint and the questionable mental state of the local law enforcement. "There's no way I can work with these people. They don't seem to give a damn about anything at all. Can't you send me some backup so we can get this thing over with?"

"Hell, no," his boss's voice boomed over the phone. "Why don't you just take out a front-page ad? Sending a bunch of suits to a town that size would immediately put Roland on notice. And having grown up in a small place myself, I can promise you that those people will not talk to you or anyone else from this agency."

"What do you mean?" Richard asked. "Who won't talk to me?"

"The damn townspeople, that's who. You better

find a way to make the local law your best friends, or you're never going to get anywhere and Roland will be gone again."

"Friends?" He looked at the photo again, but this time his vision blurred and he saw Dorie wearing short denim cutoffs and a white lacy bra. He shook his head to clear the image. "I don't think that can happen. In fact, I'm pretty sure it wouldn't be possible in this lifetime."

"Well, you have two options: Make friends with these people fast, or I send down someone who can and yank you off the case completely."

Damn it! Richard kicked a rock into the bayou and bit his tongue, holding back what he wanted to say because he knew it would only get him a transfer out of Gator Bait. "Fine," he said finally. "I'll go drinking and fishing with them if that's what it takes. But I'm not tanning in my underwear."

"The hell you won't! By God, if these people want you to run naked through town wearing a fish like a fig leaf, you'll do it and smile. I mean it, Starke. This is your last chance."

The sound of the phone slamming down resounded in Richard's ear. Holy hell, he thought as he closed his cell. Friends with Dorie Berenger? It would probably be easier to make friends with the alligator.

But he had no choice.

This case went far deeper than catching a criminal and making a name for himself at the DEA. This was personal. Richard grabbed his suitcase from the trunk of his car and walked across the street to the motel, wishing he'd thought to pack Lysol.

No one, especially a two-bit floozy in a hick town, would keep him from getting his man.

A middle-aged woman with big hair and even bigger breasts checked him into the motel and handed him a key attached to a plastic alligator chain with a crack in one side. He thanked the woman, who still hadn't said a word, and hiked up the flight of stairs to his room.

What a pit.

The entire room was barely the size of his townhouse bathroom. The shortest, most narrow double bed he'd ever seen was pushed against one wall, its middle sagging almost to the floor. A table stood just to the side of the bed, and when he threw his briefcase on it, it wobbled from side to side.

The bathroom had a toilet that wobbled just like the table, a sink missing a section of porcelain, and a shower so tiny that only an anorexic could possibly be comfortable in it. He took the single step out of the bathroom back into the bedroom and flopped down on the bed with a disgusted sigh. Somewhere underneath him, a spring gave way.

He'd flipped through his paperwork before calling his boss, but had come up with nothing. As far as he could tell, Roland never had ties to this part of Louisiana at all, but he couldn't argue about the completeness of his paperwork now.

According to his inside source—a man long entrenched with one of the New England drug families—Roland had established a new deal just twenty-four hours ago, so as unlikely a place as Gator Bait might be, there was no denying that Roland had been here setting up business. Every time Richard thought he was closing in, this case threw him a new angle. He was positive Gator Bait and Dorie would prove to be the worst one yet.

The woman couldn't possibly be qualified to run

a law enforcement agency, much less serve as game warden. And she had no modesty at all. Still, the entire café had gone quiet when he demanded to see her. That let him know that his boss was probably right and he'd get absolutely nothing out of these people unless Dorie said it was all right to speak. Just what he needed—a bunch of close-mouthed, beer-drinking fishermen standing in the way of catching one of the biggest and most violent drug smugglers of the decade.

Despite the fact that Dorie Berenger looked like a princess and was built like a goddess, Richard didn't think she was stupid. Not exactly. But she definitely was not trained to handle a man like Shawn Roland.

No, Dorie wanted the problem out of Gator Bait, but she had made the mistake of thinking the backpack was all Roland carried. Richard knew better. The backpack was Roland's private stash. The actual shipment would be at least thirty times that size.

He blew out a breath and rose from the bed. Noise outside of his motel room drew him over to the window, and he peered out to see a large, rowdy crowd entering the bar across the street. Drunk rednecks. He shook his head in disgust and started to move away from the window, then stopped.

Drunks were known for running their mouths.

He eyed the crowd again, assessing his chances of entering the bar and making it back out again. Maybe there was a way to get the information he needed and avoid Dorie at the same time. His boss couldn't complain as long as the job got done. Right?

Besides, what's the worst they could do?

He grabbed the broken key chain and his wallet off the table and left the room to find out.

It was almost an hour's drive to the nearest "big" city, Lake Charles. Dorie pulled through the gates of Southern Retirement Living, parked her jeep and made her way into the building.

"Hi, Sherry," she said to the receptionist.

"Why, Dorie," the woman said, and gave her a surprised look. "Whatever are you doing here on a Sunday?"

"I have some business to discuss with the sheriff. Nothing major. Are they off on some activity right now?"

"No. Just TV in the rec hall." Sherry narrowed her eyes at Dorie. "Are you sure there's nothing wrong? And don't lie to me. I changed your diapers."

Dorie smiled. Almost every woman over the age of fifty from the town of Gator Bait could use that line on her. "I promise, nothing is wrong. I just have a little police business I need an opinion on."

Sherry studied her for a moment more, obviously still not convinced, but nodded. "All right, then. You should find him down the hall. You know the way."

Dorie walked down the hallway to the large gathering room and poked her head through the doorway. Sunday was a big TV night, so the room was crowded. An elderly man close to the door noticed Dorie and nodded.

"Sheriff," he yelled across the room. "Your daughter's here to see ya."

Her dad looked up from his card game in the corner and smiled. Backing his wheelchair away from the table, he turned and headed in her direction. Dorie forced a smile on her face, trying to forget for a moment the reason she was here. When he reached her, she bent over and kissed his check.

"You're getting more silver," she said and fingered a lock of his salt-and-pepper hair.

"It's all the stress of being semiretired," he joked.

"Hmmm. I thought it may be the stress of playing cards with those mad New York Italians. I thought you were supposed to be watching TV."

He waved one hand in the air. "Nothing worth a damn on there anyway. Dead people, prison shows, mafia crap. Who the hell cares?"

Dorie laughed, unable to disagree. "I've got a bit of a police problem I need to go over with you. Can we go to your room? I need a little privacy for this."

He nodded and they continued all the way to the end of the hall. Dorie opened the door and stepped aside for her dad to enter. No one locked their apartment doors at Southern Retirement.

Her dad continued past the entry and toward the cozy living room straight ahead, while Dorie made a quick stop in the kitchen, snagging a beer for her dad and a soda for herself. Then she joined him in the living room, flopping down on an overstuffed chair with a sigh, not wanting to be there at all. Not for this reason.

Her dad popped the top on his beer and took a swig. Then the bomb dropped. "What the hell were you thinking?" he asked her. "I've been getting calls all weekend long—people claiming the alligators have gone mad, some of them claiming you've gone mad right along with them. But did I get a visit? Shit, no. I didn't even get a phone call letting me know what was happening. So what in the name of God is going on?"

"I don't think God had anything to do with this one," she replied, already feeling six years old and three feet tall again. "We had a situation out at Maylene Thibodeaux's on Friday."

"Maylene Thibodeaux has been a situation since birth," her dad retorted. "Tell me something I don't already know."

Dorie grimaced and continued. "This problem was an alligator in Maylene's pool. He had a backpack hanging out of his mouth. I was a little surprised the gator allowed me to remove the pack so easily until I opened it and found a bunch of baggies full of heroin. He was high as a kite."

She looked at her dad, but he remained silent, his face stone-cold and his upper body tensed. "Go on," he finally said.

"There was also a bundle of cash in the backpack, and the real kicker is, I pulled a finger out of the gator's mouth. Joe and I ran the print and came up with nothing, although I had my doubts even then about the accuracy. Then today, a DEA agent from D.C. waltzes into town and claims he's taking over the investigation."

Dorie put both hands up in the air. "We've never had a problem with drugs in Gator Bait. I don't know what to make of this."

Her dad frowned in obvious concentration. "You're sure it was heroin?"

"Positive. That DEA agent didn't even try to deny it. I get the feeling he's been looking for this guy for a while, but he's not exactly handing out information."

"No, he probably wouldn't be."

"Oh, but there's no shortage of insults, believe me."

Her dad nodded and studied her for a moment. "You know, I can't tell you what you want to hear."

"What's that?" she asked, pretending ignorance.

Her dad laughed. "You want me to tell you that you're not obligated to help him. That the problem is obviously his and he should handle it and go away. I'm afraid I can't do that."

Dorie bit her lip to hold in the string of curse words on the tip of her tongue. "But, Dad, you didn't see this guy. He's impossible."

"Yeah, I would imagine so. Still, your help will probably allow him to finish and be gone a lot quicker. The townspeople aren't likely to talk to him unless you give the go-ahead."

"I know," Dorie said and rose from the chair, the point of her conversation over and shot to hell. "It's just that he rubbed me all wrong. Coming into town with his superior attitude, telling me I wasn't qualified to run a law enforcement facility. I'm having a hard time wanting to help him at all, but I guess if it gets rid of him sooner, then that's what I'll do."

Her dad cocked his head to one side and raised his eyebrows. "He called you unqualified and he's still walking around with all of his body parts?"

"I didn't have my holster on. I was fishing."

Her dad began to laugh, knowing full well what Dorie's fishing entailed. "Guess that's a kind of welcome he ain't ever seen before."

Dorie leaned over and kissed him good-bye. "Well, I sure hope he enjoyed it because he's not seeing it again."

She could still hear his laughter as she strode down the hall.

Richard walked into the crowded bar and made a quick assessment from the doorway. Bunch of good ole boys. Hopefully, they wouldn't try to give the city boy any trouble. He really needed a drink.

He tried to sidle across the entry unnoticed, but his hopes were immediately dashed as a beefy bartender shouted to the room, "Look, everybody. It's Dick."

All conversation ceased, and everyone in the bar turned to stare. In unison they shouted, "Hello, Dick!" Then they turned back to whatever they had been doing before the choreographed greeting. Richard stared at the crowd in dismay, then made his way over to the bar. He noticed Joe seated at one end with a vacant stool next to him, so he crossed the bar to the empty stool and sat down.

"What the hell was that about?" Richard asked.

Joe shrugged. "Word musta got around about you giving Dorie a hard time."

Richard glared at him. "I don't suppose you have any idea how that 'word' would have gotten around?"

Joe gave him a blank look. "Don't suppose I would."

Richard shook his head in disgust and moved to a stool at the other end of the bar. The bartender shuffled over and asked, "You want a drink?"

"Sure," Richard said. "What do you have?"

The bartender looked a bit surprised. "Beer."

Richard waited for a longer list, but none was forthcoming. "Just beer?"

"Yeah, just beer," the bartender said dryly. "Three different kinds for anyone who wants to get picky. Guess you're one of those picky ones. I'll have to get the menu."

Richard looked up expecting another joke, but the bartender had his back to the counter, pulling a sheet of laminated paper from under the cash register. He handed the sheet over to Richard. It read "Beer, Light Beer, Dry Beer."

Some selection. He tried not to smile.

"I'll have a light beer," he said and handed the sheet back to the bartender.

"Figures," the bartender said and popped the top on a longneck. He handed Richard the bottle, smirked and strolled to the other end of the counter.

Richard took a sip of the beer and noticed the man to his right had seven empty bottles in front of him. A good place to start his inquiry. "I'm Richard Starke," he said and stuck out his hand.

The man stared at him as if he were roadkill. "Who the fuck cares."

Okay. Maybe the seven bottles had only been this round. Richard picked up his beer and left the counter. He could still feel the man glaring at him as he walked away. He looked over at Joe, who waved and gave him a big smile. Assholes. Every last one of them.

He crossed the room and leaned against a wall, assessing his options. Maybe the first guy wasn't the best choice. In fact, maybe a man wasn't the best choice. He did all right with the ladies in D.C. Maybe a woman would be a better pick. After all, the locals weren't likely to win them over with charm.

He scanned the bar, but all the women seemed to be with men. Finally, he saw one lone woman sitting at a table in the corner. Blowing out a breath, he headed that way. When he was only ten feet or so from her, someone stuck a leg out in front of him. He looked over to see Joe, shaking his head.

"Not a good idea," Joe said.

"And why not? She's sitting there alone."

Joe laughed and pointed to the corner of the room where two big, burly men were head-to-head, obviously about to throw down. "She's alone because her husband and her lover are about to get into a fight. You wanna get in the middle of that?"

Husband and lover? He stared at Joe, convinced the man was joking, but about that time, one of the big burlies threw the first punch.

"I told you about sleeping with my wife!" the husband yelled.

The lover staggered back for a second, then threw a right hook at the husband's jaw. "And I told you to do your job right, then the stupid bitch would stop calling me in to take care of your work."

Richard started to turn to Joe, wondering if he planned to break this up, when the sound of gunfire rang out right next to his ears. Deafened, he ducked and spun around, spotting Joe with his gun still in the air.

"That's enough, gentlemen," Joe said and sat back down at the bar.

Richard looked at the two men again. They stared at Joe for a moment, then backed away from each other. The lover left the bar through a side exit. The husband grabbed his wife by the arm and hustled her out the front door.

"Guess I'm done here tonight," Joe said and threw some bills on the bar.

"Keep your money," the bartender said and shoved the bills back across the counter. "This one's on me. Damn idiots. That wife has been having an affair with a woman from Lake Charles for over a year." The bartender shook his head. "It's a good thing you got those blanks, Joe. They sure do sound real enough, but it's certainly made a difference on the roof repairs."

Joe nodded and pocketed the money. He cast a

final amused glance at Richard and strolled out of the bar. Deciding now might be a good time to give up the quest for information and tie one on instead, Richard sat down at the counter again and waved at the bartender for another beer.

The bartender took his time getting back over to him, but after he served the beer, he leaned against the counter and stared, obviously ready to talk now that the night's entertainment was over.

"Word has it you been giving Dorie a hard time," the bartender said. "Why would you want to do that?"

Richard sighed. "I'm not giving her a hard time. I'm just trying to do my job. A little cooperation might make it go faster, and I could leave town sooner."

The bartender considered this a minute. "That doesn't sound like a bad idea. What kind of cooperation was you looking for?"

Richard shrugged. "I'm not exactly sure. Right now, I need to know everything I can about the bayous around town. What size boats can run in them. Where they begin and end. That sort of thing."

"*Hmpf.* You best make friends with Dorie then. She knows more about these bayous than the gators. Only person that knows more is the sheriff."

"Great," Richard muttered. "What is the deal in this town with Dorie Berenger? You'd think she was some sort of god."

"Damn near it. Dorie keeps this town running. Keeps it protected. Keeps the bayous and marshlands safe. Without Dorie and the sheriff, Gator Bait might have gone away a long time ago. She may not be a god, but she's damn close." The bartender walked away, obviously done talking.

Richard took another swig of beer. He was out of

options and more than a little pissed off that his boss had been right about the townspeople. They'd proven to be even more demented than the law enforcement. First thing tomorrow morning, he would have to worship at the throne of Dorie Berenger, and that left an awful taste in his mouth. Still, if it was the only way to catch Shawn Roland, he would do it with a smile.

He slammed the remainder of his beer and tossed some money on the counter. A god with large, perfect breasts, a small waist, tanned body and mean as a snake.

What the hell. He'd seen worse.

Chapter Four

Dorie was at the sheriff's office before dawn the next morning, hoping to get a grip on everything before Richard showed up and started making demands. She'd wrestled with the problem of Richard Starke and his drug dealer most of the night, never quite getting any real sleep. Every instinct told her that the DEA agent from hell was trouble, and she was going to regret getting involved with him, even if only on a professional level.

She blew out a breath and punched the button on the coffeepot. Unfortunately, there wasn't any real choice in the matter. Even if her legal position hadn't been made painfully clear, there was still her dad to consider. He wasn't coming out of that wheelchair. Ten years of tests and therapy hadn't made a lick of difference and living at Southern Retirement didn't come cheap.

Without Dorie as deputy, the town wouldn't keep electing her dad sheriff. Without her dad drawing the salary of sheriff, he couldn't afford to stay at

Southern Retirement. Not that Dorie resented the situation or her dad—that just wasn't the case. She resented being backed into a corner by the uptight, self-righteous Richard Starke. Backing Dorie into a corner was never a good idea. She usually came out swinging.

Resigned to her position, she turned on her computer and started to research the heroin trade. Arm yourself with information. That's what her dad always said, and he was right. Information beat out instinct every time. The screen swirled and presented her with a host of data. Settling down in her chair, she began to read.

She hadn't even poured her first cup of coffee when Richard walked through the door. Every muscle in her body tensed, including some that she would have preferred not respond to Richard in that way. Why in the world did this one man make her so jumpy, so unsure of her self-control? Just thinking about it made her even edgier. She barely nodded as he crossed the office to stand beside her desk.

"I was surprised to see your lights on this early," he said.

Dorie stared at him a moment, trying to temper her feelings. His voice was entirely too polite for six A.M., and that irritated her even more. "I'm always up at dawn, but I'd appreciate it if you'd hold off on giving orders until I've at least finished one cup of coffee."

"No problem," he said easily. Too easily. "Mind if I join you?"

Dorie narrowed her eyes. "What's the catch?"

Richard gave her a wide-eyed innocent look. "What do you mean?"

"I mean you're being too damn nice, and I don't like it. What are you up to?"

Richard sighed. "I knew this wouldn't work." He ran one hand through his hair. "Look, I hung out at the bar last night, and it was made really clear to me that if I wanted help, you were the only one who could give it to me. I also figure if you won't help me, no one else in town will either."

Dorie tried unsuccessfully to hold back a smile. "You went in Pete's Bar? Alone?"

Richard nodded and her opinion of him rose a fraction of a point.

"I'm surprised you made it out alive." Dorie poured a cup of coffee and handed it to Richard, then poured another for herself. "I've been thinking on the matter, and I've about decided that the best way to be done with you and the trouble you're chasing through my town is to help you catch your bad guy."

He started to speak, but Dorie cut him off with a wave of her hand and pointed a finger at him. "But—I still have a job to do. Two jobs, as a matter of fact. I cannot chase your man twenty-four hours a day. If duty calls, I have to respond."

It was as good a deal as Richard was going to get, and Dorie was pretty sure he knew it. Especially since he'd been in Pete's.

Finally, he nodded and stuck out his hand. "Deal."

She shook his hand and dropped into a chair, motioning him to take a seat on the other side of the desk. "Well, it happens I don't have anything pressing this morning, so first off, I want a little information about the man we're trying to catch. I can't help you corner him unless I know what his objectives are."

Richard shook his head. "I'm sorry, but it's confidential. I can't tell you anything."

Dorie stared at him in amazement. "Are you *trying* to make me mad, Dick? I can't work without information. I'm not about to waste tax dollars hunting the Invisible Man."

The pleasant expression Richard had pasted on when he walked into the sheriff's office changed to the look of a hardened, and very miffed, professional. "You know good and well that I can't give that information out. You're going to have to trust me. After all, this is *my* investigation."

Dorie shook her head, absolutely certain he'd lost his mind. "Trust you? I don't even know you. All I know is that you work for the government in D.C., and that in itself is enough to make any smart person leery. What proof do I have that you'll protect me from being injured when you won't even start by letting me know what I'm up against? Can you handle what we're up against?"

Richard laughed. "Isn't that question a bit ironic coming from you—the half-dressed, pink-nail-polished sun goddess who *claims* to have been left in charge? How do I know you didn't feed the sheriff to one of those swamp monsters and crown yourself 'Princess of Hicksville'?"

Dorie drew up straight in her chair and slammed her coffee mug on the desk, sloshing its contents on her calendar. "Is this your roundabout attempt at an insult, Dick? Hell, without even knowing the guy you're after, I've managed to get more of him than you have. Unless, of course, he's missing more digits that I don't know about."

A flash of red crept up Richard's neck and he narrowed his eyes at her. "You don't know anything about me or my job."

Gotcha. Dorie gave him a sweet smile. "Yes, Dick,

that's exactly my point. Or is your short-term memory so bad that you've already forgotten what started this little discussion?" She leaned forward in her chair and looked at him eye to eye. "Do you even remember who you're chasing? Or is that why you can't give me information?"

Richard rose from his chair and glared down at her. "I've had it with your attitude and your mouth. I can only assume from your reluctance to actually perform your job that you lack the ability."

Dorie jumped up from her chair and had just squared off in front of Richard when Joe strolled in the sheriff's office, whistling. It took him only a moment to realize that the situation in front of him didn't call for a song. More likely, it called for Mace or pepper spray.

Joe looked from one face to the other then threw his keys on the desk in disgust. "What in the world is going on with you two this damned early in the morning?"

Dorie nodded her head toward Richard, then looked back at Joe. "Genius boy over here says I'm not qualified to handle my job and has even accused me of killing the sheriff in order to obtain my position as 'Princess of Hicksville.' "

Joe stared a Dorie for a moment, a flicker of disbelief in his expression, then he shifted his gaze to Richard and all disbelief was gone. "Jesus H. Christ. One of you is no less impossible than the other." He gave Richard a hard look. "What's your problem? Didn't your trip to Pete's teach you anything?"

"Obviously not," Dorie threw in. "All that time he spent 'investigating' would probably have been better spent drinking. Maybe a hangover would loosen up his tight ass."

Joe shook his head. "Nah, he was drinking last

night and it didn't do any good at all. He was still as stiff as ever." He looked back over at Richard. "So do you want our help or not?"

Richard crossed his arms in front of him and rocked back on his heels. "I think I've decided on not. If someone will direct me to the sheriff, I'll be happy to leave you to whatever it is you usually do for your salary, and I'll take my tight ass to discuss business with someone who has a better understanding of the law *and* respect for their fellow lawmen."

Joe stared at Richard as if he'd lost his mind. "You want the sheriff's help? The man's on medical leave."

Richard set his jaw. "Is he comatose? Bedridden?"

"No," Joe answered, "but that's not the—"

"Unless he's paralyzed," Richard interrupted, "I'm sure he'll be all the help I need."

Dorie laughed and Joe glared at her. "Fine, Big City," Joe said. "We'll take you to the sheriff and you can have all the time in the world with him. How's that sound?"

"Joe, are you crazy?" Dorie asked.

He shook his head. "Not at all. I'm just following protocol. City here is stuck on the rules, so we'll play by them. Seems he's deemed you and me unqualified to assist on this case. If he wants to work directly with the sheriff, that's his right. Let him have it."

Dorie stared at Joe for a moment, but she knew he was right. She had no authority over Richard and was well aware of it. Maybe a trip to the sheriff wasn't the worst idea, even if it hadn't come from her. "Fine," she said finally, "but I can't take him there. No transportation. I came in my boat."

"Well, shit." Joe stared at Dorie in dismay. "My

pickup only holds two people comfortably." He looked pointedly at Richard.

"I don't care," Richard said, still glaring at Dorie. "I'm the one who needs to talk to him. We can take my car. Leave the princess back here with her reptilian court."

"Hell, no!" Dorie said and shoved her pistol in the holster at her side. "You want to talk to the sheriff, you do it in front of me." She pointed at the truck outside. "But I am *not* riding bitch and there's no way I'm getting in a car with you." She gave him a disgusted look. "Foreign piece of shit. Who the hell drives a Honda except someone with a stick up his ass?"

"Fine!" Richard said. "I'll sit in the middle. I'll ride in the back. I don't really care as long as I get the help I'm due."

"Good!" Dorie said and gave him a parting smile as she headed toward the front door. "Then Joe can shift that five-speed monster in your crotch and not mine." She strode out the front door, letting it slam shut behind her.

Joe stared after her in dismay. "See what you've done?"

"I only want to conduct my business here and be gone," Richard said. "If that means going over her head to do it, I won't hesitate."

Joe shook his head. "Sure, and if for some ungodly reason this foolish quest of yours is successful, I'll fit you with a bulletproof vest when we get back here. You're gonna need it."

The three of them sped down the highway in complete silence, Richard wondering all the while when they were going to stop and why the sheriff was this far from Gator Bait. Of course, there was no hospital in Gator Bait, and the sheriff *was* on medical leave. Maybe his condition was serious.

Maybe he'd had a run-in with one of those finger-snatching monsters.

As they drove through the gates of the retirement home, he looked at Joe in surprise. "Retirement home? I thought the sheriff was on leave?"

Joe glanced over at Dorie, who remained silent, staring out of the passenger window. "Sort of."

"What do you mean, sort of?"

"You'll see. Go inside and talk to the man."

Joe parked the truck and Dorie immediately jumped out, slammed the door and stalked toward the entry of the building.

"You coming?" Richard asked.

Joe sighed and stared at Dorie's retreating figure. "Yeah, I suppose. The sheriff would never forgive me if I drove trouble out here and didn't even say hello."

"I'm only trying to do my job," Richard said as they walked toward the building. "I resent being referred to as trouble."

"Then stop resembling it," Joe shot back and pushed the door open for them to enter.

Sherry greeted the deputy as soon as he walked in the door. "Why, Joe," she said, smiling happily, "we haven't seen you in here for a while. The sheriff has been complaining. What brings you around?"

"Business, unfortunately," Joe replied. He pointed a finger at Richard. "This is Dick from D.C. He thinks Dorie's unqualified to assist on his investigation and has requested the sheriff's help instead."

"Is that what all the stomping was about?" Sherry gave Richard an up-and-down look. She didn't seem impressed with what she saw. "You disturb my patient, and I'll have your hide, son. I don't care how old you are or where you're from. You understand me?"

"Yes, ma'am," Richard replied, wondering what the hell he'd gotten himself into now.

"This way," Joe said and headed off down a corridor. Richard took one last look at the frowning Sherry and followed Joe down the hall.

When they reached the end of the building, Joe knocked on a door, and Richard heard a voice call for them to enter. Joe shot Richard a dirty look that clearly said this was not going to be pleasant and it was all Richard's fault, then pushed the door open.

The man in the wheelchair was in a tiny living room just off the entry. Richard took one look at him and held back a string of curse words. The man *was* paralyzed. And apparently the two assholes he'd ridden over here with had found that information unnecessary to pass along despite his comment back at the sheriff's office. He barely controlled his anger as he scanned the rest of the room.

Dorie sat in an overstuffed chair, arms crossed in front of her, a resolute expression on her face. A collection of military weapons that would have made a third-world country envious hung on the wall behind her, and a huge alligator head was perched above the fireplace, its glassy eyes seeming to glare at him. The wall next to him contained photo after photo of camouflage-clad men, and in the center hung a single medal. Upon closer inspection, Richard realized he was looking at a Silver Star and turned his attention back to the man in the wheelchair, trying not to show his surprise at finding a war hero in such an unlikely place.

The man, whom Richard now presumed was the

sheriff, had shouted at Joe as soon as they entered the room and was currently berating Joe on his visiting habits. "Joe, where the hell you been?" the man said. "You haven't been to see me in almost two weeks. It better be that pretty Jenny that's keeping you away."

Joe stared at the man in obvious dismay. "How'd you know about Jenny?"

The man snorted. "Hell, boy, everyone in town knows how you feel about Jenny, except for Jenny. Did you really think I got this far in life being shortsighted?"

Joe sighed. "No, I guess not."

"Well? Have you been seeing her?"

Joe shook his head.

"What the hell are you waiting for? If you hold off until you're comfortable enough to ask, Jenny'll be married and have five kids. You want to live in that town for the rest of your life with another man married to your wife?"

"No, sir," Joe said and shifted his feet, obviously uneasy at the thought of Jenny married to another man. "I know it's more fun picking on me, but we've got a situation here that needs your attention."

The man in the wheelchair looked at Richard. "Are you the self-righteous son of a bitch?" The man pointed to Dorie. "Her words."

Richard stared at the man, unsure how exactly to reply to the question, and Joe nodded. "Yep, this is Dick with the DEA. He wants to see you about Dorie's refusal to follow his orders and her apparent inability to do her job in general." Joe waved a hand at the man in the wheelchair. "Dick, this is Sheriff Berenger."

"Berenger?" Richard looked at the sheriff, then Dorie and back to Joe, a feeling of dread creeping over him. "Dorie's father?"

Joe gave Richard a huge smile. "The one and only. Go ahead and tell him all about his incompetent, bullheaded daughter. I'm going down the hall to find some of those chocolate-chip cookies Sherry keeps at the front desk." He sauntered out the door, whistling.

"So, Dick," Sheriff Berenger said, smiling. "I hear you been giving my daughter a hard time."

Richard stared at the sheriff in dismay. This was not going at all like he'd anticipated. He cleared his throat and addressed the man. "It's Richard, and I don't think I've been giving her a hard time." *Not near as hard as the time she's giving me.* "I'm only trying to do my job."

The sheriff pointed to the couch and Richard took a seat as far away from Dorie as he could manage. "And that job would be using Dorie or anyone else in this town to find your man," the sheriff continued, "but not letting them know the where, when or why. Right? And just what makes you think I'd condone that kind of nonsense?"

Richard sighed. "Look, Sheriff. Surely you've been around long enough to know what kind of information I can and can't give out. This isn't personal. I have my orders the same as anyone in law enforcement."

Sheriff Berenger leaned forward in his wheelchair and looked intently at Richard. "Lemme ask you something, and I want an honest answer. Do you think my daughter is stupid?"

Richard blinked in surprise. This wasn't what he had expected at all, and he had to think for a moment to find a politically correct answer, especially since Dorie was armed and sitting only eight feet away. "No, sir," he finally said. "From what I've seen, she seems very qualified to handle the town."

Dorie snorted. "Ha."

"I see," the sheriff muttered, and Richard knew that neither of them was in the least bit fooled by the duplicity of his reply.

"Qualified to handle Gator Bait, but not anything outside of the town, right?" the sheriff continued. "You think we're all a bunch of small-town hicks, capable of competence only in our own neck of the woods."

Sheriff Berenger glanced over at Dorie, who shot him an I-told-you-so look. The sheriff blew out a breath and sat back in his wheelchair, apparently in deep thought.

"I'm not trying to insult anyone," Richard said finally, trying to smooth things over. "But yes, I do feel Dorie may not be the most qualified person to assist in an arrest on this particular crime. It's a very complicated case."

"Uh-huh," the sheriff said. "So if the local law is so 'unqualified,' as you say, why doesn't your department send in more men?" He gave Richard a keen look, and Richard was certain he already knew the answer to that question.

Richard blew out a breath. "My boss feels that too many agents in such a small place would draw attention to our investigation and cause our target to flee."

"And he's right," the sheriff said. He looked over at Dorie and back at Richard. "Seems to me that the two of you have a problem. You're stuck with each other until this man is caught or out of Gator Bait. That seems to be the directive from *both* your superiors." He gave Dorie a hard look and she dropped her eyes to the floor.

"But," the sheriff continued, "I would never ask an

officer under my command to go in blind. That goes double for my daughter. I saw enough of what happens when you go in unprepared during 'Nam." He pointed at Richard. "You better figure out a way to loosen your lips. At least enough for Dorie and Joe to feel safe helping you."

Richard thought for a moment about the time and money the agency had invested in capturing Roland. *Don't hold your breath*. "I'll see what I can do," he said.

Dorie shot him a look that said she wasn't buying a word of it, and Richard decided it was time to leave. He'd been reading people long enough to know when he could push them around. Sheriff Berenger may as well have been a brick wall. The fact that Dorie was his daughter made the situation that much worse. He wasn't likely to give at all on his direction, and Richard knew he was fast running out of options where catching Roland was concerned.

He rose from the couch and extended his hand to the sheriff, who gave him a bone-crushing handshake as he cast a final glance at the glassy-eyed monster over the fireplace.

"She's a beautiful specimen, isn't she?" the sheriff asked.

For a moment Richard thought the sheriff was talking about Dorie. Then he realized the man was looking at the alligator head. "Yes. She's a beauty," Richard replied, unsure what to say exactly about the head of a dead animal serving as decoration. "Did you shoot it?"

Dorie laughed and the sheriff gave Richard a withering look. "Wouldn't have been much sport in that, would there?"

Afraid to ask how he managed the monster's death without use of a firearm, Richard decided it was time to make his exit. "Thank you for your time," he said. "I'll see what I can do about getting a release for information."

Sheriff Berenger nodded. "Do that, and I promise, you won't regret it." He looked out the apartment window, a faraway expression on his face. "I always try to help with the law." He looked back at Richard. "It never leaves a person, you know, even if the person has to leave the law."

Richard gave the sheriff a nod and left the room, more frustrated than ever about Gator Bait and Dorie Berenger.

Dorie watched Richard's retreating figure until the front door had closed behind him before she turned to her dad. "He'll never get clearance to give me information and you know that. What are you trying to accomplish?"

Sheriff Berenger laughed. "Maybe I just like seeing you squirm a bit."

"Please." Dorie gave him a disgusted look. "Like I find Dick threatening. He's about as dangerous as a seagull."

The sheriff shook his head. "Dick may well be the only man on earth brave enough to stand up to you."

Dorie rose from the couch and leaned over to kiss her dad on the forehead. "Don't confuse being foolish with being brave," she said and left the apartment, certain that her dad had only succeeded in aggravating an already impossible situation.

Richard decided the ride back to Gator Bait was as entertaining as a funeral. It was as if everyone in the truck had taken a vow of silence, all of them determined not to be the first one to speak. Dorie stared out of the passenger window, her back turned slightly to him, but it hardly mattered to Richard, who wasn't feeling especially talkative after his less-than-stellar run-in with the sheriff.

The only one who didn't seem bothered by the almost offensive silence was Joe, but Richard had gotten the impression early on that the less he spoke around Joe, the happier the man would be. Which was yet another thing that troubled him. Joe seemed to resent his presence only because he believed it caused Dorie problems. And since most everyone in town kept throwing Jenny in Joe's face, he figured it wasn't jealousy that made the other man mad.

Richard sighed. Too many mysteries. Who would have believed such a small place could have so much angst? And he'd thought big cities had issues. He shook his head and focused on his conversation with the sheriff. Better to stick with what he knew. Sordid small-town relationships were beyond his scope.

Finally, Joe parked in front of the sheriff's office. Dorie jumped out of the truck and announced over her shoulder that she needed a part for her boat and would be in the office in a minute. Without even a backward glance, she headed across the street to the boat shop.

Richard took one look at her retreating figure and sighed. Getting answers from Dorie was not going to be easy. And despite her father's edict that she was required to help, he didn't think she would make it pleasant for either of them.

He turned around and looked at Joe, who was checking the air pressure in his tires. "What did

Sheriff Berenger do in Vietnam?" Richard asked, curious about the man and the rare medal that hung on his wall.

"Sniper," Joe replied, still leaned over, studying the tire.

Richard blew out a breath. That certainly explained his comment about shooting the alligator, and gave a whole new meaning to the collection of weaponry hanging on his wall. It also gave him a lot more incentive to tread lightly where Dorie was concerned. "How long has he been like that?" Richard asked, wondering briefly if the chair made the man less dangerous or simply frustrated him, making him more dangerous.

"In a wheelchair, you mean?" Joe straightened up and put the tire gauge in his jeans pocket. "I guess it would be about ten years or so, maybe closer to eleven. Heart problems left him partially paralyzed."

"Ten or eleven years?" Richard asked, surprised. "Why is he still sheriff? He can't possibly perform the job."

Joe studied him for a minute before answering. "People around here still elect him because they know Dorie will be here to do the job. Places like he's staying aren't cheap. He needs to draw the salary."

"What about Dorie's mother? Does she help at all?"

Joe stiffened and a sudden chill settled over them. "Dorie doesn't have a mother, and no one in Gator Bait speaks about it, least of all to Dorie. You'll do yourself a big favor to do the same." Joe turned and walked into the sheriff's office, the door swinging shut behind him.

Richard looked at the man through the plate-glass window, then back across the street at the boat shop. That woman was quickly becoming one of the most interesting people he had ever come across. And not necessarily in a good way.

Deciding he had inflamed and irritated enough people for the morning, Richard headed across the street to the motel. He needed to get permission to release some information to Dorie, and he already dreaded calling his boss.

Dorie took her time at the boat shop, silently daring Richard to interrupt her. But when seconds turned into minutes and he didn't stalk through the door demanding her attention, she grew bored with the boat-shop chatter, paid for her part, and crossed the street to the sheriff's office.

Joe was sitting at his desk when she came in, typing up a form. "Where the hell is Dick?" she asked.

Joe shrugged, never lifting his eyes from the typewriter. "Guess he had something else to do."

"Did he say that?"

"No. But he didn't follow me in here, so I figure he had something else to do."

Dorie shook her head in exasperation. "Joe, did any part of this morning's fiasco bother you at all?"

He looked up from the typewriter and considered her question for a moment. "Guess not." He turned back to the typewriter.

"And why the hell not?" What was wrong with the man? Did he *like* being insulted and bossed by Dick?

He blew out a breath and leaned back in his chair, finally understanding that he was not going to be allowed to finish his report until this conversation was over. "It was a waste of time, really. I figure the sheriff set him straight, or you straight, or quite possibly, the both of you."

Dorie bristled. "I did *not* need to be set straight. I'm fully aware of my responsibilities. But I notice you didn't feel the need to stick around."

"No point. The sheriff didn't need my help, and besides, Dick's problem is with you."

"I give up," she said and grabbed her boat keys off the desk. "I'll be out in the marsh. Hopefully, dying of exposure. If Mr. Condescending shows up, you tell him I have a job to do, and it doesn't include waiting around on him." She stalked out of the sheriff's office, slamming the door behind her.

Joe leaned back in his chair and smiled. Dorie was more than a little irritated by Big City, not that he blamed her. The man seemed to create aggravation almost instantly. But the interesting part of it all was if they took a moment to consider the situation from the outside, they'd see how much alike they were. Two more bullheaded people had never been made, and when they collided, the sparks were going to fly.

Smiling, he started filing his paperwork, happy in the knowledge he already held a front-row seat to the show of the century. Dorie Berenger was going down for the count. He would bet money on it. And she was taking Big City with her.

If she didn't kill him first.

Chapter Five

It was almost quitting time and Richard still hadn't made it back to the sheriff's office. Dorie was back at her desk, pretending to type up a report while sneaking looks at her watch every couple of minutes. The sneaking part was necessary because she was afraid Joe was on to her. The last thing she needed was Joe knowing she was waiting on Big City. Weakness was not one of her options. And even being nosy counted as weakness in her book.

At five o'clock on the dot, Joe rose from his chair, rinsed his coffee mug and grabbed his keys from his desk. He looked at Dorie. "You coming?"

"No, not quite yet. I think I'll finish up this report first so I don't have it for tomorrow," she answered, trying to sound nonchalant.

"Uh-huh," Joe said and walked toward the door. "Give that report my best when he shows up," he said and walked out of the office.

"Damn," Dorie said out loud.

This whole situation had the potential to be very embarrassing. And it was a completely new experience. She had never met a man that made her want to shoot him and rip his clothes off at the same time. Dorie was used to men who were reverent of her and perhaps even a little afraid. Certainly no man in Gator Bait but her dad would even think of demanding things from Dorie.

Until Richard.

She'd apparently met her match and didn't like how it made her feel. Kill him or sleep with him? One or the other would have been fine. Wanting to do both at the same time was downright troubling. Especially considering the man in question.

She shook her head in dismay. Why in the world was she even remotely attracted to a man who considered her an idiot? Not that Richard wasn't attractive—in an uptight, preppy sort of way. Even the starched clothes couldn't disguise the muscular build and stocky frame beneath them.

Sighing, she leaned back from her desk. Of course, attraction was attraction and a completely separate issue from respect or love. Maybe it had just been too long since she'd scratched that itch. Of course, she didn't know a single man in Gator Bait worth the scratching time and since she rarely left town except to visit her dad, her options of other men were severely limited.

It was probably like dehydration. She'd just run so short on men for such a long time, the first one who came along not missing a limb or most of his teeth started to look attractive.

"I've got to start getting out more," she said out loud.

"What for?" The voice made her jump. She

looked up and saw Richard standing just inside the doorway. She hadn't even heard him come in. Some detective.

"Into the game preserve," she said quickly. "I need to get out into the game preserve a little more. We might need to thin the alligator population. I wouldn't know except by spending time there."

Richard nodded and sat on the desk across from Dorie. "Look," he said, "I know we didn't get off to a great start. You weren't exactly what I was expecting, but that problem is mine, not yours."

"At least we agree on something," Dorie shot back before she could control her tongue.

Richard blew out a breath. "I spent the afternoon trying to get a special clearance for you so I could give you classified information."

Dorie sat up straight in her chair and stared at Richard in surprise. "Really?"

"Yeah. I didn't want to ask, but after giving the entire matter a lot of thought, I can't really blame you for your position. I would never walk into a situation like this without the facts, no matter who said it was okay. I can hardly ask you to do something I wouldn't feel comfortable with myself."

"So did you get the clearance?"

Richard shook his head, clearly frustrated. "No. The agency has been hot on this case too long, and my superiors are paranoid of losing our man now that we're so close."

Dorie shook her head in disgust. "Then we're right back where we started. I still can't help you track a ghost. And don't bother to tell me the sheriff said I have to. I could have told you that was a waste of time."

Richard put one hand up in protest. "I know. I know. And that's why I've decided to give you some information, despite my agency's ruling on the matter. Realize, of course, that if anyone finds out I gave you this information, it would mean my job."

Even though his words made sense, Dorie still wondered about his shift in attitude. Always suspicious, she couldn't quite put her finger on what caused the change. And it bothered her. "Is it worth the risk?" she probed, trying to find the answer to her question. "Why not just ask for reassignment?"

His face grew hard and his lips tense. "Reassignment is not an option. This is my takedown—period. I have my reasons and they're not open for discussion."

Interesting, but not exactly the detail she was looking for. "Fine. I won't repeat anything you tell me in confidence, unless Joe is pulled into this, too. Then he has a right to the same information I do. That also goes for the sheriff. And I can vouch for both of them."

Richard looked closely at her, but she steadily met his gaze. Apparently satisfied, he began his story. "The man I'm looking for is Shawn Roland. He's a deal-maker for the Hebert family out of New Orleans. The Heberts are the main suppliers of heroin for the New England area. They don't distribute, of course, just deliver. The New England families take care of distribution."

"So you want to cut off the supply chain because that's more efficient than busting every drug dealer in New England? Makes sense."

"Exactly. Since we knew Roland was connected with the Hebert family, we concentrated our investigation on New Orleans, thinking the drugs were coming in through the port at the mouth of the Mississippi."

"But you didn't find anything?"

Richard shook his head. "Not a thing. But we still felt the drugs were coming into the country through the Gulf of Mexico. We've been systematically checking all of the towns along the Gulf Coast. We just hadn't made it this far."

"Then I ran the print."

Richard nodded.

Dorie stared at him for a moment. Something wasn't right. He hadn't told her everything, not that she'd expected him to. But she had the feeling there was something major missing from his explanation. Cocking her head to one side, she studied the man in front of her, but he avoided looking directly at her. "How long have you been chasing this Roland?"

She saw his face flush slightly and knew she'd finally hit a nerve. This was one of the questions he'd been hoping she wouldn't ask. "Dick?" she asked again. "How long?"

"Eight years," he said between clenched teeth.

He still hadn't met her gaze, and she knew there was more to the story. "And before you?" She pushed harder. "How long has the agency been looking for this man?"

He stared at the floor and mumbled something she couldn't quite make out.

"What was that?" she asked.

"Thirty-four years," he said with a sigh. "The agency has been trying to catch Shawn Roland for thirty-four years."

"Jesus Christ, Dick!" Dorie shouted and jumped up from her chair. "That's longer than either one of us has been alive. And you people are supposed to be the best? Good God."

Richard's facial features tightened. "The best men

at the agency *have* been on this case. Unfortunately, Roland is superior at his job. He has no family, no friends and the only picture we have of him is from sixth grade, the last year he attended school."

Dorie stopped pacing and stared at him. "Tell me more," she said, her curiosity piqued by this master criminal.

"His father was a small-time pimp and pusher," he continued. "His mother was an addict and a prostitute. Both liked to slap Roland around when they got mad. Apparently, Roland wasn't interested in the family business."

He blew out a breath and ran one hand through his hair. "Roland struck out on his own when he was twelve. Child Protective Services came to check on him and the parents said they hadn't seen him in weeks."

Dorie shook her head in disgust.

"I know. They also hadn't reported him missing and didn't seem very concerned. CPS returned a couple of weeks later to follow up and found both parents dead in the house. They'd been stabbed over twenty-five times each and were lying next to a pile of drugs that had been left behind."

Richard gave her a hard look. "Roland was the main suspect, of course, but the local cops never found a trace of him. They finally gave up, figuring him for dead."

"I knew it," she said, disgusted. "He *is* a ghost. You're telling me this man has existed all those years in nothingness?"

"There was a woman once. But it was over thirty years ago. She gave the agency most of our information on him. She wanted out."

"What happened to her?" Dorie asked, pretty sure she wasn't going to like the answer.

"I don't know. The agency never heard from her again, and they never located her."

"He killed her."

"Probably."

Dorie blew out a breath. A drug dealer suspected of multiple homicides—his first as a minor—had stopped off in her town. This week was going to hell in a handbasket.

"I guess we'd better start right away," she finally said. "God knows, you need my help. At the rate you people are going, I'll never get you out of my town."

Ten minutes later, they were bouncing down the logging trail to Maylene Thibodeaux's house. For some reason Dorie couldn't fathom, Richard wanted to see the pool where the alligator had been found. If this was the way the DEA performed an investigation, it was no wonder they hadn't caught Roland. What a waste of time. Roland had never been in Maylene's swimming pool. If he had, Maylene would have bagged him and probably had him mounted on the wall over her portable television.

Still, Maylene might be a quick way to get rid of Richard. No, that was even too cruel for Dick. Best keep him away from Maylene's brew.

Dorie pointed to the house as they approached. "There's the house. And I'm giving you fair warning. Maylene is a widow on search for victim number two. Do not drink anything she has to offer."

Richard stared at her, a confused expression on his face, but nodded. "Okay. I promise I won't drink anything."

They walked up the steps to Maylene's house, and Dorie knocked on the front door. They waited a moment, but heard no movement. She knocked again, harder this time. Finally, they heard rustling inside.

"I'm coming," Maylene yelled. "I'm coming."

The door flew open and Dorie smiled. Richard's first look at Maylene Thibodeaux was a doozy. She had obviously been asleep. Her choice of night-wear consisted of a belly shirt and G-string under-wear. Of course, on Maylene, there was a lot more belly than shirt and that string on her underwear was probably lost forever.

"Damn it, Dorie. It's after five. You know I've been at happy hour since three. What the hell is so important that you're banging on my door after working hours?" Then Maylene caught sight of Richard. "Well," she changed her tone from angry to her version of sexy. "This looks important. You bringing me gifts, Dorie?"

Richard looked alarmed and took a step back, just out of Maylene's reach. Dorie bit her lip and tried not to laugh. "No, Maylene. He's not a gift. This is Richard Starke. He's with the DEA in D.C., and he's here about the drugs we found on the alligator."

Maylene looked disappointed. "City dude. *Hmpf.* City dude would never be able to keep up with me. Guess you better come on in since you're not going away."

"That's all right," Dorie said. "We really wanted to take a look at the pool. I just didn't want to go into the backyard without your permission."

Maylene waved one hand in the air. "Go on then. I'm going back to bed." She gave Richard one last lingering look. "Tell you what," she said. "I'll let you have one bottle of brew for the road. If you like it, you know where to find me." She reached for a table next to the door, picked up a bottle and handed it to Richard. "Come back soon. Plenty more where that came from." Maylene stepped back into her house and slammed the door behind her.

Richard looked at the bottle and sniffed the top. His eyes began to water. "What the hell is this stuff?"

Dorie laughed. "Maylene's man-catching brew. But don't throw it away. I use it to strip the paint off my boat, and Maylene won't give any to women."

They walked behind the house to the pool and Richard took a look around. "How far away is the nearest water supply?" he asked.

"About a mile in any direction you choose. You got the Gulf south of here and a number of bayous every other direction."

"A mile?" Richard said, obviously surprised. "That alligator traveled a mile out of the water?"

"Yeah. Surprised me, too, until I found the drugs. Gators run fast, though. I figure when the initial high hit him, he took off and ended up at Maylene's before he crashed."

"So you definitely think the alligator was from around here?" Richard asked as they began walking back toward the jeep. "Could he have come from outside Gator Bait?"

"Could have, but he didn't."

"How do you know?"

"I recognized him. He's a local."

Richard stared at her, clearly amazed. "You've included alligators in the local population?"

She climbed into the jeep. "Not really. It's just that this one had a scar on his leg from getting caught in a broken trap at the shrimp house. I remembered the scar."

Richard shook his head. "So do you have any idea where this alligator's hangout might be?"

Dorie started the jeep and gave him a broad smile. "Why, Dick? You planning on questioning him?"

Because it had been a long day and because Richard needed to consider the information he had so far to know which direction he wanted to go next, he asked Dorie to call it quits. She looked more than happy to dump him in front of the motel and sped off without a word.

He stared at the retreating lights on the jeep for a moment and shook his head. Dorie Berenger was a study in psychology. Helpful one minute and sarcastic and brooding the next. Richard didn't quite know what to make of her, and wasn't sure he had enough years left of life to figure it out. He looked at the run-down motel and thought about the long night ahead of him.

The neon light from Pete's Bar flickered in the corner of his vision. What were the odds of making it in and out of that place twice? Everyone in town probably knew he saw the sheriff about Dorie before they even got back to Gator Bait. Was all that hassle really worth a beer?

He'd just have to take his chances. Boredom was a bigger threat. Loneliness was the biggest threat of all. No one had told him how lonely this job would be. It was his only regret about his chosen profession. Hoping his luck would hold another night, he pulled open the door to the bar and stepped inside.

The night crowd hadn't made it in yet, so the room was sparsely populated. Richard recognized the same bartender from the other night and took a seat in front of the register.

The bartender, who was pouring peanuts into

plastic baskets, looked up as Richard sat down. "You need a menu again?" he asked.

Richard held in a sigh. "No, I'll just have a beer."

"Regular beer or light beer?"

"Regular beer. It's been much too long of a day to drink light."

The bartender gave him a satisfied look. "Now you're coming around. We mostly stock the light beer for women. They like to watch their figures. No self-respecting man in Gator Bait would be caught dead drinking light beer. Except, of course, if there was nothing else."

The bartender popped the top on a bottle of beer and slid it across the counter. "Word has it you saw the sheriff today. Did he put his daughter straight, or did he put you straight?"

Now Richard did sigh. "If you already know I saw the sheriff, I'm sure you also know what happened."

The bartender grinned. "'Course I do, but it's much better hearing the story from the losing end. They usually have a creative way of putting a spin on the whole thing. Kind of like a fish story, you know?"

Richard downed a quarter of the beer. "Not exactly. But I guess stories about the one that got away are fairly popular here."

"You have no idea."

Since the bartender was pleasant enough, Richard decided to go out on a limb. He extended his hand across the bar. "My name's Richard Starke, by the way. I don't think we were formally introduced."

The bartender snorted, but shook Richard's hand. "I'm Pete. This is my bar." He gave a small laugh. "Formally introduced. That's a good one."

Richard laughed also. "Yeah, I guess it didn't take long for word of me to get around."

"Word? Man, except for that locked briefcase of yours, we know everything about you down to your underwear brand. Designer label." Pete leaned over, elbows on the bar, and studied Richard. "Now why does a man want to wear designer drawers when Wal-Mart is much cheaper and no one sees 'em anyway?"

Richard considered the question and his answer for a moment. Was it really worth pursuing? Of course, on the other hand, Pete was being fairly chatty. Maybe if he told the man about his underwear, he'd give him a rundown of the people in the town. It would save him the time and trouble of asking Dorie. Mostly the trouble.

"You see," Richard finally said, "it's like this. The cotton in designer underwear is a much finer fabric. It feels better on the skin and causes less chafing."

Pete narrowed his eyes at Richard. "Finer fabric? You ain't one of them kind of guys, is you? 'Cause I don't want word to get around that I was talking to one of them kind of guys. I gotta live in this town."

Richard stared at Pete, confused. "What exactly is 'them kind of guys'?"

Pete pulled himself upright. "You know—them kind of guys. The kind that like opera and call sewing material 'fabric.' "

Richard caught on and gave the man an amused smile. "No. I'm not one of them kind of guys." Pete gave him a suspicious look and Richard held up one hand. "I promise," he said. "I've never found another man even remotely attractive."

Pete studied him a moment more and finally

nodded. "Guess it's all right, then. Not that I agree, mind you. I'll just stick to Wal-Mart or Sears when it comes to underwear. Just don't see a good reason, 'fabric' or not, to pay a lot of money for something that's going to rub on my butt all day."

Richard held in his smile until Pete turned back toward the cash register. In a strange, redneck sort of way, the man did have a point. It wasn't like anyone was actually seeing his underwear—well, except apparently housekeeping at the motel. In fact, it took him a minute to remember the last woman he'd had the pleasure of showing his finer fabric.

Shaking his head, he downed the remainder of the beer, his mind made up. When this was over and Roland was behind bars, he would have to consider a new profession. His work was thrilling and meaningful and made a difference, *but* . . . And that was where the problems were. The but.

Since joining the DEA, Richard couldn't remember a single relationship that had lasted more than three months. Women didn't like a man disappearing for long stretches of time, especially when he was unaccounted for. It was the stuff of nightmares for anyone with a suspicious mind. And Richard hadn't met a woman yet that didn't have a suspicious mind.

In the beginning, some had said they understood the work, but all had eventually left, claiming they couldn't exist in a one-person relationship. They wanted family suppers and weekend baseball games. And kids. How in the world could he be a decent father when he only made it home to his apartment five days out of any given month? He couldn't even keep a cactus alive.

The whole situation depressed him. "Give me another one, Pete," Richard said.

Pete, now finished with the peanut baskets,

popped the top off another beer and handed it over. "What are you in Gator Bait for, exactly? If you don't mind my asking?" Pete leaned on the bar, elbows resting in front of Richard, and stared.

"I don't mind your asking," Richard said. "I just can't give you all of the facts. Most of the information is classified."

Pete snorted. "Yeah, we already heard about the classified part. Got you a visit to the sheriff, which got you nowhere fast." He reached up with one hand and rubbed his jaw. "Still, Dorie took you out to Maylene Thibodeaux's this evening. I don't figure it was a social call."

Richard quickly shook his head. "No way. That woman is frightening. I was just doing a little looking around."

Pete nodded. "Yeah, the swimming pool with the high gator. Wouldn't of believed it myself if I hadn't seen the pictures over at the grocery store."

Richard groaned. "Everyone knows about the drugs?"

"Of course. You think Maylene was gonna keep gossip that good to herself? The ole gal wasn't that drunk. You don't know much about small towns, do you?"

"So much for undercover," Richard muttered. He looked back up at Pete. "Well, since you already know what I'm after, maybe you can tell me who has a problem with drugs in Gator Bait."

Pete stared at him in obvious surprise. "Drugs in Gator Bait? No way, man. There's never been anyone with a drug problem in Gator Bait. Strongest stuff we got here is Maylene's brand, and everyone knows better than to drink that. This is a beer and cigarettes kind of town."

"You know everyone in town, right?"

"'Course. Been here all my life. Served damn near everyone a beer at some time or another. Except some of the old spinster ladies. Big church people, you know."

Richard nodded. Strange as the people may seem, it *was* the Bible Belt. "I don't suppose you'd want to tell me who owns the businesses in town. You know, where the money in Gator Bait comes from?"

Pete studied Richard for a moment. "The major players. That's what you're looking for, right?"

Richard blinked at the phrase.

"Hey, we got television here. I'm a big fan of those cop shows. Investigators, DAs, forensics, you name it, I'll watch it." Pete picked up a serving tray and began to wipe it down with a clean cloth, clearly deep in thought.

"Well, we can start with Buster Comeaux. He owns the shrimp house. Employs probably eighty percent of Gator Bait, either by actual employees or buying shrimp from the locals. Without the shrimp house, there'd be no Gator Bait."

Richard nodded. It was the typical dynamic of a small town. One main source of employment keeping the entire place afloat. Richard hoped for all their sakes the price of shrimp stayed up and the shrimp stuck around town. "What's Buster like?" Richard asked.

"He's great. One of the best men around. Gives Dorie a bit of a problem by not fixing his traps properly at the shrimp house. Gators get in and Dorie has to get them out or pay Curtis to do it. She keeps threatening to bill him. Wouldn't surprise me if she did over this last time." Pete leaned back against the register, paused for a moment, then nodded. "Yeah, all in all, I'd say Buster was a great man."

Pete rubbed on the tray again, apparently lost in

thought. A minute later, he picked up his explanation. "About thirty years ago or so, best I can remember, Gator Bait ran into a big pinch. Shrimp weren't running well, and the market had dropped way off. Even though he was losing money and giving a whole lot of his inventory away, Buster never turned down a sale and never let a single employee go."

"How'd he manage that?"

Pete shrugged. "Don't rightly know. But Buster came from one of the better families in Gator Bait. He probably had a little put back from his parents. Plus, I'm sure he'd made a healthy profit from all the years before when shrimp was running better. I just know that Gator Bait stayed afloat because Buster Comeaux didn't close the doors. And for that, I am grateful. Hell, he's going on seventy now and still works every day."

Richard nodded. "And this Curtis who helps Dorie with the alligators—who's he?"

Pete smiled. "Why, Curtis is the stuff bayou legends are made of. He has a way with those creatures that you wouldn't believe unless you saw it, so I'm not even going to try and explain. You stick around long enough and you'll get a chance to see Curtis in action. I tell you, it's a sight to behold."

"So he's a specialist?" Richard asked, still a bit confused over what services Curtis provided.

Pete laughed. "Yeah, I guess you could say that. He's an extraction specialist. The gators get in and Curtis gets them out. He's the best at his job. Not even Dorie can match him."

"Does Curtis own a business here in Gator Bait?"

"Lord, no. Curtis is just a good ole boy with an incredible talent. I dare say he couldn't even balance a checkbook, much less run a business."

Richard nodded. "What about the grocery store? Who owns that?"

"Sammy Breaux. Sammy Breaux, the third, I guess I ought to say. Grocery store's been in the family for as long as Gator Bait's been around. Another good man, Sammy. Always extends credit to people who are running a little short on luck. Probably takes the stiff on most of it, but it hasn't stopped him from doing it."

"What about the motel and the boat shop?"

"Hell, you're staying at the motel, aren't you? I figured you'd already met Stella."

Richard frowned, trying to match a person with the name. "You mean the little gray-haired lady?" It was the only woman he could remember in the motel except housekeeping and Ms. Congeniality at the front desk.

Pete snorted. "Little gray-haired lady, my ass. If you was to arm wrestle, I'd put my money on Stella. Her dad was one of the founding residents of Gator Bait. He did boat repair out of his house, but stayed too drunk to ever make any real money off it. Stella took notes and did a much better job than her dad."

"So she owns the boat shop," Richard mused. "Then why is she at the motel? Did I miss that part?"

Pete shook his head. "Stella knows how to run a business. The boat shop makes money hand over fist. Only sale or repair in town and she doesn't jack the prices up over the cities. She has a captive audience. When more people started coming down here to fish, Stella built the motel next to the boat shop. She rents boats out, too, you know?"

"No, I didn't know that. I guess she's a pretty sharp businesswoman."

"Got that right. Her and Jenny. Jenny's been cooking for residents of Gator Bait since elementary school bake sales. When her momma got sick and they needed help caring for her, Jenny opened the café. She doesn't have much free time, but her momma has a full-time nurse that lives with 'em."

Richard finished his bottle of beer and put it back on the counter. Pete picked up the bottle and dropped it in a wastebasket behind the bar. Without even asking, he popped the top on another bottle and passed it to Richard.

"Yeah," Pete said, rubbing his chin again. "Seems the women in this town have been the ones to really branch out. Change things for the better, you know? Stella, Jenny and Dorie, of course. Gator Bait wouldn't be the way it is today without those three." Pete nodded to Richard and moved to the other side of the bar to serve people who'd just arrived.

Richard took a drink of beer and stared at the glass wall behind the bar. *Three women, four men and an entire town beholden to them.* Most likely, one of them was a felon.

But which one?

Dorie sat at the kitchen table on her boat, staring at the television on the bedroom wall but not hearing a word of the dribble coming out of it. The microwave dinner in front of her cooled rapidly, but she wasn't concerned about food at the moment. She was concerned about Shawn Roland. And more importantly, who Roland was working with in Gator Bait just in case Richard was right and the deal had already been made.

She tapped one nail on the table and considered the possibilities. They weren't good. The local shrimpers and fishermen weren't smart enough to hide this sort of operation from her, so they were out. Besides, they had no way to launder drug money—not the size Richard was talking about anyway. Someone else might pay them to haul the product around, but they weren't making the initial deals, that was for sure. Jenny was out. Dorie picked up her beer and took a drink. Wasn't she?

She dropped her beer back to the table and shook her head in disgust. Of course she was, but what about the others? This is why she had never wanted to work in Gator Bait. The odds were against something of this magnitude happening, but Dorie knew that when and if it did, she'd have to consider her friends and family suspects. At least in a big city, most people were strangers. It was easier to see things clearly and when the time came, not difficult at all to take people down.

But this was different. This was her town. This was her family. And one of them might be a criminal. Dorie slumped down on the bench, the food and beer completely forgotten, and cursed the day she ran the print that brought Richard Starke into her town.

Chapter Six

After a restless night, Dorie planned to go into the office the next morning and attack locating Richard's bad guy with a new resolve. More than anything, she wanted Roland captured and Richard out of her town before everything fell apart in front of her. Unfortunately, the state had other ideas and sent a mass of paperwork they wanted back the same day.

So she put Richard to work looking at maps of the bayous and he had thankfully remained in studied silence the entire time. It took her most of the morning to process the forms when she realized she couldn't complete her obligations without a trip to one section of the game preserve for photos.

Aggravated with the further delay, she told Richard in a clipped voice that whatever he had planned would have to wait until afternoon and started out the door. Richard, in an apparent fit of insanity, followed her out and asked to go along, leaving Joe standing in the front office window staring at them and shaking his head.

Dorie drove in silence, the night's sleep doing little to improve her mood. In fact, if it was possible, she felt worse than ever. At least Richard was wisely keeping his mouth shut for a change, making her wonder why he'd bothered to come along at all. Not that she was complaining. She was in no mood to discuss the conclusions she'd come to last night after her third beer.

She drove down a logging trail to a posted section of the preserve and took a couple of photos the state required, then jumped back in her jeep and headed back to town, eager to get started on the search for Roland. They were a few miles from the sheriff's office when her cell phone rang. It was Joe.

"I got a call from Mrs. Paulie," he said. "She says there's a grill going at Boudreaux's, and they are *not* grilling burgers. Do you want to check it out?"

Dorie clenched her teeth. "Don't have a choice. You can't arrest him anyway if he's doing what I think he's doing, and if he is, I'm going to use him for crab bait."

"Problems in paradise?" Richard asked as she closed the phone.

"A small one," she said as she wheeled the jeep around in the opposite direction. "And one easily solved. But I'm afraid we'll have to put off your investigation for a little bit longer. I have to go arrest an idiot."

Richard grinned. "An idiot, huh? This should be interesting. I haven't seen one of those around here yet."

Dorie's scowl turned to a look of mild appreciation. "Good one, Dick. You're coming right along on this cynicism thing. Maybe one day you can give the real professionals, like me, a run for their money."

The conversation stopped short as Dorie turned off the paved road and onto an old logging trail that hadn't been used in some time. The jeep bounced through the holes and gaps in the broken planks that made up the low-lying parts of the trail. Dorie glanced over at Richard, who braced himself with the door and the roll bar of the jeep, and smiled.

She bet this wasn't what he'd expected when he came looking for his bad guy. Richard Starke was getting a grade-A lesson in rednecks and good ole boys. He thought only the big city had issues. She smiled. A city boy like Richard wouldn't survive a weekend here alone.

Dorie finally ended the agony by cutting left, directly into the marsh. She stopped the jeep in front of a dilapidated old cabin where three men sat outside in lawn chairs in front of a huge grill, the remnants of a massive beer-drinking party surrounding them. Richard took one look at the grill and turned to Dorie in surprise. There was no mistaking the twelve-foot shape rotating on the massive spit. He noticed her flushed face and was sure it wasn't with excitement. No, Dorie Berenger was mad, with a capital M.

She got out of the jeep, slammed the door, and stomped toward the three men in front of the grill, who at least had the good common sense to look a little afraid. "Clint Boudreaux, how many times have we been through this?" she said to the man sitting closest to the grill. "I told you I had given you my last warning. This time you are going to pay, and you are going to pay dearly."

Clint raised his hands in protest. "Now, Dorie, you

know I would never kill a gator out of season unless it was in self-defense."

She gave him a skeptical look. "Uh-huh, and what exactly were you doing that required defending yourself from an alligator?"

Clint tried the wide-eyed innocent look. He didn't quite make it. "I was just watching TV. Honest. And she came busting right through the door. See?" He pointed to a mass of splintered wood and netting next to the cabin. "I'm gonna have to get a new screen door. I'm the victim here, I swear."

Richard stared at the man and frowned. He wasn't sure exactly what was going on here, but he was positive Clint Boudreaux was no more a victim than any other repeat offender. He glanced at Dorie to gauge her reaction and didn't like what he saw. Her face was tense with anger, lips drawn tightly across her teeth. Her eyes were narrow and her hand hovered over her holster. For just a moment, Richard was pretty sure she would shoot the man.

"Where are they?" she finally asked, the words coming through clenched teeth, one short syllable at a time.

Clint held up both his hands in a surrender pose. "Now, Dorie, you know I wouldn't do anything like that—"

Before he could finish his sentence, Dorie swore and strode off toward the dilapidated cabin, then barged through the front door and went inside. Richard looked at the group of men around the grill and considered his options. He could stay out here with three probable criminals or help Dorie with her breaking-and-entering job. Not that it was exactly breaking and entering. More like just entering.

Finally, curiosity won out and Richard followed Dorie into the shack. He met her in the front room on her way back outside, carrying an ice chest and wearing an expression on her face he'd once seen on a serial killer. He hustled out of the way and let her pass, not even offering to carry the ice chest. Talking was probably at a premium at the moment, and Richard was pretty sure *his* talking wouldn't be advisable at all.

He followed Dorie out of the shack and back over to where the men sat, where she placed the ice chest on the ground and opened the top. Peering inside, Richard saw five tiny alligators, wrestling around in the shallow water.

"You're going down this time, Clint," Dorie said, obviously straining for control. "You're not getting another warning." She walked back to the jeep and returned with three sets of handcuffs. Tossing a set to Richard, she said, "I'm helping you, the least you can do is help me."

"Hell, Dorie," Clint said, rising from his chair. "You ain't putting those things on me. Now, let's just talk about this for a minute."

"I was done talking the last time, Clint," she said. "Now drop the bottle and put your hands out in front of you."

Clint spat on the ground next to him and gave her a dirty look. "I ain't putting down my bottle for no woman."

His last word still hung in the air when the shot rang out, the bottle shattered and Clint found himself holding what was left of the neck. Richard spun around to look at Dorie and saw her calmly placing her gun back in the holster.

"Drop the rest of that bottle, Clint," Dorie said. "Or I'm taking the fingers with me next time."

"Shit!" Clint said, still looking down at his hand in horror. "You could have shot my hand off, Dorie."

"You know better than that. If I'd have wanted to shoot your hand off, I would have. Now drop that glass and put your hands out."

Richard was fairly certain Clint was drunk, but apparently, he wasn't wasted. He threw the remaining piece of the bottle on the ground as if it were on fire and stuck his hands out in front of him. The other two men jumped up from their chairs and did the same. Dorie looked at the men for a moment, then down at the bayou.

"Tell you what. I have a better idea." She motioned toward the pier at a large floating object made of Styrofoam and wood. "Head on down to the barge."

The men looked confused, but weren't foolish enough to ask questions. When they reached the barge, Dorie motioned them all on board and instructed Richard to start cuffing them around a metal frame with nets attached to it.

"Dorie," Clint protested. "You can't leave us here. For Christ's sake, we can't even reach our things to pee."

"Should have thought about that before you tried to black-market alligators again. I don't have room for you three idiots and an ice chest of baby gators in my jeep. I don't suppose you have to ask which I consider to be more important. And I'm talking to Judge Harvey about garnishing your sales to pay the fines. For all three of you. If I have my way, the Gator Bait game warden will be taking a third of the cut you make off shrimping for a good long time."

The three men began to curse and pull at the cuffs. Dorie fired her gun in the air and all noise and movement ceased. "Keep it up, gentlemen," Dorie said sweetly, "and I won't send Joe for you until tomorrow." She put her gun back in the holster and motioned to Richard to leave.

Dorie lifted the ice chest and gently placed it in the back of her jeep, securing it tightly with rope, then jumped in the driver's seat, her face still flushed with anger. She looked over at Richard, who still stared at her, completely confused by the entire situation.

"Are you coming or not?" she asked. Richard nodded and jumped into the jeep, glancing back at the men handcuffed to the metal frames. This option is better, he thought as he studied Dorie's face, but only barely.

Dorie shoved the shifter in gear and tore out of the clearing. She strained to get control of herself but was pretty sure she was losing the battle. *I'd better get a grip fast. The last thing I need is Dick thinking I can't handle things. Especially now.*

She glanced over and found him staring intently at her, which unnerved her a bit.

"Are you all right?" he asked. The genuine sound of concern in his voice surprised her, and she felt some of her anger fade away, replaced with a feeling of uneasiness. *What is his angle now?*

"Yeah," she finally answered. "I'm fine. I'm angry is all."

"Don't you need a warrant to take those things from his house?" Richard asked, curiosity apparently overcoming good common sense.

She shot him a derisive look. "You don't know much about other branches of the law, do you, Dick? As game warden, I can search and seize darn near anything I want in my jurisdiction. All I need is suspicion."

He nodded and studied her face, making her even more uncomfortable. "You sure you're only mad? Because it seems like a lot more than anger to me. It seems almost personal."

She blew out a breath, not wanting to get into her private views on life, but realizing that he probably wouldn't let up until he'd received a somewhat satisfying answer. "Look. I believe all infants have a right to parents, regardless of species. That gator you saw on the grill was the mother, and she tore through that screen door because her babies were in the shack. Females stay with their young for almost a year. Without a mother, they're goners."

"What do you mean?"

"The alligators in that ice chest are newly hatched. They're a prime target for most anything right now. At nine inches long, even birds will eat them. An alligator less than four feet long has a survival chance of less than seventeen percent."

"So what will you do with them?" he asked and glanced back at the ice chest.

"I don't know yet. I need to make a few phone calls. I'm hoping my friend at the zoo in New Orleans will be interested. If not, my options are limited. I don't want to send them to a farm. It goes against everything I believe as a game warden and the mother came from the preserve."

"A farm? People farm alligators?"

Dorie nodded, disgusted. "It's big business. The skin and meat are worth a ton of money, but no one wants the animal to become extinct, so hunting is only allowed at certain times and in certain areas. The farms fill in all the gaps."

"Can't they be taken care of until they're bigger, then released in the game preserve?"

"Sometimes, but it's hard to do. When I first took

over down here, I tried that. The problem is, once they're used to a handout, they don't want to look for their own food. They ended up being a nuisance down at the shrimp house. We have to make a trip there at least once a month because Buster won't keep his traps in good repair, and the gators come up the chutes and into the shrimp house for a meal."

Richard was quiet, and she glanced over at him. He appeared to be in deep thought. "I've got to deal with this," she said. "It can't really wait. I'm sorry, but we'll have to start looking for Roland later on. Maybe by this afternoon, I'll have everything squared away."

He nodded. "That's fine. I've got a few phone calls to make and some paperwork to go over. I'll be at the motel. Give me a call when you're ready."

Dorie blinked, surprised it had been that easy to get rid of him. "You should stop by the café for lunch," she suggested. "Jenny knows how to run a grill. In fact, if you wouldn't mind, I could use a favor."

"Sure. What do you need?"

"It's almost lunch time and Joe's sure to be there. Tell him I said to pick up the guys at Clint's place but not anytime soon. And be sure and tell him to bring a handcuff key."

"No problem."

Dorie pulled the jeep in front of the sheriff's office and jumped out. She grabbed the ice chest from the backseat and started toward the front door. "I'll see you later," she said over her shoulder. Richard lifted one hand in acknowledgment and walked next door to the café.

Richard pushed the door of the café open and the smell of grilled burgers and fries wafted over him, causing his stomach to rumble. Maybe eating wasn't such a bad idea.

He scanned the small room and spotted Joe sitting in the same spot Richard had found him on Sunday. He was still staring at Jenny, eyes glazed over. This guy had it bad. Not that Richard blamed him. Jenny was a joy to look at. The best-looking woman in town.

Well, except Dorie.

He shook his head and took a seat next to Joe. Where did that come from? It was probably because he'd already seen her half-naked. If he hadn't been so angry at the time, he might have been impressed. Dorie Berenger had a body on her that wouldn't quit. Unfortunately, neither did her mouth. And now that he'd seen her gun-wrangling abilities, he would have to think twice about pissing her off again.

Joe looked over at him as he sat at the counter. "You finished at Boudreaux's already?"

"Yeah, but we ran into some trouble. Dorie has an ice chest of baby alligators she has to find a home for. She asked me to tell you to pick up the guys, but not anytime soon, and be sure to bring a handcuff key. We cuffed them to some floating thing with nets on it."

Joe's expression turned from bland to disgusted. He laid a couple of bucks on the counter, downed the remainder of his coffee, and walked out the door without a word.

"Was it something I said?" Richard asked, completely confused.

"Actually, yes," Jenny said as she turned from the grill and watched Joe pass in front of the glass storefront. "You want coffee?"

Richard nodded and Jenny grabbed a cup and began to pour. "So what did I say that was so bad?" he asked.

Jenny leaned on the counter, pushing back tendrils of long black hair that were escaping her ponytail. "It's not your fault. It's just that Dorie has this thing about all babies having parents. She's real adamant about every living creature being given all the opportunities to life that God meant them to have."

Richard nodded, absorbing the information. "And Joe? Are he and Dorie . . ." he trailed off, unsure how to phrase the question, and wondering if he had misread the relationship between the deputies.

Jenny looked at Richard in obvious surprise. "No, nothing like that. It's just that when Joe's dad died, the sheriff kind of took him under his wing. Male role model and all that. Joe and Dorie are practically brother and sister."

"Oh." The possessiveness and concern made sense now. And for some reason, it made Richard happy to know for certain that Joe and Dorie had never been an item.

Not that it would ever make a difference. Dorie had made her position clear. She wanted him and his drug smuggler out of her town as soon as possible. No stops for romance. Or sex. Or fun. Or any of the twenty other things Richard could think of to pass time with Dorie if she weren't busy insulting him.

"You like her," Jenny said, and Richard jerked his head up to find Jenny studying him.

"Well, um, yes, I guess so," he stammered, surprised to admit that on some level it was actually true. "I need the help of local law enforcement, and everyone says she's the best even though she's sort of abrasive."

Jenny laughed. "That's Dorie. No one around here takes it that way, though. She's just a great mind caught in a small town. I think she gets frustrated a lot." Jenny sighed. "I really can't blame her. Running this business has shown me the shallow and sometimes idiotic side of humans that I never really wanted to know. I imagine she sees much more of it than I do."

"It's hard to believe she wants to stay," Richard said, unable to help himself. Jenny was the only other person in Gator Bait, besides Pete, willing to have a casual conversation with him at all, and for the first time in years, Richard felt sociable. Besides, maybe Jenny had another take on Dorie Berenger that he hadn't already heard.

Jenny looked at him, clearly surprised at the comment. "Gator Bait's her home. All her family's here, and her daddy needs her."

"But she's never married?"

Jenny studied the wall, a thoughtful look on her face. "No. Never even had a boyfriend that I'm aware of. She's had a fling now and then. Police conferences and such. You know what I mean. But nothing that ever lasted more than a visit or two and a couple of phone calls. Guys don't want to move here and Dorie won't leave."

She gave him a thoughtful look. "Where are you from anyway?"

"Washington D.C. right now, but I've lived all over."

"Always big cities, huh?"

"Yeah. There's not enough crime in a small place to make it worth my education and training. I enjoy the thrill of the chase. I like knowing that what I do makes a difference."

"I guess I can understand that. Are you married?"

"No. Haven't found a woman yet who could deal with the job."

"Yeah." She studied him again. "What about Dorie? She shouldn't have any problems with your job."

Richard looked at her in dismay. "What are you talking about?"

Jenny shrugged. "It was just a thought. You have the same profession and all, so I figured if you're any good at your job, you shouldn't be threatened by her. Lots of men are. Maybe the right man for her is one just like her."

Richard rapidly shook his head. "Trust me. I'm not that man. I don't like complications, and Dorie Berenger is about the most complicated woman I've ever met."

Jenny gave him a big smile. "But that's what makes it so exciting. If attraction was easy, it wouldn't be near as much fun."

Richard watched her walk away to the kitchen and frowned. Complication was one thing, but a relationship on any level with Dorie Berenger was a certain impossibility. Hell, she barely tolerated working with him, although she had been fairly polite today. If one considered barely speaking fairly polite.

He took a large sip of his coffee and leaned back in his chair, thinking about Dorie and her personal problem with the baby alligators; Dorie and her mother that no one spoke about. What the hell had happened to her?

It was midafternoon before Dorie returned to the sheriff's office, but Richard didn't mind. The maps of the bayous alone had kept him busy the entire morning and looking at all the blue swirls on the paper made him instantly aware of how smart it had been to let Dorie in on confidential information. There was no way in hell he would have ever been able to negotiate them alone. Small countries could be hidden in this maze and he probably wouldn't know it.

He looked up at the doorway as she strolled into the sheriff's office wearing a smile, her mood apparently improved from the morning. When he asked about the gators, she told him that the zookeeper friend had room for the babies and had sent someone for them right away. The babies were currently bunking down with Stella over at the boat store awaiting pickup.

"So where did you want to start today?" she asked. "You still want to question the alligator?"

Richard tried to put on a serious face. "No. I don't see any point. Since he was high, he probably wouldn't remember anything anyway."

She smiled. "That's two today, Dick."

Richard tried not to smile, but couldn't help it. He might have learned something new from Dorie after all. And he was sure his mother would appreciate his personality change.

"You say the alligator came from around here, right?" he asked. "Then he could have picked up the backpack anywhere, and not necessarily from where Roland is hiding out."

Dorie narrowed her eyes. "You don't think that guy is still around here, do you? I figured you were only trying to determine where he went next. Surely he's somewhere else making new business contacts in a less dangerous environment."

"I know you'd like to think so, but I seriously doubt it."

"You mean he would still attempt to do a job here after losing that finger? He may as well have taken out an advertisement in the *New York Times*."

"Roland doesn't appear anywhere he's not doing business. I know you say Gator Bait has never had a drug problem, but I'm telling you, Roland wouldn't be here without a reason."

"That's insane."

"Maybe, but so is crossing the Hebert family, not to mention their contacts in New England. My source told me that the deal is already established. This stuff's not coming from the U.S. We probably have a couple of days at the most to figure out where and when it's coming in."

"And your source is?"

"Confidential and not up for discussion."

For once, Dorie seemed to accept his directive and nodded her head.

He stared closely at her, carefully choosing his next words. "You know he's not making this happen alone."

He saw heat rise in Dorie's face and knew immediately that his comment didn't bother her as much as he thought it would because it had already crossed her mind. Maybe Dorie Berenger wasn't as naïve as he thought.

"I know what you're saying," she said. "I got around to that last night after a few beers. But the thing is, I don't think I can help you with this. You're asking me to investigate the people I live with. People who are like my family. I'm too close to the subjects. I can't be objective."

She placed her keys in the desk drawer and dropped into her chair. "Besides, I know you think Roland was setting up shop here, but regardless of your opinion, I know there is absolutely no way that drugs have been moving through this town for over thirty years. No way at all."

Richard nodded. "I agree it's unlikely Roland has always moved his merchandise through Gator Bait. I think you would have caught on. But maybe someone has recently decided to take a cut of the action. Maybe this was the first job, but either way, someone in your town is working with Roland. I guarantee it."

Dorie blew out a breath, obviously unhappy with the situation, but unable to argue with the logic. "Where do you want to start?"

"At the bar, people talked about camps down here, but it sounded like most are unoccupied. What's the story there?"

"Camps are small cabins, lake houses, whatever you want to call them, along the bayou. They're usually owned by people who don't live in Gator Bait, although several of the residents have some, too. They use them for weekend fishing and an occasional vacation. Other than that, they stay empty."

"How many are we talking about? Can we check them all for possible break-ins? I don't think Roland would have gone far without clamping off that finger. And if he found an empty place to stay, he might still be around."

"There are probably twenty in all. We can check them, but it will take the rest of the day at least, and we can only get to them by boat."

Richard rose from the chair. "Fine by me if it's okay by you."

Before Dorie could answer, the door to the sheriff's office swung open and Joe strolled in. "You getting ready to go out?" he asked Dorie.

"Yeah," she replied. "Dick and I are going to

check out all of the camps. See if this Roland made a stop anywhere to take care of that finger."

Joe raised his eyebrows and looked at Richard. "You might want to wear a life jacket."

"Why?" Richard asked, confused. "We don't have to swim, do we?" He looked at Dorie.

Joe laughed. "No, you don't *have* to swim, but most people who ride in a boat with Dorie end up doing it anyway." Joe sat down at his desk and put a sheet of paper in the typewriter. "Suit yourself, but I'd at least change into tennis shoes if I were you. If you want to blend in Gator Bait, you're gonna have to start dressing down."

Dorie gave Richard a critical look and he glanced down at his slacks, button-up shirt and loafers. "You *are* overdressed," she agreed. "You stand out like a sore thumb, really. If Roland sees us coming, he's going to know what you are from a mile away. Nobody in Gator Bait dresses that way except for weddings and funerals. Well, and church on Sunday."

Richard took another look at his attire and shrugged. "You're probably right. I brought a pair of jeans. I'll go change and meet you at the dock." He walked out of the sheriff's office, the door swinging shut behind him.

Joe waited until the door was completely closed and turned his attention to Dorie. "He thinks this guy's still in town?"

Dorie nodded. "Looks that way. I hate the thought, Joe. If he's hanging around, he must be doing business or at least trying to get business started in Gator Bait."

"Not a fun thing to roll through your mind," Joe agreed. "You got any ideas?"

She stared out the window and across the street. "Not a one. To pass a crime this big by me would take someone a lot smarter than anyone here."

"Or someone close to you who's been overlooked," Joe said quietly.

Dorie took a deep breath, looked at Joe and shook her head. "That's something I don't even want to think about at the moment. Not until I have to." She strode to the front door and stepped outside, knowing full well Joe could be right and not wanting to admit to him it was something she had already considered.

Dorie untied her boat as Richard made his way down to the dock, dressed in stiff jeans and a T-shirt. She took one look at him and grimaced. "Jeesh, Dick. Do you ever loosen up? I bet you iron your underwear."

Richard grinned. "Only my Sunday pair." He looked at the sheriff's boat and back at Dorie. "We aren't taking the big boat?" he asked, his expression that of a disappointed child.

Shaking her head, she tried not to smile. She kind of felt that way about the sheriff's boat, too. "If you want to play in the big boat, we can do that after your bad guy is behind bars. For now, we need the fastest way to cover every camp this afternoon. That's my boat. Some of the shortcuts I use are too narrow for the sheriff's."

She motioned him onboard and he stepped off the dock and into the boat, which rocked a moment as he caught his balance. Once he was seated, she tossed the rope in front of him and shoved the bow with her foot. The boat had already moved about two feet from the dock before she jumped inside, not wavering for even a moment.

Lifting a bench lid behind her, she pulled out a life jacket and tossed it to Richard. "You'll probably want to put that on. Just in case."

Richard gave her a surprised look. "I thought Joe was kidding."

"Joe doesn't have a sense of humor. I'd have thought an investigator of your caliber would have discovered that by now."

Richard looked at the life jacket and back at Dorie. "What about you? You're not wearing one?"

"What, and look like a pansy? No way." She started the engine and thrust the accelerator down. The boat leapt to the top of the water, throwing Richard backward off his bench and into the bottom of the hard aluminum hull. He righted himself and quickly put on the life vest.

Dorie waited until he faced forward again before she smiled.

Chapter Seven

Richard clenched the front of the bench and leaned forward to maintain his balance, not wanting another moment like the one at takeoff. *How embarrassing was that?* The woman outright called him a pansy for wearing a life vest, and there he sat wearing a bright orange, buoyant pillow. It was like deer-hunting season on water.

Still, he had to admit the life vest made him feel a little better about his longevity. Dorie cut the boat in and out of the tiny inlets of water, the aluminum sides occasionally brushing against the marsh grass next to the bank. One thing was for sure: Shawn Roland would not get away from Dorie Berenger if this came down to a boat chase. Richard was pretty sure fish couldn't get away from Dorie in a boat chase.

All of a sudden, the boat dropped its speed and he pitched slightly forward, barely managing to hold on to his seat and his dignity. Dorie pointed to the bank on the right of the boat and steered toward a small cabin on stilts just off the bayou.

"We can start here," she said. "This is the Paulie's. They live in Lake Charles and only come here occasionally. Should be empty." She motioned to the dock. "You want to grab that pylon? I'll get the rope. Just pull us up alongside."

Scooting to the right, he reached out for the giant post and pulled them close to the pier as the boat drifted to a stop. Dorie lifted the bench lid again, this time pulling out a large ring of numbered keys.

"You have keys to all these places?" Richard asked. This was an unexpected advantage.

"Sure. It makes things easier. Sometimes owners forget to turn lights off or they leave stuff in the refrigerator that would create a bad scene before they return. They give me a call and I make a stop to fix whatever needs fixing. It gives them peace of mind and me permission to be nosy if I see something out of order."

"Like what?" Richard asked, wondering what could possibly be considered out of order in a place where nothing seemed normal.

Dorie shrugged, climbed out of the boat and looped the tie-off line twice around a pylon. "Mostly it's kids. They'll break into one of the camps with their buddies to have a party. Occasionally, we get a runaway looking for a roof for the night. Oddly enough, that always seems to happen the day report cards are issued."

Richard smiled. "I guess kids are the same everywhere, huh?" He pulled himself up on the pier.

"Pretty much, just less trouble to get into in a smaller place. Plus, more people are paying attention to other people's business," she said and stared at him, not moving.

He stared back, trying to figure out what was holding up progress when she pointed to the vest. "You plan on wearing that inside? Not much chance of drowning in the camp."

Feeling the heat rise in his cheeks, he spun around and shrugged off the life vest, then tossed it into the boat. Dorie was already headed up the pier toward the camp. He trailed behind her, slowly shaking his head. What was it about this woman that made a total fool of him?

He blew out a breath and stepped off the dock and onto the dirt path through the marsh grass, thinking all the while that he probably looked as stupid around Dorie as Joe did around Jenny.

It was already evening, and the sun had just begun to set when Dorie and Richard stepped out of another camp and walked down to the pier. They'd been through the same routine well over a dozen times and had come up empty-handed.

She put a hand to her forehead and looked at the sky. "It's almost eight. We've got one more to go. You want to hit it tonight? It may be dark before we get back."

"Can you drive the boat in the dark?"

She gave him a disgusted look.

He raised his hands in the air. "All right. Stupid question. Can we get to the last camp in time to see everything before dark?"

She thought for a minute and nodded. "Yeah, but I'm going to have to take a shortcut."

"So? We've been taking shortcuts all day, right?"

She grinned. "Not like this one."

He stepped into the boat and picked up his life jacket, not liking that grin on Dorie's face one little bit. This was probably the point where passenger met water. It had been a strangely calm day between the two of them, and he wasn't about to let her get the better of him right before quitting time.

Dorie started the boat and inched away from the pier while Richard zipped his life jacket and braced himself on the bench. As soon as he was situated, Dorie pushed the throttle all the way down, and the boat leapt out of the water and raced across the bayou. They made a hard left turn into a narrow inlet, not much wider than the boat itself. Marsh grass slapped both sides of the tiny vessel as she maneuvered the many twists and turns of the cut, never reducing speed.

Richard squeezed harder to his seat, certain that any minute now they were going to hit land and launch into the bayou. He tried to scan for alligators just in case he went flying, but the wind and the spray of salt water blurred his vision.

"You might want to sit down in the bottom of the boat for this one," Dorie shouted over the wind and engine noise.

"Why?"

"Trust me."

Dismayed, he stared at her and threw one arm up to fend off the marsh grass that raked across his face as they sped along. He was fairly certain that trusting Dorie wouldn't happen anytime soon, especially when she had that grin on her face. All the same, following her advice probably wasn't the worst idea.

Resolved to riding this one out, he dropped down to the bottom of the boat, where the hard metal proceeded to bang painfully on his tailbone. He leaned to one side and looked ahead, trying to determine their course, but he saw only land. Real land. Real land with hard dirt.

And they were headed straight for it at breakneck speed.

He spun around and stared at Dorie. Her long blond hair had pulled loose from the ponytail and whipped around her face. Her eyes were bright with excitement and her smile ran from one ear to the other.

His heart dropped. She had lost her mind. The strain of investigating her friends and family was too great and now she was going to kill them both.

"Dorie!" he shouted. "What the hell are you doing?"

She braced one foot on the steering column and another on her bench. "Just hold on!"

He looked ahead of them again, but realized it was way too late to stop. They were going to hit the bank. He braced himself in the bottom of the boat and prayed gators weren't sunbathing on that stretch of dirt. When they drew within several feet of the bank, he could see that it gradually sloped up from the water. Before he could process that bit of information, they hit the slope at full speed.

Dorie turned and yanked the motor up on the back of the boat as it cruised out of the water and up the slope of the bank. Several feet later, the boat changed its course downward with a bang that jolted him off the bottom of the hard metal by a foot or two. He could hear her laughing the whole time. The boat continued its frantic slide and suddenly ended with a giant splash. Water came up from both sides of the boat and completely doused them.

As soon as they hit the water, Dorie dropped the engine, pushed down the throttle, and they raced down a narrow cut of water again. Managing to rise to an upright position, he peeked over the edge of the boat and blew out a breath of relief when he saw only water in the near future. "Is it safe to come up?"

"Yeah. You handled that pretty well, Dick. Most people scream."

I wonder why. It only looks like death. He lifted himself up from the bottom of the boat and sat on the bench. His backside stung from the giant bounce, and he briefly regretted not using the life jacket as a cushion.

Of course, now he saw the necessity of wearing the vest. If she pulled that stunt without a bottom-of-the-boat warning, he had no doubt she would have left many a passenger back in the marsh. Probably on purpose.

The boat suddenly slowed, and he planted a foot on the bench in front of him. Looking across the bayou, he saw a camp sitting among a group of trees. This was the last one. Last chance. He was beginning to think the whole thing was a dead end. Maybe his source was wrong and Roland was long gone. Maybe his appearance in Gator Bait was just a coincidence, like Dorie wanted to believe. But even as he thought it, Richard still didn't buy it. His gut told him different.

They hopped out of the boat and made their way down the pier. As they stepped off the planks and onto the hard dirt path, Dorie stopped short and Richard narrowly missed colliding with her.

"What's up?" he asked, instantly sensing her tension.

She pointed off to the side of the path. "The grass is pressed down there."

Carefully studying the ground before her, Dorie stepped slowly over the small patches of marsh grass with Richard close behind until they reached the spot she'd pointed out. "Someone docked a boat here at high tide. That would have been around midnight last night."

"Why didn't they use the pier?" Richard asked.

"Because when the tide is in completely, the bayou runs past the end of the pier. Whoever came here did so at high tide and had to pull the boat up onto the bank in order to dock." She pushed the grass in front of them to the side and studied the ground.

"See," she said and crouched in front of a large indention in the hard mud. "That's a footprint."

Richard looked at the wide, deep hole and raised his eyebrows. "Who was docking here—Bigfoot?"

Dorie laughed. "Not hardly. This spot was a bit underwater when our visitor stepped out of his boat. That mud is thin as soup when it's in water. It just hardens to concrete when the water recedes."

She studied the print again and took a measurement with her hand. "I'd say he's thin and probably well under two hundred pounds."

"Are you sure it's a he?" Richard asked, impressed with her analysis.

Dorie stood up and shook her head. "I'm not sure about anything at this point. That print was made by a set of work boots, but you're right, every woman in Gator Bait owns at least one pair."

"So what do you think?"

Dorie scanned the land surrounding the camp then looked up at the fading sunlight. "I think we better check out the camp before the sun goes down."

"Good idea," Richard agreed and they hurried to the camp in resolute silence.

The sun had begun to glow a bright orange and the light was fading fast. Dorie reached for her keys, but paused as she stared at the rope tied around the front door handle.

"What's wrong?" Richard asked, noticing the strange expression on her face.

"Someone's been here. This isn't the right knot. Buster always ties the same knot when he leaves." She twisted the knob, but the door was locked. Quickly removing the rope from the door, she unlocked the camp and pushed the door open.

Richard stepped inside, right on her heels, but at first glance, nothing appeared to be out of order. One big room made up the kitchen, dining and living area. She crossed the room and opened the refrigerator.

"There's bottled water and lunch meat in here," she said. "And I know this was empty last time Buster left. I was by here a couple of weeks ago when we had a power outage. I checked everyone's refrigerators then."

She motioned to a pantry directly behind him, and he pulled the door open. A loaf of bread and a package of crackers were on the first shelf. He took the bread out and inspected it. "It's fresh. Buster is the guy that owns the shrimp house, right?"

She nodded.

"Do you think maybe he loaned his camp out for the week?"

She considered this for a minute. "I don't think so. He always tells me when someone's coming in, and he hardly ever comes down here himself, except to do maintenance. He only keeps the place for his sons to use, and they both live out of state."

She walked past him and into the bedroom. Two bunk beds stood on opposite walls with a double bed in the center. One bunk had a blanket thrown across it. The other beds were bare. She checked the bathroom, but reported no evidence of a visitor.

"Whoever is staying here isn't on vacation," she said. "I can check with Buster when we get back, but I have my doubts he knows anyone's here."

"Why do you say that?"

She waved a hand toward the bathroom. "There's nothing in there. Even the trash cans are empty. How many people travel without any bathroom items at all? Everyone carries a toothbrush at least."

He was disappointed, but not surprised. "There's nothing at all? I was hoping we'd find the place where he patched up the finger. Or lack of a finger."

"Well, there's nothing here reminiscent of a first-aid job. And if there was any medical treatment performed in this bathroom, he was probably smart enough to dispose of the evidence in the bayou. Can you collect hair from the bed?"

"Yeah. If that's the best we can do, then that's what we'll do. I hope this doesn't turn out to be a wild goose chase."

Dorie walked into the kitchen and grabbed some plastic bags from the cabinet. "It's the closest thing we have to a lead, Dick," she said and handed him the bags. "Don't knock it yet."

By the time they got back into town, it was long past dark and way too late to make a Fed-Ex mailing. Joe was still at the sheriff's office, undoubtedly waiting on them, but Dorie noticed he remained quiet as Richard made a couple of phone calls and got a name for a laboratory in Lake Charles that could run the DNA for him. Once Richard had the address, he said a quick good-bye and dashed out of the office to make the trip to Lake Charles.

As soon as the door slammed behind him, Joe turned to her. "Well?" he asked.

She grabbed a bottle of water from the refrigerator and sat on the edge of his desk. She took a big swallow of the icy cold liquid and began to fill him in on the afternoon's events.

"Shit," he said when Dorie finished telling him about the evidence of a visitor at Buster's camp. "It had to be Buster's. His is the only camp on the bayou that's completely hidden from plain sight and unapproachable without being seen or heard light years in advance. There's no way we can watch it."

"I know. I've been thinking about that but I haven't figured a way around it yet. I'll let you know if I come up with something."

"What about Big City? He got any ideas?"

"I don't think so. At least, not yet, and I'd prefer it stay that way for a little while longer. We need to get a DNA match on the hair we picked up before we go storming in anywhere, and we damn sure can't ask Buster about this until we know for sure it's Dick's guy who's using his camp."

Joe took a deep breath and gave her a hard look. "You don't think Buster is involved in this, do you?"

She looked away, unable to meet his eyes. "I don't know what to think anymore, Joe. I never would've believed this could happen in Gator Bait, but here we are with a bag full of drugs and money." She stared out the window across Main Street and sighed. "Maybe you never really know people."

"Maybe. Or maybe Dick's guy, or whoever is staying there, got wind of the camp and managed to find a spare key. You know there's probably a hundred of them around town. We've known Buster a lot of years. If he was into anything like this, don't you think we would've caught on?"

"I'd like to think so." She gave him a small, tired smile. "I guess we're about to find out if we know as much as we think."

He nodded, his expression grim. "Are you calling it a night?"

She stared at the wall, so deep in thought that the sound of his voice barely registered.

"Dorie?" Joe asked and gently shook her.

Blinking, she tried to clear her mind. "I'm sorry. What did you say?"

"I asked if you were calling it a night?"

She slowly shook her head. "I think I'm going to take a trip to Lake Charles myself and have another talk with my dad."

"Do you want me to come?"

"No. The things I need to ask will be hard enough alone. I'll fill you in on everything in the morning."

He gave her shoulder a squeeze. "You know where to find me," he said as he left.

She picked up her keys, locked the door behind her and jumped in her jeep, not wanting to face her dad about the use of Buster's camp, but knowing if she didn't, Richard would.

Sherry was at her regular station at the reception desk when Dorie walked in. She gave Dorie a quick look and said, "Now don't give me that crap about nothing being wrong this time. I know that look on your face, Dorie Berenger. And then the two of you brought that stuffy man to visit your father. What is going on?"

Dorie tapped one foot and stared at the clock on the wall behind the perturbed receptionist. "I'm sorry, Sherry. I can't tell you. It's police business, and it's all very confidential." She looked back at the older woman and tried to put a neutral expression on her face.

Sherry narrowed her eyes. "Confidential police

business in Gator Bait? Bullshit. Nothing's ever happened in that town. I've been living there for over fifty years. I ought to know."

"I know, but everything changes eventually, and I really need Dad's advice. I think he'll know better how to deal with the problem than me. Is he up to it?"

Sherry waved one hand in the air. "Oh, hell yes. Ain't nothing wrong with that man's mind—just his legs. Aside from the fact that it's obviously causing you some distress, he'll probably be tickled to get involved in police work again." Sherry looked thoughtful for a moment. "In fact, it might help him out of the mood he's been in. Kind of broody lately. I figure maybe he's bored."

"Thanks, Sherry. I'll see you later." Dorie walked down the hall to her dad's room. She hadn't talked to him since Richard had given her the information about Roland, and the subsequent phone call to her dad explaining that bit of news hadn't been the most pleasant they'd ever had. To say he was angry with what might be going on in Gator Bait would be an understatement.

She paused for a moment outside her dad's apartment, then walked through the open doorway, calling out his name.

"Dorie," he said from his spot in the living room. "It's good to see you." He smiled at her as she took a seat on the couch across from him. "Have you straightened out that DEA agent yet?"

"No, I'm afraid not. Dick is wound so tight, you couldn't pry him loose with a crowbar." She smiled. "I did take him on a boat ride today. Got a little more than he was looking for, I think."

He snorted. "Most people who ride in a boat with you do. What were you doing out in the boat anyway? I thought Big City was looking for his drug dealer."

"He is. We did a check of all the camps on the bayou to make sure none of them were being used in an unauthorized way."

"So did you find anything?"

"Yeah, that's why I'm here. I know this is going to be difficult for you, Dad. I've been struggling with it ever since I found out what Dick was after, but I have to ask you about some of the people in Gator Bait. Starting with Buster."

He looked surprised for a moment, then frowned. "Why start with Buster? What did you find?"

"Someone was staying at his camp, but just barely. Only one loaf of bread, some lunch meat and some bottled water. One bunk with a blanket on it but no toiletries. The knot on the front door was tied wrong, but there was no forced entry. Whoever is, or was, staying there has a key."

He considered this for a moment. "You ask Buster yet?"

"No. And we don't want to. We don't want to tip our hand if it's Roland who's staying there. Dick took some hair samples from the bed and we should know the results soon enough." She rose from the couch and paced the short distance of the living room. "There's still the off chance that we could catch him, though I must admit, I haven't exactly figured out how to get to the camp without being a sitting duck for a gunshot."

He nodded and scratched the back of his head. "It'd be tough, that's for sure. There's no cover for you on the approach, yet he'd have plenty of trees to hide behind on his side."

She stopped pacing and stared down at her dad.

"What do you make of Roland using Buster's camp? If it's him, that is."

He ran both hands up and down his lifeless legs for a moment, then shook his head. "If you're asking me if Buster Comeaux could be involved in drug dealing, I'd say no way. I've known Buster my entire life. There's nothing in his life that would cause him to need more money than he's already got. And he's never done drugs. Of that, I am sure."

He fixed his gaze on Dorie. "Only thing I can figure is someone must have gotten a key. No one is very careful with that sort of thing down there. You know that. He could have lucked out on a hiding place or even stolen one out of Buster's truck or the shrimp house for that matter. Buster's got a ring of keys damn near everywhere, and they're all labeled clear as day. I've warned him about it before, but the hardhead won't listen."

"He might start listening now," Dorie said. "Especially if we find out Roland has been using his place. I don't imagine Dick is going to let that slide without taking a hard look at Buster first."

"I'm sure he will. Dick wouldn't be doing his job otherwise, so you can't blame him there."

"What about anyone else in Gator Bait?" she asked. "You think anyone else could be involved in this? I figure it would have to be someone smart enough to handle the business with Roland, which lets out all of the shrimpers and laborers. I can't see Roland trusting them with this kind of work."

"No, no. Neither can I. But then you're only left with the business owners, and you know who they are. Do you really think any of them is involved in something like this?"

"I don't know what to think. That's why I'm asking."

He gave her a hard look. "It's not like it was years ago. Years ago, you'd hear of people getting involved in the running for just long enough to make their haul, then pull out and retire somewhere far away. There's no pulling out anymore. Once you're in, it's for life. You pull out these days, it's with a bullet in your head. You know that, Dorie. You studied all this in school."

She blew out a breath and dropped back down on the couch. "I know. I've been over everything in my mind at least a thousand times and it still doesn't add up. I just can't see a reason for any of the people who I think could be involved with Roland to *be* involved with Roland. It's not worth the risk. And the people I'm thinking of aren't stupid."

Her dad slowly shook his head, his face sad. "I don't know what to tell you, honey. I know what the facts point to, but I just can't help thinking there's some big misdirection going on here, and the problem is not with anyone in Gator Bait at all. Least of all, Buster. He's getting ready to retire next year. Got a place in Florida all paid for. Why would he do this now? It wouldn't make sense."

Joe shoved his hands in his pockets and crossed Main Street to Jenny's Café. He was happy to note that a seat at the counter would afford him a look at all the comings and goings in Gator Bait. This case with Richard left a bad taste in his mouth. He was beginning to fear Dorie might come up short on this one.

Although he'd been born and raised in Gator Bait, his life was nothing like Dorie's. Until his father's death, he'd had a regular two-parent home. Well, as regular as living with a hellfire-and-brimstone pastor could be. Father worked. Mother stayed home. The other residents of Gator Bait were just friends.

Dorie, however, was another story. According to Joe's mother, Sheriff Berenger hadn't had a clue how to take care of a baby when he'd brought Dorie home with him. The residents of Gator Bait had pitched right in and helped with every little detail. Consequently, Dorie had more "family" in Gator Bait than anyone else.

No, this was going to be a real hard time for Dorie. Not that he doubted her ability to handle it. He just felt she was a little too close to the source, and it was his job to look out for her. That's why he was going to sit here in the café and wait until the store owners in Gator Bait closed shop, then do a bit of surveillance.

"Hi, Joe," Jenny said, a big smile on her face. "Would you like something to eat, or do you just want coffee?"

Joe scanned the empty street. All the store lights were still on, but Joe knew it wouldn't be long until everyone wrapped it up for the night. He looked back at Jenny. "Just coffee, please. And maybe a chicken salad sandwich to go. I might have to leave here pretty soon." He turned to look at the street again and began to formulate a plan of action.

The bar wasn't a problem. Pete would be on the job well into the night. Even on the weekdays, Pete's business didn't slack off much. Joe figured he would come back into town after he'd followed the others and take a closer look at the bar owner. He sighed and reached for the coffee as soon as Jenny put it on the table. Maybe he ought to request two cups to go. This was going to be a long night and an even worse morning tomorrow.

A light flashed off, and he saw Stella locking the door on the front of the boat shop. She put the keys in her bag and headed next door to the motel. Joe pulled out his cell phone and punched in some numbers.

"Gator Bait Motel," a voice answered.

"Hi, Susie. This is Joe. I was wondering if Tommy is going to be working tonight. I had a question for him about my truck. Darn engine noise again."

"No," she replied. "Tommy's got strep throat. Stella's gonna fill in for him until the fever breaks. I would tell you to call him at home, but he didn't have much of a voice when I talked to him earlier. You might try in a couple of days."

"Sure," he said easily, happy that the problem of following Stella was solved for the night. "I'll try him in a couple of days. Thanks."

"You all right, Joe?" Jenny asked.

He turned on his stool and found her staring at him, a concerned look on her face. "Sure," he said, his eyes darting back to the shrimp house. "Why do you ask?"

"I don't know," she said. "You just seem a little distracted, is all. I thought maybe something was up with Dorie and that DEA guy."

He narrowed his eyes at Jenny. "What do you mean 'up with Dorie and the DEA guy?' What would be up with them?"

Jenny blushed and looked down at her hands. "I don't know. I just thought they kind of fit together nice. You know, as a couple, them being so smart and all, but every time I see her, she just seems more tense."

He absorbed this information for a moment. "It's just the job. Dorie's had some big things on her plate and they're weighing her down a bit. I'm going to try and help alleviate some of that. That's why I need the sandwich to go. I'll be working tonight."

Jenny nodded, but didn't look convinced. "Okay. But you let me know if Dorie needs anything. Without her, I would have never got this place open. I'm still looking for the opportunity to return the favor."

He smiled, unable to help himself. Jenny really was a sweetheart. "I promise if I can think of anything you can do for Dorie, I'll let you know."

"Good, and you be sure and let me know if that DEA guy is giving her a hard time. If he is, I'll stop suggesting to him that they get together."

Joe's jaw dropped. "What do you mean, you'll stop? When have you been making the suggestion?"

Jenny grinned. "Almost every day. You think he'd have heard me by now. For someone who's supposed to be so smart, he seems really slow."

"No, Big City's not slow at all. In fact, I think he's very, very clever." Joe gazed back out the window. *That's what worries me.*

A movement down the block caught his eye, and he squinted to make out Buster locking the front door of the shrimp house. He pulled out his wallet and put some bills on the counter.

"I have to run," he said and grabbed the bag with the sandwich as he rose from the stool. "Thanks for the sandwich," he shouted as he rushed out the door. He was already a mile down the road before he realized that for the first time in his life, he had talked to Jenny without freezing.

"That's me," he muttered as he watched the taillights of Buster's truck fading in the distance. "Always perfect timing."

Dorie didn't bother to hurry on the drive back to Gator Bait. No reason to. It wasn't like she had a husband or kids or a pet waiting on her. Hell, she didn't even have a plant. And although she was sometimes lonely, tonight was one of those times when she was happy to be alone. Happy she lived alone. Without the pressure of putting on a pleasant face for those around her.

At the moment, she felt anything but pleasant. The situation with Richard was starting to look worse and worse for Gator Bait. As much as she hated it, Dorie realized she would have to step up to the plate and start a full-force investigation of everyone in town. The thought didn't thrill her at all.

Plus, the talk with her dad had really bothered her, though she couldn't put her finger on why. It was almost like something was said, but not said all at the same time. She didn't think her father would outright lie to her. Not even to protect a friend, but he wouldn't be above not telling her the whole truth. He'd done that before.

She rolled down the window of the jeep and let the cool night air blow across her face. Of course, the only time her dad had withheld information from her was to protect her. That meant that if he was withholding information now, it was either because it was someone she was close to or someone he was close to. Someone he thought he could reason with before things got more out of hand.

"Damn it," she said and pounded the steering wheel with her hand. Not only did she have to investigate the residents of Gator Bait, she was going to have to take a closer look at her dad. For his own good.

Joe killed the engine of his truck and coasted into a group of shrubs with an angled view of both the front and back of Buster's house. Buster parked in the middle of the driveway and entered the house through the front door. Joe shook his head in disgust. No key. The idiot is still leaving his door unlocked.

The door closed behind him, and a light came on inside the front room. Almost immediately, the light clicked off, and Joe straightened up in his seat, straining to make out movement in the house, but it was as dark inside as it was outside.

He was about to get out of the truck to make a closer inspection when the back door opened and a figure stepped out. Much too lean to be Buster. The figure scanned the backyard and headed toward a field behind the house. He made it a couple of steps when the back porch light clicked on, giving Joe a better look at the man even though the stranger's back was to him.

But Joe didn't know him from Adam.

The man froze for a mere second as the light shone upon him, then dashed into the field, never once looking back. The rear door opened again and Buster stepped out. He looked around for a moment and went back inside, closing the door behind him. What the hell was going on here? And more importantly, who was that man?

Joe started his truck and backed slowly away from the shrubs, not sure what he had just witnessed, but already certain he wasn't going to like telling Dorie about it.

Chapter Eight

It was just shy of six A.M. when Joe walked into the sheriff's office. Dorie looked up in surprise. Joe was no slouch, but he rarely came in before seven-thirty. Giving the man a quick assessment, she determined that he'd either had one hell of a rough night sleeping or hadn't yet been to bed.

"You're up early, Joe," she said as he poured a cup of coffee.

"I know," he said, his voice a bit uneasy. "The truth is I only made it to bed a couple of hours ago. And I had so much trouble trying to sleep, I finally gave up and decided to come on in. I wanted to talk to you before Big City showed up."

She straightened in her chair and motioned for him to take a seat in front of her desk. "What's up? Nothing ever bothers your sleep."

"This time something did." He took a drink of his coffee and was silent for a minute, apparently trying to decide how or where to begin. Finally, he cleared his throat and said, "After our talk yesterday,

I decided to do a little night check on our main business people. Not anything heavy. Just a look to see where people went and what they did after closing time."

"Okay," she said, not sure whether to be appreciative that he tried to alleviate the problem of investigating her extended family or angry that he did so without orders or backup. "Was there a problem with anyone?"

He tapped his hand on the desk. "Not necessarily a problem, but definitely something I don't understand."

Concern and fear flooded her senses and she felt her lower back tense. "Tell me."

He took a deep breath and began to recount what he had witnessed the previous night, beginning with following Buster home and ending with the man who had fled into the weeds. When he finished his story, he frowned. "What do you think?"

She leaned back from the desk and picked at a piece of loose leather on the arm of her chair. "I don't know what to think. You say you didn't get a clear look at the guy?"

He shook his head. "No, it was too dark, and once the light was on, his back was to me. I only saw enough to know I didn't recognize him. He was tall, over six feet probably, and lean with blond hair. I'd say he was older, but not old, if you know what I mean?"

"Forties or fifties, maybe?"

"Probably. You have any idea what Dick's guy looks like?"

"No. They don't have any photos. Apparently, he's a ghost when it comes to pictures. But Dick did say there was a woman one time who was willing to turn evidence. I bet they got a description from her. I can ask him about it when he gets in."

Joe sat his coffee mug on the desk with a bang. "I'm really sorry, Dorie. I know Buster has been your dad's best friend for a lifetime. And I know we don't have any proof that anything's going on at all. At least, not with Buster's knowledge, but I still don't like the way things are looking."

She rose from her desk and patted him on the arm. "I don't either. But I appreciate you watching out for me, Joe." She poured the remainder of her coffee in the small sink, the rest of her work forgotten. It was time for a break. The burden of her job pressed on her more than ever, and Joe's news was not what she'd been looking for when she'd come into work this morning.

As soon as Richard appeared they were going to have a conversation about giving information on Roland to Joe. Dorie was certain Joe wouldn't back off his protective stance and the more they uncovered, the more it looked like she and Richard would need all the help they could get.

"What do you say we head across the street for breakfast and some real coffee?" she asked with a forced smile. "Then maybe we can talk about you taking the afternoon off."

It was almost nine o'clock before Richard showed up at the sheriff's office. Dorie had been pacing most of the morning, worried about the news Joe had given her, worried about what her dad wasn't telling her, and wondering what the DNA evidence would show. Joe had grown weary of watching her and finally left the office to "patrol" Main Street.

"It's nice of you to make it in," she said to Richard as she glanced at the clock on the wall.

He looked surprised for a moment, then shot back, "I wasn't aware that I punched a clock here."

"You're taking up my time," she reminded him. "The least you could do is tell me if you're going to be late. This office opens at eight o'clock. There's other business I could have taken care of."

He stared at her for a moment, but must have known from her expression that arguing was a bad idea. "I was on the phone with the lab and then the agency, but you're right, I should have called."

She blinked, surprised he had agreed. "That's okay. We never really talked about working hours or anything. I'm just being bitchy. It's normal. You'll get used to it. Everyone else did."

He smiled. "Were they given a choice?"

Although she tried to hold it in, Dorie found herself smiling back at him. "No."

"It doesn't matter. Choice has always been overrated."

She nodded and took a seat behind her desk. "So what did the lab say?"

He took a seat across from her. "The tests will take up to thirty-six hours to complete. The feed into our database is much faster. Shouldn't take more than an hour to run a match once the data is in. I pulled some strings and coughed up a couple of cases of beer to make the rush less painful. A team started on the hair samples last night."

She did a mental calculation. "So by early tomorrow morning, we'll know if the hair belonged to Roland. What then?"

"I don't really know. And I wanted to get your opinion on that, because I think you'd be a better judge than me."

"What did you have in mind?"

"I wanted to see what you thought about checking Buster's camp again. We were pretty careful about placing everything back where we found it. If

Roland came back after we were there, I think we'd know."

Considering this for a moment, she nodded. "I would for sure, but then if this Roland is as good as you say he is—and after thirty years of evasion, I have no doubts that he is—then I think he'd know we had been there regardless of how careful we were. Wouldn't he have cleared out by now?"

He raised both hands in the air, palms up. "Possibly. But if that's the case, at least we'd know he was here as recent as yesterday."

"Fine. We can check it out this morning if you'd like. If we circle in off the west cut on Johnson's Bayou we can get a clear look at the camp with binoculars. At least to see if there's any movement before we go in closer. But I would rather make that trip while Joe is around. I've given him the afternoon off to get some sleep."

Richard gave her a sharp look. "Is something wrong with Joe?"

"Nothing that a couple of hours between the sheets won't cure, but I do need to talk to you about what Joe was doing when he should have been sleeping, and why I think it's time we let him in on all the details of this investigation."

An hour later, Dorie and Richard skimmed down the bayou in Dorie's boat, headed for a quick recheck on Buster's camp. Joe was posted back at the office in case they called him for backup. If for any reason they weren't back by noon, he would come looking for them. Dorie could tell Joe didn't like the situation one little bit, especially since he was now "in the know" on all the Roland information, but he only nodded and slumped down in his chair when she told him what she wanted him to do.

She chose a way to the camp that approached the structure from the only side without a window. There was no way to hide the engine noise, and it carried far over water, but it was the best she could do. When they were about a half mile from the camp, she stopped the boat and picked up a pair of binoculars.

"You see anything?" Richard asked.

"No. Everything looks quiet. Doesn't seem to be any movement inside, and I don't see any boats around the pier. Of course, if I were Roland, I'd hide my boat in the marsh grass, so that doesn't really mean anything." She handed the binoculars to Richard who lifted them to his eyes.

"What do you think?" she asked.

"Looks clear, but I don't know. Something about it makes me feel a bit uneasy."

Surprised, she stared at him. She'd felt the same way, but had always chalked her "feelings" up to female intuition. It had never occurred to her that a man could be as perceptive as she was.

"I agree," she finally said. "I don't like it, but I can't pinpoint why exactly."

Richard scanned the camp and its surrounding area again. "Maybe it's because approaching the damn thing makes us open targets."

Dorie took another look at the expanse of water and marsh around them. "There is that. But if you think the information is worth another look, we can certainly give it a whirl."

"Joe's waiting at the office, right?"

"Yeah. Don't worry about backup. Joe will stick. He's not going anywhere if he thinks I might need him."

He nodded, apparently satisfied. "Then let's go take a look, shall we?"

She started the boat and headed down the bayou toward the camp. They were about twenty yards from the pier when the first shots rang out. Reacting immediately, they bailed over the side of the boat and dove under water to avoid the spray of bullets as they hit the metal hull.

Richard dove underwater and swam directly for the bottom of the bayou. The bullets passed around him like angry mosquitoes, and he thanked God that he had gone without the life jacket that day. Otherwise, he would have been a floating target.

It couldn't have taken more than a minute to reach bottom, but it felt like hours. The faint whiz of bullets still sounded, but it was distant, and he no longer felt any moving around him. He tried to see in the murky water, but it was impossible. Knowing he had dove straight behind the boat when the shooting started, he figured the pier couldn't be too far. He hoped Dorie had the same idea since finding her in the inky sludge was impossible.

Hands in front of him, he started swimming across the bottom, searching for one of the giant pylons that the pier was built on. At least that would give him some cover in order to surface.

He hoped.

He made it twenty, maybe twenty-five yards, before his air ran out completely and he surfaced, looking frantically around him, gasping for air. He felt a momentary surge of relief when he realized he was underneath the pier and behind the seawall. For the moment, he had a hiding place. Gunfire no longer rang through the bayou but that didn't mean the shooter was gone. He might be waiting for movement.

Peering out between the boards of the pier,

Richard studied the terrain but couldn't see a thing in the marsh across from him. The last remnant of Dorie's boat sank rapidly, the current churning around it as it sucked the vessel under. He scanned the surface of the bayou, looking for bubbles or any other sign of life. He prayed that Dorie made her way to safety, knowing without a doubt the chances of finding her in this murky water were practically nil.

He wondered how long he had to wait before he could safely move, and hoped against hope that one of those reptiles from hell hadn't found this pier a good place to set up house.

As soon as she hit the water, Dorie dove for the bottom of the bayou, her mind frantically racing with the nightmare of the situation. The whizzing bullets cutting through the water sounded around her as she opened her eyes, scanning for a sign of Richard, but the inky liquid was too dirty to see anything at all. She reached out one hand in front of her and it sank quickly in the mud at the bottom. Stretching her arms as wide as possible she swept them through the water but felt nothing.

The pressure was building in her chest, so she released a little air and continued to swim slowly on the bottom, searching for Richard with her hands while straining to keep her mind focused and calm. She had been under for at least a full minute already. She had maybe another minute of air if she conserved, but after that, she had to surface. Picking what she hoped was the right direction, she started a slow swim for the pier.

A minute or so later, her left hand hit a chunk of wood and she felt a thin slice across her palm.

Reaching out with her other hand, she carefully felt around the object. It was definitely a pylon. But was it one of the pier's pylons or one of the many hundreds of old ones sunk below the bayou's surface?

There was only one way to find out.

Touching the pylon with her nails in order to avoid the razor-edged barnacles, she began a slow assent to the surface, hoping all the while that her last gasp of air wouldn't be in the face of a killer.

Seconds later, she broke the surface, releasing the last of the air from her lungs, and sucked in a deep breath. A hand reached out and grabbed her and she stifled a scream.

"It's me," Richard said.

She swallowed the cry in her throat and wiped her eyes, trying to clear her vision from the saltwater. It was still blurry, but Dorie could make out Richard and saw that they were underneath the pier and behind the seawall.

"Is he gone?" she gasped, still trying to breathe normally. Why was it that her chest felt more constricted now than it had under the water? Her arms and legs tingled and she knew they were going numb.

"I don't know," he replied and looked back out between the boards. "I never heard a boat, but he could have left before I surfaced."

"Or he could still be out there."

Richard nodded, his expression grim. "Yeah, but we're sitting ducks here as well. I think I should—"

Suddenly, she raised one hand to silence him. "Listen," she whispered.

Richard cocked one ear toward the front of the pier and heard the distant sound of an approaching boat. They peered between the boards, looking in both directions for the source of the noise, and

Richard was sure neither one of them breathed. Finally, on the west side of the bayou, two boats full of fishermen rounded the corner. They continued a short distance past the camp and anchored just east of them on a bend in the bayou.

He heard Dorie let out of breath of apparent relief. "He must be gone, right?" she asked. "It's not like he'd hesitate to kill a group of fishermen."

Richard took another look at the boats anchored on the point. "No. He wouldn't hesitate. I think it's safe to get the hell out of here." He turned to look at Dorie and was frightened by what he saw.

Her tanned face was as white as paper, absolutely no color left at all. Her arms were draped by her side and she swayed with the motion of the water, seemingly unable to keep herself still. "Dorie?"

He reached out to touch her and her body went slack.

Shocked, he rushed to put his arms underneath her and struggled to keep his balance. Once steady, he pushed through the water toward the bank on the far side of the pier, where he hoped, the fishermen would not see what was going on and come to investigate. He wasn't sure that the shooter was gone, and he didn't want to put a bunch of innocent people in the middle of the situation.

Bad enough he'd gotten them there by wanting to look at the camp again. He laid Dorie down on the edge of the bank where she would be sheltered by the end of the pier then crept slowly up the bank and scanned the marsh on the other side of the bayou. He waited several seconds, but when no shots came, he figured it was as clear as it was going to get. Moving Dorie inside where he could examine her couldn't wait any longer. He returned to Dorie, put his arms underneath her limp form and carried her up the bank, cursing himself the entire way.

This is all your fault. You want to get Roland so bad that you're compromising your instincts. Even worse, you're taking other people with you. Glancing over his shoulder, he checked the fishermen, but apparently they hadn't noticed the activity at the pier. He hurried to the camp, checking Dorie every few seconds, and desperately hoped she would be all right.

He was a little surprised to find the front door open, but walked inside anyway, certain the shots had not come from the camp. He laid Dorie on the couch just inside the door and made a hasty scan of the remainder of the tiny cabin, just in case anyone was still lurking.

The camp was clear.

Letting out a huge sigh of relief, he returned to the couch to see if he could bring Dorie around. He knelt beside her lifeless body and put two fingers to her neck. Her pulse was good. Steady. But he would have sworn it was racing earlier. Her breathing was still rapid, but not labored. Richard couldn't figure out what in the world had happened to her. Shaking her gently, he called her name. She moved slightly and tried to open her eyes.

He called her name again, and her eyes popped open, staring wildly at him. She sprang to a sitting position and he grabbed her before she could stand. "Dorie, it's me, Richard. Dick," he said, trying to calm her.

Her eyes began to lose some of their frantic glare and became more subdued, but still troubled. "Are you all right?" Richard asked. "Please say something."

"Yeah," Dorie said, clearly confused. "At least, I think so." She looked around at her surroundings in obvious surprise. "How did I get here?"

Richard let out a breath when she spoke, unaware that he had been holding it. "You blacked out under the pier right after the fishermen went by. I carried you up here."

"I blacked out?" Dorie asked, sounding offended at the thought. "I never black out. Never." Her expression grew more irritated. "I thought I could handle it." She looked down at her quivering hands then crossed her arms in front of her, covering her hands with her arms as if angry with their lapse of strength.

"Handle what?" Richard asked. "You know, it's all right to be afraid of being shot at. It's happened several times to me and every time, it takes weeks to get over it. Minimum."

"It's not the shooting," Dorie said, her voice barely a whisper. "I've been shot at before. It's the water. I reacted fine, until I had time to think about where I was. I hate water!"

Richard stared at her in complete amazement, unable to believe what she'd said. "How in the world can that be?" he asked. "You work on the water every day. Hell, you live on a boat."

"That's different. I can be on top of water. I can't be *in* water. It makes me claustrophobic. I feel like giant weights are pressing me from every angle."

He shook his head. "What are the odds? And you living in a place like Gator Bait all of your life. Where everything is about water."

"One of life's little ironies, I guess. And such fun for me." She settled back on the couch and drew her knees up to her chest, shivering. "Look, Dick," she said softly. "I'd really appreciate it if we could keep this between the two of us. No one else but my dad knows . . . well, and Joe. It would kill my ability to enforce the law around here."

He made the Boy Scouts sign. "I promise, I won't say a word."

"Thanks."

He put one hand on her arm and noted her skin felt cold and clammy. Taking a good look at her eyes, he realized that despite her fairly normal ability to converse, they weren't out of the woods just yet. He rose from the floor and headed for the bedroom.

"You're still in shock," he said as he left the living room. "We need to warm you up before you black out again."

He returned with a blanket and a couple of towels. "You need to get out of those wet clothes and wrap up in this blanket. At least until your temperature returns to normal." He set the blankets on the couch next to Dorie. "I'll be in the other room. I need to get out of these wet things myself so maybe they'll be dry by the time Joe comes looking for us. I figure we got at least an hour to wait unless you want to flag down the fishermen."

"No. I don't want anyone in Gator Bait to know what happened here. We don't want to tip our hand. It's bad enough that Roland already knows we're on to him." She stared at him. "I'm assuming Roland was the shooter."

"Unless you know anyone in Gator Bait who has a big grudge against you and a supplier for heavy artillery, I would say that's a safe bet. That was an automatic weapon he fired at us. They're not that easy to obtain."

"Not just any automatic weapon, Dick," Dorie said. "That was an M16, military issue."

Richard stared at her, momentarily surprised by her statement. "You sure?"

Dorie gave him a weak nod. "There's no other sound like it. I'm absolutely certain."

"Does anyone in Gator Bait have that kind of firepower?"

"Only my dad," Dorie replied, "but I doubt Roland dropped by to borrow a gun from the sheriff." She shook her head. "We're lucky your criminal isn't a good shot. We wouldn't have stood a chance with a professional marksman."

Richard nodded in agreement, certain that someone had been watching over them, someone with the power to make a spray of bullets from an automatic weapon miss two large targets. He looked closely at Dorie, who still hadn't made a move to change out of her wet clothes, and grew more concerned. "Do you need some help getting up?"

"What?" she asked, obviously miles away, then shook her head. "No. I'll be fine."

"Okay," he said, not sure whether to believe her or not. "I'll be in the next room. Yell if you need me."

Dorie waited until Richard closed the bedroom door behind him and struggled to rise from the couch, still unsteady. She unbuttoned her jeans and tugged them and her underwear off her wet body, hanging the garments over the plastic dining chairs. So much for doing laundry. This was not an event requiring clean underwear. *Next time, I'll save my quarters.*

She shrugged off her T-shirt and reached for one of the towels, drying her long hair as best she could, then grabbed the other towel to dry her body. When she was done, she wrapped herself in the blanket and curled up on one corner of the couch.

"Can I come out?" Richard called from the other room.

"All clear," Dorie said and he opened the door and walked into the kitchen. He wore a beach towel wrapped around his lower body, which might have covered the important parts, but left his chest open for full consideration. He must have a hell of a workout when he's not trapped in small towns.

"Would you like a drink of water?" he asked.

It took her a second to realize that one, he had asked her a question, and two, she was staring quite openly at him.

"No," she said and spun around to stare out the front window. Behind her, she heard him open the refrigerator door. She told herself she wouldn't look, but sure enough, he was just bending over to remove the water from the refrigerator when she shifted her gaze back to him. It was a hell of a view. His back and shoulders were as equally impressive as his chest, the muscles rippling gently from top to bottom. He wasn't overdone, like some she'd seen before, but he was definitely built.

Just before he turned around, she caught sight of a scar, low on the back near his waist. It was a bullet hole. She was sure of it. Although she hadn't had the pleasure of the experience, she had seen many in her lifetime. In their line of work, it was impossible not to. Living in Gator Bait, where accidental gun discharge was as common as jaywalking, only added to the odds.

Richard took a seat on the couch and looked closely at her. "You feeling any better?" he asked, and she was surprised to hear the genuine concern in his voice.

"I think so," she said. "I'm still cold, though. I can't

seem to get warm enough and it's got to be ninety degrees in here."

Richard nodded. "It's shock. It will take a while to wear off. But at least your color is coming back. You really had me worried for a minute there."

Dorie squirmed uncomfortably and looked down. "I know you're probably used to working with tougher people. I'm really sorry you're stuck here in Gator Bait with me."

"Hey," he said and put one hand on her blanket-covered leg. "You don't have to apologize to me. Everyone has weak moments. That doesn't make us incapable. It makes us human."

"I bet you've never had a weak moment on the job," she said, still unable to look directly at him.

"You're wrong," he said softly. "I had the worst moment possible on the job. I hesitated, and because of that, an agent died and the killer got away."

She raised her head and looked at him. He stared straight ahead at the wall, the pain on his face clear as day. "Do you want to tell me?" she asked.

He looked back at her for a moment and nodded. "It might help you understand why I take the chances I do and why this case is so important to me." He took a big drink of water and rubbed the side of his face.

"It was a little over eight years ago. I was still a bit of a rookie then, but the agent who had been after Shawn Roland for years asked me to back him up on a check of an abandoned building. He had received a tip that Roland was staying there."

Richard paused for a moment, fingering the edge of the towel, then continued. "His regular partner was in the hospital having his appendix removed. He didn't want to waste time asking the agency to reassign, so he asked if I'd go. I said I would."

"Did you find Roland?"

"Yes and no. Roland was there. The DNA match later confirmed it, but I never saw him. We were ambushed from the beginning. As soon as the other agent entered the stairwell, shots rang from above us. He was hit and instantly went down. I heard running on the stairwell, and he told me to go after him. Kill him if I needed to. Just don't let him get away again."

"But you didn't go?" she whispered, already knowing the answer.

"No. I started to, but I couldn't leave him that way. I radioed for an ambulance, then tried to suppress the bleeding."

"He didn't make it," Dorie said, her heart constricting.

Richard shook his head, the horror and misery of the situation etched on his face. "He was pronounced DOA at the hospital. And because I didn't follow orders, he died for nothing. Maybe I could have gotten Roland right there and finished all of this."

"Maybe. But there's no way to know for sure. The agent you were with had chased Roland for years and hadn't caught him. Do you think that agent was incompetent?"

Richard looked directly at her, his eyes beginning to turn red around the edges. "No," he said quietly. "He was one of the best we had. He was my father."

She felt a rush of blood to her head, unable to fathom what he must have felt, must still feel to this day. The pain on his face was unbearable, but Dorie knew he'd made the right decision, regardless of the outcome. She leaned over close to him and put her hand on his arm. "You did the right thing. Don't ever doubt that."

"But he died anyway. Nothing I did made a difference."

"It makes a difference to you. If you had gone after Roland and your father had died, you would have always wondered if you could have saved him. That would have been harder to live with. Roland is only temporarily out of reach. That chance will come again."

His expression hardened and he nodded. "You're right. I'll get another chance, but I've got to stop risking so much trying to force one. Coming here today was a mistake. I should never have asked you to do it."

"I wanted to be here," she said simply, knowing she would have done the same had she been in his position. "Nothing that happened has changed that."

He reached up with one hand and stroked the side of her face. "I hope you still feel that way after this," he said and leaned over to kiss her.

Chapter Nine

Dorie was surprised at the tenderness of the kiss. Soft and undemanding, his lips pressed against her own, his hand still gently touching the side of her face. The heat returned to her body in a flash and her breasts went on high alert, her nipples rubbing against the soft fabric of the blanket. The warmth spreading between her legs told her that despite her reservations, her body would not be denied.

"I still want to be here," Dorie said softly, "but with a lot less material in between us." Before she could change her mind, she gave Richard a smile and dropped the blanket from her shoulder, exposing herself down to the waist.

Richard blinked in obvious surprise and opened his mouth to speak, but before he could say a word, Dorie leaned over, grabbed him by the back of the head and locked him into a kiss.

There was no gentleness in her kiss, just a hunger akin to starvation. Their lips parted and Dorie felt his tongue on hers, all tenderness gone. Pure appetite had taken over and it felt as if every nerve ending in her body were on fire. Dorie pressed one hand against his chest, the taut warm skin causing her head to spin, but there was no stopping herself now. She trailed her hand down his chest, across his abdomen and trickled her fingers across his lap, causing him to groan. Even though her touch had been light, there was no disguising his arousal and she gave him a smile.

"It's nice to see not only your wardrobe is stiff," she teased and pressed her hand on his erection, stroking the hard length of him beneath the towel.

His body stiffened and she heard a sharp intake of breath. "What are you doing to me?" he asked.

Dorie laughed. "If you don't know, then you're in for a real treat," she said. She pushed the towel to the side, freeing the long, hard length of him. Although she hadn't thought it possible, his kisses grew more intense as he reached both hands around to cup her breasts, his thumbs making a circle around her nipples. She gasped at first and felt another wave of heat rush over her. She had no more recovered from that action before he pushed the blanket down, exposing her lower body.

"We'll see who's in for the treat," he whispered, causing her skin to tingle with anticipation.

With a gentle touch, he reached between her legs, running his hand slowly up her thigh until she thought she would cry out from the agony of waiting for his fingers to touch her where she wanted it most. When at long last he reached the moist spot between her legs, his initial touch almost sent her over the edge and she gasped for air. He smiled at her and pressed his fingers into her warmth before resuming his kiss. Softly he stroked her, over and over until she thought she would explode. With every increasing flick of his fingers, she quickened the pace of her hand on him as her own pleasure increased, and she could tell it wouldn't be long before they both spiraled over the edge.

She broke her lips from his and looked him in the eyes. "I want you inside of me, now, before we're both done," she said and felt him stiffen even more in her hand.

He ripped the towel from around his middle and pushed her back on the couch, the blanket falling around her and sliding to the floor. He stayed poised above her for just a moment, then entered her fast and hard. She gripped his shoulders and cried out, pleasure rippling through her body.

His moans matched her cries and he began to move in and out, increasing his speed and strength with every thrust. She felt the heat come and knew she was close.

"Now," she said and dug her nails into the taut skin on his back. "Now." And she gave way, the climax consuming every inch of her body.

Richard's body stiffened as he gave one final thrust. He held that position for a moment, the muscles in his frame finally relaxing. She could still feel him throbbing inside of her.

She looked up at him and smiled. He smiled back and lowered his head to gently kiss her lips, then withdrew from her and moved to her side, still holding her tightly, both of them perched on the narrow couch.

As she lay in the aftermath of the hottest sex she'd ever had, Dorie could still feel her heart racing, not yet willing to slow down from the excitement and the release. The heat from Richard's body warmed her more thoroughly than the blanket had and she nestled against him, savoring the moment she knew couldn't last.

"Well, Deputy Berenger," Richard said and planted small kisses down the side of her neck, "I'm glad to know that all your skills match your gun-wrangling ability."

"You're not so bad yourself—for a city guy," she said, trying to ignore her body's response to his feathery kisses.

Richard laughed. "And you thought I had no talent at all."

Dorie grinned and pushed herself up on one elbow in order to look down at him. "As long as you remember—this does not change anything. I'm still in charge."

Richard ran one finger down the side of her breast. "Well, I can't say it doesn't change *anything.* My stay here has improved a hell of a lot from the first day. Although, now that I think of it, I saw you naked then, too. I just wasn't in the mood to appreciate it."

"And what makes the mood different now?"

Richard shrugged. "I don't know. Maybe an appreciation for your skills, maybe the fact that everyone in Gator Bait thinks you're some kind of god." He gave her a grin. "Maybe it was just being shot at. That tends to change one's perspective."

She smiled. "Yeah, I guess that's true."

Richard reached up with one hand and pushed a stray lock of hair from the side of her face. "I can't promise you things won't change. Life always changes people, and meeting you would have had an impact on me regardless of whether or not this happened. This just makes it even better. You're a hell of a lady, Dorie Berenger. Frightening sometimes, but a hell of a lady."

He leaned over and kissed her softly on the lips.

She placed one hand on the back of his neck and gently returned the kiss.

The sound of a boat approaching made her break off the thoughts the kiss was leading to. She jerked Richard's arm up and looked at his watch. "Holy shit!" she said. "Joe would have left at least fifteen minutes ago to look for us. He'll be here any second. We've got to get dressed. I don't need that kind of aggravation."

She jumped off the couch and grabbed her clothes from the kitchen chairs. They were still damp, but her body was flushed with the heat of their lovemaking, so the wet clothes were no longer a concern. She tugged at the wet jeans that wanted to cling rather than slide, and finally managed to get them up and buttoned. She pulled on her T-shirt and quickly stuffed the thin lacy strip she called underwear into her jeans pocket.

Realizing Richard still hadn't moved, she glanced over at the couch and saw him staring at her, a goofy grin on his face. "Get a move on, Dick," she said. "Unless you want my dad to hear about this. Joe would pay money for the opportunity."

The mention of Sheriff Berenger was all it took to kick Richard into action. He wasn't about to give the old man the satisfaction of knowing exactly how he and Dorie had settled their differences. That would be far too embarrassing.

Hurrying into the other room, he located his clothes and tugged the clingy material on as quickly as possible, still amazed that things had gone as far as they did between him and Dorie.

He'd only intended to kiss her, but the touch of her lips and the knowledge of her naked body resting just inches away under an easily removable barrier had taken his breath away. Feeling like a teenager parking for the first time, he'd tried to reel himself in, afraid if he didn't show restraint, she'd throw up that wall around her all over again.

But when she'd dropped the blanket, there had been no mistaking the desire in her eyes, and there was no force on earth that could have made him resist her.

Even if he'd wanted to.

Making love to Dorie had been everything he'd thought it would be. He only hoped that when they were out of the camp and back to relative safety, she wouldn't decide it had been a mistake. There was a huge passion inside of her, but it seemed to only run outward, rarely allowing anyone to touch her life the way she'd touched theirs.

That was all about to change. Now that he'd seen an entirely different side of her, there was no way he was letting her slide back into her comfortable cocoon and shut him out. There was plenty of protected land around the D.C. area that needed watching, and Dorie seemed to have no problems at all with her game warden duties. If her disgruntled father came with the deal, then Richard would figure out what to do with him along the way.

As he slid on his shoes, he heard engine noise right outside of the camp. Peering out of the bedroom window, he saw Joe dock his boat, then pull out his weapon and proceed cautiously toward the camp.

He had just stepped off the pier and onto the path when Dorie yelled at him from the camp that everything was clear. Richard tied his shoes, threw on his shirt, and hurried to the front room just as Joe stepped inside.

"What the hell happened?" Joe asked. "Why are you wet and where is your boat?" He looked more upset than angry, and Dorie knew he wouldn't take the news of an attempt on her life lightly.

Placing one hand on his arm, she said, "I'm fine, but we have a serious problem here." She told him what had happened to her and Richard.

Joe banged his fist on the table and swore. "Damn it, Dorie! You could have been killed. It's a miracle that you weren't. What the hell kind of position would that leave everyone in?"

Joe turned and glared at Richard. "And what were you thinking?" he continued to rant. "Were you thinking at all? You knew damn good and well what you were after when you came here. Are you willing to make anyone expendable to get your man?"

She started to defend Richard, but didn't. Joe was on a real tear, and when he got that way, it was better to just ride it out. The normally mild-mannered deputy didn't get upset often, but when he did, it was a sight to behold.

"You're right," Richard said, obviously keying in on Joe's mood and not wanting a fight. "It is all my fault. I should never have asked Dorie to come out here. It won't happen again."

Joe blinked, apparently expecting an argument and caught by surprise with the apology. Dorie bit her lip and tried not to smile. Richard sure had a way of twisting things around. He even had Joe confused.

"Well," Joe said, finally relenting a little. "I guess it's not all your fault." He gave Dorie a stern look. "But you will *not* do any more investigating without proper backup. If this guy is crazy enough to take shots at a DEA agent and a deputy in broad daylight, then he won't hesitate to try again."

She shook her head. "There's only three of us. We can't stick together all of the time or we'll never cover any ground. And besides, you know better. If this guy wants me dead, he will get me. That's the odds."

"To hell with the odds," Joe said. "You know I suck at gambling so I'm not about to use you as a playing chip."

"I don't think he's going to come after me personally. What happened today was probably a fluke—we came up on him and he took an opportunity. I don't think he planned it that way. Besides, Roland has to know that we've already got an ID on him. It's not like I have more damaging information than Dick already had when he came here." She looked at Richard.

"She's probably right," Richard agreed. "In the big scheme of things, Dorie is relatively unimportant. Roland won't expend the energy to come after her. It's not worth it. But he would take advantage of an opportunity if it presented itself."

"Like today?" Joe asked. "My point is, Dorie spends her entire night and day presenting someone with an easy opportunity."

She started to protest, but Joe cut her off. "You know I'm right. You spend all day as an open target in the bayous and you live on that boat docked out in the middle of nowhere. It wouldn't take any more effort than a ten-minute drive to catch you there alone. And not a person in the world is close enough to even hear the gunshots, much less a call for help."

Joe ran one hand through his hair, the concern on his face unmistakable. "At least move in closer to town until this guy is caught," he said. "You can have the spare room at my place."

He looked at Richard, apparently expecting him to protest, but Richard nodded. "It's not a bad idea, Dorie. Your place *is* isolated. You'd be a sitting duck."

"No way." Dorie said, shaking her head. "I'm not leaving my house. I have to be there to think. I can't operate at full capacity on anyone else's turf." She gave Joe a small smile. "Besides, you snore like a freight train."

Joe swore again, but she knew he wouldn't push. He was smarter than that.

"So where do we start?" Joe asked. "I know you're waiting on the DNA results, but isn't it just a formality at this point? No one in Gator Bait would take a shot at Dorie. At least not sober. And no one but Maylene is drunk this early."

Dorie let out a breath and lowered her eyes, unable to look at Joe with what she had to say. She had been dreading this all along and now the moment was upon her. "I think it's time we questioned a couple of people in town. Dick and I will start with Buster. This is his camp, and as much as I hate to think anything bad, it's the logical place to start."

Joe stared at her for a moment, then nodded, obviously resigned to the unpleasant task. "Who do you want me to start with?"

She considered this for a moment. "Try Pete at the bar and Sammy at the grocery store. Ask if they've heard of any trouble at the camps or if any boats have come up missing lately, even if they were returned. Ask if they've seen anyone around they didn't know. Aside from Lake Charles fishermen, of course."

"Okay. I can cover both of them this afternoon. You gonna get Stella?"

"Yeah. We can talk to her after Buster and check out her rental sheets. Unless he imported it, Roland got that boat from someone in Gator Bait. I want to know who."

"What about Jenny?" Joe asked, and lowered his eyes to the ground.

Dorie glared at him. "Joe Miller, I'm surprised at you. I understand thoroughness in your job, but if Jenny Johnson is involved in this, then I'll kiss your butt right in the middle of Main Street." She looked at Richard, hoping for confirmation.

"It's not very likely," Richard agreed. "Even if I hadn't met Jenny and already formed an opinion, Roland, as a rule, doesn't deal with women. Besides, Jenny is a little young for him to trust on this kind of deal. Roland likes his partners a bit older and much more desperate."

Joe nodded in obvious relief. "How about we meet back at the sheriff's office around five? Will that give you enough time to get some dry clothes and talk to everyone?"

Dorie looked over at Richard, who nodded. "That's fine," she said.

Their afternoon of work planned, she waved Richard and Joe out of the camp and stepped out onto the porch, tugging at the ring of keys in her still damp pocket. She locked the door and started down the steps behind them, an uneasy feeling settling over her that had nothing to do with the job she was about to perform.

Her morning with Richard had opened too many doors that had been sealed for a long time—basically, a lifetime. And that frightened her. Sleeping with him was a lapse in judgment that she normally would never have made. Not that she regretted the sex. It was fantastic and quite frankly probably the best she'd ever had, but still something nagged at her, not allowing her to bask in the afterglow of their incredible passion.

The real problem was that this time hadn't felt casual to her, like the occasional ones in the past had. And since Richard was just stopping by and she wasn't leaving Gator Bait, anything more than a physical release wasn't a possibility.

She shook her head at her line of thinking and stepped onto the pier. What in the world was wrong with her? Good Lord Almighty, was she actually starting to think like a girl? Had the orgasm affected her mind? That would be disastrous. She had to focus, remember her credo—a good time for a short while. Long term was not in her vocabulary.

She needed to concentrate on the job and forget the things that had happened today. Weakness was not an option and getting involved with Richard would make her anything but strong.

Shawn Roland lowered his binoculars and frowned, unhappy that the problem he thought he'd taken care of that morning was strolling down the pier in front of the camp. How could he have been mistaken? He'd waited for almost twenty minutes after firing and never saw movement.

He shook his head in disgust. They must have hidden under the pier, although how they managed to get there unscathed was beyond him. Roland didn't believe in luck. Luck was something counted on by people who didn't plan, and he planned everything, down to his meals and the color of his socks.

There had been a time once, when he wasn't that way, and it had almost cost him his life. He looked through the binoculars again at the tall blonde climbing into the boat. Women. *A woman was almost my undoing. Can't trust them for shit, and now I've got one after me, along with that damn DEA agent.*

He sat back down in the boat. *My business in this town is over.* Killing them, while seeming to be the best option this morning, would only have brought more agents into town. What he really needed to do was keep them out of his way until his shipment arrived and was transported out of Gator Bait.

The DEA agent wasn't a huge threat as far as he was concerned. He'd already managed to evade the man for years. Getting caught now by the city slicker deep in the Louisiana bayous was highly improbable. But the woman was a problem. She knew the area—everything about it—and wasn't likely to miss the slightest change in her surroundings or her residents. His associate in Gator Bait had warned him about the woman in the beginning and feared that without anything to stop her, she'd figure out his identity and the drop location before the deal could go down.

He blew out a breath and shook his head. Last time he'd made a drop in Gator Bait, he'd been saddled with another nosy bitch. He'd taken care of that one only to have this one crop up behind her—relentless, pushy and apparently not about to give an inch. What he needed was more time, and it had come to the point where the only option was to remove them permanently, and fast.

Of course, with the heavy paperwork required in any government agency, killing them would buy him all the time he needed. It would take days to reassign a DEA agent. He'd benefited from the red tape nightmare many times. Replacing the woman with someone as good also seemed unlikely. And besides, killing was so much fun. Especially with a worthy adversary.

He watched their boat fade into the distance, his mind made up. He didn't know how the two of them had survived his attempt this morning, but it wouldn't happen again. First he'd deal with the woman. She posed the biggest threat. But this time, he would have a plan. And a plan beat out luck every time.

Joe pressed the throttle down on his boat, forcing it faster and faster down the bayou. The sooner this was over with, the better. Life for him had come to an all-time low. Forced to question his friends as suspects, worried that something could happen to Dorie—all of it weighed on him like a ton of lead. And his conversation with Dorie was far from over. He was just waiting until he got her alone to continue it.

When they got back to the dock, Richard hurried across the street to the motel for a set of clean clothes and to put a priority order on another cell phone. Dorie and Joe went into the sheriff's office where Dorie pulled out a duffle bag containing an extra pair of jeans and a T-shirt. In their line of work, a spare set of everything was always a good idea, and Dorie managed to damage or lose things faster than most. The bayou was not always as peaceful as it seemed. In the storage closet, next to the duffle bag, was a stack of cell phone boxes. Joe removed a box from inside and tossed it on her desk while Dorie dug another pistol out of her desk drawer.

Because he knew she wouldn't bother changing in the other room, he sat at his desk and turned to face the wall. He was going to get his piece in even if he had to do it backward. When he heard her unzip her jeans, he figured it was time for the questions. Nothing like a captive, naked audience.

"Anything else go on today that I should know about?" he asked.

"What do you mean?" she replied, and he heard the rustling of fabric.

"You know what I mean. I've known you all of my life, Dorie. You're like a sister to me. I know when you're holding something back."

"You're imagining things. There's nothing more to tell."

"Bullshit. You're hiding something and I want to know what it is."

He heard her sigh. She grabbed the back of his chair and swung him around. Now dressed, she perched on the edge of the desk, and looked down at him. "There's nothing else you need to know about, Joe. I promise."

He took a good look at her face and snorted. "There's nothing else you *think* I need to know about. You're keeping something from me, Dorie, and I don't understand why." He gave her a close look again. "Unless, of course, it's personal."

The color rose in her face and she stared at the floor, a rare occurrence. Obviously, he'd struck a nerve.

The realization of what had happened came over him in a flash. It was the only explanation for her silence and embarrassment. Dorie didn't talk about weakness, especially in herself, and she would definitely consider getting involved with Richard a weakness.

He placed his hand gently on her arm. "Hey, are you really afraid I would think less of you?"

She brought her head up and met his eyes. "No, I guess not. But it doesn't stop *me* from thinking less of me."

"Jesus Christ, Dorie." Joe stood and hugged her. "You gotta stop being so hard on yourself. You're human, you know." He released her and smiled. "At least most of the time."

Dorie gave him a small smile and a kiss on the

check. "Thanks, Joe. I should have known you'd understand. Although I don't know why, since I still don't. All I could think about was my dad."

Joe gave a moment of thought to Sheriff Berenger having the same inkling of knowledge that he did, however slim, and whistled. "No, that wouldn't be pretty. He won't be hearing anything from me. That's a promise. You tell him whatever you see fit, but don't be surprised if he sees right through you."

"Yeah," she said with a big sigh. "Maybe I'll just try to avoid him until this is all over. It might be safer."

"Probably so," he agreed and turned to leave just as Richard walked through the front door. The concern on Richard's face as he looked at Dorie was all it took for Joe to know that this was far from over. At least on Big City's side. Joe nodded his head at Richard and left the office, eager to be done with his interviews.

The question was, was it over for Dorie?

"You all right?" Richard asked, as the door closed behind Joe.

"Yeah," she said. "I'm excellent, considering the morning we had." And considering the job she was about to have to do. She gave him a small smile. "Can you eat?"

He thought for a moment and gave her a somewhat surprised look. "You know, I think I'm actually hungry. Guess that means we're recovering."

She laughed. "That's what Dad always used to say when I hauled home some wounded animal or reptile. If it's eating, it's probably all right."

He pushed the front door open and waved his hand. "Then let's eat. I hate asking questions on an empty stomach."

The café was busy for a weekday, so they hurried through their lunch and left immediately to talk to Buster. It was a short walk from the café to the shrimp house, and Dorie never uttered a word the entire time. Too many thoughts rolled through her head. What if Buster was in on this? What in the world would she tell her father?

Richard opened the door to the shrimp house offices and they stepped inside. A woman behind the counter looked up as they approached and smiled at Dorie. She gave Richard a quick look up and down and frowned. Dorie tried not to smile. Richard had made quite a name for himself in such a short time. It must be some kind of record.

The woman turned back to Dorie. "What brings you here, Dorie? You need to see Buster?"

"Yeah. Is he in?"

"Sure. He was just finishing up a sandwich. Let me tell him you're here." She picked up a phone and gave a quick message to the man on the other end. "He says to give him a minute, then head on up."

"That's fine," Dorie said and waved one hand at Richard. "Have you met Richard Starke yet?"

The woman sniffed. "No, and I'm not likely to want to. You give my best to your father the next time you see him." She rose from her desk and walked off into a room to her left. The smile Dorie held in broke through. She couldn't help it. The look of dismay on Richard's face was too comical.

"You're making friends fast, Dick."

He sighed. "I've never even met that woman. God, I'd hate to be on trial in this town."

Dorie laughed. "No chance of that. There's probably not enough people in Gator Bait who can read and write well enough to fill an entire jury panel."

She looked up at the clock on the wall and a feeling of dread began to settle over her. "Guess we might as well get this over with."

They walked out a side door and up a set of narrow steps. At the top of the stairs, Dorie knocked on a door with the words "Owner/Operator" stenciled on it.

"C'mon in," a voice yelled.

She pushed the door open and they stepped inside. Buster sat behind a large oak desk, but rose as they entered and walked around to give Dorie a hug. "How are you, honey?" he asked, then turned his stout frame and stared at Richard.

"I'm fine," she replied. "Buster, this is Richard Starke. He's with the DEA out of Washington. Richard, this is Buster Comeaux."

Richard extended his hand. Buster hesitated a moment before shaking it and used the time to size Richard up. "Not sure it's a pleasure to meet you," Buster said. "Folks here don't appreciate the kind of trouble you've chased into our town. Especially when it gives Maylene Thibodeaux more to run her mouth about than usual."

Richard drew his hand back in surprise. "I didn't chase him here. I didn't know where he was until Dorie ran that print. And to be quite honest, this is one of the last places I would have thought he'd be."

Buster studied him a minute more then nodded. "Maybe that's why he gets away."

Richard shrugged, clearly not wanting to get into a discussion about Roland or investigative procedure. "Perhaps."

"We have a couple of questions for you, if you don't mind," Dorie said, attempting to cut in on the testosterone festival before it got ugly.

"Hell, no," Buster replied and waved them to the

chairs in front of the desk. They all sat down and Dorie looked over at Richard, who nodded. She gave a mental sigh of relief. He was going to let her run this. Thank God. Maybe Richard wasn't as ignorant on this small-town thing as she thought.

"What can I help you with?" Buster asked.

"First of all," she began, "I need to know if you've loaned your camp to anyone."

Buster gave her a surprised look. "No. Neither one of my boys has been here in six months or so. I haven't even been down there myself in over a month, even though I should go mow the grass."

"Well, someone's been there, and it was probably that someone who took a couple of shots at Richard and I today."

Buster paled and looked her up and down as well as he could over the desk, obviously searching for any sign of injury. "Are you all right? He didn't get you anywhere?"

She waved one hand in the air. "No, no. We're both fine. He missed, but neither one of us is much interested in a repeat event. The marsh is wide open, and regardless of the situation, I still have a job that requires me to be out in those bayous. I prefer to be there with fishermen and shrimpers only, if you see what I'm getting at."

"Sure, sure," Buster said, nodding his head rapidly. "But why were you at my camp? Was there a problem?"

"A couple of days ago, we checked out everyone's camp just in case the guy we're looking for was using one as a hiding place. We found signs of an occupant at your camp, although the occupant himself was nowhere to be found. We went back today to see if there had been any change."

"And that's when someone shot at you?"

Dorie nodded. "We're certain he's not staying there any longer. We figure he realized someone had been there and was just waiting around to see who came back."

She leaned forward in her chair and looked Buster directly in the eyes. "The place wasn't broken into. Whoever stayed there had a key."

Buster stared back at her, never blinking, but not avoiding her look either. Finally, he leaned back in his chair and blew out a breath. "That could be damn near anyone then. I've got keys to that camp everywhere. Here, home, in my boats, in my truck. It wouldn't take much effort to come across one if you were looking."

"You're probably right, but the thing is, he'd have to know what he was looking for."

Buster scrunched his forehead in obvious confusion. "What do you mean?"

"He'd have to know who owned that isolated camp far back in the bayou before he could know who to steal a key from. It's not like you painted your name, address and phone number on the pier."

Buster stared at her, his eyes wavering a little as he realized what she had said. "You're saying someone in Gator Bait is helping him?" He shook his head slowly. "I just can't believe it. Why would anyone in Gator Bait get involved with anything like that, especially these days? You see that shit on the television all the time. Those drug dealers don't mess around."

"I know. It's about the quickest way to an early retirement in a pine box that I know of, but that doesn't change the facts. Someone had to know the camp was yours in order to steal the right key."

Buster shook his head again. "I can't believe it. I

don't know anyone who would do something that foolish. People here are simple, but not stupid."

"Someone here is. You haven't had any boats missing, have you?"

"No. My nephews borrowed my bass boat last Saturday for a fishing tournament, but that's the only time one of them has been off the dock."

She stared at the wall behind Buster for a moment before speaking again. "Do me a favor and stay away from your camp for a while. At least until we catch this guy or we know for sure he's gone or dead. I don't want any other incidents like today."

Buster nodded. "No problem. I'll just borrow Curtis's goats if the grass gets too tall for the lawn mower."

The phone rang and Buster scowled. He yanked the receiver from the desk and bellowed into it, "I said no interruptions. This better be important."

As Buster listened, the smile vanished and a disgusted look appeared. "I thought you fixed everything," he said, his voice getting louder. There was another pause, then he said, "Fixed means it doesn't happen again. What part of that do you not understand?"

He slammed the phone down and rose from his desk. "I'm sorry, Dorie, but we got a problem with the traps again. The guys swore to me that they repaired them all. For the life of me, I can't figure out what's going on."

"How many?" Dorie asked, rising from her chair.

"Just one," Buster said as he walked toward the door. "But he's a big one. The guys already called Curtis. He should be here any minute." Buster walked out the door and hurried down the steps, Dorie and Richard following behind.

"What's going on?" Richard asked as they rushed down the steps and through the front office.

"An alligator got through one of the traps and is in the shrimp house. Remember me talking about them finding an easy meal? The traps angle from the shrimp house into the bayou to run off water and ice, but if the grate on the end is removed, a persistent alligator can climb right up the trap and into the shrimp house."

Richard's jaw dropped slightly in obvious disbelief. "Does this happen often?"

"More than you want to know, and with everything in this town tied to this shrimp house, no one can afford this kind of problem," she replied.

"So I guess our interview with Buster is over?"

Dorie nodded. "Yeah, but I was out of questions anyway, and still didn't have a feel on it. What about you?"

"I can't think of anything we missed, and unfortunately, don't know the man well enough to pass judgment on his honesty. Do you think he lied about anything?"

"I don't know," she said, pushing open the door to the warehouse. "Something doesn't feel right, but I can't put my finger on it. Let me make sure this gets handled, and then we'll get back to our business. I'll think a bit on our conversation with Buster and maybe something will hit me later."

Richard nodded and they stepped into the warehouse to witness Gator Bait's most dangerous problem firsthand.

Chapter Ten

The smell of fresh shrimp and fish assaulted Richard's nose as they followed a crowd of people through the warehouse doors. Suddenly, everyone in front of him stopped, and he dug in his heels to keep from running into someone. Peering over Dorie's shoulder, he tried to determine what the holdup was and got an immediate answer.

A couple of feet in front of them was the alligator, and he was huge, every bit fifteen feet. Perched in the middle of a giant pile of shrimp, with a good portion of the pile hanging out of his mouth, he seemed to glare at everyone, almost daring them to make him give up his supper. Every time someone moved, he swung his head in their direction, rose up on his giant claws, and all crowd movement ceased.

A door at the far end of the warehouse opened with a bang against the metal wall, and Richard saw people scrambling to move to the side. It looked like Moses parting a sea of people, and he couldn't help but wonder what in the world was coming now. He stretched up on his toes, trying to see over the crowd of people, but all he could make out was a mop of brown hair moving slowly through the warehouse. When the hair got to the crowd in front of the alligator, everyone shifted again, and a man stepped through.

"That's Curtis," Dorie whispered. "Wildlife and Fisheries keeps him on retainer for this sort of thing. He's fantastic."

Richard gave her comment a lot of weight, considering the source, and strained to get a better look at the man Dorie called fantastic, hoping he didn't have competition he couldn't compare with. When the crowd parted just enough so he could see, he was more confused than ever. Curtis was small, maybe five-foot-four and a hundred twenty pounds with clothes and shoes—and if he stood in a monsoon.

"Fantastic at what?" Richard asked. "Being bait?"

Dorie gave him a grin. "That's another good one, Dick. Your true colors are coming through." She nodded toward Curtis, who now stood directly in front of the alligator. "You've heard of a horse whisperer?"

"Yes, I saw the movie," he replied. "How did we get off on horses?"

"Curtis is sort of an alligator whisperer," Dorie continued. "He's had write-ups in all the wildlife magazines."

He stared at her, certain she was pulling his leg, but she looked back at him, a completely serious expression on her face. He gave Curtis another good look and turned back to Dorie. "That man only has three fingers on his right hand."

Dorie shrugged. "That gator was blind. It was a fluke."

"A fluke? The man lost his fingers to a fluke?" He shook his head in disbelief and as the crowd grew quiet, he turned back to watch the clinically insane Curtis.

Curtis took a step closer to the alligator, who rose immediately on his enormous claws and looked directly at the man, obviously ready to strike. Curtis held his left hand out in front of him, palm up. Then he turned the palm to face the alligator, making a stop gesture, his eyes never leaving the alligator's.

They held in that pattern for about thirty seconds, then the alligator slowly began to lower. When the alligator lay down again, Curtis walked right up to his nose and squatted in front of him. He moved his hand in a circular pattern, then began to speak, but Richard was too far away to hear the words.

Curtis reached over and stroked the alligator on the nose, still speaking in a low voice. The alligator's eyes began to close as if sinking into a deep sleep. When his eyes shut completely, Curtis motioned to the crowd and someone passed him a duffle bag. He unzipped the bag, never disturbing the sleeping alligator, and removed a metal clamp, which he placed around the alligator's mouth. Then he reached inside the bag again and drew out what looked like plastic booties.

He placed the plastic booties around each claw on the alligator and clamped them at the top. When the last foot was done, Richard heard a collective sigh of relief, then a quiet cheer went up in the room. Realizing he had been holding his breath along with everyone else, he let out a whoosh of air.

The double doors behind them opened and a man on a small crane drove into the warehouse. Curtis rolled the alligator from one side to another and placed some belts around the creature. When the belts were attached to the crane, he motioned to the operator, who lifted the alligator off the floor and began to proceed out of the warehouse.

"What about the clamps?" Richard asked as the crane moved toward the water.

"Curtis will remove the clamp on his mouth before releasing him. The gator will work the plastic ones off in a matter of minutes. It's just a safety precaution. One of those claws could slit a man from end to end."

He nodded, still not quite believing what he'd just seen. "Why isn't Curtis in Hollywood? He could make a fortune hosting one of those silly wildlife shows."

Dorie shook her head. "He tried once to talk to an alligator in Florida. It doesn't work the same."

"Different dialect?"

Dorie smiled. "Maybe. Either way, Curtis is kept plenty busy right here. Besides, he makes sixty, maybe seventy thousand every year during alligator season. He doesn't really have to work but a couple of months out of the year. Spends the rest of it drinking beer and playing poker at the casino in Lake Charles."

"Sixty or seventy thousand?" Richard said, amazed. "Unbelievable."

"Not if you know where to find them and how to kill them without them killing you. Since Curtis doesn't use guns, there's no damage to the hides or the skulls. He gets top dollar for his catch."

"So how does he kill them?"

"He slits their throats."

He was taken aback for a moment at both the directness and the content of her answer. "And that's all right with you? I mean, I thought you were all about animal rights and such."

Dorie thought for a moment and shook her head. "It's not like that exactly. I run the game preserve. In the preserve, different rules apply. Besides, you can't let alligators populate under protection forever or you'd have ten times more of them than people in a couple of years' time. Our goal in the preserve is to keep the alligator from becoming extinct and provide them a safe place to exist, not help them take over the world."

He nodded, trying to comprehend the delicate balance Dorie must have in her mind to be able to support both preserving and hunting the same animal. "What's next?" he asked. "The boat store?"

Dorie looked up at the sky. "Yeah. We better get a move on. It took longer here than it should have. We'll be running late meeting Joe unless we hurry."

As they began to walk back up Main Street, Richard heard a big splash. He turned and saw the alligator pop up on top of the water. The creature shook his head for a moment, then submerged completely and was gone. Richard looked at the small man sitting on a crate on the dock calmly smoking a cigarette. *Ripley's Believe It or Not* had nothing on Gator Bait, Louisiana. He hoped things at the boat shop weren't quite as exciting.

Oblivious to all of the happenings at the shrimp house, Joe walked into Pete's Bar and took a seat at the counter. It was still early, not quite five o'clock, and the place was empty except for him and Pete. Which is just the way Joe wanted it.

Pete came out of the storeroom and gave Joe a nod. "What can I get you, Joe? Soda?"

"No. I think I'll take a beer."

Pete looked surprised. "Don't tell me it's after five already." He glanced down at his watch. "It's not quitting time, Joe. You having a beer before quitting time?"

"I am today."

Pete gave him a curious look and popped the cap off a bottle of beer. He walked over to Joe and sat the beer on the counter. "What's wrong? I haven't seen you this worried since your daddy caught you peeing in the baptismal at church."

Joe sighed. "I was six years old, Pete."

"I know. That's my point. So what is it that's driving you to drink at four-thirty in the afternoon on a weekday?"

Joe took a sip of his beer and thought about how to proceed. "You know about this DEA agent that's in town, right?"

"Yeah. He's been in here a couple of times. You saw him the first time he was in. He came back again a day or two after that. We had a pretty good conversation."

"Really? What in the world did the two of you have to talk about?"

Pete shrugged. "He wanted some information on the people in Gator Bait. Major players. I knew Dorie had decided to help him out, so I figured if I could give her a hand, why not. I told him the names of everyone that owned businesses and such and a little about the people themselves. Nothing much, really."

Joe took another drink of his beer and considered this bit of information. "So he had already decided before he ever arrived in Gator Bait that someone who lived here was involved. It might have been nice for him to let the rest of us in on that from the beginning."

Pete gave Joe a look. "I got the idea that he didn't want you or Dorie put out because he might be arresting one of your friends. It didn't take him long to figure out how close Dorie is with most everyone in town. If someone here is involved in something like what Dick's looking into, it's going to be a real blow to her."

Joe nodded. "I know. It already is." He put his beer down on the counter and looked Pete squarely in the eyes. "Someone tried to kill them today."

Pete dropped the basket of peanuts he was holding and it fell to the floor. "What? What do you mean tried to kill them? Where at? Are they all right?"

"Yeah, they're fine," Joe said, trying to read the expression on Pete's face for any indication of guilt, but only came up with horror and disbelief. "Someone had been squatting at Buster's camp. They went back today to check it out for any changes, and someone took a couple of shots at them." No use telling everyone that a crazy drug dealer was running around firing an automatic weapon in broad daylight, Joe decided.

Pete shook his head and leaned against the counter. "Someone shot at them during the day? That's serious business, Joe. I don't have to tell you that. What in the hell are you doing about it?"

"Exactly what Dorie didn't want to have to do—question everyone in town and try to find a motive for why anyone would be involved in this sort of mess."

"Well, look at me all you want, but don't waste too much time here. I don't want that shooter getting away. I just can't believe it. Fifty-two years I've lived in this town and nothing like this." He shook his head. "Nothing even close. If I didn't know you, Joe, I'd swear you were lying."

"I know. It doesn't seem right, does it? Anyway, I just wanted to ask you a few questions, a formality really."

Pete picked the basket off the floor and placed it on the counter behind him. "Sure, shoot," he said and realizing his words, stammered a bit, "ugh, I mean, go ahead."

"When was the last time you were at your camp?" Joe asked.

"Last weekend. I went to mow."

"Any sign of a break-in? Anything out of order? And I mean anything at all, even something tiny?"

Pete thought for a moment and shook his head. "No, nothing at all. It was the same as it always is."

Joe nodded. "What about your boat? Have you loaned it to anyone lately? Been away from the dock at any time that you didn't know where it was?"

"Buster borrowed it this morning to pick up a couple of crab traps over in the channel. He said his flat bottom wouldn't start."

Joe nodded and made another note. "That's the only time, then?"

"Yeah. Aside from mowing, I haven't had it out lately. Been too busy arranging shipping detail with Stella."

"Stella?" Joe said, feeling a bit confused. "What in the world would the two of you be shipping together?"

Pete shook his head. "We're not shipping the same thing. It's just that we both have to pay a ton extra for the vendors to deliver here in Gator Bait. Her boat parts and motors, my alcohol and frozen food, Sammy's grocery stock, too, and none of us have the storage for a full truckload. We end up paying full delivery prices for a quarter of a truck of merchandise."

Joe nodded, so Pete continued. "Well, Stella found a hotshot service out of Lake Charles that would load all of our merchandise from another delivery point and charge us half what we're paying to deliver to Gator Bait. Amounts to several hundred dollars a month between the three of us. So we've been trying to coordinate delivery times and central locations for a pickup."

"Makes sense," Joe said. "In fact, it's a pretty damn good idea."

"You know Stella," Pete said with a smile. "She knows how to make a profit better than anyone. I guess she spent enough time learning the wrong way from her daddy."

Joe nodded. "Yeah. Guess so." He looked down at his watch and realized it was about time to meet Dorie and Richard. "I suppose I better get going. You let me know if you hear anything." He tossed a couple of bills on the counter.

Pete nodded. "See ya, Joe. I'll keep my ear to the ground, or the counter, if you will. If I hear anything, I'll let you know."

Joe nodded and walked out of the bar, wondering if Dorie and Richard were making better progress.

Dorie and Richard walked into the boat shop and up to the counter. Of all the business owners, Stella was the most volatile and opinionated of the bunch, and Dorie wasn't looking forward to questioning her. A young man behind the counter smiled. "Hi, Dorie," he said. "What can we do for you?"

"Hi, Bill," she said. "I need to talk to Stella. Is she around?"

Bill shook his head. "Not right now, but I expect her back any minute. She had to run to Lake Charles this morning. Her grandson was sick and her daughter didn't have anyone to watch him."

Dorie nodded. "Is it all right if I take a look at the list of boat rentals?"

Bill looked a bit surprised at the request, but

nodded. "Sure. Help yourself. It's the blue binder at the end of the counter."

"Thanks," Dorie said and motioned to Richard. They walked over to the end of the counter and opened the rental book. There were only three rentals listed for the past two days and all of them had been returned before this morning's adventure.

"Let's check the boat launch," she said and pointed to the marina. "Make sure they're all accounted for."

He nodded and they made their way out to the marina and checked the boats, but all were present and accounted for. They took a cursory look inside each one, but didn't really expect to find anything.

As they finished inspecting the last boat at the marina, a voice sounded behind them. "What the hell is going on, Dorie?" Stella asked.

Dorie looked up from the boat and saw the older woman standing on the pier, hands on her hips and a disapproving look on her face. "Billy said you checked the rental sheets, and now I come out here and find you going through the boats."

Dorie stepped out of the boat and onto the pier, Richard close behind her. "I'm sorry, Stella. If I'd have known you'd be upset, we'd have waited for you before looking."

Stella waved one hand in the air. "Oh, hell. I'm not upset about you looking around. I'm *worried* that you're looking around. I know you wouldn't be asking questions unless there was a big problem." She gave Richard a less-than-complimentary look. "And since we all know why this one is here, I can about guess what your problem is. But please, tell me how I can help you."

"This morning someone took a couple of shots at

us down near Buster's camp," Dorie said. "We're trying to establish his mode of transportation."

Stella looked from Dorie to Richard, clearly shocked. "Took shots at you? Why, Dorie, that's just insane."

Dorie nodded. "I know. But obviously we're a little too close for someone's comfort. We're talking to people around town trying to see if anyone has seen someone that could help us. We checked here to see about boat rentals, even though showing his face in town would be a long shot. We came down to the marina to make sure none of the boats were missing."

Stella nodded, apparently understanding their unauthorized inspection. "We haven't had any rentals since yesterday. I had Billy out here this morning repainting the numbers. If one was missing, I'm sure he would have told me straight off."

"Have you seen anyone different around lately?" Dorie asked. "Anyone you didn't know, besides your fishermen rentals, of course?"

Stella looked out across the bayou, considering the question for a minute. "The rentals and motel people have been ones I've seen here before. Many times, actually. Mostly businessmen from Lake Charles interested in fishing and escaping their wives for the weekend." She slowly shook her head. "I just can't think of anything out of order."

Dorie glanced at Richard, who nodded. "Thanks for your time, Stella. Let me know if you see anything, all right?"

Stella nodded but didn't reply. "There was one thing," she said just as Dorie and Richard began to walk away. "One thing that was a little strange."

Dorie and Richard stopped walking and turned back to face Stella. "What was it?" Dorie asked.

Stella gave her a puzzled look. "This morning when I was on my way out of town, I saw Buster's bass boat going down the ship channel, but it wasn't Buster driving it." She waved one hand in the air. "Oh hell, it was probably nothing. Could have been someone who worked for him." She paused a moment again, obviously deep in thought. "Of course, Buster don't really have any business in the ship channel. All his traps and nets are back in the bayou."

Dorie's senses went on high alert, and she felt Richard stiffen beside her. "Did you get a good look at the man?" she asked.

Stella shook her head. "Not really. The morning sun was too glaring to get a good look. He was taller than Buster and thinner. Had on jeans and a T-shirt, a black ball cap and sunglasses. I couldn't really tell anything else from a distance."

Dorie nodded. "Thanks, Stella. And if you think of anything else, anything at all, please let me know. And be careful. No one in this town is out of the woods until this man is caught."

Stella sighed. "I just don't know what this world is coming to when you're not even safe in a place like this." She gave Dorie a stern look. "You make sure you get to see your dad as soon as possible. You know this shooting story of yours has probably already made it to him. He'll be a nervous wreck until he sees for himself that you're all right."

Dorie gave her a small smile. "Yes, ma'am. I'll take a drive over there tonight. I promise."

Stella nodded her approval and walked down the pier and into the boat shop.

"What do you think?" Richard asked.

Dorie considered the options for a moment then replied. "I think we should go ahead and check in with Joe as planned. See if he's discovered anything else."

"And then?"

"Then it looks like we need to have another talk with Buster."

Dorie and Richard hurried back to the sheriff's office and filled Joe in on their afternoon adventures. Then Joe took his turn and Dorie wasn't exactly surprised to hear about Buster borrowing Pete's boat, especially since all indications pointed to Buster being short a boat that morning. But the information left her unsettled. Resolved to her task, she hurried out of the office, hoping to catch Buster before he left the shrimp house. It was time to get an answer to their questions.

An answer that made everything right, if she was lucky.

Richard agreed to remain behind with Joe, all of them deciding Buster might be a little more forthcoming with information if Dorie was alone. She caught Buster getting into his truck, just about to leave the shrimp house. "Buster," she said, "I've got a bit of a problem."

He turned to look at her, clearly surprised at her tone of voice and the statement. "What's wrong?" he asked, his brow puckering in obvious concern.

"I've got a witness that says they saw a strange man going down the ship channel today in your boat. And I've got Pete saying you borrowed his boat this morning to check your traps because your boat wouldn't start." She crossed her arms in front of her and stared at him. "I guess I'm wondering how someone else was driving your boat when it wouldn't start."

The frightened look on his face was unmistakable. "Someone saw a man in my boat?"

She nodded but remained silent, waiting to see if he would volunteer the information.

He blew out a breath and ran one hand over his balding head. "I'm sorry, Dorie. I don't know what to say. I didn't tell you the boat was missing this morning because I thought it was kids." He looked straight at Dorie and slowly shook his head. "I would never have withheld that information if I'd have thought my boat was being used by that drug dealer, I swear. You've got to believe me."

Dorie studied his face and frowned. He wasn't lying, but she was sure he wasn't telling her everything. "You still should have called me the minute your boat was missing. Whether we have other problems in this town is not the issue. A stolen boat is still a crime."

Buster kicked at the ground. "Oh hell, Dorie. I'm not calling you every time some kids take my boat on a joy ride. I seem to remember you and Joe having quite a few rides yourselves when you were younger."

Dorie blew out a breath. "Things are different now. The world is changing, Buster, and taking Gator Bait right along with it. You just can't keep doing everything the way you used to." She raised one hand and pointed a finger at him. "And I want you to promise me that the first change you are going to make is gathering up all of those damn keys and locking them up. And I want you to stop leaving doors unlocked. You have a collection of rifles that could arm a small country."

Buster sighed and looked beaten. "I guess you're right. I would have felt awful if something had happened to you this morning, and I found out he used my boat to do it. I'll do as you ask, Dorie. But it's a sad day when people aren't safe in a place like

Gator Bait." He climbed in his truck and backed out of the parking lot.

Dorie watched until his tailgate was a small blur in the dust and wondered if she'd just made things harder for Roland, or had simply put him on notice. She wasn't sure she wanted to know the answer, and the last thing she wanted to do right now was talk to Richard and Joe, especially since she knew they'd jump to the same conclusion as she had over Buster's weak explanation.

Still, there was nothing to be done about it now. Buster had made his choice and Dorie could only hope that this time she was wrong in her analysis, regardless of how unlikely that may be. "Damn it." She kicked some loose gravel in the parking lot and looked up Main Street, knowing she couldn't keep Joe and Richard waiting much longer. Wishing she had taken on any profession but her current one, she headed back up the street to the café.

Dorie found the guys having a burger over at Jenny's and slumped into a chair across from them, then waved at Jenny so she could place an order. Both of them looked up from their plates as she sat down, the unspoken question written in their expressions.

She took a minute to give Jenny her order then repeated her conversation with Buster. They listened intently until Dorie finished her story, their food forgotten.

"So what do you think?" Joe asked. "Is he telling the truth? You'd probably know better than most."

Dorie sighed. "Yeah, you would think so, but lately I think everything looks suspect. Maybe being shot at has made me paranoid. Imagine that. Still, I could tell he was upset, possibly scared, but then that could have been because he realized someone could have used his boat to kill me. Doesn't mean he knew who it was, and it definitely doesn't mean he loaned him the boat."

She tapped her fingers on the table and stared over Joe's shoulder at the wall. "Still, I get the feeling he was hiding something. I just don't know what." She looked at Richard. "I'm sure you get that a lot in your investigations."

Richard nodded. "Of course. The key is to figure out if what they're not saying is relevant to your investigation or just something they would find embarrassing if anyone else knew. It's usually about half one and half the other."

"Great," Dorie said and stared at Richard. "Then there's only a fifty percent chance that my dad's oldest and dearest friend tried to kill me. That's one to sleep on."

"What about tonight?" Richard asked.

"What about it?" she asked, and looked down at her plate, hoping the attraction she felt for the man across from her didn't show plainly on her face.

Richard placed one hand on her arm, causing her skin to tingle, and she looked back up to find him staring at her. "You sure you won't reconsider staying with Joe?" he asked. "Or even getting a room at the motel? I'm sure the DEA won't have a problem with covering the expense."

Dorie frowned at the hopeful look on their faces. The offer of Joe's place was bad enough. Why in the world would Richard tempt her with the motel? The proximity alone would leave her sleepless, or even worse, committing acts she'd regret the following morning. "Sorry, guys," she said finally. "No can do. We've already discussed this. I'll be fine."

Jenny placed the burger and fries on the table and Dorie reached for the catsup bottle. She saw

Joe and Richard give each other a look. Great, she thought as she took a bite of the burger, now I have Dick and Joe siding with each other against me. What in the world had things come to if people like Richard and Joe were becoming buddies?

"Are you going to see your dad tonight?" Joe asked.

Dorie almost choked on her burger and grabbed her soda to wash it down. "No. I'm not up to it. I guess I have to call and fill him in on everything, but I figure I can be yelled at on the phone as easily as making that drive all the way to Lake Charles." *And I'll be putting that phone call off till the last minute, too*.

There was a lapse in conversation and everyone concentrated on the food. Grateful for the break, she tried to clear her thoughts. At the rate her mind raced, sleep would be an impossibility, which was a dangerous thing considering she probably needed to be in top physical shape given the shooting fiasco this morning.

"So when exactly are you going to call your dad?" Richard asked, completely ruining her focus on the remaining french fries.

She sighed and dropped the partially eaten fry from her hand. "You sure know how to ruin a girl's meal, Dick. I'd hate to be on a date with you." She gave him a dirty look. He countered by looking immediately contrite and made her feel a little guilty. Very little, but a little.

"I guess I'll call him after we finish eating," she relented, "and with your choice of dinner topics, that time is approaching rapidly."

"Sorry," Richard said. "I know I'm just getting the hang of this small town thing, but I'm pretty sure someone's already broken their neck calling him with the news of our shooting adventures this morning, and he's probably sitting on the phone right now, waiting for it to ring."

"Calling now or calling later isn't going to change the facts of what happened today," Dorie said.

"Maybe not," Richard replied, "but there's no use in pissing him off even more by not keeping him in the loop. The last thing I need is for him to yank you off this case, and he has the authority to do it. Without your help, I'd be lost in those bayous for months."

Joe snorted. "You're catching on a lot faster than you think, City."

Richard laughed. "Yeah, I guess it's all those specially honed investigative skills. Or maybe just the fact that I have no idea where to find even one camp we've looked at over the last two days, much less the one we suspect Roland of using. Give me a boat at this point and I'll probably end up in Mexico."

Dorie had to smile at Richard's comments, although she was positive there was a lot of truth in them. Her dad wouldn't hesitate to pull her off the case if he thought for one moment that Roland's motives were personal or specifically directed at her. That meant more hedging than explaining when she got around to telling her dad anything at all about the events of the day. She picked up a fry and dipped it in the catsup, making the decision that at least one beer was in order before she placed that phone call to her dad.

And a few more afterward.

More than two hours later, Dorie locked the front door of the sheriff's office and headed down to the dock. Finally giving in to Richard and Joe's nagging, against her better judgment, she'd placed the call to her dad. It went about as smoothly as she expected—which was not at all. In fact, he had taken things much further than Joe and Richard's suggestions of bunking down with one of them for the duration. No, her dad wanted her to get the hell out of Gator Bait until Roland was caught.

The fact that Roland had evaded authorities for more than thirty years wasn't something he was interested in hearing. Not even when Dorie pointed out that the potential of her never being able to return was a high possibility given the DEA's track record.

She said good-bye to Richard and Joe, hopped into the old flat-bottom boat she kept as a spare and backed away from the dock. The six-pack in her refrigerator was calling her and after the phone call, it didn't really look like enough. She might even have to dig into the frozen cookie dough stashed in the freezer.

She blew out a breath and pushed the tiny boat harder down the bayou, eager to be home and away from everything, even if only for a night. All this stress was not good for the muscle tone. She was pretty sure no one had developed ripped abs from a diet of cookie dough and beer, but this was one time she was willing to try.

She quickly docked her boat and hurried into the cabin, not wanting to leave herself a stationary target after dark, despite her brave front to Joe and Richard. Not that she was afraid exactly, but deliberately tempting Roland would be stupid, and no one had ever accused her of being stupid.

Well, except Richard, but he didn't count. There were things he didn't know about her and never would. Already, he'd entered her world just a little too deeply, and it was beyond time for her to move him out. All the thinking about Richard made her lower back tense and she went immediately to the shower and turned the knob inside all the way to hot.

She shed her clothes and stepped into the stream of water. Thank God she hadn't let the guys talk her into staying in town. Not that it was ever a consideration for her, but sometimes she did things she didn't really want to do if it meant a lot to the other person. And Dorie knew that she was the only one who wanted her to stay out at her place alone.

Except maybe Roland.

But she would rather take her chances on her own turf with Roland than stay with Joe, who would have mothered her all night, or Richard, who, well, she wasn't exactly sure what Richard would have done. And since she couldn't trust herself around him either, it was safer to stay away.

What had happened between them that morning was a big mistake. She should never have let her guard down that way and she couldn't afford for it to happen again. Irritated because Richard had entered her thoughts again, especially while she was naked, she grabbed the shampoo and shook it.

Then she heard a noise outside of the cabin.

There was no mistaking the creaking of the cabin floor and she immediately knew she wasn't alone. Reaching one hand out of the shower, she turned off the light but left the water running. The sound of the shower would give her intruder the idea that he had the edge. He might let down his guard.

She watched the hall closely, her eyes quickly adjusting to the dark. It was only seconds later when she saw a figure emerge in front of the bathroom door. At once, she jumped out of the shower, tearing the curtain with her as she went. Grabbing the intruder around the neck, she shoved her gun to his head.

Chapter Eleven

"Give me a reason," Dorie said, her finger tightening on the trigger. "Just one good reason."

"Dorie," the man managed to choke out. "It's Richard."

She lowered her gun and released him from the choke hold. Reaching into the bathroom, she flipped on the light. Sure enough, it was Richard, dripping wet from the attack of the flying shower curtain and rubbing at red marks on his throat.

"What the hell were you thinking?" she exploded. "I could have killed you."

"I'm beginning to see that," Richard said and reached behind her for a towel hanging on the wall. "I thought you were in the shower. I didn't want to disturb you. I just wanted to make sure you were all right. But then the lights went off and I got worried. Jesus, Dorie, don't tell me you shower with your gun."

Dorie gave him a derisive look. "Of course I shower with my gun. I built a special shelf for it right into the wall."

Richard gave her a look of disbelief, and she pointed to the crude tile shelf on the shower wall, placed just high enough to be out of the stream of running water.

"You're crazy," he said and shook his head.

"I'm crazy? I'm not the one who almost got his head blown off for breaking and entering someone else's private residence. Is this the kind of thing they teach you at the DEA?"

Richard finished drying his face and took a good look at her. "No, but if they'd told us that the view was always this good, I would have tried it before now." He gave her a grin.

Dorie threw her hands up in the air, turned off the water in the shower, and stalked past him to the bedroom, her only relaxing moment of the day completely ruined. "What is it with you and boobs, Dick?" she asked as she slammed the door behind her.

Richard stared at the closed door for a moment, trying to collect all of his thoughts. All day, it had been obvious that Dorie was trying to put some distance between the two of them. The question was, should he let her? Deciding that another view of Dorie's boobs was probably worth being yelled at, he opened the door and walked into the tiny bedroom.

She was sorting through a pile of unfolded laundry, tossing the rejects all around the room and looked up in obvious surprise when he walked in.

"I thought we were done talking," she said. "I don't need any protection. You'll do yourself a favor to go ahead and go back to the motel."

He gave her a smile and looked her naked body up and down. "Talking wasn't exactly what I had in mind." He took a step closer and positioned himself directly in front of her.

Dorie shook her head. "Oh, no. I thought we'd already agreed that what happened today was a fluke and it wasn't going to change things."

He ran one finger down the side of her breast and her nipple immediately popped to attention. "You agreed. I never did. Making love to you was not a fluke, although I do consider myself extremely lucky. What's wrong with a little fun between adults?"

He saw her stiffen as the words "making love" left his mouth and instantly realized his faux pas. Dorie played things fast and loose. Any indication of caring or love seemed to make her want to run for the bayou. Fine, he decided, he'd just play it her way.

For now.

"I've got enough things about this investigation distracting me already," she said. "I don't need anything else adding to my stress."

Richard reached one arm around her and roughly pulled her against him, squeezing her butt in his hand. With the other hand, he cupped her breast firmly and stroked his finger over the hardened nipple. "I'm not trying to add to your stress. I'm trying to relieve some of it." Lifting his hand from her breast, he grabbed her by the back of the head and forced her lips to his, kissing her deeply, sucking on her lip.

She gasped as he grabbed her. Then she pulled back to stare at him in obvious surprise, but as he lowered his hungry mouth to hers again, there was no mistaking the desire. And for someone who was trying to rush him out of her life, she wasn't putting up much of a fight.

Her lips and tongue answered his with a sense of urgency and he felt his body stiffen. Dorie groaned as he pressed his length against her naked, wet body. Reaching down with one hand, she stroked him through his blue jeans. A rush of heat ran through his veins and the jeans bound tighter and tighter, inhibiting further progress.

"Whoever made jeans this tight in the front didn't know about you," he said.

She looked at him and smiled. "I guess we'll have to do something about that." Grabbing his jeans with both hands, she worked the buttons loose and pushed them, along with his underwear, down his hips. Richard decided he wasn't doing his share to help out and quickly removed his shirt, tossing it to the floor behind them. He was just about to reach down and take off his shoes when she lowered herself in front of him.

When he realized what she was about to do, his body froze in anticipation. It was a good thing, he decided, because the instant she took him into her mouth, he would have buckled had his knees not been locked. Looking down at her body, still glistening wet from the shower, he almost lost control.

Those gorgeous curves alone were enough to send him over the edge. But the way she made him feel was fast overtaking her appearance, and the flicker in his chest made him briefly wonder if this was really as casual as they both pretended it was. Shifting his eyes away from the view, he tried to think of something, anything to help distract his rising need and prolong the pleasure.

Root canal, Aunt Sarah's meatloaf, stepping in gum. He groaned. It wasn't working. He couldn't take his mind off the activity below, and that activity was about to send him quickly over the edge. He made one last desperate attempt to hold himself back, but the orgasm was already building, his body a mass of nerves, his muscles locked into place.

Squeezing her shoulder with one hand, he barely managed to say, "I can't hold back much longer."

She removed her mouth from him long enough to reply, "Then don't," and returned to her task, increasing the tempo with every stroke.

A couple of seconds later, the heat rushed through him, and he climaxed.

As soon as his muscles worked properly again, he reached down and drew her up to him, eager to bring her as much pleasure as she had given him. Not willing to be outdone, he ran his hands across her breasts, then down her stomach. As he moved his hand lower and lower, he felt her tense with anticipation. Before she could protest, he lifted her from the floor and laid her on the small bed. Kneeling in front of her, he grabbed her legs and pulled her toward him, kissing the inside of her thighs as he teased his way to her center.

She gasped at the first stroke of his tongue and he felt another wave of pleasure run through him. Determined not to be the only one with no staying power, he began to work Dorie with his tongue and fingers until her legs trembled. Increasing his speed and pressure slightly, he sent her over the edge, her soft moans enough to turn him on all over again.

He rose up from the floor and stood above her, the length of him already standing at attention. Dorie eyed him for a minute and smiled. "I guess we better do something about that."

It was the only invitation he needed. Lowering himself over her, he entered her slowly and gently. All the pent-up energy had been released with his first orgasm, so there was no hurry now, no need to rush. Now was the time to savor, to enjoy every inch of the woman beneath him.

Dorie wrapped her hands around his head. She threaded her fingers through his hair and pulled him in closer for a kiss. Long and slow, he kissed her, his tongue brushing hers with gentle strokes that matched their sexual rhythm. He felt her body tighten around him and knew she was getting close again. He grew harder with anticipation and knew it was time to send them both over the edge.

She moaned softly, then bit his lip, gently at first, then moving down to his neck, increasing pressure with every nibble. Her nails dug into his back, causing him to pump harder and faster. He rubbed the engorged nipple on one of her breasts, the pressure of her teeth on his neck and her nails pressing deep into his skin about to drive him mad with pleasure.

Her body tightened around him one last time, squeezing so tightly he cried out and buried his face in her neck. With one final thrust, they climaxed together. He gasped at the intensity of the orgasm, frozen in place as he felt her body contracting around him. Her hands slid from his back and dropped to her sides, her body limp, and he knew she was in the same place he was. Heaven.

They collapsed in a heap on the tiny bed, clean clothes scattered around them, never uttering a single word, and it was only a matter of minutes before they fell fast asleep.

A couple of hours later, Dorie woke from that sleep with a start. In the dim glow from the running lights of the boat, she could see the cabin was empty, but she heard a noise outside. Lightly placing one hand over Richard's mouth, she shook him. He awakened immediately and gave her a questioning look. She removed her hand and pointed to the side of the boat next to the pier. He nodded and they rose silently from the bed, threw on their clothes, and retrieved their weapons.

She pointed to a window on the opposite side of the boat and they crept out the window and around the cabin until they had a clear view of the other side. No one was there. They held in that pattern for about a minute, and Dorie strained her eyes to make out something, anything in the blackness, but couldn't detect movement at all.

A group of clouds began slowly making its way across the sky, allowing the moon to peek through. In the dim glow, she saw a clump of brush about fifty yards from the boat sway slowly in the still night air. She tapped Richard on the arm and pointed to the brush. This had to be their intruder.

They crept around the boat and stepped off onto the pier, trying to move as quietly as possible. Despite their best efforts, the pier still creaked as they walked. Dorie muttered under her breath, but couldn't really complain. Were it not for the creaking pier, someone would have been in her boat, and with the way they were sleeping, she wasn't sure either of them would have awakened in time to protect themselves.

Guns drawn, they made their way down the narrow path to the brush. The moon had disappeared behind the clouds again and it was only the thousands of times that she had walked this path that kept them on it, but when they arrived at their destination, the intruder was gone. Dorie scanned the area, then continued quickly up the path toward the road, with Richard following close behind. They were just a hundred yards or so from the road when they heard an engine start. She began to run, desperately hoping to catch a glimpse of the intruder or the vehicle he used, but the taillights were already fading in the distance by the time they reached the parking area.

Yanking her keys out of her pocket, she ran to her jeep, hoping she could catch him by car, but pulled up short when she discovered that every tire on her vehicle had been slashed. A glance at Richard's car told her it had suffered the same fate, and it looked like their prey had escaped again.

Frustrated beyond belief, she shoved her gun back in the waistband of her jeans and began the walk back to the boat in stony silence. This wasn't going as she'd expected and she was uncertain how to handle the situation. She didn't like being wrong, and she had been very wrong in her assumption that Roland wouldn't bother with her, especially at her home. Despite all her earlier protests, she couldn't think of anyone else who would creep around her boat in the middle of the night. Well, except Richard, but he was already there.

Still pondering their next move, she stepped onto the pier and her cabin cruiser exploded.

The blast threw her backward several feet and onto the ground, a shower of splintered wood and broken glass pummeling her. Covering her head with her arms, she rolled into a tiny ball, trying to protect the most vital organs and hoped Richard had done the same. He had been behind her on the path, but she hadn't felt him fall with her during the blast.

When the shower of debris stopped, she looked up and saw Richard struggling to his feet just a couple of feet away from her. "What the hell was that?" Dorie asked. "Don't tell me Roland's gun connections also dabble in explosives."

Richard slowly shook his head and stared at what was left of the boat. The entire back and middle was gone. Only a portion of the bow remained, stuck in an upright position deep in the bayou mud.

"Explosives are a new one. I've never heard anything about Roland using explosives." His voice shook slightly as he answered. "You sure you're all right?" He stepped close to her and put his arms around her.

She gave him a squeeze and pulled away. "Well, at the moment, I have exactly seven hundred dollars in my checking account and absolutely no assets left at all, but I suppose things could be worse." She cast one final forlorn look at her previous residence and sighed. "I don't suppose you have a phone in your car, do you?"

"Yeah," he said and fumbled in his pocket for the keys. "I guess we better call Joe, right?"

She nodded. "No one else to call, and the boat's not presenting a fire threat to anyone, what's left of it anyway."

They headed back up the path to the car. Richard sighed and she looked over at him. "Something wrong? Other than the obvious."

He shrugged. "I'm just wondering who's going to kill me first, Joe or your dad. This wasn't exactly what we had in mind when we decided I should come out here tonight."

Dorie stopped dead in her tracks and stared at him. "*We* decided? And who exactly constitutes we?"

He fidgeted a bit and finally blurted out the answer. "Me, Joe and your dad. Joe and I called him after you left the station. He was plenty mad. My ears are still raw, and Joe, well, let's just say that your dad cut him no slack."

"Damn it! I ought to whip the entire lot of you. What part of 'I can take care of myself' are you people not understanding?"

He looked instantly contrite. "I didn't mean to imply you couldn't take care of yourself. But I don't want to see you hurt and if anything were to happen to you, I'd blame myself. Roland is supposed to be my problem."

"Roland is society's problem," she shot back and started to continue her tirade but the pitiful expression on his face made her back off a little from her indignation with a resolved sigh. She wouldn't want to be in Richard's position either. The last thing anyone in law enforcement wanted to do was endanger the very people they were paid to protect. Shaking her head at the entire mess, she stomped over to Richard's car. He unlocked the car door, pulled out his cell phone, and handed it to her.

"Coward," she said and dialed Joe's number. There was no answer at his house, so she hung up and dialed his cell.

"No answer?"

"Not at his house. Of course, the sound from that explosion probably carried halfway to Lake Charles. Joe would have immediately assumed that it had something to do with me and is probably already on his way." The cell phone finally made a connection, and Joe answered with a yell that could probably be heard from fifty yards away. It took Dorie a minute to explain to Joe that he was speaking to her, not Richard, and there was a moment of silence on the other end of the phone before the sound of Joe's cell phone snapping shut echoed in her ear.

The fact that Joe was obviously too angry to speak and hadn't even asked if Richard was alive or dead let her know that he was probably going to kill them both when he got there—just to save Roland the trouble.

"That went well," she said and handed the phone back to Richard. "You might want to think about drowning yourself, or making use of a firearm. Hell, at least rub some blood on your face. If you appear hurt, Joe will probably be less likely to kill you."

He laughed at first, but when she didn't join in or even smile, he sobered a bit and went back to frowning. Dorie squinted, as she looked down the shell road trying to catch sight of headlights, but the tall, thick marsh grass blocked out any light whatsoever. Out of the corner of her eye she saw Richard swipe one bloody forearm across his head and she bit back a smile.

"What's taking him so long?" Richard asked.

"I don't know," Dorie replied. Even though she knew they hadn't been waiting long, she also knew that it *felt* like forever. Not happy standing around any longer, she was about to suggest they start walking and meet Joe on the road, when his truck squealed into the parking area throwing a shower of rocks and dust. Joe took his time getting out of the truck then strode purposefully toward them.

He only took a moment to ascertain their physical health then glared. "I ought to kill the both of you right here just to keep anyone from being accidentally hurt in the cross fire."

"I told you," Dorie muttered low enough so only Richard could hear.

Joe turned his glare specifically to Richard. "And some job you managed. I send you out here to protect her, and she still almost gets killed. How in the world did you miss someone rigging a bomb to her boat?" He looked back and forth between the two of them then held up one hand. "Never mind. I don't want to know."

"We were just sleeping, Joe," Dorie said. "Honest."

Richard nodded rapidly and held up one hand. "Scout's honor. We were just sleeping."

Joe narrowed his eyes. "Yeah, well, Dorie normally sleeps very lightly, like a cat. I've been to enough conferences with her to know what it takes to make her sleep soundly and since there wasn't enough time for her to consume that much beer, then it had to be the other."

Dorie gave Richard a guilty look and couldn't bring herself to look directly at Joe. "All right, Joe, you've made your point. I'll just have to step it up a notch."

Joe shook his head in disbelief. "You two are amazing, but your ridiculous lives have made me realize two things. One, when all of this is over, I'm taking a vacation—a long one."

"And the second?" Dorie asked.

"As soon as the café opens tomorrow," Joe said, "I'm asking Jenny out. Before it's too late to be asking. Working with you two is obviously not safe."

That said, he stalked back to his truck and climbed in the cab, slamming the door behind him. Richard gave Dorie a look of dismay. "This is going to be the longest five-mile ride of my life."

She took another look at Joe, the anger still clear on his face and nodded. "Maybe we ought to ride in the back. Give him a chance to cool off."

Richard nodded and seemed relieved. "Good idea," he said and climbed over the tailgate and into the back of the pickup. He extended one hand back for Dorie, and she grudgingly took it and hopped in the bed beside him.

The engine roared to life and they sat down, their backs leaning against the cab. Joe screeched out of the parking area and floored the truck, sending them bouncing on the hard metal bottom of the truck bed. Dust swirled around them and they both began to cough, trying to breathe. Joe was really going to have his fun with this one.

"Maybe we'll choke before we get back to town," Richard said as he gasped for air.

Dorie shook her head. "I'm not that lucky."

Richard grit his teeth every time his tailbone jarred against the bed of the truck, but despite the sheer agony in his butt, he wasn't looking forward to the end of this ride. Based on the expression on Joe's face when they'd left the dock, Richard wondered if he'd even slow down in front of the hotel or if he would expect Richard to fling himself out onto Main Street and be thankful for the ride. He guessed it would be the latter, but no matter which, he considered the whole truck-riding experience merely a warm-up for the ass-chewing that was certain to ensue later on.

He looked over at Dorie, trying to interpret her expression, but Dorie Berenger was one tough read. Aside from when she was supremely pissed or when they were having sex, Richard couldn't tell what she was thinking at all, and that surprised him. He didn't expect to understand the way women worked all the time but figured he ought to have a better idea than those two extremes.

Glancing over at her again, he saw her face was completely blank. What in the world could she be thinking? Was she in some state of shock? Was she worried about explaining this second attack to her dad? Did she regret her entire involvement with Richard and this case?

What the hell. If I can't guess, I'll just ask. The worst she can do is shoot me.

"What are you thinking about?" he blurted out before he could change his mind.

Apparently, he had caught her midthought because it took a moment for his question to register.

Finally, she looked at him and replied, "I was just thinking that my association with you has been hell on boats. I'll probably have to find a new insurance company after this. But then on the other hand, I've had my eye on that new bass boat in Stella's store ever since she got it in."

He stared at her, completely amazed. So much for a deep emotional state of thought. The woman's house had just exploded, almost taking both of them with it. Joe was surely plotting sixty different ways to hold them in protective custody, probably the nearest jail cell if he could manage it, and as soon as her dad got wind of this, he'd probably have his daughter kidnapped and held at gunpoint in a safe house in Antarctica. But she was thinking about buying a new bass boat.

He sighed and leaned back against the cab of the truck. Good Lord, was his perception of women this far off the mark? Of course, if he were honest with himself, he'd admit that even at his first glimpse of Dorie, she'd given him the impression she was nowhere near normal.

The truck made a huge bounce and mercifully climbed off the dirt road and onto the highway. Between the boat ride and the truck ride, he might have to spend a lot of time standing from now on. He closed his eyes and tried to ignore the stinging pain in his backside.

Fortunately, the remainder of the ride was brief, or maybe it just felt that way since it was a lot smoother, and it was only a couple of minutes later that they made a hard right turn and the truck screeched to a stop. Richard rose up from the bed and looked around him at the row of neat little houses on stilts. "Where are we?"

"Joe's place," Dorie replied.

"Great. Why didn't he just take us to the motel?"

Dorie shrugged. "You may as well get used to it. Once Joe gets in his protector mode, it's all over but the suffering. I'll be lucky to pee unattended until Roland is caught."

She climbed out of the back of the truck and trailed into the house after Joe. Richard took one look at her departing figure and wondered if this situation could get any worse.

Dorie awakened the next morning with a sore rear end and a screaming headache. Probably from being too close to the blast. Desperate for an aspirin and coffee, and not necessarily in that order, she crawled out of bed and made her way into the kitchen. Richard and Joe were already there, sitting at the dining room table, glaring at each other, not saying a word.

"You guys should keep it down," she said. "How's a girl supposed to get her beauty rest?"

"You may as well give up on the joking, Dorie," Joe said. "I'm not taking this lightly, and I won't let you do so either."

"I wasn't making light of anything."

"You were going to try, and I'm not allowing it. This has gone way too far. It's one thing for you to go off half-cocked and think you're invincible, but there are other people in this town who could get caught in the cross fire. This Roland has got a set of balls on him that we are not accustomed to dealing with."

"So what would you like us to do—let him get away?"

"No, but we're going to have to change the way we think."

She looked at Richard, who raised his eyebrows and barely shook his head with a "you're not going to win, don't even try it" signal. "Okay, Joe. I'll agree that I underestimated the length Roland would go to get to me, but I wasn't exactly wrong."

Joe snorted, and she held up one hand to stop him from speaking. "Look, I still don't think Roland would be bothering with me if he had already moved his product through Gator Bait. The fact that he took the chance of being seen or caught by being so close to me tells me that his business here is not done. Which still gives us an opportunity to find out who he's doing business with."

"She's right," Richard said. Joe glared at both of them and turned his attention to his coffee mug.

"I'm not saying she's not right," Joe said. "I'm saying she's going to have to start being a hell of a lot more careful. And being careful starts with me going everywhere she goes." He glared at Richard. "*You* can do what you choose. I can't control you, and am under no professional or moral obligation to protect you."

Joe rose from his chair. "The first item on the agenda for this morning is a visit to your dad." He pointed a finger at Dorie. "You have got a hell of a lot of explaining to do. That explosion rocked the entire town. I'm sure he's already heard about it. After you talk to him and let him know you're all right, *and* if he doesn't kill you, then we'll ask him about this case."

Joe stalked off toward the bedroom and Dorie blew out a breath. "That went well," she said. "Just what I wanted to do first thing this morning is go see my dad. I don't even have clean underwear." She gave Richard a dirty look before he could speak. "And I'm not borrowing from you or Joe."

She downed the remainder of her coffee and got up to rinse the cup. "I guess I'll have Joe stop off at Wal-Mart in Lake Charles. I can get enough to tide me over. It's not like I'll be needing an evening gown or anything."

Richard just nodded in response.

"Are you going with us?" she asked.

He shook his head in obvious relief. "No. I need to get back to the motel and call the office."

"Chicken shit," Dorie muttered.

He had the decency to look a little guilty, but still managed to protest. "The DNA results should be in this morning. I know it's just a formality, but it will strengthen our case against Roland once he's captured."

She nodded and stared over his head out the window. "You know, with the way this thing is going, I'm not so sure I'd like to see him go to trial. I'm to the point that a cell six feet under is sounding better and better."

"Don't think for one second that I wouldn't take that opportunity if it presented itself," Richard said softly. "I'm not saying I would do anything in cold blood, and I certainly wouldn't advocate you doing so either, but if he gave me any reason, even blinking, I don't think I would hesitate for a moment."

Dorie considered for a minute how she would feel if it were her dad who was dead, and she had the opportunity to meet the killer face to face. Would her professional training and ethics be enough to outweigh the need for vengeance?

She felt her jaw tighten, and her right hand shifted automatically to her waist where she normally carried her gun. She looked at her hand and shook her head.

Obviously, the answer was no.

Chapter Twelve

Joe was silent for the entire drive to Lake Charles, which was fine with Dorie. She had enough to think about without Joe throwing his opinion into the mix. And Joe always had an opinion, even if he didn't voice it. But today Dorie wasn't interested in hearing his thoughts, especially since she'd heard enough of them since last night.

They pulled into the parking lot of the retirement home, Joe parked the truck, and they made their way through the entry and up to the front desk. Sherry was at her usual post and gave Dorie a disapproving look as she walked in the door. "Your dad has been having fits over you. If you didn't come in today, he was going to make me drive him to Gator Bait. I don't have to tell you how much work it is to handle the sheriff when he's mad."

"I'm sorry, Sherry—"

"Don't want to hear it," Sherry cut her off. "Running around with a damn Yankee, getting shot at, your home destroyed. All for what? Let that man catch his own criminal. It's got nothing to do with you."

Knowing there was no use arguing, Dorie just nodded and mumbled a quick, "Yes, ma'am." It wouldn't do to tell Sherry that Richard's criminal did involve her because someone in Gator Bait was helping him. Dorie looked over at Joe, who leaned against the counter, quietly observing the exchange, a sour look on his face.

"You coming with me?" she asked.

He shook his head. "Not for the first order of business. You're on your own for that one. When he gets done, and if you have any ass left, call me and I'll come in. Meantime, I'll be right here at the desk trying to talk Sherry out of some cookies."

Resigned to her fate, Dorie walked slowly down the hall toward her dad's room, hoping to delay the scene that she was positive was about to ensue. She was a few steps away from his door when she heard voices talking inside his apartment. Angry voices. There was a small crack in the door and she stepped closer and leaned in to try to hear what they were saying.

The first voice was her dad's and she strained a bit and made out the second voice as Buster's. What in the world was Buster doing here this early in the morning visiting her dad when he ought to be opening the shrimp house? And what were they arguing about? She had a very bad feeling about the whole thing and pushed the door open just a bit more, so she could hear exactly what they were saying.

"Damn it, Buster," Sheriff Berenger complained. "This is my daughter we're talking about. If I find out you're involved somehow, I swear to God, I'll kill you. Don't think I can't do it."

"I promise you," Buster said, his voice shaky, "I don't know anything about Roland. I didn't have anything to do with him coming back here. You know that's all in the past. I kept my end of the bargain."

Dorie felt her chest constrict and she sucked in a breath. It was her worst possible nightmare. Her dad and Roland? She leaned against the wall in the hallway, unable to think for all the blood rushing to her head. *What am I going to do? I have to confront them.*

Taking a deep breath, she stood up straight and stepped into the apartment, slamming the door behind her.

The two men jumped at the noise then looked horrified when they realized who was standing there. And with the angry expression on her face, she was sure they knew that she had heard their conversation.

"Dorie," her dad began, "let me explain."

She took a couple of steps into the living room and glared at them, the heat running up her face and neck, her hands clenched at her sides. "You actually have the nerve to think you could explain being involved with the man who is trying to kill me? You make me sick."

"We're not involved. I swear to you," Buster pleaded. "It's all in the past. I was telling your dad the same thing. I don't know why Roland is back in town, but he's not doing business with me. I swear on my children and grandchildren."

Dorie gave Buster a hard look. He looked upset and more than a little scared, but he sounded sincere. She turned to her dad, who was still red in the face from his argument with Buster. "You want to tell me what the hell is going on here? Why do you know

Roland at all? And what is in the past that has resurfaced in the town you are *supposed* to protect?"

Her dad pointed to a chair. "You might want to have a seat. We'll tell you everything, and then you can do what you need to."

She hesitated for a second, not wanting to sit down. Standing above her dad made her feel more in control, and right now, control seemed more important than ever. Sitting on his level put her back at daughter status.

"Please," her dad said softly.

She blew out a breath and sat on the edge of the chair. "Go ahead," she managed to choke out.

Her dad looked at Buster, who nodded and took a seat on the couch. "It all started right before you were born," her dad began. "The big international boats moving through the shrimp channel changed the tidal flow in a lot of the marshes. White shrimp disappeared and only small browns remained. At the same time, the economy took a bit of a dive everywhere. Restaurants weren't buying as much shrimp and started serving cheaper fish and chicken."

Dorie nodded. She knew how Buster had kept the shrimp house open and saved Gator Bait. It was the kind of thing small-town heroes were made of.

"Buster ran into big problems over at the shrimp house," her dad continued. "He was getting in a second-tier product and the orders were only ten percent of what they used to be. He held the place open for almost four months on his own savings, still buying whatever the locals had to sell at the old market price, even though he ended up dumping most of it back in the bayou. But Buster was almost out of money and without the shrimp house, Gator Bait would have become extinct."

"That's when Roland first approached me." Buster picked up the story. "He claimed he came from a family of commercial shrimpers in New Orleans and was looking to make an investment in a shrimp house."

"And you believed him?" Dorie asked, shaking her head at such shortsightedness. "You said yourself the business was going under. Why in the world would you think someone would want to put their money in only to lose it?"

A flush crept up Buster's neck and he looked down at the floor. "I was stupid. I admit it, but I was so desperate I never even stopped to think straight. Maybe if your dad had been here things would have been different, but he was still in Vietnam and I was trying to hold together the town so he had a home to come back to."

"So you took the money," Dorie said.

Buster nodded, obviously miserable. "Yeah. Worst mistake of my life. By the time I found out about the drugs, he was done with his deal."

"That's besides the point and you know it," Dorie said. "Why didn't you go to the police with what you knew?"

"Because he couldn't," Sheriff Berenger replied. "Roland had parked a ton of money in the shrimp house operating account to ensure Buster's silence. By the time I got back from 'Nam and Buster told me what was going on, Roland was long gone." Sheriff Berenger gave Dorie a pleading look. "What was I supposed to do—let my best friend go to jail for being foolish? The real culprit had already gotten away. There was no point in taking Buster down."

Dorie blew out a breath of disbelief, trying to reconcile the two men she'd loved and trusted her entire life with the story they'd told her. Finally, she narrowed her eyes at Buster. "Is that why your traps are always broken, Buster? Are those chutes a convenient way to drop drugs into the bayou for pickup?"

Buster held up his hands and rapidly shook his head. "I swear, Dorie, I ain't involved with Roland. I never would have been if I'd known what he was doing. Besides, I'm not that stupid. Maybe years ago you could make some quick money and get out. Nowadays, the only way out is dead."

"If you're so innocent, Buster, then why are you here talking to Dad?"

Buster waved one hand at Sheriff Berenger. "I came here this morning because it's apparent that Roland is back and out of control. I wanted to make sure your dad knew I wasn't the one involved."

Let's just assume for a moment that I believe you," Dorie said. "Then who is Roland working with now?"

Buster gave her a look of sheer misery. "I don't know. I haven't even seen Roland, I swear. I'm sorry. I just don't know."

She rose from the chair and looked down at her dad, trying to hold back the tears of anger, frustration and disappointment that threatened to spill over at any moment. "Do you know what kind of position you've put me in? Do you have any idea at all? This isn't something that's going to go away. Richard isn't leaving here until Roland is caught or dead. This is a federal case. Do you really think anyone else will believe this story of yours?"

Her dad lowered his head, apparently unable to face her. "I'm sorry, Dorie. Not reporting Roland was a mistake. I know that now, but there's nothing I can do to change the past." He finally raised his head and looked at her. "But I need for you to leave town until this is over. I can't afford to lose you."

"You should have thought about that before you helped cover for a drug smuggler," she snapped, unwilling to even consider the excuses her dad had given her for his lack of legal action regarding something so ugly. "No crime is without cost, even if it doesn't come at the hands of the law." She pointed a finger at him. "You taught me that, remember? Maybe your bill has come due. If anything happens to me, you can live with that."

She spun around and left the apartment without even a backward glance, unsure of anything in her life anymore.

As soon as he arrived back at the motel, Richard called the agency, anxious for the DNA results. It took a few minutes on hold before his buddy Brian picked up the phone. "Lab."

"Brian, it's Richard. You got the results?"

"Richard, I'm glad you called."

He heard papers rustling in the background, then his friend spoke again. "We got the results several hours ago, but I had them run the tests again."

Richard crinkled his brow. Surely he hadn't been wrong about this. It had to be Roland at Buster's camp. "Why did you rerun? You tested against the finger, right? Wasn't there a match?"

"Yes. The hair and the finger were a perfect match. Then I sent it through the main database under orders from your boss to double- and triple-check everything. He doesn't want any slipups this time. But there's no doubt remaining. It's definitely Shawn Roland."

Richard let out a breath. "Then what was the problem?"

"There was another match. A partial, but suspicious enough for me to ask for the rerun."

Richard's breath caught in surprise. "That's not possible. Roland doesn't have any kin that we're aware of, and even if he did, they probably wouldn't be in our databases."

He heard Brian cough, a sure sign of nerves. "There's no mistake. We tested a second strand of hair with the same results as the first. That match is Dorie Berenger." They share the same blood type too—AB negative, not exactly common. I'd bet my job they're related."

Richard's head begin to spin. It wasn't possible, yet Brian was the absolute best at his job. But how could this be? "Why would we even have DNA or blood-typing, for that matter, for Dorie Berenger?" he asked, sure that despite the test, his friend was mistaken. "Can it be an error on the admin side?"

"No. I checked that first thing. Apparently, about ten years or so ago, the agency was heavily recruiting Dorie out of college. She had already passed the medical and physical testing. That's why she's on file. You know the agency never throws anything away."

"Recruiting Dorie? What college?" Now in total disbelief, Richard stared out the window and across the bayou. "Why in the world would the agency have tried to recruit Dorie? How could they even know of her existence?"

"I know," Brian said, sounding animated for the first time. "I thought it was strange, too, so I looked into it. Apparently, your hick deputy is some sort of genius. She went to Rutgers on scholarship at sixteen. Finished her bachelor's in criminal justice in two years and her master's in a year. She was almost done with her Ph.D. when she chucked everything and left town."

Her dad. Richard knew immediately why Dorie had dropped out. She'd come back to Gator Bait to take care of her dad. Jesus H. Christ! Could this case get any more complicated? He sank onto the bed, confusion and fear coursing through him.

"Thanks, Brian," he managed to get out and threw his phone on the bed. What the hell was going on here? Was he wrong about Dorie and her father? Had they been in cahoots with Roland all along? Stretching his mind, he searched for any comment from Dorie that alluded to her education, but couldn't come up with anything even when he'd insinuated that she was stupid.

In fact, Jenny had been the only one to make a statement about Dorie's intelligence when she referred to her being a great mind trapped in a small town. But he'd thought she meant compared to everyone else in Gator Bait, not compared to most of the world. With the kind of intelligence Brian had explained, Dorie Berenger was primed to pull off almost anything she wanted, especially on her own turf.

Either one of the attempts on her life could have been staged to throw him off track. In fact, had he not shown up at her boat, the explosion would have provided a convenient way for Dorie to disappear. He shook his head, trying to make sense of it all. And what about the sheriff? He claimed to be her father, but was that the truth? And if he was, then who was her mother? Those were two questions that would require answers, whether Dorie liked it or not. But did she even have that answer? And was it possible that everyone in Gator Bait was lying as well?

He rose from the bed and strapped on his gun. It was time to have another conversation with Sheriff Berenger.

Joe drove down the highway back to Gator Bait confused about what he should be feeling. Part of him wanted to remain angry with Dorie and that idiot Richard, but something odd had happened between Dorie and her dad at the retirement home, and Joe was getting a very strange vibe. He knew that whatever was bothering her had been enough to make her rush past him and Sherry and out the front doors of the retirement home without a single word.

Joe and Sherry had looked at each other in surprise as the doors slammed shut, then Joe had rushed out after her. He caught up with her halfway across the parking lot, but all she said was that the meeting was over. One look at her face had been enough to tell him that this was a good time to shut up and drive. Still, it was a long way back to Gator Bait, wondering all the while what had happened to make Dorie run out like that.

If it were Richard sitting here with her, he'd probably just come right out and ask. *Of course, I'm still several IQ points above Richard when it comes to dealing with Dorie, so that's not a good comparison at all.* Joe sighed and tried to shut off his thoughts. Dorie would tell him when she was darn good and ready, and he knew there were no words that could change that fact.

He sighed again, and Dorie turned from the passenger window and looked directly at him. "You want to know what's wrong and you're not going to ask because you're afraid I'll shoot you." She shook her head. "Don't worry about it. I left my gun at your house."

Joe stared at her in surprise. "You're not packing? You haven't been without a firearm since you were eight." The explosion must have rattled her more than he'd thought. Dorie strapped on a gun the way most people put on underwear. The fact that she admitted she forgot her gun made him worry even more. She had no problem admitting when she was wrong, but admitting a weakness was a whole different story.

"Is it anything I need to know?" Joe asked.

Dorie looked back out the window and nodded. "Yeah, you need to know all of it. I'm just not so sure I'm up to telling it." She pointed at an exit for the next town. "Turn off here and let's find a place for a cup of coffee. I can't eat, but I need to tell you what I have to say face-to-face."

Joe exited the highway without a word, wondering what in the world Dorie had to tell him, but already certain he wasn't going to like it.

Shawn Roland exited the interstate a couple of cars behind Joe and Dorie. He followed them long enough to ascertain their destination, then continued past the breakfast shop and back toward the highway. How could he have missed killing her a second time? The explosion couldn't have left much of her boat. The only way she could still be walking around today is if she hadn't been inside when it exploded.

This woman was making things extremely difficult. His connection in the East was champing at the bit for delivery, and his contact in Gator Bait was beyond paranoid over Dorie Berenger's involvement in the investigation. Both worries put him at risk for not completing this job.

And failure wasn't an option when payment had already been made.

He cursed under his breath. For someone who didn't believe in luck, Roland was afraid he'd finally found someone who had discovered that luxury.

He was not amused.

* * *

Richard walked out of the motel prepared to pay Sheriff Berenger a visit, but stopped before he got to the parking area. There were two problems with that idea. The first was that if Dorie were in on things with Roland, then the sheriff was likely involved too. By talking to him, Richard would just tip his hand. Plus, he had no car. He'd completely forgotten that his rental, slashed tires and all, was still out where Dorie's boat used to be.

"Damn it," he said and looked up and down Main Street as if a car was going to magically appear. Deciding that he was stuck until he could get four new tires, he blew out a breath and crossed the street to the café. Maybe Jenny would know who to call about getting his car fixed.

Jenny was busy with a table in the corner when he walked in the café, but she looked up and nodded in acknowledgment. Richard took a seat at the counter. A minute or so later she stood in front of Richard, a worried expression on her face.

"Is Dorie all right?" she asked. "People have been talking this morning about the explosion. Then, when neither she nor Joe showed up at the sheriff's office this morning, I really started to worry."

"Dorie's fine," Richard said. "We weren't in the boat when it exploded."

Jenny looked at him in obvious surprise. "We? You mean you were there when it happened?"

Richard nodded. "Yes. I was there to protect her. A hell of a job I did on that one."

Jenny gave him a sympathetic look. "I'm sure no one is blaming you. Well, except maybe Joe and Sheriff Berenger."

Richard blanched at the accuracy of the statement. "I'm having a bit of a problem with my car. I need to have it towed and get four new tires. I don't suppose there's anyone in Gator Bait who handles that sort of thing?"

"Sure," Jenny said and wrote a number and address down on her pad. "He works out of his house, but he could probably get you fixed up enough to make it to Lake Charles for a better job. Did the bad guy get a hold of your car, too?"

"I'm afraid so."

She shook her head in obvious dismay. "This guy you're chasing is something this town has never seen. I never thought we could have such goings-on in a place like Gator Bait."

"Gator Bait is definitely not what I had in mind for a drug deal, either, but apparently business worked out here. It's just a matter of finding out with whom."

Jenny's eyes widened in surprise. "Oh. You think someone in Gator Bait is in on things with this guy?"

"There's no other explanation for his being here."

She considered that fact for a moment then narrowed her eyes at him. "Then who is it? You've got to have an idea."

He sighed. "That's just it. We don't have an idea at all. It could be anyone." He gave her a small smile. "It could even be you."

She was clearly taken aback for a moment but quickly realized he was trying to make a joke. "I guess you've got a point," she said and gave him a smile. "Of course, if I was really a suspect, I don't suppose you'd be sitting here letting me know that."

"I don't know," he said, considering her words. "I guess I would if I wanted to study your reaction."

"I never thought of it that way before. You must find it hard to trust people."

He crinkled his brow. "Why would you say that?"

She shrugged. "I just figure that if you take your

job as serious as Dorie, then you probably work more than anything else. And if you're always in some strange city looking for a bad guy, then everyone you talk to is a potential criminal. It's sort of depressing."

"You have no idea," he said, then quickly continued with the line of questioning he'd been holding back before he lost his nerve. "Jenny, you've been here your whole life, right?"

She nodded. "My family's been here three generations."

"I want to ask you something, but I need you to promise me that you won't tell anyone what I asked."

Her eyes widened and she nodded solemnly at Richard. "Okay."

Taking a deep breath, he made the plunge. "What do you know about Dorie's mother?"

"Whew," Jenny said and rocked back on her heels away from the counter. "That wasn't along the lines of the question I was expecting at all." She stepped back next to the counter and stared at him, indecision written clearly on her face. "I suppose it wouldn't do me any good at all to ask why you want to know?"

He shook his head.

She thought for a bit longer, then sighed. "I guess I can't see what it would hurt to tell you what I know. But you have to make me a promise, too."

"Depends on the promise."

"You have to promise to never tell Dorie that I said anything about this to you."

Richard nodded. "That's one promise I'm definitely interested in keeping."

Apparently satisfied, Jenny leaned against the counter and lowered her voice. "Now, what I'm gonna tell you is all hearsay, 'cause I wasn't even born when the sheriff brought Dorie home, but I've heard my momma and my aunts talk through the years."

He nodded and motioned for her to continue.

"Momma says it all happened so fast. The sheriff was gone from Gator Bait for a couple of days. Back then, one of Buster's cousins was the deputy, and the sheriff left him in charge. 'Course everyone knew that Buster actually called the shots when the sheriff was gone, but they were all polite and everything to the deputy anyway. Momma says the first anyone knew of Dorie was when the sheriff called Buster's wife to come over and help him with learning to prepare a bottle and diaper. Well, you could have knocked everyone over with a feather. Why, the sheriff didn't even have a special lady friend as far as folks in Gator Bait knew, much less someone serious enough to have a child with."

She stopped for a moment, in obvious thought, then continued. "Momma says when the ladies of Gator Bait heard about Dorie and the sheriff, they all pitched right in. Took turns watching her while the sheriff worked and each of them spent time with the sheriff in the evenings and on weekends teaching him how to take care of a baby. Momma says it beat all she had ever seen. There was the sheriff, so strong and gruff and such a confirmed bachelor, and you only had to look at him when he was holding that baby, and you could tell he was in love. Momma says it was the sweetest thing she'd ever seen."

Richard smiled, thinking of the sheriff with Dorie as a baby. "But no one ever asked about Dorie's mother?"

Jenny shook her head. "Not really. Folks around here might seem a little off to someone like you being from a big city and all, but when it comes to certain things, we mind our own business. That's just good manners. I guess everyone figured that if the sheriff had wanted them to know the situation, he would have told them. Momma and the other women always figured it was a one-night stand sort of deal. Someone who didn't want the inconvenience of a baby. They figured whoever she was just signed Dorie over and disappeared."

"So no one knows who Dorie's mother is," he said and considered this for a moment. "I wonder if Dorie does."

"No way. I remember her catching flack at school one time over not having a mother. One of the Miller twins was ribbing on her pretty bad. Dorie got in a good left hook and he stopped his talking, but I came across her on my walk home from school. I used to cut across the marsh even though Momma told me not to, and there she was, sitting up against a clump of brush, crying her eyes out. Now, I really didn't know her, mind you. I'm a couple of years younger and at that age, a couple of years is a lot."

Jenny took a deep breath and swallowed. "I stopped in front of her and told her that if she needed a friend, I'd be proud to be one. I remember her looking up at me and I thought for a moment that she might just stomp me right there in the marsh. But instead, she smiled and stretched out her hand. We shook on it, and ever since then, there is little or nothing that I wouldn't do for Dorie Berenger. Or her for me. You know she cosigned on the loan for me to open this place? Without her help, I couldn't have done it." She brushed one hand across her cheek, catching a teardrop.

"Dorie only said something that one time to me about her mother. She said that she didn't really understand why anyone cared who her mother was, because she didn't care at all. She said any woman that ran out on her baby was no use to anyone. I think that's why she gets so worked up over the animals that way. You know, like the baby gators the other day."

Richard nodded, completely confused. Jenny's story didn't line up at all with his thoughts on Dorie's parentage, but one look at Jenny's face, and he knew that she was speaking the absolute truth—at least as far as she knew it. Was the person she described really capable of joining up with the likes of Shawn Roland? Even if they were somehow related? Everything inside of him felt it couldn't be true, but there was one person left to speak to before he could put that thought to rest, even if it put Roland on notice.

He put one hand on top of Jenny's and smiled. "I appreciate what you've told me. And I want you to know that you did nothing to hurt Dorie at all. Everything you've told me only makes my opinion of her better."

Jenny sniffed and nodded. "Thanks. I appreciate that. I hate to think I was breaking a confidence, but I don't know where you're going with all this. I guess maybe if it all works out then you can tell me. Or maybe not. I just know that I want this guy out of Gator Bait. And I want Dorie back in the café griping about everything and Joe too scared to speak to me."

She looked directly at him. "What I'm trying to say is I want my life back. And if talking to you helps things along then I'm willing to do it."

He nodded in understanding. "You've helped me make up my mind on a very important issue, Jenny, and for that, I'm in your debt. I want nothing more than for your town to get back to normal." He rose from the counter and started toward the door, certain that the next conversation he needed to have was with Sheriff Berenger.

Joe dropped his cup of coffee to the table with a bang, and narrowly missed sloshing his hand. "I don't believe it," he said.

Dorie sighed and set her coffee mug on the table, the hot liquid doing nothing to calm her nerves. "Do you think I want to believe it? This is my worst nightmare, Joe. All this time I've been worrying about having to arrest someone in Gator Bait, and the way it stands, my dad and Buster are the prime suspects."

His eyes flashed and he stared intently at her. "Are you planning to tell Richard about this?"

She shook her head, feeling miserable. "I don't know. I don't think so. I don't think they're involved with Roland this time, but it wouldn't look good for them anyway. If I thought the information would help Richard at all, I'd tell him, but I don't see how it could." Could it?

Joe considered this for a moment then nodded in agreement. "I'm with you. I don't see how it could help at all, but it certainly could hurt a lot. If this got out in Gator Bait, the sheriff would be ruined, which affects you."

Joe took a deep breath and ran one hand down the side of his face. "I don't know where it would leave Buster. People around here gotta make a living. But I still say it could be made miserable enough for him that he takes an early retirement or sells out completely to one of the big commercial firms."

"I know. No matter how you slice it, if this got out, it would cause a lot of problems in Gator Bait. And I'll admit—problems I'm not ready to deal with."

"Me either. And I don't want you feeling guilty about this, Dorie. It's too far in the past to be an issue now, and there's nothing we could do to change it anyway."

She blew out a breath. "I know. But it doesn't stop the hurt, Joe. My own father." She pounded the table with one fist and brought a few looks from the other diners. "For Christ's sake," she said, lowering her voice a bit, "it was his job to keep anything like this out of the town, and instead, he covered it all up and pretended it had never happened. All for money. It makes me sick."

Joe shook his head. "It wasn't really for money. It was to protect a friend. Besides, if they'd kept the money, some of it would still be around. Your dad did what he thought was best for Buster and Gator Bait. I don't agree with his decision, but I don't see where it was motivated by any personal gain."

"The reason still doesn't change the facts. By not reporting Roland to the authorities, they committed a crime. Because of what they did, that man felt safe enough to come back to Gator Bait, and the rules are different now." She looked Joe straight in the eyes. "With the attempts that have been made lately, I can't help wondering just how close I am to the person involved with Roland. Someone doesn't like where I'm headed with this investigation, and they apparently have a bigger problem with my involvement than yours or Richard's."

Joe nodded and looked miserable, clearly wanting to disagree but unable to argue with the facts. "So what do you think is going on?"

Dorie blew out a breath. "I think that Roland's partner is scared I'm on to him and he's sent Roland into action to rectify the problem. Which can only mean it's someone close enough to me to think I'd figure them out."

Joe nodded.

"I don't think he's going to quit until I'm dead," she said. "There's too much on the line for them to screw this up."

Joe stared back at her and nodded once. "Then we'll have to see that he doesn't get a shot at you. And that means we have to hunt him down. I know how you feel about justice, Dorie, but I have to tell you that this is one case where I will not shoot to injure."

Dorie stared out the window at the highway, realizing that Joe had just suggested they hunt a man down and kill him in cold blood. "The worst part is," she said finally, "that's the best idea I've heard all week."

Richard waited at the small garage while the young man pulled the tires off of his car. "Whew," the young man blew out a breath. "Someone did a real number on these. I can't patch this at all. Whoever did this knew what he was doing."

"Lucky for me," Richard said. "I always wanted a car with no tires."

The young man laughed. "I'll see what I can find for you. We don't have anything like this and definitely not in a set of four, but I can probably find something that will get you to Lake Charles so you can get a matched set, although it might ride a bit rough."

Richard nodded. "That would be great. When I get them changed, I'll bring the others back. Charge me double whatever you normally do. My company's footing the bill for this one."

The young man's eyes widened in surprise. "Cool. Thanks a lot, man."

Giving the man a smile, he stepped out of the garage, pulled the cell phone from his pocket and dialed the agency. "This is Agent Richard Starke," he said to the woman who answered. "I need all the information you have on Dorie Berenger."

"Oh, yes, I pulled that file this morning. Do you want it faxed?" she asked.

"No. I don't have access to a fax at the moment. Just read me what's in the files and I'll take notes on anything important."

"Agent Starke, there are over twenty pages of information in this file."

Richard looked into the garage. The young man had at least forty different tires scattered on the floor, trying to find anything remotely matched. He pulled a small pad of paper and a pen from his pocket. "I've got time," he said. "Go ahead."

Dorie and Joe spent most of the afternoon attempting to salvage anything from Dorie's boat. They made it back to the sheriff's office toward evening. The message light blinked on the antiquated phone system and Dorie pressed the button on the machine. Sherry's voice immediately poured out. "Dorie, I just want you to know that DEA agent is here talking to the sheriff. Now, I don't know what got you so upset this morning, and I couldn't exactly refuse him a visit, but I don't like all these goings-on. It's not good for your daddy's heart."

The message stopped and Dorie gave Joe a frightened look. "What is Richard talking to Dad for? He didn't say anything to me about talking to Dad."

He slowly shook his head. "I don't have any idea, but I don't like it."

"Neither do I. You don't think Dad would be stupid enough to tell him about Roland, do you?"

He blew out a breath. "God, I wouldn't like to think so. But then, if he thought Richard would make you leave town like he wants, he might."

"Damn it!" She banged her hand on the desk. "What the hell is Richard doing?"

Chapter Thirteen

Richard knocked on the sheriff's apartment door and was told to enter. He pushed the door open and stepped inside the living room where the sheriff sat in his favorite spot. Sam Berenger looked surprised to see him and continued to stare at the door, even after Richard closed it behind him.

Was he expecting Dorie? Doubtful. She and Joe had been there that morning, but based on the anxious expression on the sheriff's face, Richard knew something was definitely up. Studying the man in front of him, he wondered exactly what had transpired between Dorie and her father that made the man so nervous.

"Dorie's done been and gone if you're looking for her," the sheriff said and took his gaze away from the door.

"No," Richard said and took a seat on the couch. "Actually, I came to talk to you."

Sheriff Berenger stared at him for a moment and nodded. "Go ahead, then."

Taking a deep breath, he began. "I need to know about Dorie's parentage."

Sheriff Berenger stared at him in obvious surprise. "Ain't nothing to know about her parentage. I'm her father and her mother is long gone and irrelevant."

Richard shook his head. "That's not good enough, Sheriff. The DNA results on the hair samples from Buster's camp came back this morning. There were two matches—a full on Shawn Roland and a partial on Dorie."

Sheriff Berenger gave a start and the blood drained from his face. "That's impossible," he said, his voice barely a whisper.

"They ran the tests twice to be sure. Blood tests too. There's no mistake." He stared at the sheriff and was fairly sure the man wasn't breathing. For a moment, he wondered whether the sheriff was about to have another heart attack. That would be a nightmare. But just when Richard began to rise from the couch to call for help, the sheriff waved a hand to stop him.

"I'm fine," he said, coughing a little. "Well, as fine as I can be, given what you just told me."

"Sheriff, I need to know what this means. You understand my position here? How this looks to me and my superiors?"

Sheriff Berenger nodded. "I understand. I just can't believe this is happening. What are the odds, right?" He gazed past Richard and stared at the wall, his face full of sorrow.

"Can I get you anything?" Richard asked, still worried about the pale color in his face.

"No, no. I best just tell you since you're all off in the wrong direction. It's not gonna get any easier with a drink." He gave Richard a small smile. "Especially since I had to get off the good stuff a long time ago."

Richard nodded and settled back on the couch, hoping if he looked relaxed, it would encourage the sheriff to tell his story.

The sheriff sat in silence a moment longer, as if deciding how to start, then cleared his voice and began. "Of course, it was over thirty years ago when it happened. I was a hell of a lot younger then and still full of piss and vinegar—like most young men are when they come back from the war a decorated hero. There wasn't a woman who could hold me. Everyone called me The Heartbreaker, and the name was well-deserved."

He gave Richard a broad smile. "Man like yourself ought to understand that." His smile faded and he shook his head. "Still, I had no intention of settling down. My mother hadn't been any prize. She ran around on my father back in the days when women just didn't run around. When I was six, she left completely. I've never seen or heard of her since."

He looked at Richard, a hollow expression on his face. "It makes a man think twice," he continued. "You know, about women, relationships. I had plenty try to get me, but I wasn't having any of it. I had my work and an occasional woman in Lake Charles, and that was more than enough for me." He nodded. "Yep, that was more than enough for me. Until that Tuesday—the day my life changed forever. That was the day I met the girl I would love for the rest of my life."

Richard shifted to a more comfortable position and nodded for the sheriff to continue, sure he was about to reveal the truth about Dorie's mother.

"I'd been out in the marsh most of the day. Gators had been breeding in some odd areas that year, and I was doing my best to keep them contained. Didn't want some unsuspecting fisherman to happen across a female and her nest. We'd already had two attacks that year, and I wasn't wanting a third.

"The day had been long and hard," the sheriff said, "and there was nothing I wanted more at that moment than a hot shower and a cold beer, but they were going to have to wait. It was late evening by the time I got home and I could see something next to my door when I pulled in the drive. Hell, I was always ordering something by mail, so I didn't think nothing of it until I got out of the car and heard the crying."

"Dorie?" Richard asked.

Sheriff Berenger nodded. "There she was, all wrapped up in a pink blanket and sitting in a cardboard box next to my door, wailing like the dickens."

"What did you do?"

"I grabbed her up right away, thinking maybe she was hurt and that was the reason for all the noise. As soon as I got her inside I checked every inch of her, but didn't find so much as a scratch. There was a small bag in the box with her and I opened it up. Inside was a can of formula, a couple of diapers and the letter."

Richard sat up straight. "What did it say?"

The sheriff looked Richard eye to eye. "I remember the exact words to this day. It said 'I can't keep her safe. Please find someone who will.' That was it. No signature, no indication of who the mother was or why she couldn't care for the child." Sheriff Berenger shook his head. "I'm not a fanciful sort of man, but something about those words gave me a chill and I wondered what in the world that woman had gotten herself into. And why an infant would be at risk."

"Did you try to track down the mother?" Richard asked.

Sheriff Berenger narrowed his eyes. "Of course I did. What kind of lawman do you think I am? Any woman who's got to give up a part of herself has bigger issues than raising an infant alone. I aimed to help her if possible, but couldn't find a thing. I checked the hospitals for recent births, but everyone on record was happy at home with their families. Meantime, I left the baby with a friend of mine in Lake Charles who worked for Social Services. He and his wife fostered kids, and they were more than happy to help."

"So you never found anything?"

"Not a thing. It's as if the woman appeared in Louisiana by a puff of smoke and disappeared the same way."

Richard nodded. "So how did you manage to keep her?"

Sheriff Berenger blew out a breath and lowered his head. "I lied. I broke the law, pure and simple." He looked up at Richard, his eyes beginning to redden around the edges. "After a week with absolutely no success on locating the mother, I went to my friends, intending to take the baby and make her a ward of the state. When I walked in the house, she was wailing, just like she had been that day on my doorstep. Linda was trying to soothe her, rocking her slowly in a chair, but it wasn't doing a bit of good. I stepped next to the chair and put one hand on her head."

Sheriff Berenger cleared his throat and took a deep, unsteady breath. "She looked up at me and stopped screaming," he said. "She stared at me with those big blue eyes and tried to grab my hand with her tiny fingers. I lifted her from Linda's shoulder and held her in my arms. I knew right then that I had fallen in love for the first time and the last time in my life. And I was willing to do anything to keep her."

The sheriff paused a moment and dropped his gaze to the floor. Richard remained quiet, giving the man time to compose himself and his thoughts.

Finally, he continued. "I had my friend at Social Services do the paperwork for me. A fake birth certificate got me a social security card, and Dorie was mine. With all the time I'd spent away from Gator Bait trying to locate Dorie's mother, the townfolk thought I had some woman on the side that I'd gotten pregnant. They figured she didn't want the baby and I had been gone to get her and make arrangements to keep her. No one ever asked, and I never offered to tell. Not even Buster knows. My best friend."

"And the couple in Lake Charles," Richard asked. "You didn't worry about them telling?"

"Hell, no. They were happy enough to see the baby going to someone who would love her. Having dealt with the foster care system for so many years, they weren't exactly eager to see an infant go into it."

Richard nodded. "So you kept her, and all the women in Gator Bait pitched in to help you care for her."

The sheriff looked at Richard, his eyebrows raised. "Who told you that?"

"Jenny. She's worried about Dorie. She had no idea why I was asking her questions, but if it was going to keep Dorie safe, she was willing to tell me what she knew."

Sheriff Berenger nodded. "Jenny's a good girl. She looks after her own and still feels like she owes Dorie. Dorie doesn't feel that way, mind you, but it hasn't stopped Jenny from trying to repay her all these years. She's a good girl. As good as my Dorie."

He looked Richard straight in the eye and drew himself up in his wheelchair. "I did what I thought was best for Dorie. Always have. If I had to do it all over again, I'd do the same thing. Don't really matter who fathered her, if that's where you're going with this. I'm her daddy. There's a big difference."

"I agree, but do you think Dorie's going to see it that way? She's spent her entire life under the assumption that you are her biological father and her mother abandoned her. She's only half right. The odds of Shawn Roland having fathered Dorie are very high—damned near one hundred percent. And if that woman had a baby with Roland, she was definitely in danger. So now the man who actually fathered Dorie most likely killed her mother and is now trying to kill her." He blew out a breath and ran one hand through his hair. "That's too much, Sheriff. Too much to ask anyone to deal with. Even someone as strong as Dorie."

"I know," Sheriff Berenger said. "That's why I was kind of hoping we could keep this between us. There's no need for Dorie to know about it. At least, not that I can see."

Richard shook his head. "You're wrong. Dorie deserves to know. She may very well have to face Roland. Do you want her to make a decision without a full set of facts? She may never forgive you for it if she does."

Richard paused a moment and took a deep breath. "I can agree to buy you a little time by trying to keep Dorie out of the worst of this, but you know I can't guarantee success. And even if I can hold her off, it won't be for long. You know your daughter, Sheriff. She's not going to let this go. Roland's attacked her on her home turf. It's personal now."

The sheriff nodded. "I understand. And I know

what you're up against. My Dorie's as hardheaded as they come."

Richard cleared his throat and rushed forward with his next statement before he could change his mind. "There's something else, Sheriff. Another reason why I can't lie to your daughter."

The sheriff looked at him and beckoned him to continue.

"I care for her," he said. "More than I should. More than I wanted to. But there's no way we have any future if this secret is between us."

Sheriff Berenger looked at Richard and slowly nodded. "I kind of figured it would get around to that between the two of you. I never seen anyone get under Dorie's skin the way you did. It was bound to happen." He leaned forward in his chair and looked closely at Richard. "I tell you what. I'll make you a promise if you make me one."

"What's the promise?"

"I promise to tell Dorie everything when the time is right if you promise to get her out of that godforsaken town and put her talent to better use. Since she popped up in your databases, I'm sure I don't need to go into her background and education. I didn't mean to keep it all from you before, but Dorie's never really wanted anyone knowing about her brains. She said it gave her an edge if people thought she was stupid. Hard to argue with her when she's right."

"What about you? You know Dorie won't leave here given your condition."

"I can take care of myself just fine. I know Dorie's worried about money and the cost of my care, but I have a plan to cover that. I'll let her know when everything is in order."

Richard blew out a breath, not exactly pleased

with the vague plan, but smart enough to know it was the best he was going to get. For now. "Okay. If you tell her the truth, and she's willing to leave, I'll see that she's taken care of with a game warden or law enforcement position somewhere else. Will that do?"

Sheriff Berenger nodded and slumped back down in his chair. "Then I guess you best get to catching your criminal. You've got a life to get on with." He pointed a finger at Richard and gave him a stern look. "And you best remember that life you're getting on with includes my daughter. I just ask that you keep her out of catching Roland. Your criminal has been far too aggressive where Dorie's concerned."

"You have my word, Sheriff, that I'll do everything possible to protect her."

The sheriff nodded and Richard rose from the couch and walked out the door, wondering how in the hell he was going to act normally around Dorie now that he was keeping this secret. Pulling back from her after the way they'd been together would probably hurt her, but it was what he was going to have to do.

There was no way he could continue to be so intimate with Dorie and not let everything spill out. No, he was going to have to make a huge adjustment. Go back to the standoffish, sarcastic Dick. At least, until this was over and everything was out in the open.

As he climbed into his car and set off in search of tires, he wondered how Dorie was going to feel about him when she found out about the lie he'd helped her father perpetuate, even if only for a brief time.

* * *

Sheriff Berenger reached for the phone on the end table beside him. He pressed speed dial and spoke as soon as the man answered on the other end. "Buster, it's Berenger. It's time to get on with our plans. I've held my daughter back long enough. You've got things covered on the other end now, so there shouldn't be any problems."

"If you're sure," Buster said. "I'll start making arrangements. I found someone in Florida on my last trip who said they could take care of things down there."

"Well, best get going then. But I have a favor to ask before we start." He told Buster what he had in mind. There was silence on the other end, but he knew Buster wouldn't refuse him. Hanging up the phone, he opened the drawer on the end table and removed his .357, weighing it in his hands. It felt good, he decided. It had been too damn long since he'd enjoyed the brush of the metal against his palm.

Removing a soft cloth from the drawer, he gently began to clean the weapon, and hoped that this time would be the last.

Dorie and Joe eyed Richard suspiciously when he entered the sheriff's office. Dorie tried to study him, but found herself unable to look him in the eyes. Even though she'd already made a vow to distance herself from Richard, she was afraid it was going to prove impossible. Just the sight of him had her nerves jumping and her heart racing—for all sorts of reasons.

It only took one look at him for her resolve to waver. *I am not capable of lying, and hiding the truth is no different.* She looked over at Joe, who frowned and shook his head, apparently keying in on her warring emotions. Dorie took a deep breath and struggled to get control. Her dad's future depended on it.

"You find out anything, Dick?" she asked, trying to sound normal.

"Not really," Richard said. "Well, except that the DNA was a match, but then we already knew that. And I got my car patched well enough to get me to Lake Charles for a new set of tires. What about you?"

She shook her head. "No. We went over the boat and the surrounding area with a fine-tooth comb, but came up with nothing." She shrugged. "Not that I expected anything. We knew it was a long shot. So what's next?" She looked expectantly at him, still waiting for him to mention his visit to her dad.

He stroked his jaw for a moment, apparently considering her question. "It looks like we've stalled on figuring out who Roland is in business with. Maybe we need to come at this from another angle."

Dorie shrugged, and tried to control her rising aggravation. She didn't care about Roland right now. She wanted to know why Richard had visited her dad and what the old fool had told him, but it looked like that bit of information was something she was going to have to get from the sheriff—the last person she wanted to speak to at the moment. "Okay," she said finally. "What angle?"

Richard sat on the end of Joe's desk. "We've been focusing on who Roland was dealing with and how they were going to get the drugs in Gator Bait. Maybe we should consider how they're going to get them out."

She raised her eyebrows and looked at Joe, who nodded. "That's actually a pretty smart idea," Joe said. "If the shipment is as large as you say, it will take far more than a pickup truck or a bass boat to move it out of here. And I can only assume Roland would be planning one trip in and one trip out. I can't imagine him moving the product out in small pieces."

"He wouldn't," Richard said. "No time for that. Roland is not part of a small operation. The people he works for have timetables. And they don't like to wait."

"No, I don't guess they would," Dorie said. "So what do we have to go on? We've talked to the major players in town. Anyone have an idea as to how someone could move that much product out of Gator Bait without looking suspicious?"

"The shrimp boats are out," Joe said. "No shrimper is going to be headed up the channel into Lake Charles. That would attract too much attention. Lake Charles game wardens would be all over him."

"He's right," she agreed. "Anyone that far up from the gulf risks being stopped and searched in a big way."

Richard considered this for a moment. "What about cabin cruisers? Anyone have a boat large enough to haul the product while still appearing to be taking an outing?"

Dorie didn't like the answer to this one. She looked over at Joe, who barely nodded, giving her the go-ahead to tell Richard what they knew. She supposed it would be easy enough for Richard to find out the information on his own, and they would look far worse for not telling when they had the opportunity.

"Buster has a cabin cruiser," she said. "It's about thirty feet. Would that be big enough?"

"Probably," Richard said. "And that should be a very easy thing to watch. Anything else? What about enclosed trailers? Anyone have horses?"

Dorie and Joe shook their heads. "I can't think of

any enclosed trailers at all," she said. "Flatbed, yes, but that wouldn't work."

"What about his own transportation?" Joe asked. "Couldn't Roland be arranging to rent a truck or trailer and move the stuff out himself?"

"It's possible," Richard said. "But not very likely. We've caught some of his shipments at the delivery point, but Roland was never anywhere to be found. I think he arranges things, then steps conveniently to the side. Plus, you could hardly move an eighteen-wheeler through a town like Gator Bait without attracting a whole lot of attention. Ditto for a big boat. In a town this small, a different hairdo is a big event."

"True," Dorie agreed. "Still, he's got to have a plan or he wouldn't be here. And he definitely wouldn't be taking time out of his schedule to chase after me if the deal was over."

Joe opened his mouth to speak when the phone on his desk rang. He answered the phone and Dorie heard loud obnoxious cussing all the way at her desk. Joe held the phone about six inches from his ear and waited for a pause in the yelling. Finally, there was a break, and he put the phone back up to his ear. "I'll come out right now, Mrs. Thibodeaux." He hadn't even completed the sentence when the yelling and cussing began again. Joe looked at Dorie. "She's asking for you. How do you want me to handle this?"

Dorie sighed. "I guess I better go. Whatever has her that riled will probably take at least an hour of my time and a bottle of her brew to solve." Dorie looked at Richard. "You going or staying?" she asked, hoping at the same time that he would both go and stay.

Richard hesitated for a moment then replied, "I think I'll go. I need a break from this case. Mrs. Thibodeaux is quite a refreshing form of entertainment compared to Roland."

Dorie laughed. "That's the first time I've heard anyone refer to Maylene as refreshing."

Joe smiled. "And it will probably be the last." He rose from the desk and followed Dorie and Richard out the front door. "Since Richard has security detail covered, I think I'll make a pass around town while you're taking care of Maylene. See if anyone acquired transportation large enough for what we're looking for."

"Be careful, Joe," Dorie warned. "We can't afford to create another target."

"You're the one who needs to be careful," Joe said, and Dorie knew by his tone that he wasn't only talking about Roland.

"I've got it covered, Joe," Dorie said, trying to keep her voice steady and sure.

"Well then, don't worry about me," Joe continued with a smile. "Dick just thinks Maylene is safer than Roland."

Dorie slowly shook her head at his retreating figure and hoped this time he wasn't right, then jumped into her jeep, Richard in tow, and headed out to the Thibodeaux place.

For as big of a snit as she was in, Maylene had managed to put on more clothing than Dorie had expected. Her T-shirt came almost all the way to her waist and her shorts just missed covering her entire rear. The remainder of both front and back were hanging out of the garments in full display. Dorie took one look at Richard and knew he was rethinking his position on Maylene Thibodeaux being entertainment.

"Hello, Maylene," Dorie said, trying to sound pleasant. "What seems to be the problem?"

Maylene lowered the bottle of brew long enough to wave one hand in the air and start a stream of words. "Too much noise. Day and night. Damn boats. No one should be driving that fast. Don't understand it. Should be against the law."

Dorie raised her eyebrows at Richard and waited for the tirade to end. Maylene's mouth must have gotten dry, because finally she took a break from griping and put the bottle back to her lips.

"So what you're saying is that boats are running past your house all hours of the day and night and you would like it to stop. Is that correct?"

Maylene lowered the bottle and stared at her. "Of course that's correct. Weren't you listening to a damn thing I said? Now, I want those boats to stop."

Dorie nodded, not sure whether to be alarmed or amused. "Okay. And which night exactly did you hear the boats?"

"Last night, damn it," Maylene yelled. "I already told you. Last night. Loud as hell. Shook all my bottles."

Dorie nodded and pretended to make a note on a pad of paper. "Okay, Maylene. I'll check that out right away and see that it stops. Is there anything else I can do for you today?"

Maylene lowered her bottle again and shifted her gaze from Dorie to Richard, who began to squirm. "No. There's nothing else you can do, unlessing you'd like to leave your man here while you take care of business. I've got business of my own he could attend to."

Richard choked back a laugh and cleared his throat. "Not this time, Maylene. Dorie might need help finding those boats, and a woman with your incredible looks shouldn't have her beauty sleep disturbed."

Maylene shrugged and looked a bit disappointed.

"Guess not. Smart of you anyway, Dorie, to keep him on the job." She gave Richard a wink. "Once a man has a bit of Maylene, it ruins him for other women."

Richard smiled back. "I don't doubt it," he said, and somehow managed to keep a straight face until the were back at the jeep. "Jesus," he said and made a face like he'd just taken in a mouthful of saltwater. "That was a close one. What was her husband like?"

"Before or after the fall?" Dorie asked with a grin.

"After."

"Drunk."

"What about before?"

"Pretty much the same."

He smiled. "I guess that would explain it. So what are you going to do about this boat thing? You can't tell people when to operate a boat, can you?"

"No, nor how fast to drive them," she said and jumped in the jeep. "And wouldn't have to even if I could."

Richard followed suit and gave her a questioning look. "Why not?"

Dorie smiled. "Because it's obvious that Maylene is hallucinating. Remember, I told you that the nearest water source to Maylene's is over a mile in any direction. There's no way she heard boats, especially closed up in her house and drunk as hell. More likely she left her TV on NASCAR, and got a bit confused. One time, watching *Animal Planet* had her convinced there were elephants in her living room. It took us almost two hours to get her to come out of the bedroom closet."

Richard laughed and looked past Maylene's house down the narrow shell road. "What about this road? Does it go through to anywhere?"

"Not really. It dead-ends right smack in the middle of the game preserve. I let the grass grow over it as much as possible. I don't want anyone getting any ideas of trying to fish back there. The place is loaded with gators."

She looked down the road and squinted her eyes in the sunlight. "Still, I guess I wouldn't be doing my job if I didn't check it out. Prepare for another bouncing ride," she said and gave Richard a smile.

"At least I'll be on the seat this time. Tell me. How is it that you have four perfectly matched tires, and I had to drive all the way to Lake Charles on something I can't even describe?"

Dorie snorted. "In my line of work? Hell, I learned real early to have spares. I probably have four or five sets still over in Joe's garage."

Richard stared at her in obvious surprise. "You go through that many tires here? What happens to them? Is there a lot of trash in the roads?"

"Nah. It's gators mostly. They don't really like people coming into what they consider their home. I usually lose seven or eight tires a year to gator bites."

She put the jeep in drive and squealed out of the driveway, leaving a shower of dust behind.

"And are we on our way right now to one of those tire-biting locations?" he asked.

Dorie grinned.

"Great. Nothing death defying has happened in a couple of hours at least. I was starting to get bored."

Chapter Fourteen

Joe walked up and down Main Street, taking a critical look at the town around him. Everything looked normal, but yet it couldn't possibly be. Everyone in Gator Bait went about business as usual, completely unaware the town was under siege. Well, that wasn't exactly accurate. People were more than a little concerned about Dorie's boat being blown to bits, but as soon as they found out she was all right, it would just be another day.

Joe shook his head. What was wrong with these people? Did they really brush up against death so often that someone else's misfortune was merely conversation for Pete's Bar? Or were they like Dorie and resigned to the fact that everyone had to go sometime? Joe looked at the church and sighed.

All those years of his father preaching about the hereafter—at church, at home, on vacations. It had never made Joe comfortable with death, and he was the one person in town who ought to be. After all, he probably knew more about heaven than the angels.

He shifted his gaze to the diner. Now was the time. If he was going to cast his lot with Dorie and Richard, he'd better ask Jenny out while he was still breathing. With a new resolve, he strode across the street and pushed open the door to the café.

Jenny looked up in surprise as the door banged on the inside wall. "Sorry," Joe said sheepishly. This was starting off well.

Jenny smiled. "It's broken. It's supposed to be fixed this afternoon."

He nodded, relieved he wasn't destroying her restaurant, and took a seat at the counter. It was too late for lunch and too early for supper, so the diner was empty.

"Can I get you some coffee?" she asked. "Or maybe a soda?"

His mind raced over the simple question. Coffee gave you bad breath. He reached up to his shirt pocket. Damn. No mints. "Soda, please."

She fixed the soda and set the glass in front of him. "How's Dorie doing?"

"She's fine. As far as I can tell anyway. Hell, you know Dorie."

Jenny nodded. "Yes, I do. That's why I worry about her. She keeps things all bundled up inside. It's not healthy. I'm afraid one of these days she's going to blow."

He took a gulp of the soda and swallowed, trying to clear his throat. "Let's just hope if she blows anytime soon, it's around Dick's bad guy."

Jenny stared at him, her face drawn tight. "I'm really worried about her this time. This is worse than anything I've ever seen and I probably don't even know the half of it. You would tell me if there was a problem, right?"

Joe looked her straight in the eyes and considered his answer. He opened his mouth and tried to let the lie out, but couldn't speak at all. Finally, he sighed and dropped his gaze to the counter. "If something was wrong with Dorie that she didn't want known, I'm afraid I wouldn't tell you."

He raised his gaze back up to Jenny's face, expecting anger, but instead, she smiled. "You're a good man, Joe Miller. Will you do me the honor of escorting me to the Contraband Days Dance in Lake Charles?"

Before the last words left her mouth, he choked on his soda and tried to swallow, but it was impossible. Unable to breathe, he finally spit the soda back in his glass and coughed. Jenny laughed and dumped his glass in the sink behind the counter.

"Did you think I was going to wait forever?" she asked. "If you're gonna keep hanging out with Dorie and Richard, I figured I better get my time in fast."

Joe laughed. "The funny thing is, I was thinking the same thing on my way over here. I came in with the specific intention of asking you out."

"Well, then why didn't you?"

He shrugged. "I don't know. Nerves, I guess." He lifted her hand from the counter and held it in his. "You're something special, Jenny. I guess I've never been sure I deserved something that good."

Jenny sighed. "Just make me one promise."

"What's that?"

Although they were all alone in the café, she leaned across the counter and whispered in his ear. "Promise me you won't take so long to get around to *everything*."

The jeep screeched to a halt in front of a tall barrier of marsh grass, and Richard gratefully relaxed his grip on the roll bar above him. Dorie stepped out of the jeep, walked to the edge of the marsh, and took a look around.

"I don't like it," she said as he made his way over to her. "Someone's been out here. Recently." She pointed to a section of broken grass off to the left.

"Fishermen?"

She shook her head. "I doubt it. City people wouldn't know how to find this and the townspeople are smart enough to keep away."

"Is it safe to follow the trail and see where it goes?"

She grinned. "No, but that's never stopped me." Pushing the remaining grass aside, she stepped into the marsh.

He hesitated for a moment, studying the thick wall of grass that could be hiding darn near anything. "Oh, hell," he finally said and followed her into the muddy water.

They pushed their way about a quarter mile or so through the grass and came to a small clearing of hardened bayou mud that rose just far enough out of the water's path to stay dry. Dorie stepped onto the dirt and pointed to a section of broken grass just off to the left of the clearing.

"Whoever it was continued through there," she said. "And based on the boot prints in the soft mud at the edge of this clearing, it was definitely human and not animal." She looked around again and blew out a breath. "I don't know about this, Dick. I don't think we should go any farther on foot. We probably ought to come back with a small boat. At least that would get us out of the water."

He looked around and suddenly realized he couldn't see a thing beyond the small circle of dirt they were standing on. Maybe a boat was a good idea. Besides, if Dorie wasn't comfortable, he ought to be worried as hell. "Whatever you think."

Dorie nodded and had just stepped off the dirt and into the marsh when the alligator charged at Richard. The animal had been hidden in the grass just to the right of them and apparently didn't appreciate them disturbing his resting place.

Richard whipped his head around and stared at the alligator, completely horrified and frozen in place. Before he could even contemplate movement, gunshots rang out, and the gator dropped dead at his feet. He spun around and looked at Dorie, but her gun was already holstered, and she was standing calmly in a foot of water shaking her head. It was like *Gunsmoke* on the bayou.

He let out the breath he'd been holding with a whoosh. "Jesus Christ! I thought you couldn't kill anything in the game preserve."

She raised her eyebrows and gave him an amused look. "Did you expect me to cuff him and read him his rights?"

Realizing how ridiculous his comment sounded, Richard laughed nervously. "No, I guess not. I guess I was just expecting to die," he said in complete honesty. "I really didn't think beyond that point."

Dorie nodded and her expression turned serious. "That's why I said no one in their right mind would be out here." She looked across the dirt at the trail extending deeper into the marsh. "You know what that means?"

"Someone in his *wrong* mind made this trail?"

She gave him a small laugh. "Now, that would describe darn near everyone in Gator Bait, but yeah, that's the idea. Except even people in Gator Bait have more of a mind about the game preserve than to go wandering around it on foot. This had to be someone stupid enough, or desperate enough, to try to make it through here, and I don't know of a single person who fits that bill."

"Roland?"

Dorie stared at the dead alligator and shook her head. "Maybe you *are* chasing a ghost, Dick."

Joe left the café, a huge grin on his face when Jenny rushed out the door after him. "Joe, wait," she yelled. "Sherry at the retirement home is on the phone looking for Dorie and she sounds in a bad way."

Joe's heart immediately dropped. *Please, God, no. Don't let anything have happened to the sheriff.* But as he rushed to the phone, he wondered already if this morning's confession might have been just the thing to send the sheriff's heart over the edge.

He grabbed the phone from the counter. "Sherry, it's Joe."

"Oh, Joe," Sherry wailed. "I don't know what to do. I just don't know what to do."

"Calm down, Sherry. You've got to tell me what's wrong."

"It's the sheriff," Sherry cried, her voice rising in panic.

Joe felt every muscle in his body tighten and he braced himself against the counter. "What's happened to the sheriff, Sherry?"

"He's gone," she shrieked. "He's gone!"

Joe got what little information he could from the frantic Sherry, dropped the phone and raced out to his truck, trying to make his voice sound normal as he called for Dorie. "Dorie, call in." He waited a moment then pressed the button again. "Dorie, are you out there?" He waited another moment, but the radio remained silent.

"Damn!" He looked at Jenny, who was standing next to the truck, hand clenched by her side. "Dorie headed out to Maylene's earlier. I'm going to drive that way. I'll keep trying her on the radio. You try her on her cell and give Maylene a call, then keep a lookout in town. If you see her, tell her to get to the retirement home immediately."

She nodded as he threw his truck in gear. "Joe," she said and leaned over to kiss his cheek. "Be careful."

He gave her a grim smile, floored the truck, and squealed down Main Street.

Dorie and Richard were wading out of the marsh, when she heard Joe's voice come over the radio. It didn't sound good. She rushed to the jeep and grabbed the radio. "Joe, it's Dorie. What's wrong?"

"Dorie, thank God. I've been trying to reach you for almost ten minutes. There's a problem with your dad."

Dorie sucked in a breath and Richard placed his hand on her shoulder. "What kind of problem?" she asked.

"He's missing. Sherry can't find him anywhere, and she's in a panic. We need to get over there. I'll meet you in town."

Dorie flung the radio into the jeep and jumped in the driver's seat. Richard barely made it around the other side before she put the vehicle in gear and tore off down the road, making the drive back to Gator Bait in record time. They slowed just enough on Main Street for Joe to jump in the back of the jeep, and then she floored the vehicle again, and raced toward the highway.

Sherry was standing in front of the building, worry etched on her face, when Dorie screeched to a halt in the middle of the driveway. Completely ignoring the no parking rules, she jumped out of the jeep and rushed into the building after Sherry, Richard and Joe not far behind.

Dorie passed the distraught Sherry in the hallway and was the first to enter her dad's apartment. "I just know something awful has happened," Sherry cried. "Oh, Dorie, please forgive me for not keeping a better eye on him." She put her hands over her face and burst into tears.

Dorie patted her on the arm. "This isn't your fault, Sherry. If Dad wanted to go, he would have gotten around you regardless of how closely you were watching him." She pointed to the empty wheelchair and looked at Richard and Joe.

Richard glanced at the chair and his eyes widened. "Good Lord. You think he wanted to leave, or did someone force him?"

Dorie slowly shook her head and studied the room. "There's no sign of a struggle, and Dad's upper body all but makes up for his legs." She walked over to the coat closet in the living room, yanked the door open and peered inside. "His manual wheelchair is gone."

Joe whistled. "Not a good sign."

Richard looked from Joe to Dorie. "What does that mean?"

Joe blew out a breath. "It means someone else was with him, and they wanted to move fast and easy. The motorized wheelchair is heavy to push, if necessary, and not easy to fit in some places."

Dorie closed the closet door and did the one thing she'd been putting off since she stepped into the apartment—she opened the drawer on the end table and looked inside. "It's gone," she said, her voice choked with fear. "Joe, it's gone."

"What's gone?" Richard asked, his voice rising with Dorie's obvious panic.

"His pistol," Joe replied, his voice grim. He

turned to Sherry, who was still weeping quietly and said, "I need you to pull a phone log. See who the sheriff called this morning and last night."

Sherry nodded and hurried out of the apartment. Joe and Dorie began to systematically check the rooms for missing items, leaving Richard standing helpless in the midst of chaos.

"His stash is still here," Dorie said and waved a wad of cash she'd removed from the dresser.

"Looks like all his clothes are here," Joe said and began to close the closet door, then paused and stared at the floor. "Except his boots. Why the hell would he need rubber boots?"

Dorie was struggling for an answer when Sherry rushed back into the apartment, a long sheet of computer paper trailing behind her. "It's here," she said breathlessly. "The only place the sheriff called today was the shrimp house."

"Buster," Dorie said and looked at Joe, who blew out a breath, and slumped against the wall. "What if they lied to me again, Joe? What if the whole story was a lie?"

Joe shook his head and darted a glance at Richard, then at Dorie. "We don't know that and shouldn't jump to conclusions."

Dorie looked at Richard, who was obviously aware that he'd missed something important, but wasn't about to ask. She knew Joe wanted her to keep everything quiet, at least until they figured out what was going on, but this had gone on long enough—thirty-something years too long, as a matter of fact. And it was going to end here, regardless of what Richard thought of her after she'd had her say. "First thing we have to do is find Buster," she said and looked back at Joe, who nodded.

She returned her gaze to Richard, but couldn't quite meet his eyes. "And I have a few things to explain to you on the ride back to Gator Bait."

After Dorie's confession, the remainder of the drive was completed in silence. Dorie was dying to know what Richard thought, but wasn't about to ask—not in front of Joe. Unfortunately, the agent's opinion mattered far too much to her, and she didn't want to hear that he suspected her dad was involved with Roland's latest drug run. Especially since she didn't know herself that her dad *wasn't* helping Roland.

Dorie dropped Joe off at his truck and he raced off to Buster's house to check things out. Dorie and Richard continued to the shrimp house.

The secretary was at the front desk when they burst in the door. She frowned at Richard and gave Dorie a brief smile. "Help you, Dorie?" she asked.

"Is Buster here?" Dorie asked, trying to keep the panic out of her voice.

The secretary gave her a confused look. "Why, no. He got a call from your dad earlier today and raced out of here. I figured it was an emergency or something with the hurry he was in. Is your dad all right?" She stared at Dorie with obvious concern.

"I'm not sure. He's gone from the retirement home, and no one knows where he is. If you see him or Buster, please call me."

The woman straightened in her chair and nodded. "Absolutely. And I'll take a stitch out of those men if I find they've worried you this way over some silliness. Bunch of old fools."

"Thanks," Dorie said as they left the shrimp house and stepped into the warehouse to question the workers. A couple of minutes later, they were back outside with no more information than they'd come in with.

Dorie stared down Main Street, then across the bayou and blew out a breath, remembering the receptionist's comment. If only silliness were the answer. Right now, she'd give anything for her dad and Buster to be on a bender at a topless bar in Lake Charles, but she knew that wasn't the case. Topless bars hadn't required rubber boots and a sidearm for years.

She reached into the jeep and picked up the radio. "Talk to me, Joe. What do you have?"

"Not a damn thing," Joe replied. "The house is empty, and the idiot left it unlocked again. No sign of his truck, but all the boats are still here."

"Boats, damn it," Dorie said. "Thanks, Joe." She threw the radio down in the jeep and hurried around the shrimp house to the dock. "I'm thinking like an amateur. We need to check the boats." She stared at the line of crafts tied off behind the shrimp house.

"Are they all here?" Richard asked.

She studied the row of boats for a moment, certain something was wrong. "No. One of Buster's old flat-bottomed aluminum boats is gone."

"Wide enough for a wheelchair?"

She stared at the empty slip and nodded, unable to speak.

"Well," he said and glanced back at the shrimp house, the gleaming row of windows reflecting the sun onto the bayou. "He didn't load your dad up here or someone would have seen him. Where would he do that if he didn't want to be seen?"

Dorie scrunched her brow in concentration. "Not any of the marinas, that's for sure." She shook her head in frustration. "There's just nowhere to load someone in a wheelchair from a car to a boat without risking being seen by someone." Then a thought hit her like lightening. "Except my place. It's completely isolated. That's the only answer."

They raced back around the shrimp house, jumped in the jeep, and tore out of the parking lot. Dorie radioed Joe on the way to tell him where they were headed. "I still don't understand why they need a boat. What the hell are they doing?"

Richard shook his head at the question and clutched the roll bar of the jeep. His mind had been swimming with possibilities ever since Dorie had told him the story of her dad and Buster's past with Roland, and none of them were good. Further complicating the whole mess was the other lie that only he and her father knew about. Another lie that had been perpetuated for more than thirty years. What would stop the man from lying about everything? And how would they know when he was telling the truth?

What if the sheriff had been involved with Roland all along? What if the story he told about Dorie's "adoption" was just another lie created to cover up his part in Roland's drug trade? And how would Dorie feel if Richard was single-handedly responsible for taking down her father *and* her dad?

At least he no longer suspected Dorie of direct involvement with Roland, but the knowledge was poor consolation at best.

He blew out a breath and looked out over the bayou. So deceptively peaceful. The tide rolled gently out toward the gulf. The marsh grass swayed with the rhythm of the water with the sun reflecting down on it all, creating bursts of color. And in spite of the view, this sleepy little town held secrets no one could imagine.

All of which centered on Dorie Berenger.

He looked over at her and didn't like what he saw. Her face, usually flushed with anger or excitement, was unusually pale. There was no doubting the strain she was under. Not that he blamed her, but he was afraid it would take her edge off. And if her dad was dealing with Roland, they were going to need all the edge they could get.

It was long after midnight before they returned to Joe's house. Dorie and Richard found Buster's truck and trailer at Dorie's place, but the boat was nowhere in sight. And despite spending the remainder of daylight and half of the night in the bayous, they had come up with nothing. Joe dropped onto the couch in exhaustion, Dorie headed to the shower and Richard went into the kitchen for a much-needed beer. "Do you mind?" he asked.

Joe waved a hand. "Go ahead. Hell, bring me one while you're at it."

He nodded and carried two beers into the living room. Slumping into a recliner across from Joe, he tossed a beer over to him. "We should probably eat something. Last thing we need is a middle-of-the-night emergency on a stomach with only beer."

Joe nodded. "Yeah, and unfortunately, the odds of a middle-of-the-night emergency have increased dramatically ever since you came to town."

Richard blew out a breath. "I know. Damn, I never thought things would get this complicated. All these years, I've been chasing a one-dimensional criminal. I never considered how it might affect other people."

Joe nodded in understanding.

"I never even imagined that people, like the sheriff or Buster, could have been involved with someone like Roland." He ran one hand through his hair in frustration. "It's like a bad horror movie, with me starring as The Asshole."

Joe snorted. "No one's blaming you. It's true this town's been sitting on things that were best left sat on. But that's not the way life works. Life has a way of uncovering secrets, usually at the worst moment possible. How we choose to deal with them is what makes us better than those who kept them in the first place."

Richard considered Joe's words for a moment, then nodded. "Anyone ever tell you, Joe, that you're damn smart sometimes?"

Joe shook his head and smiled. "Not very often. I try not to let that information out."

Richard studied the man for a moment. "You've spent your entire life in Dorie's shadow, and it's never bothered you, has it?"

"No, it hasn't," he said immediately. "But then you know Dorie better than some people who have lived here all their lives. Would it have bothered you?"

Richard considered this for a moment. He thought about Dorie's dedication to the town and her family, her passion for the animals under her care and her absolute conviction for the truth, even at her own expense.

"No," he replied softly. "It wouldn't have bothered me at all."

The three were sitting down to a very late supper of grilled-cheese sandwiches and chips when the phone rang. Everyone jumped from their chairs, but Joe made it to the phone first and answered, almost breathless. Dorie watched his face for any sign of the information he was receiving, but quickly realized the call had nothing to do with her dad. Joe's expression went from expectant to exasperated in under two seconds.

"It's Maylene," he said, putting his hand over the receiver. "She says the boats are out making noise again." He moved his hand. "I'll be out there in twenty minutes or so to take care of the problem."

A burst of sound came out of the receiver that Dorie could hear clearly from where she stood. Joe put his hand over the phone again and looked at Dorie. "She wants you specifically. Do you want me to tell her you're not available?"

Dorie sighed. "No. I'll probably never hear the end of it since she's already complained once and apparently is still hearing things. I'll take a ride out there. It's probably nothing."

"Nothing a decade of coffee drinking couldn't fix," Joe agreed and told Maylene to expect Dorie shortly.

Richard rose from the table and followed Dorie to the front door. "Where do you think you're going?" she asked.

"With you," he said. "You're not going anywhere alone. That was the agreement."

She sighed and motioned to Joe to hand her what was left of her sandwich. "At least eat on the way," she said to Richard. "This night has been far too long already and morning is coming up fast. Neither one of us can afford to be tired and weak."

Richard didn't even bother to argue. He grabbed his sandwich from the table and the two headed out the front door.

"Call if you need me," Joe yelled from the kitchen as the door slammed behind them.

* * *

The road to Maylene's house was much worse at night than during the day. At least during the day, Richard could see the giant holes coming. It was too damned late to be awake, and he was definitely not in any condition to see Maylene half-naked again.

Dorie swung into Maylene's driveway and parked in front of the house. Maylene was standing outside in all of her glory—and that was about it. Dorie tried to hold her laughter and Richard choked on the last bite of his sandwich, convinced that his mother was right when she said God had a sense of humor.

When Maylene saw the jeep, she hurried down the steps toward the driveway. No human being should have to suffer through watching this, he thought as her body bounced up and down. He was still trying to figure out what the hell she was wearing when she tripped on the last step and came to a rolling stop in front of the jeep. Dorie jumped out and peered down at her.

"You all right, Maylene?" she asked.

"Oh, hell," Maylene replied. "I'm probably going to have to redo this wrap now. I bet it's all off-kilter."

Richard peeked around the other side of the jeep, still trying to decide what exactly was covering Maylene's rotund figure. Whatever it was, it was see-through, and although he had no idea what a "kil-ter" was, based on the display in front of him, he was pretty sure that it was off.

Maylene grabbed the front bumper of Dorie's jeep and struggled to her feet, wrenching the bumper off the jeep with a loud screech. "What in the world are you wearing?" Dorie asked, confusion mixed with aggravation written all over her face as she gazed from Maylene to her fallen bumper.

"It's Saran Wrap," Maylene replied, trying to smooth the sticky plastic back down over her mammoth thighs. "You don't think I keep this figure by just sitting around, do you? I wrap up at least three times a week. It sweats off the fat and keeps me lean and sexy."

Richard took one look at the expression on Dorie's face and was pretty sure she wanted to shoot Maylene. Hell, he kind of wanted to shoot her, too, but he didn't want anyone back in D.C. to get wind of his presence at the Saran Wrap parade.

Dorie shook her head and looked around in the darkness. "What about the noise, Maylene? I don't hear anything."

"There was noise all right," Maylene said indignantly. "I called just after it started. And I went light on the brew tonight, so I know what I heard."

"Ummhmm," Dorie said and looked skeptical. "So what direction was this noise coming from?"

"Up."

"Up?" Dorie repeated.

Maylene nodded rapidly, the Saran Wrap starting to droop under one of her chins. "Up. And I got to thinking. Maybe it wasn't boats. Maybe it was a plane."

Dorie nodded her head and sighed. "I'm sure that was it. It was a plane." She looked up at the sky. "Doesn't appear to be around any longer. I'll have to check with the airport in Lake Charles tomorrow morning."

Maylene blew out a breath. "Well, if that's the best you can do."

"That's it."

"Then I guess I'll be going on back inside. I gotta redo this wrap and that takes time." She looked over at Richard, who was still wisely crouching alongside the jeep. "Unlessin' of course, you'd like to help me out." She gave him a sexy smile. "But then with a man like you around, I wouldn't be so much interested in putting stuff on as I would be taking stuff off."

Richard held back a smile. You had to hand it to the old girl for persistence. "Sorry, Maylene, but I'm dreadfully allergic to plastics. Can't even carry a sandwich in a baggie or I break out in a huge rash when I eat it. It's a very rare but serious disorder."

"Hmmm," Maylene said and put her hands on her hips. "Guess there's no use having you around me if you can't touch anything good. I'll catch up to you once I've been through the shower a couple of times." She glared once more at Dorie, gave Richard her version of a sexy smile and turned around, Saran Wrap in tow.

Dorie grinned and picked up her bumper, tossed it in the back of the jeep, and climbed in the vehicle. Richard jumped in beside her, still shaking his head. "That woman is a detriment to society."

Dorie laughed and put the jeep in gear. As she backed out of the driveway, she turned and looked at him, still grinning. "You sure you don't want to stay? I could pick you up a box of Benadryl for those allergies. Look what you're turning down."

He knew he shouldn't have, but he looked. God help him, he looked.

Maylene started up the stairs, all the wrap that used to cover her behind hanging just below her cheeks. At that very moment, the clouds cleared and he found himself staring at the biggest, whitest butt he'd ever seen in his life—with more wrinkles than a Shar-Pei.

"I'm sure," he said, slamming his eyes shut. "I may need counseling after this. There has got to be something you can arrest that woman for."

Dorie laughed again and began the bouncing journey back up the road. "People in Gator Bait know better than to go around Maylene. Unfortunately, it's my job."

Richard shook his head and looked out of the jeep into the black sky. "What do you think about the plane idea?"

"I don't think about it at all. She's drunk. That's all there is to know."

He was silent for a moment. After all, Dorie wasn't exactly wrong—Maylene *was* drunk. But for some reason, her complaint still bothered him. He had that nagging feeling in the back of his mind that something important was happening. "I don't like it," he finally said.

Dorie stared at him in obvious surprise. "You're serious? Two weeks ago Maylene Thibodeaux called and reported a Mardi Gras parade passing by her house, complete with floats and a marching band playing 'When the Saints Go Marching In.' Does that sound reasonable to you? The woman is out of her head about ninety-nine percent of the day."

He shrugged. "Call it intuition. Hell, call it indigestion, but I think there's something to what she's saying."

"Okay. If you don't like it, we'll check into it first thing in the morning. Lake Charles should be able to tell us if anything showed up on radar, but they don't have anyone answering the phone in the tower until the morning shift comes on at six."

He nodded, studying the strained expression on her face. For the millionth time he hoped that the morning would bring news of the sheriff. The kind of news that didn't require an arrest warrant or a body bag.

Despite Richard's "feeling" about the plane and her own worry about her dad, Dorie insisted on going to sleep when they got back to Joe's. "There's nothing we can do about either of them right now," she said, "and I'm too damn tired to think anymore."

Richard pulled her close and kissed her gently, wrapping his arms around her. "This will all be better tomorrow. I think it's all about to come to a head."

Dorie nodded and buried her head in his chest, relaxing for a moment in his strong arms, hoping his words came true and her dad came out of this alive. Finally, she pulled back and tried to smile. "We'll get on it first thing in the morning. But right now we've both got to get some sleep."

Richard nodded and gave her one more kiss, then trudged off to the living room couch, apparently too beat to disagree. Joe was already asleep, the cordless phone still clenched in his hand. Dorie pulled the phone from his grasp and placed it on the nightstand, then made her way to the guest room, where she collapsed on the bed, not even bothering to undress.

She awoke the next morning with a cramp in her shoulder and a pain in one foot, probably due to sleeping in her boots. Oh well, it cut down on getting-ready time. She stepped into the small bathroom and quickly washed her face and neck.

Richard was already awake when she walked into the living room, but not yet to the moving-around phase. "Morning," he said from his spot on the couch.

Dorie waved a hand in greeting and went to the kitchen to put on a pot of coffee, then slumped into a chair in the dining room, still half-asleep, as Richard headed for the bathroom. The coffee was almost done brewing when Joe finally rose from the dead and made his way into the kitchen with a freshly showered Richard close behind.

"What's the plan for today?" Joe asked as he

poured a large cup of coffee and passed the pot to Dorie.

"Not sure," Dorie replied and poured both herself and Richard a cup of the steaming brew. "I need to call Sherry and give her an update. Then we need to check the shrimp house and Buster's place again, although it will probably be a waste of time. After that, I guess the only thing to do is start questioning every damn person in town about seeing Buster or my dad yesterday. There's no way they made it out of Gator Bait without someone seeing them. It's just a matter of finding the right person."

"What about the plane?" Richard asked.

Dorie sighed. "You and that damn plane. I'll call over to Lake Charles and see if anything passed on radar during the night."

"What plane?" Joe asked.

Dorie rolled her eyes. "The one Maylene *says* she heard. The one Dick *thinks* she heard."

Joe raised his eyebrows. "Not very likely, but I guess we ought to check it out. Was she drunk?" He waved a hand in the air in dismissal. "Never mind. Stupid question. Was she dressed?"

Richard choked on his coffee and Dorie had to smile. "Kinda," she said as she walked out of the room to get the phone, "but I'll let Dick tell you about it. I've got some phone calls to make."

Chapter Fifteen

Dorie picked up the cordless phone in the bedroom and dialed the retirement center. She knew it was stupid, but she didn't feel like making the call in front of Richard and Joe, even though she knew Sherry wouldn't have anything to report. Sherry answered on the first ring and confirmed her thoughts. There had been no sign of the sheriff or Buster.

Sherry had spent most of the previous day questioning everyone in the center and found two residents who had seen the sheriff leaving with Buster, but neither man mentioned where they were going, and the residents hadn't asked. Dorie hung up the phone in disgust. What ever happened to nosy old people? First time she needed them to be in her business, they didn't know a damn thing.

She lifted the phone again, dialed Information, and asked for the number to the Lake Charles airport. While waiting for a connection, she walked slowly back into the living room. It was almost a minute before someone answered and a little bit longer than that to transfer her to the air traffic division. Finally, someone picked up.

"Traffic, this is Larry."

"Hi, Larry, this is Deputy Dorie Berenger of Gator Bait. We had a noise complaint last night after midnight. Lady says a plane passed over her house. Mind you, this particular lady starts happy hour somewhere around nine A.M., but I wouldn't be doing my job if I didn't at least ask. Is that something you can check on for me?"

Larry laughed. "Sure, I can check. I wasn't on shift last night, but there will be a log. Let me take a look."

She heard paper rustling and a couple of seconds later the man was back on the phone. "Yep. Looks like you had a pass-over at about 12:20 A.M. No one contacted us establishing a flight pattern, so I can't give you any information on the plane."

"It didn't land in Lake Charles?" she asked, a bit confused. Richard sat up straight on the couch and looked expectantly at her.

"No way," Larry said. "We'd have the info if it had. It looks to me like it came in from over the gulf and headed back out the same way after circling. Kinda strange, but we get a lot of rich, bored people playing with private planes. That's probably what it was."

"Hmmm, maybe so," she said, even though the explanation didn't sit right on her.

"Let me know if you have any other complaints. If it keeps occurring, we'll look into it. We don't like unestablished flight patterns over the gulf with all the choppers coming in from the oil rigs. That's a recipe for disaster."

"I'll be sure to tell you if it happens again. I had one complaint before, but I can't say for sure if it was the same problem."

"Same happy lady?" Larry asked.

"Yeah. Same happy lady. Thanks for the information, Larry. I'll get back to you if I hear anything else."

Frowning, she hung up the phone. "Well, Maylene's not crazy. At least, she wasn't last night," she said, then relayed the rest of the information Larry had given her.

"Is that our drug drop?" Joe asked. "I know we've been thinking about boats, this being the heart of the shrimping industry and all, but a plane's not a bad idea. Especially if the drop is in a fairly isolated spot." They both looked at Richard.

"A plane is a damn good idea actually," he said. "Maybe whoever was using that road down at Maylene's was looking for a way to retrieve."

Joe whistled. "That's smack in the middle of the game preserve. You're talking about thousands of acres of marsh to cover."

"Maybe not," Richard said and flipped open his cell phone. "There's a guy in D.C. who owes me a favor. I think I can narrow down our target." He rose from the table and left the room.

Feeling exhausted all over again, Dorie slumped down into a chair at the dining table. She was in desperate need of more sleep, but not like the sleep she'd had—littered with wild dreams of betrayal and lies. No, what she needed was the kind of sleep she had after a few beers or really great sex. Like sex with Richard.

She tried to block the image of her and Richard, locked together in a frenzy of physical need and the feeling she had when it was over and she was snuggled against him, her body pressed tightly into his. That feeling of oneness—completeness. A feeling she'd never had before.

She shook her head. It was a complete waste of

time to go there. With all the trouble her dad was in, Richard probably wanted to catch Roland and get the hell out of Gator Bait as soon as possible, conveniently forgetting he ever met her. And the worst part of it was, she could hardly blame him.

Frowning, she looked over at Joe. "Why is it, Joe, that sometimes the law and justice don't seem to walk the same lines?"

Joe shook his head. "You know nothing's black and white when you're dealing with people. And people made the system. People run the system. You knew it was flawed before you ever got in it."

She sighed. "Yeah, you're right. But it's hard sometimes, you know? Reconciling what I'm bound by law to do and what my heart and mind is telling me is fair to do. I don't like being put in this position."

She looked Joe straight in the eyes and calmly said, "When all this is over, I'm resigning from my position as deputy. If things turn out all right with my dad, I'll figure out some way to see he gets the care that he needs."

Joe nodded, not seeming at all surprised by her announcement. "You planning on going big time?" he asked.

She shook her head. "I'm not sure exactly. I just know I don't want to work in law enforcement any longer. I want to focus on the animals, the wildlife. That's where my heart is. That's where I feel I can make a difference. This other—I'm afraid if I stay in much longer, I'll end up doing the wrong thing."

"You know, you're going to have to leave Gator Bait to do that."

"I'll deal with that when the time comes," she said quietly and stared over Joe's shoulder out the window, not wanting to get into a deep conversation with Joe about the idea that had been niggling in the back of her mind, pestering her even before Richard had come to Gator Bait and turned her life upside down.

Besides, now wasn't the time to think about the future. The present was far more important.

A couple of minutes later, Richard dashed back into the dining room, whooping. "He's going to do it," Richard said, unable to contain his excitement. "In a couple of hours we'll have a satellite photo of the entire area. Infrared and everything—the best the military has to offer. He's sending it to your e-mail."

Joe and Dorie looked up at Richard in obvious surprise. "That marsh is right next to the Strategic Oil Reserve," Dorie said. "I'm surprised your request didn't mobilize the marines."

Richard smiled. "Yeah. He was a little upset about that part too, but he's still going to make it happen."

"Damn!" Joe said. "That must have been one hell of a favor you did this guy."

Richard winced. "You don't even want to know. Suffice it to say that this guy is breaking seventy major laws to do this."

"I'm impressed, Dick," Dorie said. "A photo is a sight better than tromping through every square inch of the marsh. What will it show exactly?"

"The kind of photo he's requesting will show the marsh in light grays and anything solid, like houses, boxes, piers in black. The wildlife will come through as white."

"That should narrow things down a bit," she said. "I have a site map of every square inch of that preserve. We can compare the two and eliminate the structures I have on my map. Then all we have to do is—"

The ringing of Dorie's cell phone interrupted the conversation, and she grabbed it off of the table and flipped it open. The conversation was brief, but as the color drained from her face, Richard knew it was far from pleasant. Bracing himself for what was surely coming, he waited as she slowly closed the phone.

"It was the hospital," she said, her voice hollow. "Someone brought Dad in thirty minutes ago with a gunshot wound."

Dorie, Joe and Richard rushed into the emergency room. A nurse behind the front desk recognized Dorie and walked around the desk to speak with them.

"He's being prepped for surgery," the nurse said, "but he should be all right as long as his heart holds. The bullet went into his side, but it looks like it missed all the vital organs."

"Who brought him in?" Dorie asked, trying to assimilate all the information at once and figure out at the same time the most important questions to ask.

"A fisherman found him over in a cove off Rabbit Island. He was alone in the boat." The nurse gave Dorie a curious look. "What's going on, Dorie? There's no way your father got into a boat by himself. What in the world was he doing out in the bayou?"

She shook her head. "I don't exactly know. I've been looking for him since yesterday. Can I see him before they take him in?"

The nurse cast an anxious glance toward the double doors to the emergency room. "I'll take you back, but just for a second or two. I'm not supposed to do something like this."

"I understand. Is the fisherman still here?"

"Yes. We told him he had to wait for the police to arrive. He went down to the cafeteria to get a cup of coffee."

Dorie nodded at Joe and Richard, who left in the direction of the cafeteria. Taking a deep breath, she walked through the double doors and into the surgery area. The nurse pointed to a door on the left, and Dorie slipped inside.

The room was empty except for her dad, but Dorie knew that wouldn't be the case for very long. She needed to talk to her dad and get out before the surgeon showed up and the nurse caught hell for letting her in. She walked over to the bed and looked down at her dad. He was pale, and for the first time in her life, he looked really old.

"What were you thinking, Dad?" she asked and stroked his head with her hand.

Sheriff Berenger's eyes flew open, and Dorie could tell he was trying to focus, but was under heavy sedation. "Dorie?" he finally asked.

"Yes, Dad. It's me. The nurse says you're going to be all right, but a doctor is going to have to see to that gunshot wound. Can you tell me who shot you?"

He looked confused and disoriented, as if he still wasn't quite sure where he was and why, then stared at her and tried to speak, his mouth moving but no sound coming out. She leaned in closer, hoping to hear what he was trying to tell her.

"Careful," he said, his voice barely a whisper. "Friends betray you. Don't trust friends."

She heard him sigh and lifted her head to look at him, but he was out cold. "Dad," she said and watched his shallow breathing.

The nurse stuck her head in the door. "We've got

to get out of here. They just paged the doctor. He's on his way down."

Dorie nodded and hurried out of the room with one last look back at her dad. She closed the door and hurried with the nurse down the hall and into the waiting room where they arrived just seconds before the surgeon.

"Ms. Berenger?" the doctor asked when he saw her standing beside the nurse.

"Yes," Dorie replied.

The doctor extended his hand. "I'm Doctor Walker. Your dad's prognosis looks good, considering. I'm not anticipating any problems, but I'm sure you understand that with his heart condition, I have no way of being certain."

"Life doesn't hold guarantees, Doctor," she said. "I'm painfully aware of that."

He nodded and clasped one hand on her shoulder. "We'll be in surgery for about an hour. I'll let you know something as soon as we're out." He dropped his hand, nodded to the nurse, and walked through the double doors.

Richard and Joe returned while Dorie was speaking to the doctor, and she turned to address them as soon as he was gone. "Did you get anything?" she asked.

Joe shook his head. "The guy is a regular fisherman in that area. He saw the boat and didn't think anything of it at first, but when he was passing and started to wave, he realized that your dad was in a wheelchair and was slumped down. He pulled alongside and saw the blood, checked for a pulse, and tried to start Buster's boat, but it was a no-go. Not having any other choice, he said he tilted the wheelchair to the side, and dumped your dad out into the bottom of his boat. Then he hauled ass to the docks and called 911 from the marina."

"He didn't see anyone else around?"

"Not a soul," Joe replied. "He said it was dead quiet out there. No sight or sound of other boats."

"What do you think happened?" Richard asked. "Was your dad awake? Did he say anything?"

"I don't know what happened. Dad was heavily drugged, and I'm not sure how much of what he said he really understood, but what he did manage to say bothers me." And she told them what the sheriff said.

Joe blew out a breath. "Do you think Buster was still in on everything, and the sheriff found him out?"

Dorie looked at him and slowly shook her head. "At this point, I can't assume anything," she said and sat down on a couch to wait while Joe went to make some phone calls, letting all concerned parties know what was happening.

Richard paced the floor back and forth a few times and finally came to rest on the couch next to Dorie. "You okay?" he asked. "All things considered, I mean."

Dorie shrugged. "I guess I'm as good as I'm getting for the moment." She looked at him and tried to control the wavering in her voice. "I never wanted to do this again. Sit at the hospital, wondering whether he would live or die."

Richard took her hand and held it in his. For a moment, she felt better, the strength of the man beside her coursing through every nerve in her hand.

"He's going to be fine," Richard said. "I'm sure of it. He's a tough guy, you know that. Pretty soon he'll be out of that bed and raising hell again, just like before."

Dorie shook her head. "Not just like before. Something's got to give. If all of this turns out all right, Dad has got to quit law enforcement altogether."

He stared at her and finally nodded. "If you're worried about the cost of his care, I can pull some strings. I heard about your education, and I know the DEA would love to have you on board. The salary would more than cover your expenses and help take care of your dad."

Dorie was momentarily taken aback at Richard's comment about her education, but it only took a second to realize her dad must have spilled the beans. She lowered her head and looked at the floor, desperately wishing for the first time in her life that things could be different—that she could be different. "I appreciate the offer, really I do, but I can't leave here."

"Why not? You only came home to take care of your dad. If you can do that somewhere else and better your position at the same time, why wouldn't you?"

She looked him straight in the eye and whispered, "Because I can't breathe anywhere else."

Confusion was written all over Richard's face. "What do you mean?"

Dorie blew out a breath and scanned the room. She'd managed all these years to hide it from everyone else, and Richard had already witnessed entirely too many of her breaking points in only a few days time.

But it also wasn't fair to let him think there was even the slimmest possibility of her leaving Gator Bait. And even though he'd mentioned the job offer casually, Dorie could see the expectant, hopeful look in his eyes.

"Dorie?" Richard said gently.

She looked back at him and tried to hold back the tears threatening to flow. "The whole time I was at school, I was miserable. Oh, I was a great student. All my professors thought I was going to go on to a prominent career with a national agency, but I just couldn't."

She took a deep breath and continued. "I think it really hit me when I did an internship with a local police department. I couldn't take the misery of the victim's families, the sheer evil that one human being could perpetrate on another. It was all so senseless, so wasteful, and I knew I'd never be able to handle all of the sadness that the crimes created. It pressed on my chest until I felt like I was suffocating from the pressure."

"A lot of people feel that way at first, Dorie," Richard said. "I promise you it gets easier."

She shook her head. "I knew then that I wasn't cut out for that line of work. Here in Gator Bait is one thing. Until this Roland problem, we didn't have much going on here. And besides, being back here I got to work in the preserve with the animals. That's what I really care about."

Dorie rose from the couch, walked to the window across the room and stared outside. "When I received the phone call of my dad's heart attack, do you know I was actually relieved? How horrible is that? But finally I had a reason to chuck the city and return to Gator Bait. A reason that no one could argue with."

"It's not terrible," he replied and gave her a sad smile. "I think it's sort of wonderful that you have a place where you belong so absolutely. I've never had that."

She turned from the window to face him. "Why not?"

He shrugged. "You know how big cities are. People are so absorbed in their own lives, their own problems. They don't take the time to get to know anyone else's."

Dorie nodded. "I guess not."

He grinned. "Hell, until I came to Gator Bait, I didn't even know a place like this existed—where people actually looked out for their neighbors and considered the whole community family. It's really nice. A little too personal sometimes, but still nice."

She smiled back at him. "Yeah, it's hard to keep a secret in this town," she said, but even as the words left her mouth, she thought of all the secrets that had been kept. Secrets that had caused the trouble they were in now.

An hour passed, and Dorie and Joe were still waiting at the hospital. Richard, under much protesting, had finally gone back to the station to get the satellite photos from his friend. As soon as Dorie was sure her dad was all right, she and Joe would head out and meet him at the station. Joe had called Jenny and asked her to come to the hospital and sit with the sheriff after surgery, and she'd agreed to close the café and hurry to Lake Charles. She arrived at the same time the doctor came out of surgery.

"He came through just fine," the doctor said, immediately putting their fears at rest. "His heart is stable and showed no signs of stress during the procedure. There was no damage to his internal organs, so the worst thing to watch for is infection. I closed the entry wound and the stitches will dissolve; however, I still want to see him back here a week after he is discharged. And he should have someone watching him."

Dorie nodded, relieved at the doctor's words. "He

lives at Southern Retirement. I'll give one of the women there a little extra to ride herd over him."

The doctor smiled. "That's about the best setup I can imagine." He put one hand on her shoulder. "It was nice meeting you, Ms. Berenger. I've heard a lot about the work you and your father have done. I'm glad he's okay."

He walked across the room and started to push the doors open, but paused a moment. "Don't feel guilty, Ms. Berenger, if you need to leave. Your father is in excellent care, and I'm sure there's a more pressing matter you need to see to. Perhaps before I notify the Lake Charles police of a gunshot wound?" He gave her a smile and left.

Dorie hugged Jenny and thanked her again for coming. "Are you sure you're okay with this? I don't want to cause you any problems down at the café."

Jenny rolled her eyes. "Dorie Berenger, you are not causing me problems. Now, get the hell out of here and get that bad man out of town. I'm getting a little tired of this nonsense, and since Joe has finally agreed to go out with me, I'd like to manage at least one date before the year is over."

Surprised, Dorie looked at Joe and saw a slow blush creeping up his face. Jenny leaned over and kissed him on the cheek, causing him to blush even more.

"Go on and get out of here," Jenny said and gave them a shove. "And Joe, you better watch Dorie's back or you'll have to answer to me," she shouted as they were walking out the door.

"I didn't know you and Jenny were dating," Dorie said as they pulled out of the hospital parking lot.

"We're not really dating," Joe said. "Haven't exactly had a chance."

Dorie grinned. "Are you trying to tell me this investigation is cramping your life? You're going to have to learn to work your way around that if you want a relationship with Jenny. The job is not going to stop, although, I admit, something this bad will probably never happen again."

"You mean I should be more flexible, like you?" he asked dryly.

She knew he was referring to her relationship—or whatever—with Richard, but she wasn't about to get into that discussion. Not now. Probably not ever. And definitely not with Joe, who wouldn't understand the turmoil she was feeling. Joe thought love made everything better. And although Dorie wasn't convinced that what she felt for Richard was love or even the beginning of it, she was sure it wasn't a passing fling. No, from where Dorie was sitting, love or the possibility of it only made things complicated and stressful.

"Maybe flexible isn't the worst thing to be," she finally said. "If this entire mess has shown me anything, it's that nothing is forever and you better get the good stuff in before you run out of time."

"Yeah, but when the bad guy is locked up and the adrenaline rush is over, what do you have?"

She stared out of the truck and down the highway. "I guess that remains to be seen."

Richard looked up when they walked through the door of the sheriff's office. "How's your dad?" he asked, an anxious look on his face.

"He's going to be fine," Dorie replied. "Jenny will let us know if there's any change, or if he says anything else once he's awake. I lied and said she was family so she could get into his room."

Richard gave her a small smile. "Not really much of a lie."

"No, not much," she said, his words making her feel a bit better.

He pointed to the printer where photos were spitting out. "Your timing is great," he said. "I just sent all the photos to print. We have a total of twelve, covering from Gator Bait all the way to the next town, in every direction, and the gulf."

"I'll get the preserve maps," Joe said and stepped into the back office, returning a minute later with a thick set of rolled documents. Richard grabbed the printouts, Joe unrolled the maps, and they all hunched over the desk to look.

The first ten photos were fine, nothing out of place, and Dorie grew more anxious each time Richard turned to another photo. *We can't be wrong about this. We just can't be.*

Richard shook his head and continued to flip through the pictures. "Whoa," he said. "What is that?" He pointed to an area on the photo that contained a cluster of black dots. "Is there anything solid in this section that you are aware of?"

Dorie scanned her preserve maps for the coordinates and pointed to the matching area. She looked at Joe and saw that he understood immediately what she was pointing to. Looking back at the photo, she pointed to the white spots that outnumbered the black spots ten times over. "There's not supposed to be anything solid in that area of the preserve, unless you want to count all of those white spots."

Richard looked at the photo again and frowned. "There must be at least a hundred white spots on here. What the hell is this place?"

"Breeding ground," Joe said. "That's where the alligators go to lay their eggs."

* * *

Richard stared at the two of them in horror. "Breeding ground. You've got to be kidding me." But the look on their faces told him they weren't kidding at all. "But that's crazy," he protested.

"It's more than crazy," Joe said. "It's suicide. Someone must have made a mistake with the drop. We may not have to worry about this Roland if he tries to pick up his shipment in this location. Of course, we'll never find evidence of his death, either, which might be a problem."

"That's not even the beginning of the problems," Dorie said, her voice beginning to rise. "What about the possibility of hundreds of high gators if someone doesn't get those drugs out of the marsh? Jesus Christ!"

"Holy crap," Joe said. "We can't have this, Dorie. There's no telling what those gators are capable of if they haul any of these bags out of the preserve and bite into one."

"I know," she said and looked at Richard. "No one understands more than I do how much you want to catch Roland, and believe me, I want to catch him, too, but I have to get those drugs out of the game preserve right now, even if it means we blow our chance."

Richard nodded. "I understand. And as much as I hate it, I agree. This entire town would be at risk. I want Roland, but that's one risk even I am not willing to take." He blew out a breath and slammed one fist down on the desk. "Damn it! I was so close this time."

Dorie placed her hand on his arm. "We'll get him. I'll help you, even if it means leaving Gator Bait. This is one part of my past that I want shut away permanently."

Richard looked at her, surprised, but then took a moment to think about her words. Dorie had as much of a stake in Roland's capture as he did. Roland didn't leave loose ends, and he would consider both Berengers a liability. The real irony was Dorie was trying to capture her father to protect her dad.

The weight of that fact grew heavy in Richard's mind. He should never have agreed to keep the sheriff's secret. The way things stood now, it might be awhile before the sheriff could live up to his end of their bargain and tell Dorie the truth. Dorie was never going to forgive him for withholding this, and there was no way he could blame her.

"What about the town?" he finally managed to ask. "If you leave, who'll take care of everyone?"

"Joe can take care of Gator Bait," she replied. "He's been standing in my shadow long enough."

Joe raised his hands to protest. "Dorie, you know that's not true. I've never had cause to complain about my station. I'm happy working here with you, and I don't want you to leave. You've got to know that."

"I do know that, Joe," she said softly. "And that's why you're going to make a great sheriff."

Joe rapidly shook his head. "Oh, no. I'm not running against your dad. I can't do that, no matter what you say."

Dorie reached into her desk and pulled a small revolver from the drawer. She bent over and pulled her jeans up over her ankle. "My dad won't be running again," she said. "He hasn't earned that right."

Joe was silent, and Richard could see the conflict racing through the man's face. Shawn Roland had caused so much trouble in this town. And to good people. It made Richard angry all over again to think about it.

"What do you need me to do now?" Joe finally asked.

"Check around town," Dorie said as she secured the holster around her leg. "I'd still like to find the transport vehicle. It might get us information we can use to locate Roland later on. Make sure you keep your radio on you at all times. And take the keys to the other airboat with you. If we get into a bind, I'll need backup."

Joe nodded, his expression grim.

"And go to scramble on the radio, or we'll have everyone in Gator Bait listening in on their scanners. We don't need any amateur help on this one." She straightened up, checked the gun at her waist, and looked at Richard. "Are you ready to do this?" she asked.

Richard took one last look at the photo on the desk, the white spots whirling through his mind like a disco. "I'm as ready as I'll ever be."

Dorie nodded. "Then that will have to do."

As soon as they left, Joe gave Jenny a call at the hospital, and learned that the sheriff was still in recovery and hadn't yet been moved to a room. He brought Jenny up to date on the situation and asked her to make any calls directly to him and only in the case of an emergency. There was no telling what kind of situation Dorie and Richard might get into, and Joe needed to keep all channels of communication clear.

Jenny promised to limit her calls to drastic changes only and said she was headed straight to the hospital chapel to start praying. Joe hung up the phone and stared at the church across the street.

Aside from his earlier investigating with Dorie, he hadn't set foot inside since his father had passed, but Jenny's words had touched him somewhere he thought was closed. Maybe she had the right idea. Praying couldn't hurt. Determined to put his past to rest once and for all, Joe set his shoulders, strode across the street and opened the door to the church.

The elderly pastor looked up at him in surprise as he entered. "Joe. How can I help you?" he asked with a smile. "Are you planning a wedding? I sure would be happy to hear it."

Joe shook his head. "Not yet, Pastor Don, but I'm hoping to. We've got to have a date first, though."

Pastor Don nodded. "Dating is probably a good thing if one is contemplating marriage. I haven't heard of anyone trading their daughter for cattle in many years." He smiled again. "So if it's not a wedding you're wanting, then what can I help you with?"

Joe's hands started to sweat and felt sticky in the humidity. He took a look around and blew out the breath he'd been holding, trying to figure out where to begin. Pastor Don waited patiently, a friendly smile on his face. Finally, Joe found his voice. "I'm sure you heard I haven't been to church ever since my father passed. I've never had much use for organized religion, although that doesn't mean I don't believe in God."

"Of course not," Pastor Don said.

"Everyone thought my father was a great man, and there's no denying that was true for the church," Joe said. "But he didn't have much use or time for my mother or me and I guess that's why I've resented him and religion all these years."

Pastor Don nodded his understanding. "It's a hard

thing for a child to reconcile that his father can have so much love and time for others but not his own." He patted Joe on the hand. "When you receive a call from God, it's overwhelming. Some men never figure out how to balance their parish and their family. But rest assured, that neither God nor the religion called your father to abandon you. That was his choice, and it's something you will have to learn to accept if you expect to move forward."

Joe nodded. "I think I finally have, but it's taken a long time to get here."

"The journey is what makes us stronger. But I have a feeling that something else is bothering you."

Joe looked Pastor Don directly in the eyes. "There is something else. The truth is, I'm worried about Dorie. She's had some major issues to deal with in the past week, and even Dorie is not strong enough to handle everything alone. But she won't let anyone help either."

Pastor Don nodded.

"And beyond being worried about her mental health," Joe continued, "I'm worried about her physical safety. I'm sure you've heard the talk. This guy the DEA agent is chasing has taken a couple of shots at removing Dorie from law enforcement permanently. It's only due to skill and some sheer luck that she's still alive."

Pastor Don let out a sigh, a grave look on his face. "I have indeed heard the rumors, and I'm sure that even as fantastic as they sound, they border on the truth. I know Dorie is like a sister to you and I don't blame you for worrying. The truth is, I'm worried about her also."

He knelt before Joe and extended his hand. "Would you pray with me, please?"

Joe breathed a sigh of relief at the offer and sank

down onto the floor. He clasped his hand in the pastor's and bowed his head, feeling like he'd come home again.

"Dear Lord," Pastor Don began.

Dorie untied the airboat from the dock, tossed the rope in the boat, and motioned for Richard to get in. He stepped in and took a seat on one of the high chairs across the back. He'd been completely silent since leaving the sheriff's office, and he was pretty sure Dorie thought that had to do with the alligator situation.

If only that were the case.

Not that he was completely comfortable with the alligator situation. Truth be known, he was scared to death of those damn things, and his experience the day before hadn't helped his opinion. He tried to look at Dorie as she backed the boat away from the dock and started down the bayou, but couldn't meet her eyes.

No, this was about feeling guilty. Guilty that he was keeping a secret from her. A secret that never should have been.

He could feel her staring at him and knew she had to be curious about his silent state, but he looked away before she asked.

Coward. You're no better than the sheriff. And what if by some miracle you run into Roland out in the marsh? What then? Are you willing to run the risk that this woman, who you care about, might kill her biological father without knowing the truth?

Because no matter the rules of law enforcement, Richard had no doubt that if they came face to face with Roland, it would be the last time. Roland would not surrender quietly.

Things had changed so rapidly Richard hadn't

even had time to assess his own feelings. He was chasing a man who had killed his father, and he had already fallen for the woman who was the killer's daughter but didn't know it. And that same woman had been raised by the man who helped cover up Roland's business in Gator Bait in the first place. Did the fact that Roland had fathered Dorie have to change the way he felt about her? It shouldn't, but he wasn't positive that it didn't.

They were halfway to their destination and quickly closing the gap, when he put one hand on Dorie's arm, unable to hold it all in any longer.

"Something wrong?" she asked.

He nodded. "There's something I have to tell you. Your dad was supposed to do this, but I guess he got other ideas about how to handle things first. And I can't let you go into this without knowing. It wouldn't be right."

She killed the engine and looked at him, a worried expression on her face. "What do I need to know? What else did my dad keep from me?"

He stared at her and hoped the first bullet she fired today wasn't at him. "It started over thirty years ago," he began.

Chapter Sixteen

Joe had just finished his trip out to Buster's place and was pulling back into town when he saw the truck parked in front of Pete's Bar. It was a medium-sized moving truck, not one of the eighteen-wheelers he usually saw making deliveries. He screeched to a stop in front of the sheriff's office and hurried across the street to take a closer look.

A guy was unloading crates from inside the truck and carrying them into the boat shop. Joe took a closer look at one of the boxes. Boat oil. He scanned the rest of the boxes and saw similar items. Then he remembered Pete's comment about the hotshot driver Stella had been coordinating to save them all some money. He glanced over at the bar and saw a light on inside. Maybe he'd just step across the street and have another word with Pete.

The front door of the bar was unlocked, so Joe let himself inside. He figured Pete would be in the storeroom, so he called out for him. A couple of seconds later, Pete rounded the corner from the back of the bar and gave Joe a look of surprise. "What brings you here so early, Joe? I'm glad to hear the sheriff's going to pull through. Is anything wrong?"

"Everything's wrong," Joe said, "but that's not why I'm here. I was just wondering about something. I remember you talking about the truck driver Stella found. I saw him outside, so I guess everything went through all right with that deal?"

Pete nodded. "Yeah. Today is his first delivery. Any particular reason you're wanting to know? I mean if something's wrong with the guy, I don't have a problem getting rid of him."

Joe shook his head and forced a smile, not wanting to tip his hand. "No, nothing like that. At least, not that I'm aware of. I was just wondering if it would be a good deal for Jenny to get in on." He barely managed to get the lie out and sound normal.

Pete's face cleared in understanding. "I get it. Yeah, Stella asked her about it, but Jenny wanted to wait a few runs and make sure everything worked out okay with the guy."

Joe nodded. "Makes sense. Did everything go okay that you could see?"

Pete scratched his head. "Yeah. Everything seemed all right. I mean the orders were right, and he was on time and everything."

"But?" Joe asked, certain by Pete's tone that there was a "but" buried somewhere in his reply.

Pete shuffled his feet a bit. "I don't know. I hate saying anything about a person if I don't really know anything for sure."

"Oh hell, Pete, you spend most of your days and nights in this bar talking about people. Don't give me that crap. If you've got a problem with this guy, I want to know about it."

Pete gave him a sheepish look. "It's not exactly a problem. I just didn't like the feeling he gave me."

Joe saw a bit of red rise in Pete's face.

"Damn," Pete said, "I sound like a woman. That's just the kind of thing they always say."

Joe nodded. "Yeah, and they're usually right when they say it."

Pete considered this for a moment and nodded. "Guess that's true enough."

"So is there anything in particular you can put your finger on that bothered you?"

Pete stared at him for a moment and stroked his chin. "Well, it didn't seem like he was all that great of a driver for one. I mean, this guy is supposed to have been doing this for years, but it took him three tries before he could back into my loading dock." Pete shook his head and waved one hand. "Oh, hell, it's probably nothing. I'm probably just being stupid. So maybe the guy exaggerated a little about his experience. Lots of people are looking for jobs. He wouldn't be the first one to lie about his qualifications."

Joe stared across the bar, considering Pete's words. "And Stella found this guy, right?"

Pete nodded.

"Maybe I'll talk to her. Just to put my mind at ease."

Pete shrugged. "Couldn't hurt."

Joe left the bar and walked down the street to the boat shop. The truck was parked out front, but the driver was nowhere to be seen. Maybe he's inside, Joe thought, and pushed open the door.

Stella was behind the counter opening boxes and looked up at him in obvious surprise. "Joe, what are you doing here? I thought you'd be down at the hospital with Dorie."

He shook his head. "I need to take care of some business. It couldn't wait." He didn't bother to tell her that Dorie wasn't at the hospital either. Maybe if people assumed she was there, Roland would, too.

Stella put down her box cutter and gave him her full attention. "How's the sheriff? And I don't want any bullshit. I want to know the truth."

He smiled. "He's all right. I swear." He held up one hand. "He came out of surgery just fine. No internal organs were hit, and his heart stayed stable the entire time. The doctor only said to be careful of infection."

Stella nodded. "That's good to hear. Dorie has had enough problems going on here lately without her daddy acting a fool. What the hell was that man thinking, leaving the retirement home? And what the hell was Buster thinking, taking him out of there? Do you have any idea who shot him? Damn poachers, probably. Those city folk are going to kill us all someday."

He blew out a breath and shrugged. "We're not really sure what they were doing."

She gave him a sharp look, and Joe knew she was aware he was leaving out a big hunk of the story. "What about Buster? Anyone seen him yet?"

"No."

She scrunched her forehead and thought for a moment. "What the hell is going on in this town, Joe?"

"I don't know, but I'm trying to find out. In fact, I have a question for you, if you don't mind?"

"Sure."

He looked out front and saw that the driver had returned and was smoking a cigarette out by the truck. "The driver you hired—where did you find him?"

Stella looked at Joe in surprise. "I didn't find him."

"Pete said you found the guy and negotiated the deal."

She narrowed her eyes. "I don't know where you're going with this, but I can assure you that I did not find the driver. He contacted me and said that he had talked to Pete at a bar in Lake Charles. Said Pete had given him my name and number as a contact because I was better at figuring out the business end of things than him."

Joe stared at Stella, a bit stunned at her comment. What in the world was going on here? Joe looked back out at the driver, still leaned against his truck smoking a second cigarette. "What's he waiting on?"

"I got some boxes in the storeroom that need to be loaded, returns and recycling and such. He said loading wasn't part of his job, but he'd get to it in a minute."

Joe glanced back outside at the driver. He showed no signs of moving anytime soon. "I don't suppose you'd mind if I took a look in a few of those boxes."

Stella threw her hands in the air in surrender, apparently deciding he had lost his mind. "Of course, you can look in the boxes, but when all is said and done, Joe Miller, you're going to owe me one hell of an explanation."

"Yes, ma'am," Joe said and followed her back into the storeroom.

Dorie sat rigid in the boat, unable to speak. Her mind was whirling with the information Richard had given her. At first, she hadn't wanted to believe it, but his story filled in too many missing elements in her past. The mother that no one spoke of, the difference in appearance between her and her dad and his silence all those years when she was a little girl and wanted to know about her past.

How could he? How could he have done this to me? And knowing all the time that she was chasing Roland—the man who had fathered her and most likely killed her mother?

"What I don't understand," she finally said, "is your excuse for not telling me the truth." She focused directly on Richard.

He looked at her for only a moment before averting his eyes. "I promised your dad I wouldn't. I was giving him the opportunity to tell you himself. He was supposed to do it soon. How was I supposed to know that he was going to disappear and get himself shot?"

She narrowed her eyes. "You weren't, but after he disappeared and I told you about his past with Roland, you could have told me then. I told you my secret—and at no small expense, I might add. What was stopping you?"

He shrugged but didn't look at her. "I don't know. I guess I didn't want to tell you any more than your dad did. It wasn't a pretty story." He finally turned his gaze to her. "You have to understand, Dorie, that I never intended things to get this out of control. I didn't want people hurt, especially you and your father. I've spent all these years tracking Roland to try to prevent people from being hurt. Or at least that's what I've told myself. Maybe it was all just a convenient lie in order for me to justify my revenge."

She sucked in a breath, never having considered it that way, and wondered how she would feel if the situation was reversed. Would she have used everyone around her at any expense to avenge a loved one? She tried to imagine it, but her emotions were already too clogged to process anything else. And why had Richard been so reluctant to tell her the truth—regardless of how sordid it was? Was it possible that he cared for her more than he let on? Was his concern for her more than it would have been for anyone else in the same situation? Her chest constricted at the thought. She wasn't ready for this. Not now. Too much in her life was unsettled.

And that was a gross understatement.

She looked at him again and took in his miserable expression, the apprehension in his eyes when he looked at her. He's not sure either. All these secrets had probably put an end to something before it had ever really gotten started.

And maybe it was best that way. Richard was going to keep trying to catch Roland. He'd be far from Gator Bait, maybe even as soon as tomorrow. Despite her offer to help him apprehend Roland if he left Gator Bait, she knew he wouldn't or couldn't take her up on it. The DEA would close up shop before they allowed any assistance from the biological daughter of the man they were after.

"I'm sorry, Dorie," he said. "I didn't want to hurt you any more than you already have been, but there's still the possibility we might face Roland before this is over. I couldn't allow you to do that without knowing the truth."

She nodded. "I understand. But the truth doesn't change what I have to do."

"Maybe not, but it might change how you do it."

She gazed down the bayou for a moment and considered his words. Did knowing that Roland had fathered her make a difference in how she would handle a confrontation? Instinct told her it didn't, but how could she be sure? Realizing there was only one way to find out, she started the boat, and hoped that Roland was still around.

The truck driver opened a cell phone and dialed. "We might have a problem," he said. "That deputy was at Stella's and Pete's asking questions."

He paused for a minute waiting for instructions.

"No, not the woman. This was the guy. I haven't seen the woman or that DEA agent anywhere. Maybe they're still at the hospital. So do we move now or what?"

The driver listened for a moment, then closed the phone. It was time to get this over with, collect his money, and disappear. This deal had obviously gone sour and although he had no real aversion to killing a man—or woman, for that matter—it wasn't really something he wanted following him around when the job was done and he was all set to relax.

"Dorie, come in." Joe radioed out from the sheriff's office.

"Go ahead, Joe." The reply came quickly.

"I think I've found our transport, and it's leaving town today."

"What have you got?"

Joe told her about the truck driver and Stella's and Pete's comments. "It looks like someone set the driver up to play off each of them, both thinking the other had made the initial contact. And to have done that, we're right back to someone from Gator Bait. Someone very clever."

"But Stella and Pete were clean?"

"As far as I can tell. Stella was a little ticked that I had her open her return and recycle boxes, but they were clear. She'll get over it as soon as all this is said and done. Pete didn't have any returns at all, so

Stella was the only one sending anything back with the driver."

There was silence for a couple of seconds, then Dorie said, "Can you watch him and see where he goes without him catching on?"

He considered this for a minute. "I could probably track him within fifteen miles or so from the top of the motel. The guy's already noticed me asking questions, so I'm sure he'd catch a tail."

"Do that, then. Try the top of the motel and see if you can find where he lands. Call in backup from Lake Charles. Do not try to arrest this guy alone. Do you understand me, Joe?"

"Yeah, I understand," he said, although he didn't like it. "I'll call Lake Charles right away and get to the top of the motel as soon as he leaves."

"Call if you get a fix on him."

"Yep," he said and placed the radio on the table. Call Lake Charles. Damn it, he didn't want backup. Dorie ran around risking her life all the time without backup, and he wasn't even counting on Richard. A big help he had been so far. He looked at the phone on the desk and sighed.

"Shit," he said as he picked up the phone and dialed.

Dorie and Richard were a couple hundred yards from the preserve when she cut the throttle on the boat, pulled out a pair of binoculars and scanned the preserve.

"Anything?" Richard asked.

She shook her head. "Not that I can see. Of course, the grass is pretty high in the breeding ground. It would be easy to hide in a small boat."

"So what do you think?"

Pulling her gun from the holster, she checked it one last time. "I think it's time to end this."

He drew his firearm, gave her a nod, and took a deep breath as she approached the breeding grounds. They were only fifty yards or so from the location on the map when he saw the alligators. Joe was right. They were everywhere.

A head or tail stuck out of every piece of brush and the water surrounding the boat was filled with them—not a spare foot or two between them. He looked down just as a big one, probably fifteen feet or so, drew alongside the boat.

They were definitely outnumbered. Not in his wildest nightmares did he think pursuing Roland would ever come down to this. He looked around again. Maybe Roland was losing it. There had to be easier ways to do business than hiding things here.

He was just about to tell Dorie to turn around and call in the National Guard when she pointed to the right of the boat. Looking out over the bow, he saw a stretch of dirt rising up out of the marsh. Smack in the middle of that stretch was a stack of duffle bags.

"Unless some of the gators are planning a vacation," she said, "I think we've found the drugs."

He nodded. "Yeah, but how do we get to them? And don't tell me you're walking up there."

She shook her head. "I'll pull the boat as far up the bank as we can go. I have a supply of flares in the equipment box. The gators hate them, and I should have enough to create a path to the drugs. We'll have to hurry, though."

The understatement of the decade.

"Yeah, we'll hurry," he said, looking once more at the hundreds of alligators surrounding that small spot of land and wondering whether there was a world record for the fifty-yard dash while carrying heroin.

It had taken a bit of explaining, but Joe was finally perched on the rooftop of the motel with a set of binoculars pinned on the delivery truck. The driver had left Gator Bait just ten minutes earlier, and Joe had waited until he turned the corner off Main Street, then hustled across the street and convinced Stella to let him sit on the roof of the motel. At first, she'd thought he was crazy and insisted on him sitting inside in the air-conditioning and having a glass of water.

Joe had explained the situation in a rush only for Stella to yell at him and ask him what the hell he was waiting for. He hustled to the roof, found a spot to sit, and waited for the driver to stop. Lake Charles was sending two backup units, but it would take them at least an hour to get there. He had already decided, orders or no orders, if he thought he could take this guy down, that's just what he was going to do. Dorie would have to get over it. After all, he'd been putting up with her dangerous stunts his entire life. He was due one of his own.

The truck made a right turn off the highway and Joe scanned the area for something familiar. "Damn," he said out loud. The driver was traveling down the road in front of Maylene's house. No wonder Maylene had been complaining about noise lately. Between the plane and someone scouting the road for a getaway, her quiet little world had probably been very busy. If she hadn't been such a drunk, they might have caught on a little sooner.

But it was too late now for wishing. There was only one way out of that road by vehicle and Joe could easily have that way blocked. He waited until the truck reached the end of the road and parked, then grabbed his portable radio and called Dorie.

The screech from the radio made Dorie and Richard jump. "Shit," Richard said.

Dorie reached for the radio. "You got something, Joe?"

"Yeah, the truck stopped down the road from Maylene's. That must be the pickup. You find the drugs yet?"

Dorie looked at the stacks of duffle bags surrounded by hundreds of gators. "Oh, we found them all right. Smack in the middle of the breeding ground. There must be a hundred gators on that patch of land."

Immediately, Joe started protesting. "Damn it, Dorie! You're not thinking of setting foot on that piece of dirt, are you?"

"No other way to get the drugs off. I have a bunch of flares. We're going to create a pathway and get the stuff into the boat as fast as possible. Then we're getting the hell out of here."

There was a moment of silence, and she knew Joe was trying to contain himself.

"You do realize," he said, "that if the driver is in position, then someone else is going to be coming after those drugs? What do you want me to do about the truck?"

"Hold tight and wait for Lake Charles to back you up. If he moves before Lake Charles gets there, then try to follow. But don't be obvious. This guy might be able to lead us to Roland if we don't get the opportunity to meet out here. I want that driver alive and talking."

"Fine. But do me a favor. Duct tape the radio open.

If you two get into any trouble, you might not be able to make it back to the radio in time. I'll take the portable with me. If you get in a bind, just holler, and I'll head that way."

"You got it," Dorie said and nodded at Richard who passed her the duct tape.

"That's really not a bad idea," Richard said. "At least if things get hairy, we'll know backup is on the way."

She stared at him. "Dick, if things get hairy, we're not even going to have time to yell."

He shook his head and sighed. "You know, it's so comforting working with you."

Grinning, Dorie lit the first flare and tossed it out of the boat about three feet in front of them and to the right. The gators immediately retreated from the burning object, hissing their disapproval. She motioned to Richard, and he tossed a flare a few feet from the boat on the other side. Again, the gators scattered, but remained within looking distance, their tails flicking back and forth in anger.

Dorie drew her gun and stepped over the side of the boat, a second flare in her hand. "If you see one of them rise up on his legs, shoot him. They're ungodly fast, even with all that length behind them."

Richard nodded, a grim expression on his face, and pulled out his own firearm. Gun in one hand and flares in the other, he followed her out of the boat and into certain hell.

Chapter Seventeen

Joe strained to hear Dorie and Richard, but finally decided that the signal was coming through fine. They had just stopped talking. He was sure he knew what had created the lull in conversation and was equally as sure he didn't like it.

He turned the radio up all the way, placed it on the ledge next to him, then picked up his binoculars for another check on the driver. He scanned the road in front of Maylene's house. The truck was still parked at the end in the same spot as before, but the driver was now out of the vehicle, talking on a cell phone.

Maybe things are about to happen. He checked his watch. The Lake Charles police were at least twenty minutes away. If Dorie and Richard ran into problems out there, they were going to be cutting it real close.

He looked through the binoculars again. The driver had finished his call and leaned back against the truck smoking a cigarette. A good sign. He was there for the duration. Or a bad sign. That meant someone is definitely going after the drugs.

For a moment, he considered calling Dorie but then remembered he couldn't. The radio was taped open on her end and the cell phones never picked up that far into the preserve.

"Damn it," he said, mad at himself for not realizing the limitation he'd put on communication. "I should have thought of that earlier." He took one final look at the truck before climbing down from his perch. He needed to verify the location of the Lake Charles police, just in case things went bad. He could only hope Dorie and Richard got the drugs and got the hell out of there before Roland, or his mystery partner, showed up to collect their merchandise.

Dorie stepped carefully into the middle of the cleared path, lit another flare, and threw it a couple of feet in front of her. Richard did the same on the other side. They were almost to the bags, and so far, the flares had kept the alligators at bay.

She lit the last flare and threw it ahead of her. As soon as Richard's matching flare hit the ground, she walked steadily to the pile and hoisted two bags onto her shoulders. Richard managed four—the show-off—and they hurried back to the boat, careful not to further aggravate the alligators.

Their first trip over, they tossed the bags into the bow of the boat, and began back down the narrow path. "We ought to be able to get it all this time," Dorie said, keeping her voice low.

Richard nodded, his eyes flashing from left to right, watching the alligators. "You know this is insane?"

"I know," she agreed. "Someone must have screwed up big time. There's no way anyone local would consider this a good place to hide something."

"Oh, it's a grand place to hide something," Richard said as he lifted the last of the bags from the ground, "just not if you're planning on wanting it back."

They were halfway back to the boat when the shot rang out. Dorie spun around as Richard stumbled to the ground, blood already seeping from a hole in his pants. Dropping immediately to the hard dirt, she searched the brush looking for the shooter. "Get to the boat," she said. "I'll cover you."

He started to move and the second shot rang out, grazing his right arm and causing him to drop the bags. Only a couple of feet away from him, the gators began to stir, the scent of blood making them restless. As they started to move toward him, Richard looked up at Dorie, the fright etched clearly across his face.

"Run," she said as she dropped the bags and ran for the boat. They were almost there when the airboat exploded, showering them with a thick cloud of white powder.

Joe grabbed the radio at the first sound of gunshots. He strained to hear anything, but could only make out the rustling of marsh grass and the water hitting the side of the boat. He tucked the radio under his arm, hustled down the ladder and ran toward the dock. The sound of the second shot brought him up short, and he strained again to hear any sign of life out of Dorie or Richard.

"What the hell was that?" Pete asked as he rushed out of the bar and over to Joe, followed a mere second later by Stella, firing off the same question.

"Dorie's in trouble," Joe replied. "Pete, do you still have that barge trailered behind the bar?"

"Yeah," Pete said, confusion written all over his face, "but that thing hasn't run in years."

"I don't need it to run," Joe said as he checked his gun for bullets. "I need you to hitch it to your truck and park it across the entrance of the road to Maylene Thibodeaux's. Make sure a vehicle can't get around it. Then head up the highway and intercept the Lake Charles police. Show them where to turn and don't let that hotshot driver get away."

Pete nodded and rushed off behind the bar, obviously not about to question Joe's instructions after hearing the noise from the radio.

Joe shoved his gun in his holster and ran to the dock, leaving Stella yelling behind him. "Wait a damn minute, Joe," she cried as she hurried behind him.

"What?" Joe asked as he yanked the tie line for his boat off the pylon.

"Take my airboat," Stella said and tossed him the keys. "You can cut straight across the marsh and get there faster."

Joe snagged the keys and jumped into the airboat. "Thanks, Stella," he yelled as he backed away from the pier.

Stella waved and yelled back, "You go get our girl, Joe. Don't let anything happen to Dorie."

Joe had just swung the boat around and was about to lay down the throttle when he heard the explosion, and the radio went silent.

"Shit, shit, shit!" he cried and pushed the throttle as far as it would go, racing away from the dock. Once he had leveled out, he yanked his cell phone from his pocket and called the Lake Charles police. He quickly relayed the situation to the dispatcher and ordered him to have that backup haul ass. An officer was down.

Even as he said it, he hoped against hope that it wasn't true, but whatever was happening out in the marsh didn't sound good.

* * *

The blast from the explosion threw Dorie and Richard onto the ground a good twenty feet from the bank. Thank God the flares were still going, Dorie thought as she looked around. The alligators had scattered after the explosion, but it wouldn't be long before they were back. Remaining on the ground, she searched the brush in the direction the shots had come from. "This doesn't make sense," she whispered. "There's no channel back there. Whoever is shooting is on foot."

"That's not possible," Richard said, staring at her as if she'd lost her mind.

The answer washed over her, quick and painful. "Maybe my dad wasn't talking about *his* friend betraying him," she whispered. "Maybe he was talking about *mine*."

"None of your friends are foolish enough to walk into the game preserve," Richard argued.

"They are if they can talk to alligators."

Joe had just entered the preserve when he heard shouting. Scanning the marsh, he saw Maylene Thibodeaux wading through several feet of water and waving frantically at him. *What the hell is going on now?* He couldn't think of a single reason in the world why Maylene would haul her large frame through the marsh, toting a sawed-off 12-guage, but he wasn't about to ask. He barely cut his speed and yelled, "I don't have time, Maylene. It will have to wait."

"Boy, you better pick me up," Maylene yelled back. "I'm ass-deep in gators out here and not in the mood."

Joe cursed and drew alongside Maylene. She rolled over the side of the boat and Joe sped off into the game preserve. "I have to tell you, Maylene," he said once she had righted herself. "Someone is shooting at Dorie and Richard, and there was an explosion. It's not safe for you to be here."

"Is that what all the racket is about?" Maylene asked. "I've just about had it with all the goings-on around here. You go on and do your job, Joe Miller. I'll just ride shotgun and help you out."

Apparently, Maylene meant that literally, because she took a position in the raised seat located right in the middle of the boat, shotgun cocked and ready. The seat strained in protest, and Joe hoped to God it held until they found Dorie and Richard.

"You're even smarter than I thought, Dorie," Curtis said as he stepped out of the brush and into the clearing. He raised his left hand and signaled, and the alligators moved quickly away from him. "But then all them brains has got you into a load of trouble."

"Curtis," Dorie said, her voice choked. "Please tell me this isn't true."

Curtis slowly shook his head. "Sorry, Dorie. Things weren't supposed to go this way. I ain't got any beef with you, personally, but you kept sticking your nose in my business. Just one more day and I'd have been gone with my money. Why couldn't you just leave it alone?"

"You know why."

Curtis gave her a small laugh. "Yeah. High and mighty. Dorie Berenger and her dad. Gator Bait's pride and joy, protecting everyone from the bad guys." He stared down at her. "'Course, I'm sure you know now that dear ole dad wasn't the righteous man he claimed to be. If only you could've followed suit."

"I don't agree with what my dad did," she said.

"I reckon not," Curtis said and sighed. "You really are different than most, Dorie. It's a shame you couldn't take a warning and back off. I didn't want to kill you, but now I ain't got no choice. Roland doesn't like loose ends."

She stared at the man she thought was her friend and felt her stomach turn. "How could you?" she asked, her voice barely a whisper.

"How could I?" Curtis replied, his voice rising in both volume and range. "How could I? You, of all people, should get it. You're trapped in Gator Bait too. You really think I wanna spend the rest of my life in this hellhole?"

"No one's stopping you from leaving."

Curtis laughed. "These critters are what's stopping me from leaving. I can't talk to 'em anywhere else. You know that. I make my money from killing my family." He waved one arm toward the alligators moving restlessly around them.

"I go on a two-month bender every year after hunting season," he continued. "And I can't do it anymore. Now, I don't have to. Roland offered me more money than I'd make in two lifetimes. I can disappear and go someplace where I never have to see a gator again."

"You can still do the right thing," Dorie said. "You know I care about these animals. There aren't many who do. What will happen to them if I'm gone?"

Curtis paused for a moment. "It's a shame, but I ain't got no options. You should've stayed away." He lifted his gun and pointed it at her, his finger tightening on the trigger. "I'm really sorry."

"I've known you my entire life, Curtis," Dorie said, desperately hoping to stop his whitening finger. "The least you could do is give me a moment to say my piece. The outcome is the same anyway."

Curtis stared at her for a moment, his eyes wild, and Dorie knew she couldn't reason with him. The best she could hope for was to stall for time. Surely Joe had heard the gunshots and was on his way. It was the only chance she and Richard had, and she intended to make full use of it.

"I s'pose you're right," Curtis said finally. "Go ahead and say what you want. I've got a little time before I meet up with Roland, and I guess I do owe you something." He grinned down at them. "After all, if your daddy hadn't hidden all the evidence of Roland the first time, I'd never had gotten the deal now."

Dorie bit her lip to hold back the words she wanted to say to Curtis. Those words would only get them shot sooner, and time was everything. She looked over at Richard who stared back at her, uncertainty written all over his face. "I love you, Richard Starke," she said.

Richard's face went to dumbfounded, then incredulous, and Dorie knew he thought she was as crazy as Curtis, taking a time like this to profess her love when there was a gun pointed at her head. "You challenged me in ways that no one else could," she continued, "and you didn't treat me like a helpless female. The bond I felt with you is like no other I've ever experienced and I just wanted you to know that."

Richard continued to stare, casting furtive glances at Curtis.

"If we'd only had more time," Dorie said and stressed the word "time" while cutting her eyes back to Curtis. "You and I could have been great together—just like those superhero cartoons from when we were kids. You know, racing in to save the day and making those last-minute escapes while leaving everyone on the edge of their seats. But without tights. We wouldn't wear tights." *Good Lord, I'm ram-*

bling. Get control. She took a deep breath and looked Richard hard in the eyes, willing him to catch on to her plan to draw out the moment in time for Joe to get there.

Richard stared at her, incredulous. "If only we had more time," she repeated, stressing her words again.

It only took a second for his expression to clear in understanding, and he reached over and placed his hand on hers. "We were already great together, and there's not a superhero in the world who could match you. You're the woman I always dreamed of, Dorie Berenger. I just didn't know it until now."

Dorie squeezed his hand and gave him a small smile. She was just about to speak when Curtis interrupted.

"Jesus Christ, are you two done yet?" he griped. "This is worse than one of those God-awful soap operas. I was feeling bad about killing you, but I'm gonna be doing the world a favor."

"Just one more minute," Dorie pleaded. "I only have a bit more."

Curtis shook his head. "No way. I'm done with this. You can talk again on the other side. Capes and masks are optional." He directed the gun straight at her head and his finger whitened on the trigger.

Dorie closed her eyes and waited for the pain she knew was coming. She felt Richard's hand squeezing hers and instantly regretted everything in her life that she would never do. Forgive me for all of my sins, Lord, she thought as her body tensed, waiting for the shot. And when it came, she almost collapsed from fear, waiting for her brain to process the injury.

Instead, Curtis began screaming in pain. They jerked their heads from the ground and saw Curtis clenching what was left of his right hand. An airboat burst into the game preserve, Joe driving and

Maylene Thibodeaux perched on the high seat aiming her shotgun directly at Curtis.

Joe cut his speed on the boat to avoid full-out contact with the land, and Maylene pitched forward into the bottom of the boat and shot off her own hat.

Curtis stopped screaming and Dorie turned back to look at him. He was staring at her, his eyes cold and blank. "I'm taking you with me," he said and lifted his left hand in the air, signaling the alligators to close in.

Before he could even think about reaching for his gun, a shot rang out, deafening Richard with its blast. He turned and saw Dorie staring at Curtis, gun drawn and her expression grim. He looked back at Curtis and realized her shot was the most deadly possible. Curtis's only hand left was badly wounded. He had lost his method of communication with the beasts circling them.

With the blast from the gun, the alligators had backed away several feet and now all heads turned to Curtis, waiting for the signal that would never come. Curtis stared in horror down at the alligators just inches away from him. "No," he screamed as they began to rise up on their legs, the scent of blood already drawing them to him.

Richard leapt up from the ground, pulling Dorie with him with one hand and grabbing one of the remaining duffle bags with the other. Dorie hesitated only a moment, her gaze still locked on Curtis, before grabbing the remaining bags and rushing for the boat.

Joe had already reversed the engines and was starting to back away from the island of alligators as Dorie and Richard flung the duffle bags into the boat, narrowly missing Maylene, who was still face-down in the bottom, apparently trying to roll herself over. They leapt in beside the duffle bags and grabbed onto the sides of the boat, which lurched violently as Joe tore away from the bank.

As soon as they were a safe distance from the bank, Dorie buried her head in Richard's chest and covered her ears. Richard looked away from the disturbing sight on the small piece of land behind them and tightened his grip around her as he tried to block out the sounds of tearing flesh and breaking bones that even the noise of the boat couldn't drown out.

Joe focused straight ahead, never looking back, his jaw set and his eyes still flashing with anger. When the boat leveled out on top of the water, Maylene retrieved what was left of her hat and struggled to right herself in the bottom of the boat, using the shotgun for leverage. Richard hoped she was out of bullets.

Finally back in a sitting position, Maylene looked around the boat at everyone and glared.

"Would anyone like to tell me what in damnation is going on?" she asked. "And who the hell is the guy I've got locked in my kitchen pantry?"

Dorie stared at Maylene, not believing what she just heard. "You have a man locked in your pantry?"

Maylene nodded. "Came around earlier. Talking all nice and stuff, but he couldn't fool me. I knew he was up to something. As soon as I opened the door wide enough to invite him in, he pulled out a gun. Almost got me, too, but I was holding a jug of 'special' and clocked him a good one."

"What time was this?" Dorie asked, unable to keep the excitement from her voice.

"About an hour ago. I figured anyone pulling a gun on a defenseless woman that way was up to no good. It's not like I'd turn down any reasonable offer," she said indignantly. "But forcing a woman in her own home just isn't my idea of a fun romp, regardless of those damned role-playing games people are into nowadays. So I figured I'd teach him a bit of manners."

She smiled gleefully.

"And you locked him in your closet?" Dorie asked.

"Yep. Hog-tied him up and dumped him in the pantry. It's real solid, that wall. All wood, no Sheetrock at all. Then I locked him in. That's where I keep the good stuff, see. It's got excellent locks."

Richard and Joe grinned at Dorie and she knew they were all thinking the same thing. There was a huge possibility that Roland was locked in Maylene Thibodeaux's pantry. Joe increased his speed and veered off to the right, headed as close as possible to Maylene's house.

"Then I go outside," Maylene continued to rant, "and I decide to take a look around his truck, since I was suspicious and all. And what the hell do you think I found in a bag in the back?"

"Drugs?" Dorie said.

"Money?" Joe threw in.

Maylene shook her head. "Hell, no. I found Buster Comeaux all trussed up like a Christmas turkey, barely breathing at all. Just as I stalked back into the house and called 911, a delivery truck went racing by my house, and then I heard the explosion. Well, that was it for me. I got my gun, jumped in the truck and headed down the road to the marsh. I don't have the patience for this much activity. Damn it, that's private property. I was trying to track down the source of the explosion when Joe picked me up."

Joe pointed to the edge of the game preserve closest to Maylene's house. The delivery truck was still there, and Lake Charles police cars surrounded it. Dorie heard Joe give a sigh, apparently relieved that Lake Charles had made it on time. He forced the boat as far up on the bank as it would go and they jumped out and identified themselves to the officers on the scene.

Giving a hurried explanation of the situation in Maylene's pantry, they hopped into police cars with the Lake Charles cops, and raced up the road to Maylene's house. Taking several deep breaths, Dorie tried to calm her nerves. *Don't get too excited. There's always the chance he could have gotten away. He's been doing this a long time. This is an expert you're dealing with.*

Still, her heart was racing as they rushed into Maylene's kitchen and saw the locks securely in place on the pantry door. Maylene hustled into the room as only Maylene could and made everyone face the other way as she twirled the combination on the lock. When it clicked open, everyone spun around just in time to see Maylene swing open the pantry door and the thin, blond man inside fall out onto the floor, still passed out cold.

Shawn Roland, captured at last.

Dorie rushed into the hospital room and hugged her dad. He was awake now and sitting with Jenny, waiting for her to arrive. Not very patiently, based on the exhausted look on Jenny's face.

Joe had called from Maylene's and told the sheriff that everything was fine. Roland was in custody, and Richard had been sent to the hospital for his gunshot wound. He also explained that they'd had to call in help from the Lake Charles game warden and arrange for armed patrol in a wide circle around the breeding area in case any of the gators ingested what drugs had been left.

As soon as Dorie was done greeting her dad, Jenny rushed around the bed and hugged her, eyeing her from head to toe.

"Thank God you're all right," Jenny said. "Where's Joe?"

Before Dorie could answer, the man in question bolted into the room, picked Jenny up at the waist and twirled her around in a circle while kissing her senseless. When he'd run out of arm strength, or maybe air, he lowered her to the floor and received a round of cheers from Dorie and Sheriff Berenger.

Joe grinned at the startled expression on Jenny's face. "Jenny Miller," he said, "will you do me the honor of being my date this Friday night for dinner and a movie?"

The smile on Jenny's face said it all as she replied, "I thought you'd never ask."

Joe let out a big whoop and threw his arm around Jenny's shoulders, pulling her close to him. Dorie took one look at their joyous faces and felt for the first time since leaving the breeding grounds that everything might turn out all right after all. Time would heal all the old hurts and hopefully the new ones, too.

"What about Richard and Buster?" Jenny asked.

"They're going to be fine," Dorie said. "Buster has a good bump on his head and is dehydrated, but no other injuries. Dick's wounds were superficial, the kind that look worse than they are. He's lucky Curtis wasn't a better shot—" She stopped for a moment, her composure lost after saying Curtis's name.

Her dad reached out and took her hand. "You don't have to tell us everything, honey. It's all right."

"Someday, maybe I'll be able to," she said and sniffed. Thinking of everything that had happened that day, she couldn't help the smile that finally came to her lips. "I *can* tell you about Maylene. And you're going to love it."

A little later, Dorie slipped quietly into Richard's room. His eyes were closed, but as she eased closer to the bed, they fluttered open. "Dorie," he said.

"You're just a little woozy from the drugs, but the doctors say you're going to be just fine. They were only surface wounds."

"Roland?"

Dorie couldn't stop the smile on her face. "Locked up in the Lake Charles jail. Your buddies in D.C. are already celebrating."

He gave her a hard look. "How are you doing with that?"

Dorie shrugged. "It doesn't matter really. Roland is nothing more than another criminal to me. It's unfortunate that we're related, but that's all it is—unfortunate. We're *not* family, and never could be."

"You sure?"

"Absolutely," she said and gave him a firm nod. "I was wondering, you know, how I would feel if I saw him face-to-face." She shook her head and laughed. "But then the moment came, and it was like the whole situation had been this massive buildup for nothing. I looked down at that man and didn't feel a thing except relief that he wasn't going to be free any longer."

"I'm glad," Richard said, and Dorie could see the relief in his expression. "I've been afraid of what might happen, how you might feel, ever since I found out about Roland. I tried to put myself in your place, but I couldn't come up with anything except anger. I guess I was worried you might feel the same way."

Dorie tilted her head to one side and thought about his words for a moment. "I guess I can see that," she finally acknowledged, "and don't think for a minute that I'm not angry, but I would've been angry about Roland no matter what. His kind tends to bring out the worst in me." She paused for a moment then smiled. "But you have no reason to worry. I have all of Gator Bait to surround me, and coddle me and wear the living hell out of me making sure I'm all right. The phone lines are probably buzzing already."

Richard nodded. "I guess you do. How's Maylene?"

Dorie grinned. "All fired up about being the one to take Roland down and telling anyone who'll listen." She sobered for a moment and shook her head. "She was really lucky, you know."

"Yeah," Richard agreed. "With all the police calls that Maylene made, Roland wasn't about to take a chance of ruining his deal over another nosy female. Between you now and your mother years ago, I think he'd had enough of women to last a lifetime."

Dorie nodded. "I'm just glad it all turned out all right. Maylene's a royal pain in the ass, and a complete nut, but she's still family."

"God forbid," Richard said and smiled.

"What about Buster? How's he doing?"

"He's going to be fine. He'll have a headache for a couple of days—at least until he and my dad are back to normal. Then I'm going to kill them both for going after Roland themselves instead of telling us about the shack on Buster's duck lease that Roland used as a hideout the first time."

"Yeah. I wouldn't want to be in either of their shoes right now." He gave her a puzzled look. "What I still can't figure out is why Roland didn't kill Buster straight away."

Dorie nodded. "Simple really. He was going to keep Buster away long enough to pass some money through the shrimp house account, then turn him loose to take the fall."

Richard shook his head. "And given what we now know about Buster and Roland's past, no one would have believed his kidnapping story, especially if that fisherman hadn't gotten to your father in time."

Dorie nodded. "It was his biggest mistake, leaving them alive, but I'm glad he made it. He should have just left Curtis wide open for accusation, but I guess he didn't trust him either."

Richard gave her a small smile and took her hand in his. "I'm sorry about Curtis," he said gently.

Dorie nodded and looked away, trying to stop the tears that were threatening to break through. "I miss him already," she said. "Even though he wanted me dead." She looked back at Richard. "Is that stupid?"

He shook his head. "No. It's not stupid. It's tragic, really. If only Curtis had confided in you before he got involved with Roland, maybe you could have found something else for him."

"I don't think so," she said. "And I've thought about little else since I left Maylene's. I mean, I could have gotten Curtis a job with Wildlife and Fisheries. In fact, I'd offered him jobs many times. The money just wasn't there, and it turns out Curtis had a big gambling habit . . ."

"Making it easy for him to launder large amounts of money," Richard finished.

Dorie nodded. "But I never knew that he felt that

way about the killing in hunting season. I swear I had no idea." She brushed the back of her hand across her eyes.

Looking down at Richard, she tried to smile. "So you finally got your man, Agent Starke. What are you going to do now?" She tried to keep her tone light, but was positive that her eyes gave her away. Every step of the way from her dad's hospital room, Dorie had rolled around the image of the ecstatic looks on Joe's and Jenny's faces. That expression of pure love. A love she thought she'd never find.

Until now. Then it hit her like a freight train as she stared at the man in front of her. All the things she'd said at the breeding grounds stalling for time were the truth. She *did* love Richard. And she'd only figured that out in time for him to leave.

Well, shit on a stick. She was in love with Richard. This was a turn of events she'd never seen coming, and for someone as perceptive as she was, that was an appalling thought. How had this happened? When had it happened?

She drew in a breath and tried to clear her thoughts. The sex had been great, but then it wasn't like she hadn't had great sex before Richard. Okay, maybe not as great as with Richard but still not anything to complain about.

Usually.

But if it wasn't the sex, that only left the alternative: Dorie Berenger had fallen completely and madly in love with the most aggravating man on the planet, despite her best judgment.

Well, hell.

Finally accepting reality for what it was, she looked at Richard, anxiously studying his expression and trying to decipher what he was thinking and at the same time trying not to place so much importance on his answer. The answer that would make or break the rest of her life. Because, after all, he still had a job to do, and it wasn't over yet. At least not for the DEA.

Richard stared at her for a moment then blew out a breath, still looking slightly dazed that it was all over. "I'll head back to D.C. first. Put together an air-tight case against Roland." He looked out the hospital window and shook his head. "After that, I don't know. My entire adult life has been defined by this one man. I don't have any idea what to do. It's like being freed from prison."

Dorie nodded, understanding exactly what he was saying, because she was in the same position. For so long they'd both operated with a single-minded purpose—Dick to avenge his father and Dorie to take care of hers. Now, Dick's lifelong quest had been fulfilled, and in its pursuit, Dorie had realized that caring for her dad didn't have to mean sticking with a job she really didn't want.

"Your buddies from D.C. should be here in an hour or so," she said. "The hospital agreed to release you to them." She looked at him and choked back the tears. "So I guess this is good-bye."

Richard reached up and gathered her in his arms. "It's only good-bye for now. As soon as things are settled, we'll figure out what to do about us. I promise."

She hugged him tightly, wanting his words to be the truth, but couldn't ignore the feeling that everything she thought she knew had suddenly and drastically changed.

Chapter Eighteen

Three weeks later, Dorie sat in the Gator Bait sheriff's office and blew out a breath of frustration.

After Roland's arrest, things had changed so rapidly. First, her dad had officially resigned from his job as sheriff, and the special election for his replacement had turned out every sober resident in Gator Bait—a new town record. The townspeople were still celebrating their newfound notoriety for aiding in the capture of one of the most wanted drug dealers in history, but Dorie couldn't seem to jump on the party wagon.

"You've got your feet on my desk." Joe smiled at her as he walked in. Of course, Joe hadn't stopped smiling ever since Jenny had agreed to marry him. Being elected sheriff had just been the icing on the cake. She grinned and moved her feet to the floor.

"Old habits," she said.

He sat down in a chair across from her and nodded. "Maybe it's time to get some new habits."

"Don't start on me again today, Joe. I'm not in the

mood. Between you and my dad, there's just no peace in my life anymore. The only person who respects my wish for silence is Jenny."

Joe's face softened at the mention of his true love, but narrowed back into focus a second later. "Don't try and distract me. It won't work this time. You're wasting away here. Why haven't you applied for a game warden position in a big district?"

She shrugged. "I don't want to make a rash decision."

"Rash?" Joe said. "It's been weeks. Jesus Christ, Dorie, I've gotten engaged and become an elected official in the same time frame. You, on the other hand, are living in a room at the motel and still traipsing around the same marsh you grew up in."

"Are you trying to get rid of me?"

"No, I'm not trying to get rid of you," Joe said, his frustration apparent. "Well, hell, maybe I am trying to get rid of you." He gave her a hard look. "You're wasting time, Dorie. Stop worrying about what might have been. If you want something, then take it. It's not like you have your dad to worry about any longer."

Dorie blew out a breath. Her dad's lack of financial dependence on her was still a sticky point. Apparently, Buster and her dad's foray into covering up drug running had yielded more money than they needed to keep the shrimp house open. Buster had squirreled away the extra in one of those nonreported banks on an unknown island somewhere in the Bahamas. Unfortunately, just as they were ready to retire, a new government had taken over the island and seized all the funds. It had taken them more than twelve years to get a portion of it back.

That "portion" had equaled well over two million.

With Roland's arrest and all other past indiscretions now known to law enforcement, they figured it was time to cash in the funds and retire in style.

They used the money to add handicapped features to Buster's retirement home in Florida and hire a full-time housekeeper/cook/nurse, and the two of them had gone off to the Sunshine State a week earlier, happy as pigs in shit. Dorie had been furious over the money, but there was nothing to be done about it. Buster had laundered it through the shrimp house, so as far as anyone else knew, he'd earned it all.

But the biggest surprise had been when Buster asked Jenny to take over running the shrimp house and made her a partner. She'd stepped up to the challenge, hired someone to work the diner, and was fast becoming the sharpest businesswoman in Gator Bait. Stella was busy telling everyone how Jenny had learned everything from her.

"It just so happens, Mr. Know-It-All," Dorie said with a smug smile, "that I have a new position starting in August."

Joe stared at her in obvious surprise. "You're kidding me. Where? What will you be doing?"

Dorie laughed. "Don't get all excited just yet," she said. "I'm still staying in Gator Bait as the game warden. I'll just be commuting to Lake Charles a couple of days a week for my other job."

"What job?"

"Lake Charles University has offered me a teaching position in their brand-new criminology department. Before I left Rutgers, I'd finished all of my required course work for my Ph.D., and the faculty agreed to extend the deadline for submitting my dissertation. By the end of the year, you'll have to refer to me as Dr. Berenger."

A huge smile broke out on Joe's face. "That's fantastic, Dorie. You'll be perfect for the job."

Dorie smiled back at him. "Just a minute ago, you wanted to get rid of me," she teased.

Joe laughed. "Not exactly. I just wanted you to do something more with your talent. This is the best of both worlds. You're finally using that mind of yours for something besides beating me at cards, and I get to keep my best friend close by."

"That's what Jenny said."

For a moment, a crestfallen look appeared on Joe's face and Dorie had to smile. "Jenny knew before me?" he asked.

"Now don't go pouting on me, Joe," Dorie said. "You know I type like crap. Jenny's been helping me polish up my dissertation since she's a wiz with all those charts and graphs and fancy computer things. I didn't want to tell anyone else until I knew for sure. You understand, don't you?"

Joe smiled. "So that's what you two have been doing all those evenings I had late patrol."

"Guilty as charged," Dorie replied, and the smile begin to vanish from her face. She felt her eyes cloud and turned her gaze out the window, hoping Joe wouldn't clue in on the hurt that lay underneath the excitement of starting her new life.

"Have you called him?" Joe asked, breaking into her thoughts.

She sighed as Joe hit on the one topic she'd been trying to avoid. "Of course I've called."

"So?"

"So what?"

Joe took a deep breath. "So what did he say?"

"He didn't say anything. He wasn't home."

Joe stared at her in surprise. "And he didn't call back?"

She shook her head and avoided his eyes, but it didn't work.

"You did leave a message for him, didn't you?"

"Not exactly," she said, trying to work around the truth.

"What do you mean, not exactly?"

She threw her hands up in the air in exasperation. "Hell, no, I didn't leave a message. The man has been gone three weeks and aside from two calls to get information for his case files, hasn't even tried to contact me. And don't say I didn't make an effort. I might not have left a message, but this is the technology age. How many people do you think he has on caller ID hailing from Gator Bait, Louisiana?"

Fortunately for her, Joe knew when to throw in the towel. He sighed and shook his head. "Well, then move on, Dorie. You're on to something new with your career. Maybe it's time to change other things too. You've been mooning around this town for too long. Even Maylene has taken to inquiring as to your welfare on a daily basis. That's just not right."

Dorie smiled. Ever since Maylene had been given a special award for bravery by the DEA, she had trailed Dorie and Joe as often as possible, insisting she was destined for a career in law enforcement. "No one has to inquire about me, Joe. I'm fine. Just a little bored. That's not against the law, is it?"

"Not the last time I checked," Richard's voice came from the doorway behind them. They both whirled around and stared. "Of course," he continued, "I know how you small towns operate. It's entirely possible you changed the laws after I left."

"Dick," Joe said and jumped up from his chair to offer his hand. "How the hell are you? What brings you back to town?"

"I'm fine," Richard said. "In fact, I'm better than fine. The case against Roland is solid as a rock. He'll never see the light of day. As for why I'm here . . ." He cast an apprehensive look at Dorie. "I have some unfinished business to attend to."

Dorie sprang from her seat and glared at him. "Unfinished business! You've got some nerve, Richard Starke, to call what went on between us business. And I have news for you—that business was finished when you never called."

Richard didn't even try to look sorry, and she saw Joe cast a sideways glance in her direction, probably trying to figure out if she was armed.

"I was busy," Richard said and smiled.

Joe whistled. "Boy, you're never gonna learn."

"Busy? You were busy?" Dorie stared at him, incredulous. "What the hell kept you so involved that you couldn't even pick up the phone and make a call?"

"Being busy is not what kept me from calling," Richard said softly. "Not being prepared is what kept me from calling. That's why it's taken until now for me to come here. I had to make arrangements."

"What arrangements?" she asked, instantly suspicious.

He gave her a broad smile. "Well, for starters, there was my transfer to negotiate with the Gulf Coast division of the DEA. I'll be based out of Lake Charles."

"Really?" Dorie asked, afraid the punch line was coming.

Richard nodded. "After my big Roland capture, they were ecstatic to have me. I didn't tell them about my secret weapon." He gave Dorie a wink.

Dorie stared at him, too shocked to say another

word, too scared that the moment was a dream and any minute it would vanish. But when she blinked her eyes, Richard was still there, right in front of her, smiling at her like it would last forever.

"And besides," he continued, "now that you'll be working in Lake Charles part of the time, I figured we could carpool. That is if you're willing to drive around in that foreign piece of shit I have."

Dorie's mouth dropped open in surprise. "How did you know about the teaching job? I just told Joe a few minutes ago."

"A little bird told me," he replied with a smug smile.

Dorie looked over at Joe and they both shook their heads. "Jenny," they said in unison.

"Here I thought she was respecting my need for privacy, and the whole time she's been passing out information behind my back," Dorie said. "You just wait until I get a hold of her."

"Now, don't be mad at Jenny," Richard said. "She was only trying to take care of you, as usual, and I needed information so I could go about finding a place to live—a place for both of us to live."

"You want to live with me?" Dorie asked, trying not to show any excitement. "You mean, like domesticated living?"

"That is the generally accepted form," Richard said, his voice serious.

"Well, I don't know about all that," Dorie said. "There's still some things I have to take care of first. It's not like I can just up and move."

"Oh, for Christ's sake, Dorie," Joe exclaimed. "Everything you ever owned has sank in the bayou or blown up on your boat. All you have left will fit in a duffle bag."

"Well, me and my duffle bag still have our standards. And I'm not so sure that domesticated is part of my vocabulary."

Joe snorted and rolled his eyes at Richard, who smiled, and pulled a photo from his shirt pocket. "I was kind of hoping that this would do for living quarters." He handed the photo to Dorie. She reached out and hesitantly took the photo, then stared down at it.

It was a picture of a boat. A really, really big boat. All sparkling white, with three levels and a hot tub, of all things, right there on the deck. "Oh my God," Dorie whispered. "You actually bought this?"

Richard nodded. "The hot tub was the major selling point. I figured we could work out your water submersion issues in a couple of different ways. Strictly for scientific reasons, of course." He grinned at her. "Check out the back," he said and handed her another photo.

Trying to control her shaking hands, she took the photo and read the name printed in bold black letters across the back, *Dorie's Pleasure*. She looked at Richard and tried to hold back the tears that were welling in her eyes.

"You're not exactly like other women, Dorie," Richard said and ran one hand gently down her cheek. "I figured jewelry wouldn't impress you at all, so it had to be the boat."

"Are you sure?" Dorie asked, her voice shaking. "Are you sure you can be happy here?"

"I've never been more sure of anything in my life." He looked deep into her eyes and gave her a sad smile. "Do you know what happened to me when I got home three weeks ago?"

"What?"

"I was carrying case files into my condo to work on at night and my neighbor across the hall asked if I was moving in. Ten years I've owned that condo, and the guy across the hall from me still didn't know who I was. Hell, everyone in Gator Bait knows what kind of underwear I have."

"Designer brand," Joe threw in. "Because of the finer fabric and all."

Dorie grinned. "Are you trying to tell me you want to move to Gator Bait because we all know about your underwear?"

"No," Richard said and leaned down to brush his lips gently across hers. "I'm trying to tell you that I want to move to Gator Bait because you all *care* about my underwear. Do you know since the day after I left, my D.C. office has been flooded with phone calls from Gator Bait residents? They sent flowers and cards and told my boss and anyone else who would listen how great I was and how it would be a 'damned shame' if I didn't at least get a raise and an extended vacation out of it."

Dorie laughed. "That sounds like some people I know."

Richard laughed along with her. "Yeah, it was pretty overwhelming. It didn't sound like anyone I'd ever known and at first, I had no idea what to think about it, especially since I wasn't exactly Mr. Popularity around here. Then I realized that all of those people loved you so much that they were willing to do their best for me because of you." Richard grinned and ran one finger down her check. "You've got one hell of a family, Dorie Berenger. You think there's room for one more person in their lives?"

Dorie wiped at the tears that spilled from her eyes and smiled up at the man she loved more than she'd ever thought possible. "I think they can fit in just one more. So it looks like I've got a duffle bag to pack."

Joe whooped and Richard grabbed Dorie and enclosed her in a hug, twirling her around the office. Then Joe broke into the moment and grabbed Dorie up in a hug, crushing her sides with enthusiasm.

"I'm sorry to interrupt this," Joe said, "but I'm so damn happy." He put her back on the ground and grabbed Richard's hand, pumping it like he was trying to raise oil from the ground. "I've got to run and tell Jenny. She's gonna have a stroke."

Joe dashed out the door, both Dorie and Richard staring after him in amusement. "You think everyone in Gator Bait can handle both you and Joe blissfully coupled off?"

She smiled up at him. "I think everyone in Gator Bait will be thrilled."

He threw one arm around her shoulders and drew her toward the door. "I am curious about one thing, though," he said, a confused look on his face. "Was that Maylene Thibodeaux I saw on Main Street wearing a deputy's uniform and a feather boa?"

Unlucky

Jana DeLeon

Everyone in Royal Flush, Louisiana, knows Mallory Devereaux is a walking disaster. At least now she's found a way to take advantage of her chronic bad luck: by "cooling" cards on her uncle's casino boat. As long as the crooks invited to his special poker tournament don't win their money back, she'll get a cut of the profit.

But Mal isn't the only one working some major mojo. There's a dark-eyed dealer sending her looks steamier than the bayou in August. Turns out he's an undercover agent named Jake Randoll, and for a Yank, he's pretty darn smart. Smart enough to enlist her help to catch a money launderer. As they race to untangle a web of decades-old lies and secrets amid a gathering of criminals, Mallory can't help hoping her luck's about to change....

ISBN 10: 0-505-52729-4
ISBN 13: 978-0-505-52729-5

To order a book or to request a catalog call:
1-800-481-9191
This book is also available at your local bookstore, or you can check out our Web site **www.dorchesterpub.com** where you can look up your favorite authors, read excerpts, or glance at our discussion forum to see what people have to say about your favorite books.